P9-AGU-838

ANGEL FALLS

SAND AND SHADOWS BOOK 1

COLLEEN HELME

M̶B

MANETTO BOOKS

Copyright © 2021 by Colleen Helme.

All rights reserved. No part of this publication may be reproduced, distributed or transmitted in any form or by any means, including photocopying, recording, or other electronic or mechanical methods, without the prior written permission of the publisher, except in the case of brief quotations embodied in critical reviews and certain other noncommercial uses permitted by copyright law.

www.colleenhelme.com

Publisher's Note: This is a work of fiction. Names, characters, places, and incidents are a product of the author's imagination. Locales and public names are sometimes used for atmospheric purposes. Any resemblance to actual people, living or dead, or to businesses, companies, events, institutions, or locales is completely coincidental.

All trademarks and brands referred to in this book are for illustrative purposes only, are the property of their respective owners and not affiliated with this publication in any way. Any trademarks are being used without permission, and the publication of the trademark is not authorized by, associated with, or sponsored by the trademark owner.

Book Cover Art by Damonza.com Copyright ©2021 by Colleen Helme

DEDICATION
To Melissa

This book wouldn't have been possible without your inspiration and enthusiasm!

ACKNOWLEDGEMENTS

It's always a challenge to begin a new series. It feels like I'm an explorer taking a journey into unknown territory. With any new expedition, there are hopes and dreams as well as fears and worries. This new series has been in my mind for a long time, and I'm so grateful to finally tell the story I've dreamed of for so long. I have poured many hours of effort, heart, sweat and tears into this adventure, and I hope it is something you will find worthwhile. If it brings you a moment of escape, quiet reflection, or enjoyment, I will consider it a success.

I'm so grateful for my daughter Melissa, to whom I have dedicated this book. You are a wonderful source of inspiration and support. Your involvement has been instrumental in helping me shape this story in the way it needed to be told.

Thanks to my wonderful husband, Tom, for believing in me, even when I struggle. To my awesome family for your continued encouragement and support. I love you all!

A big thanks to Kristin Monson for editing this book and making it better. You are the best!

I'm grateful to my amazing audio producer, Stevi Incremona, for bringing Ella's story to life on audio. Thanks for teaming up with me! You rock!

To all of my readers who have taken a chance on this new adventure. I hope you love the book! Thanks for reading! You keep me writing.

BOOKS BY COLLEEN HELME

SAND & SHADOW SERIES
Angel Falls
Desert Devil
Twisted Fate (coming soon)

SHELBY NICHOLS ADVENTURE SERIES
Carrots
Fast Money
Lie or Die
Secrets that Kill
Trapped by Revenge
Deep in Death
Crossing Danger
Devious Minds
Hidden Deception
Laced in Lies
Deadly Escape
Marked for Murder
Ghostly Serenade
Dying Wishes
High Stakes Crime

Devil in a Black Suit ~ A Ramos Story

A Midsummer Night's Murder ~ A
Shelby Nichols Novella

NEWSLETTER SIGNUP

For news, updates, and special offers, please sign up for my newsletter at www.colleenhelme.com. To thank you for subscribing you will receive a FREE ebook: *Behind Blue Eyes: A Shelby Nichols Novella*

CONTENTS

1. Chapter One   1
2. Chapter Two   27
3. Chapter Three   45
4. Chapter Four   71
5. Chapter Five   93
6. Chapter Six   119
7. Chapter Seven   141
8. Chapter Eight   161
9. Chapter Nine   179
10. Chapter Ten   201
11. Chapter Eleven   219
12. Chapter Twelve   241
13. Chapter Thirteen   265
14. Chapter Fourteen   287
15. From the Author   309
16. Desert Devil   311
17. About the Author   317

CHAPTER ONE

I leaned against a large boulder and glanced up at the endless blue sky, framed by red sandstone rocks and white fluffy clouds. It was a perfect day for a hike.

Even though I wouldn't have chosen this place, getting sent away could have been worse. Instead of this desert wilderness, I could have ended up somewhere cold, where the sun didn't shine for months. At least here, the sand and shadows, coupled with the vibrant hues of red and blue, brought me more peace than I had a right to.

The heat could be brutal though, but it wasn't enough to stop me from venturing out at the end of my workday. I'd discovered this little gulch a couple of days ago, but this was the first time I'd ventured further than I could drive my Jeep.

From the map I'd learned that this narrow slot canyon trail took an impressive climb through huge boulders and red sand, winding a short mile up the mountain to end at a spectacular waterfall. I thought it ironic that the slot canyon was called Devil's Gulch, and someone with a sense of humor had named the waterfall Angel Falls.

It reminded me of my predicament and the reason I'd been sent here in the first place. Upper management hadn't liked my attitude when it came to doing my job. Maybe they had a point, but I'd balked when it came to helping a killer. I'd let him die instead of doing all I could to save him. The Hippocratic Oath just didn't seem to apply after all the people he'd killed.

But... apparently, that wasn't my call to make. For my disobedience, I'd been sent to the small town of Sandy Creek, in the middle of nowhere, to "meditate" about the sacredness of life and my duty. Go figure.

I came to a narrow gap of loose sandstone between two sheer rock walls. Deep within the gap, I felt dwarfed by the red stone walls. Glancing up, I saw only a crack of blue sky directly above my head.

I continued the climb, each boulder a steep vertical step, and slowed to catch my breath. Climbing onto the last remaining boulder, I left the rock walls behind and stepped into a beautiful, open grotto. My heart swelled at the magnificence of this cozy space nestled at the top of the gulch.

A waterfall cascaded several feet from a ledge high above me, catching the light just right so that a rainbow reflected through the mist. The remaining water fell into a small pool surrounded by bright green vegetation which grew from the sandy earth.

The contrast between the red rock, falling water, and blue pool, surrounded by lush, green plants, filled me with wonder. This spot was like a piece of heaven, and the tension drained out of me.

I stepped to the edge of the pool and noticed that the shallow water trickled into the rocks and disappeared into the soil. I shivered slightly, the sweat on my back turning cold from the lower temperature inside the grotto.

Closing my eyes, I breathed in the fresh scent of earth and water. My heart expanded with pleasure to be in this amazing place, away from my troubles. I found a large rock where I could sit and enjoy the solitude and hear the trickling sound of falling water.

Several minutes later, another chill ran down my spine, and I became aware of a subtle change in the temperature. Shivering, I glanced above the waterfall's edge to the sky. Dark storm clouds were gathering, blocking the sun's heat. Where had they come from?

Sudden dread washed over me, punctuated by the low rumble of distant thunder. I glanced at my surroundings with new eyes, realizing that a downpour would turn that small waterfall into a raging beast.

This serene grotto was about to become a death trap. Seth had warned me about flash floods in these canyons, but, without a cloud in the sky, I hadn't even thought about it happening today. I had to get out of here—now.

I rushed past the pool to the trail and traversed the small gap between the steep rock walls. It took longer than I liked, but the boulders were too big to go any faster. At least it was all downhill, which should give me enough time to outrun the storm. At the end of the gap, the trail widened, giving me a better view of the sky.

I glanced up and my stomach tightened. Dark clouds surrounded the highest peaks of the mountain, and I knew I would soon be in the path of a rushing river.

With my heart pounding, I traversed the steep, sandy trail as quickly as I could, knowing I couldn't afford to twist an ankle. The wash dipped and descended down a narrow gully of large boulders and rocks. Jutting stones and loose gravel caused me to slip and skid, but I managed to stay upright.

The sky darkened, and rain clouds completely covered the sun's light. A flash of lightning and the crack of thunder roared overhead. A moment later, thick drops of rain pelted me. With panic tightening my chest, I picked up the pace.

My Jeep wasn't too far now, but even if I reached it, I wouldn't be out of danger. I'd driven the Jeep up the wash as far as I could. But I still had to drive it out of the wash before I'd make it to safety.

I hurried down the last bend and skidded on loose rocks, lurching to find my balance. The pitch of the trail changed. It wasn't as steep, so I picked up the pace, running as fast as I dared. After a few more twists and turns, accompanied by near falls on the loose rocks, I came to a break in the trail and caught sight of my Jeep below. Luckily, I'd parked it facing downhill, which increased my odds of survival.

Another flash of lightning ripped through the sky, and the answering thunder shook the ground. With a burst of speed, I ran down the steep path and reached the Jeep. Wrenching the door open, I fumbled to get the keys out of my pocket and jumped into my seat.

As I slammed the door, the rain began to fall in big, fat drops. I slipped the key in the ignition, and the Jeep came to life. I'd only learned how to drive a clutch from Seth after I'd arrived here. I didn't even have a car in New York, and the clutch in the Jeep hadn't been easy to learn.

After popping into first gear, I stepped on the gas. Letting out the clutch too fast, the Jeep stalled. With my hands shaking, I tried it again. This time I got it right, and the Jeep lurched forward down the steep creek bed.

Taking it slow, I glanced in the rearview mirror and found the first stream of water flowing down the wash. Panic swamped me, and I sped up, shifting into second gear and driving more recklessly than I should, only slowing enough to take the corners without spinning out.

The wash narrowed to a long, tapered descent, and I picked up speed, shifting into third gear. Letting the Jeep go faster right before the next turn, I hit the brakes and shifted into first to take the corner. The engine whined, and the tires skidded on the loose, wet rocks, but I managed to straighten the Jeep out without stalling the engine.

As I continued my flight down the wash, I approached a large boulder, and my grip tightened on the wheel. The rushing water hit the rock before taking the path of least resistance around it, right where I needed to go.

I slowed, barely managing to maneuver around it in the deepening flow of water before turning the wheel sharply to round the next bend. I swerved and nearly lost control on the wet sand before clearing the curve.

The wash ahead widened, and I shifted from second to third gear and pushed on the gas. The rushing water had overtaken me, and my back tires spun out, spewing wet gravel before catching enough traction to propel me forward. Just ahead, the wash continued downward, and I caught sight of the small fork in the road.

As water churned around my tires, I cranked the wheel to take the fork on the right and fishtailed out of the wash up onto a dirt road. The road too steep to make it up in third gear, I had to shift into second to continue, but the Jeep lost traction and began to slide back down into the wash.

Shifting into first gear, I took my foot off the brake to stomp on the gas. Sliding back into the wash, I managed to let out the clutch at the right time, but water rushed around my back tires, and the wheels began to spin. "Come on. Come on!"

The tires finally took hold, shooting me back up the small incline and out of harm's way. Breathing heavily, I continued my flight up the steep path to reach the dirt road above the wash. Finally making it to the highest point, it leveled out, and I slowed the Jeep to a stop. I swallowed, glancing over the edge of the road to watch the water roar into a deep ravine.

Unclenching my jaw, I peeled my sweaty hands off the wheel. I'd outrun the flood, but the rain was catching up. After shaking out my cramped fingers, I slid the Jeep into first gear and started off down the narrow, dirt road beside the ravine.

Glancing into the rear view mirror, I took in the heavy, dark clouds over the gap. The sudden sound of crashing water caught my breath, and I slowed to glance over the edge again. The brown, churning water filled the ravine and collided through the gulch with amazing speed and power.

The loud sounds of crashing rocks, propelled by the sheer force of the water, turned my blood cold. I'd barely made it out of there alive. Taking a shaky breath, I pushed on the gas, going a little faster than was probably necessary. Leaving the slot canyon, and the roaring water behind, I could finally breathe normally again.

With the storm gaining on me, I followed the small, dirt lane in a straight line to the main road. In the distance, the highway that crisscrossed the valley came into view, and I let out a sigh of relief. A few minutes later, I reached the lone stop sign.

My hands trembled and my legs shook, so I turned off the Jeep and sat to recuperate from my near-death experience. After several seconds, I reached into the backseat for a bottle of water and took a long pull. The water helped revive me, and I finally felt calm enough to drive home.

I started the Jeep and glanced both ways, not expecting to see another car, but, after nearly dying, I wasn't taking any chances. I even managed to shift into first gear without a problem. The smooth pavement beneath the tires felt wonderful after the bumps and rocks of the dirt wash, and I relaxed into my seat.

It was fifteen miles back to town, and this was about the loneliest stretch of highway in the valley. A gust of wind rocked the Jeep, signaling that the storm had caught up to me, and the clouds came pouring over the mountains. Within minutes, they veiled the valley in darkness as far as I could see. Occasional gusts of wind and rain buffeted the Jeep, and I slowed to keep control.

Low growing grasses and sagebrush dotted the flat landscape around me, leaving plenty of dry ground and sand in the spaces between. The wind picked up and began to play with the dry, sandy earth. In the waning light, the dust lifted from the ground and began to spin like small-sized tornados.

I watched as one touched down beside the road. It spun out into nothing, only to re-form again. I loved watching these dust devils, and my eyes widened to find several more of them twirling beside me on both sides of the road. I'd never seen this many at once.

A sudden gust of wind slammed against my Jeep, causing me to swerve into the oncoming lane. Fighting to control the wheel, I brought the Jeep back into the right lane and slowed. Grains of sand shot into my windshield in little bursts, sounding like pellets. Then the rain hit in a sheet of water, making it even harder to see where I was going.

I slowed down even more and turned on my headlights. A dark shape came up on my right, turning into a car parked halfway in the road. I swerved around it, grateful I hadn't hit it. Who would leave a car parked in the road like that?

I glanced back at the car, but couldn't see anyone inside. Shaking my head, I turned my attention to the road, and a dark form materialized right in front of me. I slammed on the brakes, but couldn't stop before a sickening thud against the front of the Jeep turned my blood cold.

"No, no, no!" I swerved to the side of the road and slammed to a stop. With barely controlled panic, I wrenched the door open and ran to the body on the side of the road. The man let out a low groan, and my heart quivered with relief that he wasn't dead. His head and shoulders rested on a duffel bag, which I hoped had saved his head from any serious damage.

I knelt beside him, immediately checking his pulse and looking him over. The rain plastered his wet, dark hair to his forehead, and I leaned over him to shelter his face from the deluge. His eyes fluttered open, dark and deep blue, then narrowed with pain. His strong jaw clenched, while his lips pulled into a tight grimace.

"Where does it hurt?" I had to shout over the storm. Without waiting for an answer, I checked his prone form. He wore a dark t-shirt that was now soaked and plastered to his well-muscled chest.

"What... what happened?" Confusion clouded his eyes, and I noticed his pupils were dilated. He moved onto his side and pushed into a sitting position.

"Whoa... you should lie back down," I told him. "You were hit by a car. We need to make sure nothing's broken."

Not listening to me, he stayed upright, but his breath came fast, and he hung his head in pain.

"Does your head hurt? I think you might have a concussion."

He closed his eyes and let out a breath, taking stock of his injuries by slowly moving his body. As he shifted his right leg, he let out a hiss of pain and reached toward his calf, just below his knee. He leaned forward to look at it, and I pushed against his chest. It was like pushing against a wall. With a grimace, he sank back to the ground, his head resting on the bag.

"Stay put. I'm a trauma nurse; let me take a look." I ran my hands over his huge thigh to below his knee. Along his shinbone, something felt off, and I pushed his pant leg up to expose the bruised and swelling flesh. I couldn't tell if the bone was broken, but it was bad enough that I knew he wouldn't be walking on it anytime soon.

"Does it hurt anywhere else?" I asked, still shouting to be heard over the storm. "Any neck or back pain? How about your ribs or your chest? Does it hurt to breathe?" I wished I had a neck brace in the Jeep, but I'd come empty-handed.

"No. It's mostly my leg that hurts." He pushed himself back into a sitting position.

Not wanting him to move, I placed my hand on his chest again. "Wait. I'd better call an ambulance. You might have internal injuries."

"No," he said, sharply. "I'm not hurt that badly. I just need to get out of this rain and get my leg looked at." His determined gaze caught mine, and I knew arguing was pointless.

"Okay. Let's get you into my Jeep. I'll take you to the clinic in town."

His shoulders relaxed with relief. While gritting his teeth, he pushed onto his good knee and managed to get his foot under him. I knelt beside him and pulled his arm around my neck. "Okay. Lean on me and try to stand, but don't put any weight on your injured leg."

He leaned heavily against me, and I staggered under his weight. I had no idea how much he weighed, but, from the look of him, none of it was fat. Shifting into a better position, I pushed up with my legs, pulling him with me. His good leg took the rest of his weight, and I managed to help him hop to the Jeep.

I got the door opened, and he slid onto the edge of the seat, letting out a groan. Using his upper body strength, he pulled himself fully inside. I helped him lift his injured leg into the Jeep. Heaving out a breath, he closed his eyes and leaned against the back of the seat. I pulled the seat belt across him and buckled it up. Before I moved away, his hand caught my arm. "My duffel bag—"

"Right. I'll get it." I shut the door and hurried back to the bag. For such a big bag, I expected it to be heavy, and I wasn't disappointed. I heaved it over my shoulder and stepped to the back of my Jeep, grateful I could swing it open, and shoved it inside.

Back to the driver's side, I jumped in and wiped the water from my eyes. My soaking hair dripped down my face, and I pushed it back so I could see before starting the engine.

As I pulled away, guilt swept over me. I'd hit this poor guy—in the middle of a rainstorm—and now he was suffering. At least he wasn't dead. It could have been so much worse. I should probably apologize, but telling him I was sorry right now didn't seem like a good idea. Instead, I concentrated on driving through the heavy storm to the clinic.

Since I was the only medical specialist in town, I ran the clinic in this little community. The hospital was an hour away, so, unless it was serious, I took care of the small town's health needs. Knowing I could treat his injuries eased some of my guilt.

I glanced over at him. He cradled his leg, trying to hold it up so there wasn't any pressure on his ankle. I grimaced, knowing I should have splinted it, or, at the least, made him sit in the back so he could put it up on the seat. What kind of a trauma nurse was I? "How are you doing?"

His dark, chiseled face seemed a little pale, making the short, black stubble on his jaw stand out. I couldn't see any sweat on his brow, but that didn't mean much, since he was soaking wet from the storm.

"Where are we going, again?" he asked, his deep voice barely above a whisper.

"Uh... like I said, I'm taking you to the urgent care clinic in the nearest town. In fact, I'm the person who runs it. If you're hurt worse than we think, I might have to call an ambulance and send you to the hospital back in Richmond. It's about an hour west of here."

"No. No hospitals. Just patch me up. I need to keep going."

From the finality in his voice, I knew it wouldn't do any good to argue with him. But something about his tone sent a wave of unease through me. Was he running from something?

Out of the corner of my eye, I studied his clothes for clues, remembering that I hadn't noticed a gun in his jeans as I'd run my hands over him. Still, he looked rugged and more than a little dangerous. Maybe it was his longish hair and the few days' growth of beard that gave him that vibe.

His dark gaze caught mine, and I jerked my eyes back to the road. "So, where are you headed?" I asked, trying to sound casual.

Wouldn't it be my luck to run into a wanted criminal out here in the middle of nowhere? Or did God have a sick sense of humor? I glanced heavenward and let out a breath. I might not be on the big guy's good side right now, but he wouldn't do that to me, would he?

The man didn't answer, so I glanced at him again. His eyes were shut in pain, and I could almost feel the agony coming off him. Guilt swamped me, and I couldn't keep my remorse down. "I'm sorry... uh... I guess you figured it out by now—that I'm the one who hit you, but I didn't see you. The storm made it hard to see the road, and I was looking at your car. That was your car back there, right?"

"Yeah." He lowered his head and winced in pain. "Are we almost there?"

"Yes. Just a few more minutes. Uh... I'm Ella... Ella St. John." He didn't answer, and I wasn't sure if he'd heard me.

"Creed... Aiden Creed."

I smiled, hoping to put him at ease. "It's nice to meet you... Aiden Creed. I mean... not under these circumstances of course. And I'm really sorry you're hurt, but I'll do my best to patch you up. You know... so you can... uh... be on your way."

His brows rose and he stared at me, then his lips quirked up. Was that a smile? "Okay... Ella St. John. Is... uh... Ella short for something?"

"Yeah. It's short for... uh... Gabriella." Why was I stammering? Having all of his attention focused on me was messing with my brain.

I caught his nod out of the corner of my eye. Then he closed his eyes like the nod hurt his head, and a shiver ran over him. Was he in shock? The rain had slowed down a bit, so I turned on the heater and cranked up my speed to get him to the clinic as fast as I could.

Ten minutes later, I pulled into the driveway of the large, two-story house where I lived. The front of the house had been turned into a medical clinic, while my living quarters took up the back, kitchen area and the second-story bedrooms.

Instead of pulling all the way to the garage, I stopped next to the covered porch. Jumping out, I hurried to his side of the Jeep and pulled the door open. Creed eased slowly from the seat, and I slid my shoulder under his arm. Taking his weight, I helped him hop up the steps to the house. Holding him steady, I unlocked the front door and helped him inside, taking him past the waiting room and into the lone exam room.

As I moved him toward the exam table, he balked. "The chair. Let me sit in the chair."

I wanted to object, but moving him anywhere he didn't want to go was probably a losing battle. After he sat down, I pulled another chair over and sat in front of him. Carefully,

I raised his leg to rest across my lap. Pushing up his pant leg, I examined his injury and winced.

"How does it look?"

I squirmed under his intense gaze. But, hoping he could take the bad news, I gave it to him straight. "You have two bones in your lower leg. And it looks like the tibia, or what we call your shinbone, might be broken, but I won't know for sure until I get an x-ray. Your ankle is swollen as well, but I don't think it's broken, probably just sprained."

He shook his head and swore under his breath. "How long before I can walk on it?"

"It depends on how bad the fracture is. After I take an x-ray, I'll know more and we can figure it out."

"How long if it's bad?" He insisted.

I shrugged. "Four to six months before you're fully healed and able to do everything you could before." At his shocked expression, I continued. "But that's the worst case scenario. Let's get that x-ray and then we'll know more."

Not waiting for an answer, I gently lowered his leg and hurried to the large supply closet to get the wheelchair. I grabbed a couple of towels as well, using one to dry my face and hair. Pushing the wheelchair next to him, I handed him a towel to dry his face.

He glanced at the chair like it was something vile and let out an irritated breath. After he scrubbed the towel over his face and hair, I helped him maneuver into the seat.

Striving for professionalism, I wheeled him to the x-ray machine in the back room. Now came the hard part. "You're soaking wet. If you want to take off your shirt, I've got some scrubs you can wear. We also need to take off your shoe and... your... uh... pants."

His eyes narrowed. "What?"

I sighed. "I can push your pant leg up, but I need it above your knee to take the x-ray, and I'm not sure I can get it up that far." He didn't seem convinced, so I went with option B. "Or I can just cut the pant leg off."

He swore under his breath, not happy with either option.

"I'll go get the scrubs. Okay?" He didn't answer, so I continued. "I can help you take them off. I do things like this all the time, so it's no big deal."

"Fine."

His rough tone didn't scare me, and I untied his athletic shoes and pulled them off his feet. "I'll get the scrubs. Don't move."

I hurried back to the supply closet and searched a box for the right size, finally finding a large, standard-issue, light-blue pair. Coming into the room, I found Creed standing on one foot and leaning against the x-ray table. His chest was bare, and he began to unfasten his belt, stopping as I entered.

"What are you doing? I told you not to move."

A challenging gleam entered his eyes. Keeping his gaze on my face, he unbuckled his belt, then flicked the top button of his jeans open and slowly lowered the zipper. My breath caught, and I couldn't help the blush that crept up my neck.

I'd been trying to ignore how attractive I found him, but seeing him unzip his pants was almost more than I could take. Sure, he was in great shape with his taut stomach, toned chest, and all those muscles... but I was a professional. I shouldn't be reacting like this.

"Sit back down. If you fall, you could make it worse."

"But I can't get my pants off if I'm sitting down."

Watching his pants hit the ground sent a little spasm through me, and I swallowed before taking in his black, stretchy boxer briefs.

"Are you going to stand there and gawk all day?"

Gasping, I jerked my gaze to his face and instantly regretted it. That challenging gleam was still there, but now his lips were twisted into a small smirk. He knew exactly what he was doing, and my blood began to boil.

Pursing my lips, I set the scrubs down and stepped to his side.

Taking his arm, I pulled the wheelchair closer and helped him ease into it. His jeans were still in a puddle around his feet, and the belt buckle hit his swollen ankle. He let out a groan, and I tried not to smirk, but it served him right.

Crouching beside him, I gently tugged the pants off his feet and folded them up. I found his shirt and added it to the pile, deciding to wash them later. Reaching for the scrubs, I handed him the top first. Moving slowly, he slipped the shirt over his head, grimacing with pain, and I caught sight of a couple of ugly bruises and some scrapes along his arms. I winced, knowing I was the cause.

Done, he reached for the bottoms, but I held them back. "Nope. Before you put these on, I need to take the x-ray."

"Seriously?"

"Yes, and now you're going to have to stand back up and lie down on the table for the x-ray." I shook my head in exasperation. "You know... If you'd waited for me, we could have done this all at the same time."

He shook his head, but winced from the movement. "Fine. Let's just get his over with."

After getting him situated for the x-ray, I grabbed a hospital gown to drape over his lap and got to work taking the pictures. I'd taken a lot of x-rays, but this was the first time I found it hard to concentrate on my job. It didn't make sense. Sure, he was good-looking, but it wasn't like me to get so flustered by a handsome man.

Relieved to be done, I helped him back to the wheelchair. Once he was seated, I shook out the scrubs, expertly scrunching them up. Crouching beside him, I pulled them over his foot and injured leg. I did the same for the other leg before lifting them to his knees.

I caught his gaze and raised my brows. "Lift yourself up on the handles."

With his head bowed, he let out a breath and pushed up with his arms. I eased the pants up his legs, but had to step closer to finish the job. With my nose nearly touching his chest, I caught his fresh, earthy scent. Pursing my lips against the distraction, I continued to pull the pants up to his waist.

As he settled back down, I stepped back and swallowed, surprised at how rattled the whole process had made me. I moved to the back of the wheelchair, grateful he couldn't see my flushed face, and took him back to the exam room.

Leaving him in the chair, I hurried back to the machine and processed the film. Finished, I snapped it onto the light screen, relieved to find that the break wasn't too bad. A stress fracture broke through the bone, but everything was still in place, so he wouldn't need surgery. It was the easiest break to treat, so at least that was good news.

As a precaution, I'd also taken an x-ray of his ankle and found he had a bad sprain, but nothing was broken. He would still be unable to walk on that leg for a while, and I needed to fit him with a special brace that would hold the bone in place.

I was glad that I could move the healing process along with my gift. I figured it was the least I could do, since I was the one who'd hit him in the first place. I entered the exam room and found him with his head slumped over and his eyes closed.

Panic caught my breath. Had he hit his head harder than I'd thought? I should have taken better care of him. "Creed?"

His head straightened, and he opened his eyes. "Yeah?"

I sighed with relief and studied his face. Now that I wasn't so distracted, it was easy to see that he looked totally exhausted. His eyes had taken on a hollow shine, like he hadn't rested for days. And getting hit by a car had only made things worse. Not wanting to dwell on that part, I smiled. "I've got some good news."

I explained his fracture and the treatment he'd need. "How's your head?" I picked up the pen light and instructed him to look at me while I flashed it in his eyes. "You've got a bit of a concussion."

"I'm not surprised. My head's killing me."

"Yeah... I've got some pain pills I can give you. I don't keep many here, but I have enough for a few days."

"I'd appreciate it."

"Sure. Uh... you're going to need to take it easy for a while and stay off your leg for a few weeks at the least. Is there someone I can call, or somewhere I can take you?"

"No. Just patch me up and I'll be on my way."

"I'm afraid it's not that simple."

"What do you mean?"

I sighed. "You can't go anywhere for a few days. You're hurt too badly."

He slumped in the chair, his eyes shut against the pain. "Then what am I supposed to do? Is there a motel around here?"

"You're in no shape to be on your own for a while. Look... you can stay with me. I have an apartment in the back of this clinic. The bedrooms are all upstairs, but you could stay on the couch down on the main floor until you're feeling better and we can figure something out."

He studied me for a moment, then glanced at his broken leg. "Well... since it's your fault I'm here... I'll take you up on it. It's not like I have a choice."

I huffed out a breath. "Look... I didn't mean to hit you, but you were walking in the middle of the road... in a rainstorm... it's not like I did it on purpose."

He shook his head, then winced, closing his eyes in pain. "I know... I'm just mad... all right? My head's killing me, and my leg's not much better."

"Sure... I'll get the brace and come right back. Don't move." It only made sense that he'd be in a bad mood, so I shouldn't take it personally. I'd be upset too if it had happened to me. Giving him a place to stay was the least I could do, even if I didn't know anything about him.

I hurried to the supply room and found the brace, picking up some antiseptic gel and tape while I was at it. This time, he didn't complain about lying down on the exam table with a pillow under his head. After getting him situated, I pulled out several strips of tape to hang from the edge of the table, ready to wrap his leg.

Holding his leg steady, I pushed the scrubs above his knee. The gel wasn't actually needed, but it gave me an excuse to touch his leg, and that was the best way for me to help him without causing suspicion. I squeezed a large amount of gel into my palm and closed my eyes to center my energy. Concentrating on the source of light from deep inside me, I pushed the healing energy outward to my hands, feeling them warm up.

With a gentle touch, I placed my hands over the broken bone and transferred the energy into his leg. Then, using light pressure, I stroked the strained muscles and bruised skin around the break, moving downward to rub his swollen ankle and foot.

The heat in my hands expanded outward to his leg and soaked deep into his bones and the soft, swollen tissue. I heard him sigh as the pain subsided. A few minutes later, I used alcohol wipes to remove the gel so the tape would stick.

At the sight of his hairy legs, I had second thoughts about the tape. It would hurt like crazy to yank it off. On the other hand, he'd been kind of grouchy about this whole thing. I mean... sure I'm the one who hit him, but it wasn't all my fault.

But honestly, since I'd used my healing gift, he probably didn't need the tape, so I skipped it. He was in enough pain already. I fit the brace onto his leg, carefully tightening it around his lower and upper shin, just below his knee and above his ankle, making sure the break was supported and held in place. For now, that was the best I could do. I'd consider a cast later if he needed it.

Finished, I sat back to admire my handiwork and glanced at Creed, noting that his color had improved. "Okay, that should do it for now. Let's get you situated on my couch. You'll be more comfortable there."

After helping him into his wheelchair, I pushed him through the connecting door and into my living room. This part of the house was the most modern, as it had been added onto the original structure. The kitchen and dining space took up one side, with a short hallway to the back door.

A small laundry room was on the other side of the hallway, and next to that was a bathroom and shower combo. The other side of the space was the living area. The open layout was simple, but homey, with a large-screen TV and entertainment center along the wall.

A cozy arrangement of a wrap-around couch and a lazy-boy chair faced the screen. The artwork on the surrounding walls held prints of the famous scenic wonders of the Big Five National Parks, as they were called around here.

Delicate Arch was the most identifiable photo, but there were several others that stood out, all of them capturing the beauty of this vast spot of earth. I'd only visited one of them so far. If John didn't call me back home anytime soon, I'd probably have plenty of time to explore the others.

As fun as that sounded, I'd rather go home tomorrow. That probably wasn't the best attitude, but I'd tried to do better. Hadn't I gone on that hike today? Until the flash flood, it had been amazing. There were probably plenty more like it right around here, so I should take advantage of the opportunity while I had the chance. I'd just have to check the weather for storms first.

I pushed Creed to the couch and removed the pillows from the back, which made it wide enough for him to lie down comfortably. After moving him out of the chair, I helped him recline on a couple of pillows and piled the rest under his broken leg to keep it elevated.

As he lay back on the pillow, he winced with pain and touched the back of his head.

"That must be where you hit your head," I said.

"Yeah," he agreed. "There's a big bump back there."

"Let me take a look." I moved behind him, turning his head to the side so I could get a better look. The knot was bigger than I liked, and I wondered how he'd managed to stay conscious.

Gathering my remaining energy, I pushed it through my fingers and gently touched the lump without using any pressure. Moving my fingers to stroke down his neck, I gently massaged the muscles there, continuing down to the tops of his shoulders in a sweeping motion.

After repeating the motion several times, I pulled away. Using so much energy had drained me, but I was pretty sure it would help him.

He opened his eyes to squint at me. In a barely audible voice, he said, "That was amazing."

I smiled. "Go ahead and close your eyes. You'll feel better after some rest."

"My bag?"

"I'll bring it in."

His eyes fluttered shut, and his breathing deepened. I took the soft blanket from the edge of the couch and tucked it around him, careful of his leg. It may be hot during the day here, but it cooled down in the evenings, and since the air conditioning worked great in this part of the house, I didn't want him to take a chill.

I glanced outside, surprised to find the rain had stopped. The clouds parted, allowing the sun's setting rays to turn them into shades of red and orange. I hurried outside for the full effect and marveled at the beautiful sunset. The colors turned pink and purple on the landscape behind me, leaving orange and molten red in front of me, just above the horizon.

I inhaled the air, fresh after such a heavy rainfall, and stood a few more minutes to take it all in. It was beautiful here, but I still missed the city. There was just too much open space, and it was so quiet. I'd enjoyed it the first couple of weeks, but now that I'd been here a couple of months, I'd had enough. I wanted to go home.

Returning inside, I gathered Creed's shoes and socks, along with his discarded shirt and pants. They were still damp, so I took them to the laundry room to throw in the wash. Feeling a heavy weight in his jeans pocket, I took out his wallet and cell phone. Curious, I glanced through the wallet, finding his driver's license and a few credit cards, all under his name. Not that I expected anything else, but it relieved me just the same.

In the other pocket, I found a set of keys, reminding me of his car still sitting in the road. I set his wallet and phone on top of the washing machine and started the cycle. Next, I stepped out the back door to put a call through to the only car repair shop in town.

"Hey Seth, it's Ella. I wondered if you have time to tow a car to your shop." I explained what had happened and told him I had Creed's car keys.

"So... you hit this guy with your Jeep?"

"Yeah, but it wasn't my fault. I mean... he was walking down the middle of the road in a rainstorm. I could barely see him."

Seth snickered. "Well, as long as he doesn't sue you. Where is he now?"

"Asleep... on my couch."

"Huh. Are you sure you're safe with a stranger there?"

"Yes. His leg is broken, so I'm fine. It's the least I can do. I'll pay for the tow."

"What were you doing out there anyway?" he asked.

I explained my little excursion up Devil's Gulch and my run-in with the flash flood.

"Damnation, girl. I told you to check the forecast before you went up there."

"I know... but there wasn't a cloud in the sky, so I didn't think about it. At least you should be glad to know I handled the Jeep pretty well. I only stalled it once." I heard him sigh and continued speaking before I got an earful. "Anyway... how soon can you come?"

"I'll be there in a few minutes."

"Great. Thanks."

With my patient out cold, I pulled my Jeep into the garage and lugged Creed's duffel bag into the house, setting it on the floor by the back door. After locking the door, I crossed through the clinic to wait on the front porch with Creed's car keys. Seth pulled up, and I ran them out to his tow truck. "Thanks. I owe you one."

"No problem. Just... be sure to call me if you run into trouble."

I smiled. "I will." Seth had started looking after me right after I moved here. He was an older, grizzled man with old fashioned ideas that a woman shouldn't be on her own. Rather than letting it bother me, I appreciated his fatherly concern, especially when it came to the Jeep.

Everyone around here needed a car, and I'd bought it off him just after I'd arrived. He'd nearly had a heart attack to find out I didn't know the first thing about driving a clutch, so he'd included teaching me as part of the deal.

I was grateful for his friendship, since he was about the only friend I'd made so far. I hadn't put much effort into fitting into the community, mostly because I'd hoped to be back home long before now. After this much time, I was starting to wonder if it would ever happen.

Grateful for Seth's help, I hurried back inside for something to eat. It was after eight, and I didn't want to wake Creed, so I grabbed a box of cereal. After setting my dish in the sink, I debated if it was okay to wake him up before I went to bed.

He might have to go to the bathroom, and he could probably use some water and a couple of pain pills. I hurried to the supply closet in the clinic and returned with a pair of crutches. After setting them down near the couch, I got a cold bottle of water from the fridge, along with the pain pills, and brought them over.

I sat on the coffee table beside him and studied his face, surprised to find that he only looked a little less threatening. His dark, tousled hair hung over his forehead, and I had to fight against the urge to push it away from his eyes. As I watched, he twitched, and his brows and mouth tightened in a grimace. His breathing came faster, and a soft moan escaped his lips.

I placed my hand on his forehead, feeling the heat of a low-grade fever. Concentrating, I pulled the extra heat into my fingers until he cooled down. After he quieted, and I took my hand away, I found his eyes wide open. Startled, I jerked my hand to my side.

"What are you doing?"

"You were restless, so I was just checking to see if you had a fever."

"I feel kind of hot. Maybe it's this blanket." He shoved the blanket off his chest. "My head still hurts, though. And my leg is killing me."

"I have some water and the pain pills right here for you."

"Oh... good. Thanks."

He pushed into a sitting position, carefully lowering his broken leg to the floor, and took the pills, drinking most of the water. After setting the water on the coffee table, he glanced my way. "I need to use the bathroom."

"Sure. I found a pair of crutches for you, and the bathroom's just back there." I pointed toward the back of the house. "I'll give you a hand."

It took some effort to get him standing. The crutches didn't quite fit, but they worked well enough for now. "I can adjust the crutches for you tomorrow."

He nodded, and we moved slowly to the bathroom. Once there, I didn't offer to help him, hoping he could manage alone. Still, I left the door slightly ajar and told him to call me if anything happened.

While waiting, I turned on the light above the stove. Noticing his duffel bag, I picked it up and carried it to the couch. The bathroom door opened, and I helped him return to the couch.

"Your duffel bag is right there if you need anything from it."

"Good. Thanks for bringing it in."

"Sure." After I helped him get comfortable and propped up his leg, I draped the blanket back over him. "I'm going to bed. Is there anything else you need?"

"Uh... yeah... there is. Could you rub my neck again?"

Was he taking advantage of me? I studied him, finding only pain-filled eyes and deep weariness. My heart softened. "Sure." I stepped to the end of the couch by his head. "Can you turn to your side a bit? It will be easier."

"Yeah." He moved his head and shifted his upper torso as far as possible without jostling his leg too much. It wasn't ideal, but it would work.

I inspected the bump on his head, happy to find it less swollen, and began at the base of his neck. Starting with small movements, I massaged the muscles there and continued down to the tops of his shoulders.

I closed my eyes and sent warmth into my fingers. It wasn't enough to call attention to it, but I hoped it would help relieve the soreness in his neck muscles from the accident. Satisfied that I'd done what I could to help him, I pulled my hands away.

His breathing had gone deep again, but he roused, shifting onto his back where he was more comfortable. With his eyes half-opened, a slight smile turned his lips up. "I could get used to this."

His eyes closed, and his breathing deepened. I shook my head and hurried up the stairs to my bedroom. Closing my door, I stepped into the bathroom for a shower. My clothes were still damp, so I hung them up on a hook to dry.

Glancing in the mirror, it surprised me to find a spark in my eyes that hadn't been there for a long time, and I knew that Creed was the cause. I'd enjoyed that little moment of intimacy rubbing his neck. I had to face it—I was lonely.

That meant I'd have to be careful that I didn't enjoy his company too much, or I'd be a mess once he left. Maybe it was time to find more friends here, even if that might keep me from going home for a long, long time.

CHAPTER TWO

I woke from a sound sleep. It was still dark outside, but starting to get light. The clock read six a.m. A noise from downstairs sounded like someone swearing. Slipping out of bed, I crept to the stairs and down to the landing.

Creed wasn't on the couch, and I couldn't see him anywhere. Hearing a couple more swearwords coming from the kitchen, I hurried down the stairs and found Creed sprawled on the kitchen floor. A bowl of cereal sat on the counter, but the box had tipped over and showered him in toasted flakes.

"What's going on?"

As he glanced up at me, several flakes fell off his head, and I burst out laughing.

"It's these damn crutches." He brushed the remaining flakes off his head and tried to get up. His lips turned down, and his jaw clenched.

Recognizing his pain, my laughter dried up. "Oh geez. Did you hurt your leg?"

"No... I don't think so."

"Here, let me help you." He slid his arm over my shoulders, and we both staggered a little, but he managed to get his good leg under him to stand. His face had paled, and I worried that he might pass out. "Let's take it slow." We shuffled back to the couch, and I helped him sit down. He took a few shallow breaths, panting from the pain.

I wanted to scold him for getting up, but I knew that wouldn't help, so I stood beside him until his breathing evened out. "Want to lie back down?"

He nodded, and I helped him get situated with his leg propped back up on the cushions. Leaning over, I caught him staring, and realized I was still in my white tank top and short pajama bottoms.

"Uh... I'll go get dressed and fix you some breakfast, okay? Then maybe you can take another pain pill."

I didn't wait for his nod, but flew up the stairs. My tank top wasn't see-through, but it still left little to the imagination. After shutting my door, I quickly changed into my boring uniform of light-blue hospital scrubs.

My shoulder-length, light-blond hair was a little poufy from going to bed with it wet, but not too embarrassing. As I wet it down, I realized that the blue highlights had faded to silver, but it actually looked good like that, especially around my face. With my dark eyebrows, the lighter blue tones in my hair brought out the almost-purple hues in my dark blue eyes and gave me a mysterious vibe.

After I'd arrived here, the daughter of the only hairdresser in town had been more than happy to put a few blue highlights in my hair. I'd done it on a whim, mostly because my hair was about the only thing I could control in my life. I'd also had her cut it to just above my shoulders, so I could still pull it back into a ponytail if I needed to, although I preferred it down.

I normally didn't wear makeup, but having Creed downstairs changed my mind. My naturally warm skin tone had tanned a bit, so I only needed to add a little mascara and some color on my lips to do the job. Finished, I hurried back downstairs to cook breakfast.

Creed cracked his eyes open as I passed, but otherwise didn't move, so I got busy cooking. Soon, I had a plate of eggs and toast, along with a cup of coffee and a glass of orange juice on a tray. I carried it over to the coffee table and set it down in front of him.

That roused him, and he straightened. "Oh wow... that looks great."

"Do you want the tray on your lap?"

"No, I'll just pick up the plate." He thanked me again and began to eat, holding the plate close to his mouth and taking big bites. "This is good. Thanks."

"You're welcome." I returned to the kitchen for my plate of food and sat at the counter to eat. From what I could see, he looked like he was starving, and I wondered if I'd made enough. "Do you want more toast or anything?"

"Maybe some more juice?"

"Sure." I'd already finished my egg, so I grabbed the juice and filled up his glass, then set it on the coffee table in case he wanted more. Eating my toast, I perched on the end of the couch by his feet. "So where are you headed?"

Since his mouth was full, it took a minute for him to answer. "Colorado."

"Oh... nice. I've never been there."

I waited for him to continue, but he took his time chewing his food, and I figured he was using it as an excuse to keep from answering. After finishing all the food on his plate, he set the plate on the tray and finally spoke. "I hate to be a bother, but I'm worried about my car. I have a few things inside, and I don't want anyone to steal it."

"Oh, I... uh... took care of it. I asked the repair shop owner to tow it to his shop. I'm sure it's locked up on his property. It's early enough that I can run over there before work and get anything you need, if you want."

His brows rose with surprise, and the worry left his face. "Oh yeah? I'd appreciate it." Letting out a sigh, he sat back against the couch and closed his eyes. Sitting up and eating had taken a lot out of him. I suspected falling on the floor may not have helped much either.

"I'll get you a pain pill, and then I want to take a look at your leg to make sure the brace is still good. I'll get your things after that." I took his dishes back to the kitchen and returned with a bottle of water and his pill. With pain etched in his taut features, he took it eagerly, and I was sorry he hurt so much.

Leg breaks like his were usually quite painful, even with my special touch. "The pain pill should kick in pretty soon." He nodded slightly, but the movement seemed to bother him. "How's your head? Still have a headache?"

"Yeah, but it's getting better."

"Good." I sat on the edge of the couch by his foot and lifted the scrubs, deftly pushing the pant leg up and over his brace. His leg was still swollen and bruised at the break point, but, from what I could see, it was in place, so that was good. "You haven't walked on it, have you?"

"No, not once."

I nodded. "Good. I know you might be tempted, but it would make things a lot worse. You were lucky that it was a clean break, but putting any weight on it could do further damage that might require surgery."

"I get it. I won't."

I chewed on my bottom lip, knowing it was my fault he was suffering and wanting to make up for it. "Oh... I washed your clothes from yesterday. They're in the laundry room. I'll be right back."

I jumped up and hurried to the laundry room, hoping I'd remembered to throw his clothes into the dryer last night. Luckily, I had, and I pulled them out and folded them up, grabbing his wallet and phone before I left.

I set his things beside him on the coffee table. "Here's your phone and wallet, too. Do you need me to find your charger? Is it in your bag?" I moved toward his bag and knelt to unzip it.

"Wait. No. It's not in there. I... uh... I'm pretty sure I left it in the car."

"Oh... okay." I abandoned the bag and straightened, noticing the relief that fell over him. My neck tingled with curiosity. What was in the bag that didn't he want me to see? Or was he just a private person and didn't like people pawing through his stuff?

My cell phone began to ring from upstairs where I'd left it on the charger. "I need to get that." I made a mad dash up the stairs to my room. I recognized the number, and a little thrill went through me. "John. Hi."

"Hey Ella, how are you?"

"I'm good. How about you?" My heart thumped with hope. Was this the call I'd been waiting for?

"Doing well, thanks. I'm just calling to see how you're doing in the new place. How long has it been? A couple of months now?"

"Yeah, that's about right." I paced around my room, unable to hold still.

"So, how's it going? Things working out okay?"

"Uh... sure, but I'm okay to come back home now. I mean... it's nice here and all, but I think I'd be more useful back in New York. I could help a lot more people... people who really need me, you know?" John didn't answer, and my hopes sank.

"That's why you're finally calling, right? Because you want me to come home?"

He blew out a breath. "I'm afraid not."

"What? Why not?"

"Ella, you know you broke the rules... quite a few of them. I did the best I could for you, but certain protocols have to be followed, and you left them no choice. I'm sorry, but nothing's changed yet. I just wanted to check up on you."

"Oh." I couldn't hide my disappointment.

"At least it's nice there, right? You could have been sent to a worse place."

I sniffed. "Yeah... I know. It's beautiful here. It's just... not how I thought things would go."

"I get that."

I sank down on my unmade bed and asked the question I'd been holding inside since I got here. "Do you know how long I'll be here?"

"No. But if I hear anything new, I'll pass it along."

Really? He had nothing to say that would give me a little hope? "That's it? Can't you at least ask them? I mean... it would be nice to know how long I'm going to be stuck here so I can make plans."

"Uh... yes, of course I'll ask. But you haven't actually been there that long, so you shouldn't plan on anything changing for a while."

My breath caught. He didn't think two months was that long? "How long is a while?"

"I don't know... a few more months... maybe longer."

"Are you kidding me?" I huffed out a breath. "But... that's ridiculous. Can't you at least put in a good word for me?"

"Ella... it doesn't work like that."

I knew it didn't, but I was desperate. If he wasn't going to help me, what was the point of this conversation? "So what took you so long to call me anyway?"

"If you want to know the truth, I wasn't sure how angry you'd be, so I put it off."

"Well, I guess you had that part right. I am angry. This is so unfair. I don't belong here. Are you sure there's nothing you can do? I know I'd be more useful anywhere else. Even if it's not New York, there are other places with a lot of people who could use me."

John sighed. "I totally agree, but it's not up to me."

"But you could tell them—"

"Gabriella. Stop. This isn't helping. Look, I know you may not like it, but try and make the best of it, okay?"

I took a deep breath to control my frustration. "I am trying. But it would help to know how much time this is going to take."

"You know... I get that, but all I can tell you is that it will take as long as it needs to."

"What's that supposed to mean?"

"Just that you may not understand why you're there right now, but the answer will come. There's a reason you were sent there. I don't know what that reason is, but if you're looking, you'll figure it out."

I sniffed back my tears. "You mean this is one of those times I won't move on until I've learned my lesson?" When he didn't answer, I stood and began to pace, letting the anger fill up my chest. "You know that's not necessary. I understand what I did. I get it. It won't happen again. You didn't need to send me away to the middle of nowhere to figure that out."

In his answering silence, I knew I wasn't helping my cause by getting angry. I opened my mouth to apologize, but the words got stuck in my throat, and I just couldn't do it. "Uh... I'd better go. We can talk later when I'm not so upset." I almost said, *when I've learned my lesson*, but I managed to hold it in.

"Yes. That's a good idea. You call me when you're ready, just don't take too long, okay?"

"Sure." I ended the call and glanced out my window, taking in the barren countryside. Sure it was beautiful in a quiet, empty sort of way, but I'd never felt so alone in all my life. And here I was, stuck in the middle of nowhere for who knew how long?

Two months had already passed, and this was the first time John had called me. Instead of encouragement, all I got were cryptic messages. What was I doing out here, anyway? As far as I could tell, there was no good reason except as a form of punishment.

What did he think I was? A child? My career was my life. I'd devoted everything I had to it, and sending me here was like a slap in the face. It wasn't fair.

With a heavy sigh, I hurried down the stairs. In order to make it to the car shop before work, I needed to go now.

Creed glanced at me, his eyes narrowed with speculation. It hit me that he'd probably heard my side of the conversation. Great. Just one more thing I had to worry about. Hopefully, he wouldn't pry, because it wasn't any of his business.

"Is everything all right?" he asked.

"Yes. What do you need from your car?"

His brows rose at my clipped tone. "There's a small grocery bag with some things I picked up at the store. If you wouldn't mind getting that for me, along with the phone charger, I'd appreciate it."

"Okay. I'll be back soon."

It was close to seven-thirty, and Seth always opened by seven, so I knew he'd be there. I found him tinkering with a car in the garage. "Hey."

He glanced up and smiled. "Glad to see you survived the night. Are you here about the car?"

"Yeah. I need to get a couple of things out of it."

"The keys are hanging inside the door. I put a yellow tag on them. The car is out back."

"Have you had a chance to look at it?"

"Yep, and it's not good. I'll have to order the parts to fix it, and it might take a week or two. But since your guy has a broken leg, I don't imagine he's going anywhere soon."

"Yeah... probably not."

"It should cost about a grand. Why don't you ask him if I should go ahead and order the parts?"

"Okay... I'll let you know."

"Sounds good."

I found the car keys and headed to the back of the property where he'd left Creed's car. The phone charger was plugged into the console, and I found a plastic bag in the back seat. It held a toothbrush and toothpaste, along with some deodorant and other toiletries—all new.

This little trip of his must have happened pretty quickly if he hadn't packed the basics. I scoured the rest of the car for anything else he might need and found a sales receipt from a couple of days ago. It looked like it was from a gas station in Las Vegas.

Had he come from there, or had he just passed through? At least it was a clue. Shutting the car door, I checked the license plates. They were from Nevada, so maybe Las Vegas was where he'd come from. A shiver ran down my spine. My earlier worries that he was on the run from something seemed more than a possibility. But if it were true, would he tell me?

I locked the car, even though it wasn't going anywhere, and put the keys back in Seth's office. After a quick goodbye to Seth, I drove back to the clinic. Carrying the grocery sack inside, I shut the door behind me and took it straight to Creed. As I approached, he opened his eyes, blinking several times.

"I got your stuff."

"Great... thanks."

"Do you want me to put your toiletries in the bathroom?"

"Um... I guess." He sounded a little groggy, so at least the pills were working.

I set everything out on the counter, and a sinking feeling came over me. He was stuck here for at least two weeks... maybe more. Did that mean I'd have to take care of him for that long? He didn't seem to want to call anyone for help, so that left it to me. But who was he? I needed to know more about him.

Was this what John was talking about? Was Creed the reason I was still here? That hardly seemed right, unless he really was a criminal. My heart sank. It better not be true, or I might just decide that none of this was worth it.

I could always work for someone else. An RN with trauma experience like me could have her pick of jobs anywhere she wanted to work. I'd be done with John and his board of directors. It was an option I'd never considered, and just thinking about it tightened my stomach. I couldn't do it.... at least not now, but I wouldn't rule it out, either.

Feeling better, I took the phone charger into the living room. "Here's your charger, and there's a plug right next to the couch." I plugged it in and handed it over.

"Thanks." His low voice sounded rough around the edges, and for some stupid reason it sent butterflies through my stomach. He connected the charger to his phone and set it on the coffee table. "Did the mechanic have a chance to look at my car?"

"Uh... yeah... if he's going to fix it, he's got to order some parts. It might take a week or two."

"Did he say how much it would cost?"

"Yeah, about a thousand dollars. Do you want me to tell him to go ahead?"

He closed his eyes and sighed, running his hand through his hair. "Yeah, I guess so. I was hoping it wasn't going to be that bad. I guess I'm stuck here for a while."

I couldn't help my sarcasm. "Uh... yeah. But it's not like you can drive anywhere with a broken leg anyway."

His lips twisted. "I guess not." He studied me. "It's a good thing you're taking care of me."

I huffed. "Yeah... I guess I'm stuck with you now."

He grinned, looking inordinately pleased. It changed his handsome face into the drop-dead-gorgeous-category that sent little tremors down my spine.

Unnerved, I frowned. "What are you smiling for?"

"I kind of like it here. I mean... I have someone to do my laundry, run my errands, and cook for me. So... even though I got run over by a car, and ended up with a broken leg and a concussion... it seems like a decent trade—although not entirely fair."

My lips tightened into a thin line. "I didn't run over you."

He grinned, then his brows dipped together. "There is one more thing you could do though."

My eyes widened. "What?"

"Can you adjust the crutches for me, so I can get around a little better? If you're going to be gone all day, I might need to get up on my own."

I huffed out a breath, still a little miffed at him. "Sure." He had asked me nicely, and it was hard to refuse him when he looked at me with such a hopeful expression. "You'll have to stand up so I can get the placement right."

"Sure, I can do that."

It took a minute to help him to his feet, but, since the pain pill had kicked in, he was a lot more relaxed. I helped him balance on one foot and made the adjustment. After tightening the screws, he made his way to the bathroom.

A few minutes later, he came back to the couch, and I helped him get comfortable before I had to go to work. "I've got to open the clinic, but I'll check in on you in a bit. Okay?"

"Yeah... sure."

I left him there and hurried through the apartment, shutting the door behind me. I checked the clinic to make sure nothing was out of place before moving to the main door and unlocking it. I was a few minutes late, but, luckily, no one waited for me.

In this small community, I never knew what to expect. Some days were filled to the brim, and others had only one or two patients. Most people saw the doctor in the next town, but a few had come to see me for more urgent needs, although most of them tended to be tourists visiting the parks.

I spent most of my days treating cuts and bruises, with the occasional broken bone and sprained ankle or wrist. It hardly compared to the work I'd done in New York. I'd saved several lives there, and it was the best feeling I'd ever had. Here, my gift was just wasted. It was stupid.

After slipping on my white jacket, I took a seat at the desk, and I turned on my computer, checking my emails. Next, I called Seth about Creed's car. "Hey Seth, Creed wants you to go ahead and order the parts."

"All right. Did you tell him it might be a couple of weeks?"

"Yes."

"And you're okay that he's staying with you for that long?"

"Yeah, sure."

"Hmm... is he good-looking or something?"

"Seth... stop it."

"Hey... I gotta watch out for my girl, you know. I worry about you being over there all alone, and now you've got some stranger sleeping on your couch."

"Seth... I'm fine. Really... he's helpless."

"If you say so. I'll call you back when I know how soon the parts will get here. I hope you don't mind if I put a rush on them, then he'll be out of your hair quicker."

He hung up before I could respond, so I shook my head and finished getting things set-up for the day.

A car drove up, and a woman hurried inside carrying a screaming child. I met her at the door and ushered her into the exam room while she explained that her two-year-old had gotten his finger slammed in the car door.

Frantic tears ran from the mother's eyes, and I knew it was she who'd done the slamming. She'd wrapped the child's hand in a towel, and I pulled it away to take a look. Blood soaked the towel from a cut that needed stitches, but the bone wasn't broken, so it wasn't too serious.

I explained that her son only needed a few stitches, and he'd be fine. Relieved, she sat in the chair with the toddler on her lap. By this time he was pretty worn out from crying so hard, and it didn't take much to calm him down. I kept a plastic tub, filled with stuffed animals, in the supply closet and chose a little dog for him to hold.

I stroked his little arm with my healing touch, and he quieted right down, allowing me to treat his wound without too much of a fuss. A few minutes later, I was done, and I sent him and his mom off with the stuffed dog and a smile.

The rest of the day was more of the same, with four more people coming to the clinic before I got a chance to check on Creed. I managed to fix him some lunch in between patients, and didn't return to the apartment until closing time.

After locking the clinic up, I stepped inside the apartment, ready for a break. Creed was still lying on the couch, but the TV was turned on to a sports channel, with the sound turned down low. His eyes were closed, but he opened them as I walked in.

I knew right away that he was in pain, and I stepped to his side to feel his forehead. "Your fever's back."

He scrunched his eyes. "Back?"

"Yeah. You had a fever last night. I'll get you something for it."

"Why do I have a fever?"

"Sometimes a broken bone causes inflammation, which can trigger a low-grade fever. It's just a sign that your body is trying to repair itself. Do you have any numbness or tingling?"

"No."

"That's good. I'll be right back." I got the correct dose of medication and took it to him. After he swallowed the pills, I checked his eyes, neck and the bump on the back of his head. It was still there, but not as bad. Later, I'd have to use my gift on him again. It would probably help with the inflammation as well.

"You should feel better soon, and the pills should help your head, too. I'm going to go change, and then I'll make us some dinner."

He gave me a slight nod and closed his eyes again. I hurried up the stairs, throwing my scrubs into the hamper, and decided to take a quick shower before I got dressed. Feeling refreshed, I touched up my makeup and slipped on my favorite comfy shorts and a plain, purple tee.

At the last minute, I spritzed on a dash of my favorite perfume. These days, I wore perfume for my own pleasure, simply because I liked to smell good. And of course, it didn't have anything to do with the handsome man downstairs... nope... not a thing.

Descending the stairs, I caught Creed watching me, his lips tilting up in an appreciative smile. I'd seen that look yesterday when I'd pulled his pants down, and my mouth went dry. Thankfully, I didn't stumble, so that was good. Still, I had to admit that a part of me enjoyed his attention—probably a lot more than I should.

I hurried into the kitchen, trying to decide what to make for dinner. I wasn't much of a cook, and my tastes were simple, so I didn't have a lot on hand. I'd have to ask Creed what kind of food he liked and make a run to the grocery store.

Finding a couple of servings of my favorite tomato-bisque soup, I decided to warm that up and make a couple of grilled-cheese sandwiches to go with it. Creed wasn't ready to sit at the table, and I hoped this wouldn't be too hard for him to eat.

With everything prepared, I loaded the tray with his food and took it over to the coffee table. His eyes jerked open, and he glanced at the tray. "Soup?"

I frowned. "Yes soup... and a grilled cheese sandwich. Is there something wrong with that?"

"Uh... no. It's fine."

From his tone, it didn't sound like it was fine. "Is there something else you'd rather have?"

His brows rose, and his gaze went from me to the tray a few times. "This is fine... but I might want a burger later."

I didn't know what to say, so I set the tray on the coffee table and turned to leave.

"Uh... Ella." He waited for me to turn around before continuing. "I can't reach that."

Groaning under my breath, I stepped to the coffee table. "You want it on your lap?"

"Uh... I don't know. It might be easier if I sit up, but I don't want to put my leg down. It's throbbing a lot right now."

His serious expression and tone of voice showed no signs that he was trying to goad me, and my heart softened. "I'll help you sit up against the armrest, and we can move the pillows to keep your leg elevated. Then maybe I can put the tray on your lap."

"Okay."

He moved into a sitting position, and I shoved a couple of pillows behind his back to prop him up. I moved the pillows under his leg closer to him, so his leg rested easy, and set the tray on his lap.

"How's that?"

"That should work."

"Good." It was on the tip of my tongue to ask him if he could feed himself, but I held back. No need to fuel the fire, especially if he wasn't trying to be a jerk. On impulse, I reached over and touched his forehead.

Surprised, he froze, waiting for me to pull my hand away. "It feels like your fever is gone."

He took a swallow of soup and licked his lips. "This is good. Thanks."

I nodded, watching him take another spoonful.

After swallowing, he hesitated. "Uh... you want to bring yours over and we can eat together?"

"Oh... sure." His request caught me off guard, and I felt bad that I'd been grumpy about helping him. I hurried back to the kitchen and brought my plate and bowl over to the coffee table. I sat on the floor and began to eat, figuring now would be a good time to find out more about him.

He surprised me by talking first. "It sounds like you had a hectic day in the clinic. Is it always like that?"

"You must have heard the screaming kid."

"Yeah. It was hard to miss. What happened to him?"

"He got his finger shut in the car door."

"Oh... ouch."

"Yeah... and it was his mom who did it. I think she took it worse than he did. But he just needed a couple of stitches, so it all worked out."

"Do you ever treat anything really bad?"

"No... not here. Those cases go straight to the hospital. I've patched a couple of people up before they headed there, but that's about it."

He nodded, dipping his sandwich into his soup and taking a bite. Swallowing it down, he continued, "So you've been here a couple of months?"

I nodded, knowing he'd picked that up from my phone call with John this morning. Was that why he was asking so many questions?

"And before that?"

"I worked at a hospital in New York."

His eyes lit up with understanding. "Oh... that makes sense. So what's a trauma nurse doing out here?"

"It's just a rotation kind of thing. I needed a break, so I'm here for now, but I'll be heading back soon."

Before he could comment on the lie I'd just told, I turned the tables on him. "So where are you from?"

"Los Angeles. My mom and my sister are still there, but I've been living in Las Vegas for a while."

"Oh yeah? What do you do in Las Vegas?"

He finished his sandwich and set down his spoon. "Just a few odd jobs here and there."

"I've never been to Vegas, but I hear it's pretty wild with all the lights and people and... stuff."

Pain flashed through his eyes. "Yes... it is. You can find people there from all over the world... and I guess you could say they're up to all kinds of... stuff."

I took a drink of water, hoping to find out more about him. "I'm sure, after all the lights and excitement, this place is kind of a shock. It's about as far from that kind of life as you could get."

"That's true." A frown marred his face, and weariness settled over him. In fact, he seemed totally worn out, much more than his injury accounted for. What he was running from? Whatever it was, it had jaded him somehow, and talking about Vegas had brought it all back. His eyes seemed haunted, like he'd seen too much of the bad side of the world.

Before I could ask him any more questions, he picked up the tray. "Thanks for the food. It was good."

I jumped up and took the tray from him. Setting it on the coffee table, I added my dishes to it and carried it back to the kitchen. "Can I get you anything else?"

"I was hoping to take a shower... or a bath. Is that possible? Can we take the brace off?"

I came back to the couch and sat on the armrest by his feet. "Uh... not tonight. I'm not sure you're well enough, and I'd hate for you to pass out on me, but maybe we can tackle it tomorrow." At his crestfallen expression, I continued. "For now, I could give you a sponge bath."

His eyes widened. "You mean here? On the couch?"

"Yes." I shrugged like it wasn't a big deal.

He arched his right brow. "Would I have to take off all my clothes?"

"No." I huffed. "Just your shirt. I'm not washing below the belt."

"Oh." He sagged with feigned disappointment, then caught my gaze and smiled. "Okay. I'm game."

I couldn't help smiling back, amazed that I'd agreed to give him a sponge bath. How had that happened? Had he manipulated me into it? Maybe, but I was the one who'd offered. Me and my big mouth. Heaving out a sigh, I shook my head.

"I'll get the stuff."

"Looking forward to it."

At his low, sexy tone, a thrill shot through me, and I knew I was an idiot.

CHAPTER THREE

I filled up a small bucket with hot water and grabbed a couple of clean towels and a washcloth. Even though I tried to quiet my inner anticipation, I lugged everything over to the couch with a hint of excitement.

Schooling my tone so I would sound totally professional, I began. "While you're propped up on the couch, why don't you take your shirt off?"

Creed's gaze caught mine, and his eyes darkened. "Okay. But you might have to help me. I'm kind of stiff."

My brows rose, but he'd already begun to tug at the scrub top he still wore. As he lifted his arms, I helped him pull the shirt over his head.

"I'll get your back while you're sitting up." Wringing out the washcloth, I gently washed his bare back and neck, noticing several bruises around his ribs and lower back. Since I was the cause, I sent a pulse of healing power into my hands, gently running my fingers over his back.

Without his gaze on me, I could admire his toned muscles and broad back all I wanted. I spent more time than was actually necessary to do the job, but he probably enjoyed it too, so I couldn't feel too bad.

Finished, I slipped most of the pillows out from under him and put a towel beneath him. "Okay. You can lay back now." I made sure his leg was still propped up, and he was comfortable. I dipped the washcloth in the hot water and wrung it out. "I'll start with your arms."

"Sure. Have at it."

Determined not to get distracted, I washed each of his strong arms, needing to lean over him a little to wash his other side. A contented smile played over his lips, and I couldn't help my remark. "Enjoying this?"

His half-lidded gaze met mine. "Immensely."

Ugh. What was I doing? I enjoyed it too... way more than I should, but I didn't want to stop, especially as I ran the washcloth over the contours of his toned chest. After the warm cloth left his skin to the chill air, a shiver rippled through his muscles, and I watched them with fascination. I rubbed the cloth over his chest several more times before realizing I was taking shallow breaths through my open mouth.

Mortified, I snapped my jaw shut and turned my head away to swallow, dipping the cloth into the hot water as an excuse. Creed's eyes were closed, and it disappointed me that he didn't seem as affected by my touch as I did, so I decided a little teasing was in order. Taking hold of his forearm, I lifted it to rest above his head on the couch.

His eyes flew open, but he didn't resist, not even with a small jerk. He had to know what I intended, so he either wasn't ticklish, or he wanted to prove he could take it. Chewing on my bottom lip, I rubbed the wet washcloth across his armpit, holding back a smile as his breath caught.

Still, he didn't budge, so I lowered that arm and leaned across him to grasp the other one. My face hovered precariously close to his. Holding my breath, I swiped the cloth across that side, rubbing several times for good measure.

He didn't even flinch. Since I wanted to get the best of him, I moved the cloth slowly down his side. He gasped, jerking his hand from my grasp, and squirming from my touch. "Okay... okay... you win... you got me."

I straightened, laughing. "That'll teach you."

"Teach me what?" His brow rose with a challenge.

"That you can't mess with me."

He flashed a smile. "Oh yeah... you New Yorkers are so tough... nothing like a sissy from L.A."

I grinned back. "You got that right."

"Well, where I come from, we don't let a challenge go unanswered."

I huffed. "You can't tickle me."

"Why not?"

"You might hurt yourself."

He froze and his eyes narrowed. Knowing I would be in trouble for that, I pounced first. This time, I tickled him with abandon, and I had no intention of letting up, especially since there wasn't much he could do about it.

He let out a groan and flinched, taking it for a few more seconds before his powerful arms pinned me against his chest. He held me so tightly that I could hardly move, even to struggle.

"Okay... okay. You got me. Time out." He loosened his hold, and I pulled away to smirk. "You west siders talk too much, that's why you lose."

He sucked in a breath and clamped me against him. Holding me down with one arm, he began to tickle me with the other, surprising me with his strength. I'd underestimated him, and now I was paying for my mistake.

I shrieked and squirmed to get away. He quickly let me go, nearly shoving me off him, a grimace of pain tightening his face. "Ow. My leg."

"Oops. Too much?"

"Yes." He clenched his teeth, and remorse filled me. I started rubbing his arms, hoping it would soothe him. His taut muscles began to relax, and his panting slowed.

"Better?"

"A little, especially if you keep that up."

Without thinking, I moved my hands to his chest. Then I froze and watched his eyes darken and his lips part. Unbidden desire rushed over me. Kissing him seemed like the most natural thing in the world. I leaned forward, ready to taste his full lips.

Whoa. What was I doing?

I pulled back a bit, and the anticipation in his eyes turned to disappointment. The realization that he'd wanted a kiss from me raised my confidence. Now that I had the upper hand, I straightened beside him. "I can't believe you let me wash your armpits."

He gasped. "You little devil..."

I chuckled, and he grabbed me tightly, pinning me against him. My breath caught with surprise, but I didn't dare struggle, knowing it might hurt him. His eyes blazed with desire, and my heart raced. Giving in, I lowered my mouth to his, and our lips met in a searing kiss.

Heat rose from my stomach to blossom in my chest. The feel of his bare skin beneath me sent my head spinning. Kissing him was like being thrown into a blazing inferno. He consumed me to the point that I lost myself in his touch. We merged into one, and there was nothing else but this moment.

A ringing phone penetrated my consciousness, pulling me back from the edge of total abandon. My eyes flew open, and I jerked upright, panting for breath. Creed's dazed eyes cleared as the sound registered. I licked my lips and reached for my phone where it sat on the coffee table.

"Hello?"

"Hello... we've been trying to reach you concerning your car's extended warranty. Your warranty will expire soon. This is your final call—"

"Ugh." I stabbed the phone to end the call and dropped it on the table.

"Wrong number?" Creed asked.

"No, just a stupid telemarketer. They drive me crazy."

"Yeah... that was... really bad timing."

I sucked in a breath and jumped to my feet, needing to put some distance between us. What had just happened? I wasn't supposed to kiss him. My lips still tingled. In fact, my whole body hummed. My heart raced, and even my legs were a little shaky.

"I'd better... uh... make sure the back door is locked."

As I rushed to the door, Creed called out behind me. "Aren't you going to finish? I think you missed a spot."

That stopped me in my tracks. I headed to the kitchen sink and filled a glass with cold water. Pouring it over his face might teach him a lesson in manners, and it would certainly make me feel better. Taking it back to him, I smiled. "You're right. I forgot to wash your face." I poured the glass of water onto his face. He sputtered and wiped the water from his eyes, his mouth open in shock.

I held back a smile and grabbed the extra towel to dab at his face. "That should do it, unless you need a dose of cold water somewhere else?" I eyed his stomach and my gaze dipped a little lower before jerking away.

He snatched the towel from my hands and pushed up on one arm. Wiping his face and neck, he picked up the scrub top. It was wet, along with the towel I'd draped behind him.

"Here... let me get that." I took the towel and washcloth, along with his shirt, and set them down beside the bucket of water. "I can put these in the wash. Do you have another t-shirt in your bag?"

I began to unzip the bag.

"Wait."

Creed's words came too late. I froze. Several rolls of hundred-dollar bills filled the bag. My breath caught. What the hell? Did he rob someone? Hold up a bank? Was he running from the law?

He twisted his head to look at me. "It's not what you think."

Anger, and a touch of fear, unfurled in my chest. "How... how do you know what I'm thinking?"

"I can see it in your eyes. You're judging me. You think I did something wrong, and I didn't."

I sat back on my heels. "Okay. Then what is it. Why do you have all that money?"

The openness on his face shuttered. "I won it. No stealing... it was nothing illegal. I won it fair and square."

"How?"

"Playing poker."

Surprised, it took me a moment to answer. "Are you serious?"

He sighed. "I am... but most of it is seed money... you know... to buy into the game. The good ones start at ten grand, and I cashed out my chips before I started losing." He shrugged. "I may not be too popular at that particular casino for a while."

"I'll bet... I mean... right."

He flopped back against the cushions. "Could you get me a dry shirt now?"

"Uh... yeah... sure."

"My clothes are on the other side of the bag."

I knelt down and finished unzipping the bag. A few t-shirts, along with another pair of jeans and several pairs of socks and boxers, filled the opposite end. Too bad the money hadn't been on that side, and I would have totally missed it. Of course, then I wouldn't know what he was up to... not that I did now. He could still be lying.

While I poked around, I couldn't help sizing up the amount of money sitting there. If all those rolls were made of hundred-dollar bills, it had to come close to somewhere between thirty and fifty grand, and that guess was probably on the low end. That seemed like a lot of cash to be carrying around in a duffel bag. No wonder he was so concerned about it.

Swallowing, I tugged a black t-shirt from the bag and handed it to him. While he worked to put it on, I zipped the bag up and took the bucket of water to the sink. After emptying it, I threw the towels and his t-shirt in for a quick wash.

Doubt crowded my mind. I wanted to believe him, but why should I? What if he was a dangerous criminal? What if the police were looking for him right now? Would he want to hurt me, now that I knew, or try and take off in my Jeep? Wait. He couldn't do that. He had a broken leg, so he was pretty much at my mercy.

I sighed. He seemed like a good person, and I wanted to believe him. A part of me wanted to give him the benefit of the doubt. And... it had nothing to do with that amazing kiss or the vulnerable gleam in his beautiful, blue eyes. Nope, nothing at all.

There was an easy way to test his story. I could get him to teach me how to play poker. Then, later, I could check the news for someone running from the law in Las Vegas. Of course, the smarter thing might be to call the police... and ask them to check him out. But... I could do that tomorrow. For now, he wasn't going anywhere.

Sticking to my plan, I rummaged through the kitchen drawers for a deck of cards. In the bottom drawer, I found them, and a small smile broke out over my face.

Taking them to the couch, I sat down and held them up. "Look what I found."

His cautious eyes widened. "Nice. Does that mean you know how to play?"

"No. But I'd like to learn. If you're the card shark you say you are, it will give me a chance to learn from the best."

Surprise washed over him, but he ruined it by smirking. "Okay... I'll bite. But what are you willing to wager?"

"Wait a minute. I'm not betting anything until after I learn how to play."

He shrugged. "Playing without betting doesn't work, even for a first-time player. There's got to be something around here you're willing to part with."

Why did that make me nervous? The gleam in his eyes came back, and he took the deck of cards from me. After getting them out, he realized his stomach wasn't a good place to shuffle them or deal them out. "If you're serious about playing, I think I can sit at the table for a little bit."

I shrugged. "Works for me."

I helped him up, and it took several minutes to get him settled at the table, especially since I had to help him prop his leg up on a chair. "While you're shuffling, I'll find something to use for poker chips, since I don't have any."

"When I first started learning, we used pennies. But anything will work."

"I might have something." I stepped into the kitchen and pulled open a cupboard door. Inside, I found a bag of wrapped, chocolate truffles. "Will these work?"

"Is that your favorite?"

"Uh... it's chocolate, creamy and delicious... so yes."

"Then they're perfect."

Creed shuffled the deck like a pro, and I knew he hadn't lied about that. He explained the betting with the small blind and the big blind before explaining the winning hands. I couldn't keep it all straight, but he was patient with my questions.

We played a few games, and Creed won every time. I hated to see my chocolates disappear, but he didn't eat them, so I hoped to get them back. After the fourth game, Creed rubbed his brow, and his eyes became dull. He didn't say anything, but, after the round, I put my hand over his.

"That's good for tonight." He glanced at my hand, and I quickly pulled it away. What was I doing?

"You're right. I'm going to use the bathroom and lie down. Is it time for another pain pill?"

"I think so."

"Good."

I moved the chair and helped him up, walking with him to the bathroom door. He went inside and shut the door. While he was occupied, I took all the chocolates he'd won and put them back into the bag before he noticed. With that done, I finished cleaning up the kitchen and wiped down the countertop.

The bathroom door opened, and I helped him back to the couch. After he was settled, I fixed the pillows, so he was more comfortable, and got him another pain pill, along with a bottle of water. Thanking me, he swallowed it down. "I had no idea a broken leg could be so painful."

"Yeah."

"How long did you say it would take to heal? I'm a little fuzzy on that part."

"It's going to take a while... probably about six weeks before you can walk on it again." I knew I might be able to speed up the process with my touch, but I wasn't sure by how much.

"Six weeks?" At my nod, he shook his head. "What about a walking cast? Would that work after a couple of weeks?"

"Maybe. I'll have to see how it's doing by then."

He took a deep breath. "Oh."

"Don't worry about it right now. Just get your rest. That will help you more than anything. And... maybe we can play poker again tomorrow?"

He smiled. "I'd like that. But next time, you're not taking my winnings."

My eyes widened. "Dang... you noticed that?" At his raised brow, I shook my head. "How about next time we play, you just keep half, since I'm only half as good as you? I mean... as it is, you have the advantage."

His lips twisted. "Angel, I'll always have the advantage. And I wouldn't say you're half as good. It's maybe an eighth or even less. But I might bargain with you for some of my winnings, if you make it worth my while."

I snapped my mouth shut, surprised by his audacity. "Wow... you're certainly full of yourself." I folded my arms. "Maybe I'll surprise you."

He grinned. "I look forward to it. Goodnight Ella."

"Night."

Before I turned to walk away, he grabbed my wrist. "Hey... I uh... told you the truth about the money, but I don't blame you if you want to check out my story. Call the police if you want... it's fine with me."

He let go of my wrist before continuing. "You should check me out. I mean... even though you hit me with your car... and broke my leg... and gave me a concussion... I'm not going press charges, because you're trying to make up for it."

I pursed my lips. "Right."

"Exactly." His lips turned into a sexy smile. "But don't get too attached to me. I can't stay here forever, you know."

I huffed out a breath. "Well... you certainly don't have to worry about that."

He chuckled, and I rushed to the back door before he noticed that he'd rattled me. After locking it, I hurried up the stairs to my room and washed my flushed face. Finishing up my nighttime routine, I slipped under the covers, but lay awake for a long time.

I knew he'd leave as soon as he could, and part of me didn't like that idea. But that was stupid. I didn't want to get attached to him, I wanted to go home. Still, if it made the next two weeks of my life bearable, how could I complain? For now, I would enjoy his company while I could and try not to worry about what happened after he was gone.

After a restless night, I got up early, unable to sleep any longer. I dressed for the day, taking extra time with my hair before heading downstairs. At the bottom of the stairs, I glanced Creed's way and found him looking at me. "Oh... good morning... I hope I didn't wake you."

"S'okay. I need to get up anyway." He sat up, cringing with pain as he eased his leg to the floor. Gathering his crutches, he wobbled toward the bathroom.

I got out a box of cereal, a bowl, and the milk, and sat at the counter to eat. As I finished up, Creed opened the door and took a seat at the table.

"You want some cereal?" I asked.

"Sure."

I took the box and a bowl over to the table, then returned with the milk and a spoon. It wasn't much, so I made him some toast to go with it. After buttering the toast, I took it over, along with the orange juice container and a glass. He mumbled his thanks between bites.

"How did you sleep?"

He shook his head. "Not well. It's hard to get comfortable with a broken leg, especially since I have to keep it propped up."

"Yeah... I'll bet. Maybe after work today, you can take that shower. That might help you feel better."

"I wouldn't mind another sponge bath."

I laughed. "That can be arranged." He smiled, but his eyes had lost their sparkle. "You look like you could use another pain pill."

"I'm afraid so."

I got the pill and a bottle of water out for him. It wasn't time for work, but I had some things I wanted to do before the day began. "I've got to go, but help yourself to anything you need around here. If you watch TV, just make sure it's not too loud. And, if you need anything else, I'm just right through that door."

He nodded, so I continued. "I don't know how busy it will be... but I'll be back for lunch."

As he finished up his breakfast, I slipped through the connecting door to the office. After unlocking the front door, I booted up my computer and searched the news outlets in Las Vegas, looking for anything that spoke of stolen money, a bank robbery, or a manhunt, going back to a couple of days before Creed showed up.

I found a couple of interesting stories, but nothing to indicate him, or anyone like him, who'd run off with a bunch of stolen money.

I contemplated calling the local police here in Sandy Creek to have them check Creed out, but that seemed like overkill. Plus, he had a point that I didn't want to make a fuss, since that meant I'd have to explain that I'd hit him and broken his leg in the first place.

Satisfied that he wasn't a threat, I finished getting ready for the day. Only two people showed up in the morning, leaving me with time on my hands. My neighbor, Evelyn, who lived across the street, picked that time to come over. She'd probably been watching and knew no one was here. In her arms, she carried a large, brown paper bag.

We greeted each other and she set the bag down, taking out a beautiful, golden delicious apple. "You probably don't know this, but this town and the surrounding area is known for its apple orchards. So I wanted to bring some over. These are some of the best apples you'll ever taste."

"Wow... thanks so much. I can't wait to try one. That's real nice of you."

She shrugged. "I'm happy to share. You haven't been here very long, but I thought you should know that we're grateful you're here. That was my grandson you treated yesterday, and my daughter was beside herself that she shut the door on his poor little finger. She was fit to be tied."

I smiled. "Yeah... she seemed almost worse off than him."

"I can imagine. Well... I wanted to thank you for taking such good care of him."

"Of course."

"Oh... before I go... I was at Seth's garage this morning, and he told me you had somebody staying here with you. Is he a friend from New York?"

Now I knew why she was really here, and I lifted my brow. "Did Seth tell you to keep an eye on me?"

She had the good sense to duck her head. "Uh... well... he might have. You know how he is."

I nodded, knowing all about it, but I couldn't be too upset with him. I just wish he hadn't told anyone about Creed. "Well, you don't need to worry about me. He's a friend, so it's all good."

"Oh... okay... good. Uh... that's nice for you to have some company. Well, I'll be on my way then. Enjoy the apples."

"Thanks. I will."

She hurried out the door, and I shut it behind her. Now she'd probably tell everyone I had a man staying with me, and who knew what rumors would come of it?

Since it was nearly time for lunch, I put the buzzer out on the front desk and took the apples back to the apartment. Creed was asleep on the couch, but stirred when I came in. "It's early for lunch," I told him. "But there's not much going on right now and a neighbor brought these apples. You want one?"

"Sure."

"I'll make you a peanut butter and jelly sandwich to go with it if you want?"

He nodded, but stayed put on the couch. I washed an apple and handed it to him to eat while I fixed his lunch. I set his sandwich on the coffee table and took a bite of apple. "Wow. These really are amazing." He agreed, but, before I could finish it, the buzzer rang, and I had to get back to work.

The rest of the day was about the same, with only a couple of sore throats that came back negative for strep. At five o'clock, I locked up before heading back to the apartment.

Creed wasn't on the couch, and the bathroom door was open and empty. I stepped to the back door, finding Creed sitting on the steps with his leg propped up beside him. Hearing me, he glanced my way. "I couldn't sit inside for another minute."

It was almost too hot to sit outside, even in the shade, but I didn't blame him. The back porch had a small, covered patio off to the side, and I'd planted a few flowers in a couple of pots. I kept forgetting to water them, so they were barely alive.

"If you're going to sit out here, you should sit in one of those nicer chairs. That cement is hard. Come on... I'll help you."

He didn't seem too excited to move, but with my help, he made it to the cushioned chair in the shade. Next, I helped him prop his leg up on the other chair and noticed the tension leave his body. He laid his head back on the cushion and groaned. "Yeah... that's much better... thanks. At this rate, we might be even by the time I'm ready to go."

I huffed out a breath. He grinned back, transforming his handsome features into serious hotness. It nearly took my breath away. Luckily, his eyes were closed, and he didn't notice my flushed face.

"It's nice out here," he continued. "So quiet. I never realized the constant noise in the city could be so... draining, you know?"

I nodded, hoping he'd open up a little more, since it would be nice to know why he'd left. The warmth in his eyes caught at my heart, and I smiled. Noticing a tuft of dark hair sticking up from the side of his head, I wanted nothing more than to smooth it down, just so I could touch him.

Unfamiliar longing unfurled in my stomach, so I glanced away, taking in the barren countryside. "Yeah... that's how I felt when I first got here. Now that I've been here a while, it's a little too quiet... and... so empty."

His brows drew together, and he studied me. Was that pity in his eyes?

"I'm going to head inside and change my clothes so I can go to the grocery store. If there's anything you want, or anything special you'd like to eat, let me know."

He nodded, and I beat a hasty retreat to my room, throwing my scrubs into the hamper and changing back into my shorts and t-shirt. In the kitchen, I wrote up a quick shopping list and slung my purse over my head. As I came out, I glanced Creed's way. "Did you think of anything?"

"Yes. I did." He paused, so I nodded at him to continue. "First, I'd like something better than cereal for breakfast... like eggs, hash browns, and bacon. Then there's lunch... how about some ham and cheese for sandwiches, and for dinner I'd like something more substantial than soup.

"I was thinking of steak. I love a good rib-eye steak with a loaded baked potato. Chicken's okay too, as long as it's got some kind of sauce on it, or if it's breaded. And... I could always go for a burger and fries, so you should put that on the list too."

My lips twisted. "Wow... uh... don't hold back or anything."

Trying not to smile, his mouth twisted. "Okay... then how about a cold beer? Bud Light's okay, or Corona, if they have it. I'm happy to give you some cash if you need it."

I shook my head. "I'll see what I can do." I stepped toward the garage.

"Oh... Ella, one more thing."

Letting out a sigh, I turned back to face him.

"You'd better get some more of those chocolates if we're going to keep playing poker, especially if you want any for yourself."

I shook my head and entered the garage, not even bothering to reply. As I backed out, he sent me a wave. I just shook my head and drove to the little market in town. Most people drove an hour to Richmond to fill their pantries, but I didn't have time for that. This little market had all of the essentials, but the prices weren't cheap, so I knew they'd be happy to see me.

Nearly an hour later, I drove home with four bags of groceries and no beer. I did manage to score a couple of steaks, but they were New York steaks instead of rib-eye, which suited me just fine. I pulled into the garage, checking to see if Creed still sat on the deck, but he wasn't there.

I lugged a couple of the bags inside, finding Creed back on the couch watching some kind of sports game.

He sent me a wave. "I'd help you bring those in if I could."

That sounded way too chipper for my taste. Once all the groceries were inside, it took me a good fifteen minutes to put everything away. I'd already decided to cook up our steaks tonight, and cranked the oven up for the potatoes. After slipping them in the oven, I made a green salad before taking the steaks out to my grill to cook them.

That was the one thing I'd learned how to use after I'd arrived. Cooking inside on a hot day made my upstairs bedroom too hot, even with the AC. When the grill was ready, I slapped on the steaks, grilling them on both sides before turning down the heat and setting the timer.

Back inside, I set the table, realizing that I usually sat at the counter and ate whatever was easiest to fix. This was the first proper sit-down meal that I'd shared with someone since I'd come here. Was that pathetic, or what?

Soon, everything was ready and I called Creed to the table. As he hobbled over on his crutches, his eyes seemed brighter. That meant he either had a fever, or it had run its course, and it was anticipation to eat the food that brightened his eyes.

His anticipation spread to me. I hadn't had a meal like this in ages. Being on my own, I never felt like cooking much, so this was a treat for me as well.

"This looks amazing." Creed smiled at me, taking in the green salad, baked potato, butter and sour cream.

"I'll get the steaks." I'd left them to sit for ten minutes, and now they looked tender and juicy enough to make my stomach growl. With their mouth-watering aroma, I glanced Creed's way and smiled at the eagerness on his face.

To say Creed demolished the food would be an understatement. He moaned his way through the steak and sent me a smile that made fixing him a good meal totally worth it.

Finished, he sat back in his chair. "That was amazing. Thank you so much. Everything was great."

I nodded. "You're welcome." Not used to compliments on my cooking, I got busy clearing the dishes. Creed stacked the plates and did what he could to help me. "Go ahead and lie down. I'll finish up."

"Are you sure?"

"Yes."

He sat down on the couch and put his leg up, but watched me instead of turning on the TV. "You must be feeling a little better."

"Yeah... I think I'm ready to try taking a shower."

I nodded. "Okay. Let me finish up, and I'll help you." I'd said that like I didn't care, but just thinking about helping him shower did something to my nerves.

Hopefully, good planning would save me from anything embarrassing, and I thought about how to do it while I finished up the dishes.

Ready to begin, I put my plan into action and placed an old folding chair from my storage closet in the shower stall. It barely fit, but there was just enough room to put the soap and washcloth within reach. I set the shampoo bottle on the floor and found a towel, which I placed on the toilet lid.

The showerhead might be a problem in the small space, so I moved the chair as close to the end of the stall as I could. Still, it would probably end up spraying him right in the face, but there wasn't much I could do about that.

Just thinking about what was coming sent my heart rate through the roof, and I had to take a couple of calming breaths to cool off. What the hot damn hell? I was a professional. I could handle seeing a naked body.

Too bad I'd kissed him yesterday. If that hadn't happened, maybe I wouldn't be feeling this way. Ha. Who was I kidding? Even without the kiss, he was too good-looking to make this anything but torture. Still, it was the kind of torture I was willing to endure.

I came back to the couch and explained what I'd done. "Okay, everything's ready. There's a chair inside the shower stall for you to sit on. I thought you could take your clothes off in the bathroom after you're sitting down on the chair… uh… with a little help."

His brows rose, and he sent me a knowing smile. Before he could make a snide remark, I continued. "Then I'll turn on the water and you can wash up. The only problem is the brace. We can't take it off, but I have a plastic leg cover we can put over it to keep it dry."

"Okay. Let's do this." Creed rose to his feet and hobbled into the bathroom on his crutches with me right behind him.

I helped him maneuver over the lip of the shower stall and steadied the chair as he sat down. I leaned his crutches against the wall and turned to face him. The stall seemed to shrink with him sitting inside. "Okay… go ahead and take off your shirt."

After he pulled off his t-shirt, he had to stand again on one leg to get the scrub bottoms off. "Here, lean on me, and I'll pull them down."

I bent over, keeping my head down, and tried not to think about how close my face was to his rock solid abs. Still, my cheek brushed his stomach, and I tried to keep my composure.

"What about my boxers? Are you going to help me with those, too?"

"Ha... you wish... but no. I'll turn my back while you do it. You can use my shoulder to help you balance, then I'll give you a towel to cover yourself until I close the curtain."

"Okay... but you're missing out."

I huffed. "Not when you stink so bad."

"Whatever."

I turned away from him while he kept one hand on my shoulder and got to work. "This is kind of tricky. I can't get them down very far."

"That's okay. Just get them down as far as you can and then sit down on the chair. After you've got the towel covering you, I'll do the rest."

Still holding my shoulder, he sat down, letting out a big sigh. "Where's that towel?" With my back turned, I handed it to him and waited while he got it situated. "Okay. I'm covered up."

I turned slowly, just in case he was pulling a fast one, and let out a breath. Working together, we managed to get his boxers off, and, once they were out of the way, I slipped the plastic leg cover over the brace, careful to keep my eyes from straying too much, although I did slip in a look or two. What can I say, I'm not perfect.

"Okay. That will keep the water off the brace. Now we can turn on the shower. You ready?"

"Yeah."

I pulled the curtain closed and held out my hand for the towel. He handed it over, and I reached in to turn on the water. "Okay... here goes. It might be a little cold at first."

With that warning, I turned it on, cranking it to the setting between hot and cold while a blast of cold water sprayed over him. He sputtered and gasped, and I tried not to laugh out loud.

"Shit. It's freezing. Can you lower the spray? It's hitting me right in the face."

"I'll try." I pushed it as low as I could, but it wasn't much. "Is that better?"

"Not really. You need to make it warmer."

I turned the knob. "How's that? More?"

"No... that's good."

"Okay." I pulled back and tightened the curtain before sitting down on the toilet seat. "The soap and shampoo are next to the chair."

"Yeah... got it."

"Let me know if you need anything. I'll be right here." The scent of soap filled the room, followed by the mint shampoo smell I liked.

A few minutes later, he spoke. "Okay. I'm done. You can turn off the water." I reached in and turned it off, then slipped a large towel to him while leaving the curtain closed. I listened to him dry off and waited for him to finish.

"Okay... I'm as dry as I can get. Sitting down, anyway."

"Why don't you wrap the towel around your waist? Then I can get the plastic covering off your brace. After that, we'll get you back to the couch, and you can get dressed there."

"Sure. Go ahead and open the curtain."

I pulled it back, taking in the sight of his muscled chest and abs, down to his lap barely covered with a towel. It was enough to give my poor heart palpitations. I sucked in a breath and quickly dried off the plastic cover with another towel and gently pulled it off his leg.

"There... that should do it. Ready to go?"

"Just about... can you hand me my deodorant first?"

"Sure... especially since it will help with the smell." I handed it over. Not about to let the opportunity slip by, I let my gaze wander over his perfect body while he put it on. "You must work out... a lot." Did I just say that out loud?

He smirked, handing me his deodorant. "Can't keep your eyes off me, can you?"

I set the deodorant on the sink without looking and shrugged. "I could take it or leave it."

His lips twisted. "Fine. Now what?"

"Uh... go ahead and put your arm around my shoulders. Then stand on your good leg while I brace you." As he stood, the towel slipped just a bit. "Keep the towel on!"

Letting out a huff, he caught the towel right before it fell. I slipped my shoulder beneath his arm and wrapped my arm around his waist. Grabbing one of his crutches, I held it out. "Okay. Now slip the crutch under your arm, and hop over the rim."

"If I do that, you know that I'll have to let go of the towel, right?"

I swallowed. "Uh... yeah, I can see that. I'll hold onto the towel."

He huffed out a breath. "I don't think that will work."

"Yes it will. Just take the crutch."

"Okay." He let go of the towel, and it promptly fell to the ground, long before I could catch it.

I gasped, getting an eyeful, and jerked my gaze away, trying to focus anywhere else. That worked for about two seconds before I looked again. "Dammit."

He chuckled, hardly bothered at all. "I told you."

"All right, all right. Just... lean your weight on me, and put the crutch outside of the shower. Then you can hop over the rim."

He followed my instructions and managed to hop over the rim. I steadied him until he caught his balance, and let out a relieved breath. "Okay... you steady?"

"Yeah... I think so."

"Okay... good. I'm going to move out from under your arm now and hand you your other crutch."

I ducked out from under his arm and turned behind me for his crutch. I handed it over, and he placed it under his arm. Once he was steady, he hobbled through the door, with me following behind. I hated to admit it, but I couldn't pull my gaze away from all that magnificent, bare flesh.

I stood in the bathroom doorway, admiring his progress all the way to the couch. He rounded the corner and sat down. I sighed rather loudly... through puckered lips... which might have sounded like a whistle, but I couldn't help it.

Creed glanced over the back of the couch and shook his head. "Did you plan that?"

"What? No... of course not."

"Uh-huh. Do you want me to get dressed now? Or is there something else you wanted me to do?"

"No... I mean yes... get dressed."

His mouth twisted. "Sure... but, you realize I'm going to need some help, right?"

"Of course." I stepped toward him, but stopped. "Uh... you have to cover up first."

He rolled his eyes and chuckled. "Okay... I'm decent."

Fighting down a shiver of anticipation, I swallowed and stepped around the couch. The blanket covered him, and I stood there for a minute, not sure where to start. Part of me wanted to move closer to him, but another part warned me to stay away.

He let out a disgruntled breath. "I just need help getting my boxers over the brace, I can do the rest."

"Uh... right."

He handed me a fresh pair of boxers, and I knelt at his feet, pulling them past the brace and up to his knees.

"You might want to turn around while I pull these up." Not waiting, he began to pull them up, and I quickly turned away. "Okay. I'm covered." He eased back down and motioned to his cargo shorts. "Can you help me with those too?"

"Yes."

Pulling the shorts over his brace wasn't too hard, and his t-shirt went on pretty fast after that. He relaxed back against the couch and let out a breath. "That was exhausting."

I smiled. "Yeah... do you feel better?"

"I do... everywhere but under the brace."

"Right. I've been meaning to take a look at your leg. As long as you hold still, I can take the brace off and wash your leg."

"I can do that."

"Okay, I'll be right back." I quickly filled my bucket with hot water and grabbed a clean towel and a washcloth. I grabbed some gel as well, since I planned to use my gift again. I didn't know how much it would help a second time, but there was no reason not to try it out.

I carefully removed the brace, making sure his leg was secure on top of the pillows. "It looks like the swelling's gone down, so that's good."

Next, I washed his leg and foot, careful not to jostle the bone or push too hard. After his skin was clean, I applied a little gel to my fingertips and brushed my hands over the bone a few times, stopping to lay my palms directly over the break.

Closing my eyes, I sent a surge of healing power into the bone and surrounding tissue. As the heat left my hands and sank into his leg, I imagined the bone knitting together. A few seconds later, I pulled my hands away, dizzy and out of breath. Whoa... that had never happened before. I blinked, surprised at how weak I felt.

I glanced at Creed. His eyes were shut, and his face held peace. As his eyes fluttered open, I reached for the brace and put it back on, hoping he didn't notice my shaking hands.

"That's strange... it doesn't hurt as much."

"Really? That's good."

His brow puckered. "Did you put something on it? Like some lotion or something? It feels hot and cold, like that icy-hot stuff."

"Oh... yeah... I did put some gel on it."

"That must be it." His eyes lit up. "If it helps that much, maybe you'll have to put some more on tomorrow."

"Yeah, I can probably do that." Still feeling a little weak, I rose slowly. "Uh... I'm going to get a drink of water. Do you want something?"

"Did you get the beer I wanted?"

I shrugged. "Afraid not, but I did get some diet soda. You want one?"

"Eww... no."

I smiled and stepped toward the kitchen. The room tilted, and I caught the side of the couch until it stopped moving. Taking a breath, I continued walking, hoping that Creed hadn't noticed anything. He didn't comment, so I poured out a glass of water and drank it down.

That seemed to do the trick, so I drank another glass of water. Feeling much better, I turned toward him, holding up the bag I'd left on the counter. "I got some more chocolates. You want to play some poker?"

He chuckled. "You bet."

CHAPTER FOUR

Starting with twenty chocolates each, we began a game of poker. I tried my hand at shuffling and didn't do too badly, but I wasn't anywhere close to Creed's level. Creed won the first round, but instead of adding the chocolates to his pile, he ate them.

"Wait, what are you doing? How will we know who won if you eat your winnings?"

He shrugged. "Yours will be gone, and I'll still have twenty left to eat later."

My mouth dropped open. Snapping it shut, I unwrapped one of my chocolates and stuck it in my mouth, letting it melt on my tongue. At his raised brow, I shrugged. "Hey, if you're going to eat them anyway, I might as well have some too."

"But you're defeating the purpose."

"Maybe, but if I don't win soon, I'm stopping. I know better than to lose them all."

He grinned. "Maybe there is hope for you yet."

I won the next game, but that's because he folded. Had he done it on purpose? I won the next game too, making my stash bigger than his. Exhilaration that I'd won caught me on fire, and I didn't want to slow down, even during the next several games when my chocolates began to dwindle.

Three games later, I only had four left. Still, all I needed were a couple of good cards, and I could win it all back. Creed had stopped eating the chocolates long ago, and his pile was huge. I wanted them back, but nothing I did seemed to be working.

With two left, I let out a disgusted breath. "Okay... you win. I'm out."

"But you still have two."

"I know, and I'd rather eat them than lose them to you."

His lips twisted. "I guess that's fair." He set his cards down and leaned against the back of his chair. "I need to lie down anyway. My leg is starting to ache."

He scooted his chair back and picked up his crutches. "Uh... will you put my chocolates in a bag for me? I wouldn't want them to disappear before I got to eat them."

I shrugged. "Whatever."

His smug smile stayed on his face all the way to the couch. I put the cards and the chocolates away, then finished up the dinner dishes and wiped down the kitchen counters. Finding it close to ten, I decided to call it a night. "Do you need anything? I'm going to bed."

"How about another pain pill? You've been kind of stingy with those."

"That's true, but it's for your own good." I grabbed a bottle of water from the fridge and pulled out the pack of pain pills. With two left, that meant one for tonight and one for tomorrow. That should probably be enough, especially because I'd been able to speed up his healing process.

I handed him the pill and water and watched him drink it down. Finished, he glanced my way. "Thanks for dinner, and... for taking care of me."

Was that real sincerity in his eyes? "Uh... sure." Self-conscious, I glanced away. "Good night."

"Night."

I turned out the lights, leaving only the lamp beside him on. He wasn't in his pajamas, but I wasn't about to offer to help him. I'd done enough already. As I climbed the stairs, I couldn't help thinking about his naked backside and how much I'd admired it. The rest of him wasn't too bad either, and I got a little flushed just thinking about it.

Needing something to relax me, I took a nice, hot shower and went to bed. He'd only been here a couple of days, and it astonished me how much I liked having him here. He helped fill that void in my life, and that was dangerous, because, after he was gone, how would I manage?

I was more vulnerable than I liked to admit, but that was only because I was here and all alone. I didn't need a man to be happy, especially one who looked like Creed. He probably had women falling all over him, and that made him dangerous. Guys like him were nothing but trouble.

I sighed, turned over, and closed my eyes, trying not to think too hard about Creed, or his backside. Maybe I didn't need a man to be happy, but that didn't stop me from imagining his arms around me. Grabbing my pillow, I held it to my chest and tried to think of anything but him. That was harder than I thought, but, eventually, I drifted off to sleep.

The next morning, I found Creed asleep in his clothes. He'd either been too exhausted or too lazy to change. Or...

maybe he didn't normally wear clothes to bed? I did a mental head-slap. It was better not to think about that.

While he used the bathroom, I fixed a breakfast of eggs, hash browns and toast. He wasn't real talkative, but neither was I. After finishing breakfast, I took the dishes to the sink. "I ordered you a better brace. It should be here sometime today or tomorrow."

"Oh... that's nice."

"Yeah. It's smaller, and should fit under your jeans if they're not too tight. After a week or two, you might be able to walk with it on. That way you won't need a cast, and it's easier to put on and take off for showering. How's the leg feeling today, anyway?"

His brows dipped. "You know... it's not so bad. I think that lotion you used really helped, but that doesn't make any sense. How could lotion help a broken bone?"

"I think you had some deep tissue damage as well, so the cream probably helped with that."

He nodded. "Oh... right."

"Well, I've got to get to work. See you at lunchtime."

I headed into the clinic, grateful I had something else to think about besides him.

The day started quietly enough, but, around ten, I got a call from a rancher, telling me his teenaged son had been bucked off his horse and was bleeding from his ears and nose. I told him to stabilize his neck, call nine-one-one, and that I'd be there soon.

I made it in less than six minutes. Kneeling beside him, I found the boy's face ashen and his breathing labored. He'd hit his head hard, and it looked like his skull was fractured. If that were the case, he could end up with brain damage... if he lived.

I got the neck brace on him quickly. "Call nine-one-one again, and tell them we need life-flight." While his mom made the call, I gently touched the back of his head, not liking what I felt. The skull was shattered, and the broken pieces could easily kill him.

Gathering all my strength, I pulled the light from deep inside me and pushed it into the wound. After several seconds, I felt the skull depression pop back out. Taking a deep breath, I reached deeper into the soft tissue of his brain, mending the bruised and swollen tissue and pulling away the pooling blood.

Opening my eyes, I glanced at the parents who knelt beside their son, watching me with widened eyes. I gasped in a breath and spoke. "Can you tell if he's doing any better?"

His mom put a hand to his chest as it rose and fell. "He's breathing easier, and his color's back."

"Good. He has a massive head injury, so I'm going to keep my hands on his head for now. Will one of you look at his eyes, and tell me if his pupils are still dilated? Is he responsive at all?"

"His pupils are dilated, but they did get a little smaller when I pulled back his eyelid."

"Good. Talk to him," I said. "Call him by name, and tell him you're here."

His mom began talking to him, and I poured what little energy I had left into his head. Her voice was like a soothing balm, and I was grateful she wasn't falling apart. He needed to hear her voice and focus on her strength. Completely empty, I could barely hold my head up.

"Mom? What happened?"

She let out a sob, but quickly controlled herself. "Blaze threw you, and you hit your head pretty hard. But you're going to be okay. Just hold still and don't move."

His eyes closed, and he let out a tired sigh. "The light... so bright..."

Her gaze met mine. Then she glanced back at her son and continued to speak encouraging words, holding tightly to his hand. Soon, the sound of the helicopter came. There was plenty of room in the open field for the chopper to land, and a group of medics carrying a stretcher hurried to us.

I told them my diagnosis and relinquished him into their capable hands. His mother got on the helicopter with him, and his father ran to his truck and raced off.

I sat back on the ground, dizzy and disoriented. I hunched over my knees, waiting several long minutes until the dizziness passed. Feeling a little better, I rolled to my hands and feet before pushing into a standing position. The world tilted a bit, and I kept my head down with my hands on my knees.

A few minutes later, my head cleared, and I shuffled to the fence, leaning against it until my legs quit shaking. A horse with an empty saddle stood at the far end of the enclosure, and I wondered what had spooked him.

Knowing he'd be fine for now, I turned toward the gate, using the fence to steady me. Shuffling to my Jeep, I found my stash of bottled water and drank my fill, emptying one and starting on another before I could even think about driving home. I used the rest of the water to rinse most of the blood off my hands.

I drove home slowly. Luckily, no one waited at the clinic door for my help, and I pulled the Jeep into the garage. I headed inside through the back door, and Creed sat up with raised brows. "What happened?"

I trudged to the kitchen and finished washing the blood from my hands. "A kid got thrown from his horse. They had to life-flight him to the hospital." After drying my hands on a towel, I pulled an apple from the bowl on the counter and took a bite, letting the tangy sweetness fill my mouth.

"Will he be okay?"

"Yeah... I think so... but it was kind of scary."

"You look exhausted. Come sit down."

I stepped to the couch, and he sat up, patting the space beside him. With relief, I sat down and melted against him. His arm came around me, and I rested my head on his shoulder. As his warmth flowed into me, I closed my eyes and relaxed.

I must have dozed for a couple of seconds, because a noise brought me awake. I opened my eyes, unsure of where I was for a moment.

"I think that's your phone," Creed said.

I sat up, pulling the phone from my white jacket pocket. "Hello?"

"Is this Ella?"

"Yes."

"This is Heather... Wyatt's mom."

"Oh... how's he doing?"

"He's going to be fine. I just wanted to let you know, and I wanted to thank you for coming so quickly."

"Of course. I'm so relieved."

"You... I think you saved his life. The doctors... they said it was a miracle he survived. From the scans, it looked like his skull was fractured, but, for some reason, his brain didn't swell or have any bleeding that they could see. Wyatt... he keeps talking about a bright light. Do you know what he's talking about?"

I held my breath. "Uh... no, not really. But I'm glad he's okay. Do you know how long they're keeping him?"

"So far, they're talking about a few more days. With a fractured skull, they want to make sure his brain doesn't have any new bleeding or swelling. They said the next few hours are critical."

"That's true. I'm sure they'll take good care of him."

"Yes, I'm sure they will. Well... uh... thanks again."

"You're welcome." I ended the call, grateful Wyatt was okay. I'd never been able to use so much power before. Usually, I only had enough to help in small ways, but this was different. I'd actually healed him. Maybe not completely... but pretty close. A chill went down my spine. What was going on?

"So he's okay?" Creed asked.

"What? Oh... yes. He's going to be fine, especially if he can get through the next few days without any bleeding or swelling in his brain."

"That's great."

I glanced around the room. "How long was I asleep?"

"Forty-five minutes."

I gasped. "Are you kidding me?"

"No. I think you would have slept longer if the phone hadn't woken you. You must like sleeping next to me." I opened my mouth to reply, but he continued. "I liked it... quite a bit, but I was a little worried. You were out cold."

"I... I was tired, that's all."

"Yeah... I could see that. Feel better?"

"Actually... yes. A lot better." That surprised me, but I wasn't about to complain. "I guess I'd better get back to the clinic." My half-eaten apple sat on the coffee table, and I automatically reached for it. Even though it was a little brown, I took a bite, and it seemed to rejuvenate me even more.

"These are so good." I glanced at Creed. "You want one?"

"Yeah. But I can get it."

"No... it's okay. I'm feeling better, and I don't mind." I slowly stood, hoping my head didn't swim. Feeling steady, I headed to the kitchen. "Looks like we missed lunch. You want a sandwich?" He said yes, and I quickly assembled two ham and cheese sandwiches.

We ate them at the table with some chips, and nothing had ever tasted so good. Feeling better by the minute, I finished the last bite, just as the buzzer sounded from the clinic.

"Oh... that's me. I'd better go. I'll clean up later." I hurried to the clinic and unlocked the door, finding my neighbor, Evelyn, standing there with a melon.

"I thought you could use this. It's from my garden."

"Oh... thanks. It looks wonderful. What kind is it?"

"It's called a canary melon, because of its bright, yellow coloring. They're usually quite sweet."

"Nice. Thanks so much."

"You're welcome." She smiled, then her brows drew together. "I heard about the accident. News around here travels pretty fast. Do you know how Wyatt is doing?"

"Yeah, his mom called to tell me he's doing really well, all things considered."

She shook her head. "We don't have much cause for life-flight around here, but when it happens, we know it's real serious. One of my daughter's friends knows one of the flight crew medics. She said it was a miracle Wyatt survived with his skull fractured so badly."

She caught my gaze. "They think it's because of you." At my widened eyes, she continued. "There's been talk around here that you have a real special... touch... some have said you have healing hands."

She glanced at my hands holding the melon, and I opened my mouth to refute her claim, but she waved me off. "I'm not passing judgement, dear. I'm just telling you what they're saying. Anyway... I hope you enjoy the melon. And... I'm real glad you're here."

Before I could say a word, she turned away and hurried off my porch. I watched her until she'd crossed the street, then I stepped back inside and shut my door. That was nice, but it also worried me. I'd never stood out like this before, and I didn't want to start now.

That was why working in a big hospital in New York had its benefits. I could help people without being so conspicuous. Here, it was much more obvious. Of course, my gift had never healed someone like that before, and I couldn't understand what had changed.

I'd felt him dying, and it had taken everything I had to save him. I still had a raw place inside where my power usually rested. What if I'd used it all up and it didn't come back? I didn't want to think about that. It would come back. I just needed to give it time.

The rest of the day passed uneventfully, and I spent most of my time catching up on the paperwork that I loathed. My head nodded from fatigue a couple of times, and it was a relief to quit a little early.

I locked up and took the melon into the house. Creed wasn't on the couch, but the back door stood open, so I figured he was out on the patio. I passed the table, noticing the lunch dishes had been cleared and the kitchen straightened.

Hmm... maybe Creed wasn't totally useless after all. Leaving the melon on the kitchen counter, I headed outside to find Creed relaxing on the cushioned chair in the shade with his leg up. "Hey. I'm done for the day. I'm going to take a quick shower, and then I'll figure out dinner."

"Yeah... uh... I was thinking. It might be nice to eat out. My leg's not hurting so much, and you could use a break. What do you think?"

Surprised by his thoughtfulness, I nodded. "You know what? That's a great idea."

"Yeah? Good. I'm getting restless just sitting around here."

"Right." I should have known he was thinking of himself, but I couldn't blame him. After sitting for a few days in a strange place with nothing to do, I'd be feeling the same way.

After a hot shower, I spent a little extra time on my hair and makeup. Although still tired, excitement to be going out for dinner energized me, and I wanted to look my best. Pulling on jeans and a favorite blue shirt helped a lot, and I realized I hadn't worn this shirt once since I'd been here.

Of course... when had I gone out to dinner last? Probably not since the first week of my arrival, and definitely not with such a handsome man. Thinking about Creed like he was my date sent a little thrill through me. It may not be a real date, but I could still enjoy being out with a hot dude.

I spritzed on my favorite perfume and checked the mirror one last time, noting that my cheeks were a little pale. I remedied that with some blush and added a pair of dangly earrings. That seemed to help, and I didn't look half bad.

As I stepped down the stairs, my stomach twisted with anticipation. Creed waited at the table. With his tousled hair and unshaven face, he pulled off that naturally rugged look that was so appealing these days. His blue eyes met mine, and my heart lurched. Then he smiled, and I knew I was in trouble.

"You look amazing." His gaze roamed over me in a tantalizing way that made me feel like a million bucks.

"Oh... thanks... uh... so do you."

He grinned and got his crutches under him, following me to the back door. I helped him get inside the Jeep, stashing his crutches in the back, and backed out of the driveway. Before pulling onto the street, I glanced his way. "There are only a couple of places to eat in Sandy Creek. One is a burger joint, and the other is a café. Which one do you want to try?"

"Let's go with the café."

"Good choice." I pulled onto the road. The café wasn't far, and my smile widened at Creed's reaction to the neon sign with flashing lights.

"Café Diablo?"

"Yes. That's it. Kind of fitting in this desert town, don't you think?"

"Yeah." He sent me a warm smile, and I tried not to drool. Self-conscious, I slipped out of my seat to get his crutches from the back, and we shuffled to the door. Inside, the café was mostly full, but the hostess found a booth for us in the back. After handing us our menus, she left to get some water.

"This place is kind of rustic, but I like it." Creed looked over the wooden beams and log walls. A few animal skulls hung on the walls, along with some elk and deer antlers. Red vinyl cushions covered the seats in the booths, and the tables were covered with red checkered tablecloths.

"What have you tried here?"

Grateful I could answer that, I pointed to the menu. "They have a wicked Philly-Beef-and-Swiss, but that's all I've had, so you're on your own."

"What do you think you'll get?"

"The Philly-Beef-and Swiss." At his raised brows, I shrugged. "It was really good."

The waitress came back for our orders, but hardly glanced my way. She stood closer to Creed than I thought necessary, and she seemed more than happy to help him decide on which dinner item to order.

While they spoke, I studied Creed, drinking in his dark good looks. The waitress did too, but I couldn't blame her. He was like a magnet, pulling attention to himself without even trying. He gave her a smile at the end of their conversation, and I think she got a little drunk from having it directed her way.

"I'll take the Philly-Beef-and-Swiss," he said. Glancing my way, his eyes twinkled, and he sent me a wink.

I couldn't help smiling and hardly noticed when the waitress left. Needing a distraction, I looked around the room. "It's nice to be out. It's been a while." Crap... why did I have to say that? I didn't want him to think I never went out. "I mean... not that I don't have friends, or go out... I've just been really busy."

He slipped his hand over mine, giving it a little squeeze before pulling away. "It's been a while for me too. When I haven't been working, I've been way too busy with... other things."

"You mean like playing poker?" He nodded, so I continued, wanting to know more about him. "So are you taking a vacation from your job? I mean... you're not a professional gambler, right?"

"No... but it does take up a lot of my free time."

"Yeah... I'll bet." I waited for him to tell me about his job, but, when he didn't, I opened my mouth to ask, only to have him cut me off.

"So... I never asked you... did you call the police about me?"

"No... but I checked you out. I guess your story holds up for now."

His lips twisted. "That's nice to know."

"Yeah... but that doesn't mean I won't call them if you get out of line."

He lifted both hands in surrender. "I'll be good."

My brows rose. "That's what they all say."

He chuckled. "Tell me about you." His curious eyes burned with intensity. "You said you were from New York. Is your family there?"

This was a sore spot for me, but, since I wanted him to open up, I had to start somewhere. "No. I don't have a regular family. I have a lot of brothers and sisters, but we're not related." At his raised brows, I continued. "My mom died when I was a baby, and I became a ward of the church... mostly because my real father is a priest."

His eyes widened, and I couldn't help smiling. "I know... it's a big no-no, but I guess he got approval from the higher-ups to raise me. Still, it's not like a traditional family, so I guess you could say I was raised by the church."

"That's fascinating. I think I've been to church once or twice in my whole life, but that's it."

Our food order came, and we began to eat. After a few bites, Creed nodded. "You were right. This is really good. I'm glad I got it."

We ate for a few more minutes, each of us enjoying our sandwiches. Feeling full, I set mine down and took a drink of water. "Okay... I've told you a little about me. Now it's your turn. I know you grew up in L.A., but I don't know anything else. When did you move to Las Vegas and start playing poker?"

"Oh... I haven't been there long. Maybe a couple of months."

"Then what did you do in L.A. before that?"

His lips thinned. "I can't act worth a damn, but I've managed to be an extra on a lot of TV shows and a few movie sets."

"Oh... wow. That's cool." It wasn't what I'd expected to hear, but now his toned body made more sense. And he was certainly good-looking enough for Hollywood standards. "Have you met a lot of big movie stars?"

He frowned. "Enough to be glad I never made it big like they did."

Before I could respond, our check came, and Creed seemed happy for the interruption. He took it, insisting on paying. "You've done enough for me. Now it's my turn." He leaned closer to me, speaking so only I could hear him. "But you're not off the hook yet."

He smiled to let me know he was mostly joking, and pulled out his credit card. After paying, we stood to leave. Creed grimaced with pain, but smoothed his features and hobbled out on his crutches. Sitting for so long had probably been hard on him.

As we left, I noticed several people watching me and whispering to one another. I didn't recognize any of them, but I could have treated one or two. Word of Wyatt's accident must have spread fast. One woman caught my gaze and smiled. I smiled back, but quickly turned my attention back to helping Creed out the door.

Luckily, the drive home only took a few minutes. As we pulled into the driveway, I noticed a box on the porch with a medical symbol on it. "Oh look. Your new brace is here. Want to put it on?"

"Sure."

Inside, Creed put his leg up on the couch, while I got the box off the porch. Pulling it open, I took out the white brace and the stocking that went with it. I took it over to the couch and sat down. I carefully loosened the old brace before pulling it off.

"Hey... before you put the new brace on, do you mind rubbing some more gel on my leg? I think it made a big difference last night."

"Yeah. Good idea. I'll go get it." I wasn't sure I could do anything with my healing powers after such an exhausting day, but now that I'd eaten, I felt a lot stronger.

I squeezed some gel on my hands and gently brushed them over the bone a few times, stopping to lay my palms directly over the break. Closing my eyes, I concentrated on pulling the warmth from inside me. A tiny surge of heat flowed into my hands, and relief washed through me. It was still there, but not nearly as powerful as before.

I sent the small wisp of healing power into Creed's bone and the surrounding tissue. As the heat left my hands to sink into his leg, I imagined it spreading over the broken bone like a mesh and knitting it together. A few seconds later, I pulled my hands away, panting like I'd just run a marathon.

"What did you just do?" Creed's puzzled gaze locked on mine.

"Oh... uh... I rubbed gel on your leg." I lowered my head, feeling a little dizzy.

"That's not what I meant. It feels so much better now... because of you. You did something with your hands when you touched me."

Grimacing, I knew I had to tell him something. "Ever since I was young, I've had a special healing touch with injuries. That's why I went into medicine. My supervisor said I had healing hands... so that's what I call it."

He nodded, but his brow puckered. "But how do you do it?"

"I don't know. It just happens when I treat an injury."

He shook his head. "And you don't know why? Is it like a gift from God?" At my shrug, he continued. "Maybe it's because of all that time you spent in church."

I chuckled. "I honestly have no idea, but we can say that if you like."

He smiled. "If I'd known about all the perks, I might have gone to church more often."

"Your loss." I swallowed, not quite strong enough to move yet.

"Are you okay?" Creed sat up. "What's wrong?"

"I'm just a little light-headed. It will pass in a minute."

"Does this happen all the time?"

"No. Not until..." Realizing my mistake, I froze.

Creed's eyes widened. "Today? With that kid? Did you..." He raked a hand through his hair. "Did you heal him?"

"No... I just helped. I had to do something, or he would have died, but I'm not a miracle worker. I just helped him enough to keep him alive until he could get to the hospital."

Creed's brow furrowed. "So... tell me this... if someone was injured months ago, could you heal them?"

I shook my head. "No." That wasn't exactly a lie. I'd never tried anything like that before. Of course, I'd never had the juice to help anyone as injured as Wyatt was before either, so I didn't know what was going on. "Look... I'm fine now. Let's try out your new brace."

I took the stretchy tubing and carefully tugged it over his foot and up the length of his lower leg. The brace came next, fitting his leg perfectly. I tightened the Velcro so it cinched around his leg, supporting the bone and muscles. "There. How does that feel?"

"Pretty good. Can I walk on it now?"

"No." That came out a little forcefully. "It may feel a little better, but it's not healed. Like I said, I have a nice touch, but I'm not a miracle worker."

His shoulders slumped with disappointment, so I continued. "But I think in your case, you might be able to walk on it in a couple of weeks. I'll take another x-ray before you leave, and it will give us a better idea. But at least this brace is better than a cast. You can take it off to shower... or, actually a bath would probably be easier for now."

"So, your 'healing hands' just helps to speed things along?"

"That's usually how it works."

"So... why did they send you out here to the middle of nowhere? With what you've got going on, it seems like you'd be more useful in a bigger place."

My brows dipped. "How did you..." Realization hit me that he'd heard some of my conversation with John. "Just how much of that phone call did you hear?"

He opened his mouth to protest, but quickly shut it. "Enough to know you're not happy here... and you might be in trouble."

"Trouble? Why do you say that?"

"Because I heard you say something about making a mistake, and that you were sent here to learn your lesson."

I scoffed. "Wow... you really were eavesdropping. Thanks for your concern, but it's none of your business."

If I could have jumped to my feet and left, I would have, but I was just too darn weak to do anything but give him a dirty look.

"You're right. I'm sorry. I was out of line." He sat up and moved his leg to rest on the coffee table. "Come and sit down by me. You look like you're about to fall over." I hesitated, until he patted the couch. "Come on... I won't bite."

The desire to be close to him was stronger than my anger, and I slid onto the couch beside him. He promptly circled his arm around me and tugged me close. "Let's watch a movie." The remote was on the armrest beside him, and he clicked it on. "What do you feel like watching?"

"Honestly, I really like those super-hero shows."

"Yeah? Me too. Let's see what we can find."

We began one of the comic book movies, and it was easy to get caught up in the show. As the movie progressed, it seemed like the most natural thing in the world to snuggle against his side and get comfortable.

At some point during the two hour movie, my eyes drifted shut, and I fell asleep. A loud explosion coming from the sound track roused me, and I managed to sit up in time to see the end of the show. As the credits rolled across the screen, Creed clicked the TV off.

I pulled away to face him. "Sorry I fell asleep."

"Don't worry about it. You were exhausted, and I didn't mind, even if you drooled a little." He frowned, but his eyes held a teasing light, and I shook my head.

"Guess I'd better get to bed." I checked the time, finding it close to midnight. "It's a good thing tomorrow's my day off."

"It is? Hey... maybe you could show me around? Not that I mind staying here in the house, but I wouldn't mind seeing a little more of the country. I've been looking at all those posters of the national parks. Now that I'm stuck here for a bit, it might be nice to take a look."

"That's a great idea. I've got the perfect place, and it's not that far, especially since I can drive my Jeep most of the way up the canyon."

"Sounds great."

I knew I should get up and go, but I found it hard to leave his side. Sitting so close to him felt good. Almost how I imagined an addiction would feel, which didn't bode well for me. "Well... I guess I'd better go."

"Maybe you don't have to." He sat up and touched my hair, then ran his fingers through my silken strands. "So soft. I've wanted to do that all night." His hand moved to cup my cheek, and his thumb skimmed over my lips. "And I've wanted to kiss you ever since the last time. It's all I've thought about."

His gaze searched mine, silently asking the question. In response, my lips parted, and I turned my face into his palm. He leaned closer and tilted his face to capture my lips, his hand moving to the back of my neck. His tender touch filled me with desire, and I kissed him back, tentatively at first, then with more abandon.

He deepened the kiss, filling me with an ache that left me breathless. His lips left mine, trailing kisses along my jaw and down my neck. My breath caught, and his lips found mine again, insistent and demanding.

His hands stroked my back, my waist, and slipped under my shirt. His touch on my bare skin sent shivers over me, but it triggered alarm that this was going too fast. I placed my hands on his chest and pushed away.

My breath came in short bursts, but the desire in his eyes wore down my resolve. Still, deep down, I knew this couldn't happen. Not now anyway. I had too much to lose. I wasn't a one-night-stand kind of person, no matter how desirable he was.

He tilted his head closer to mine. I felt his breath on my cheek, and his lips brushed across mine again. Closing my eyes, I barely stifled a groan. As the tentative kiss deepened, I pulled back, my breath heaving, and touched my fingers to his mouth. "I... I can't."

He froze, his gaze searching mine. "I want you, Ella. More than anything." Desire burned deep in his eyes. "So... if you don't want this, you'd better go to bed; because, if you don't leave now, I'll do everything in my power to change your mind."

His declaration froze me in place. My breath caught, and shivers ran down my spine. He cupped my cheek again, before slowly trailing his fingers across my jaw and down the side of my neck. Without thinking, I tilted my head back to give him better access to my throat. His gentle touch continued to trail along my collarbone before coming to the dip in my throat.

I closed my eyes in response, and his lips captured mine, sending shivers through my chest. I'd never felt so helpless or so alive. His hands slipped beneath my shirt, and I arched my back to get closer. Breathless, he pulled away to capture my gaze. "Does this mean you're staying?"

My body screamed to stay, but my head knew it was a terrible idea. Did I want to pay such a high price for this short time with him? Yes, I wanted him... but I needed more than one night. "I can't."

My chest heaving, I scrambled away. He gazed at me, his lips parted and his breath coming fast. Even standing a few feet away didn't curb my need to rush back to his side. Before my traitorous body overruled my head, I retreated up the stairs to my room.

After shutting the door, I leaned against it, suddenly woozy. I stepped into the bathroom and splashed my face with cold water. As water dripped from my chin, I glanced into the mirror. My pupils were dilated and my lips were swollen.

What the hell was going on? I'd never responded like that to anyone. It was like he had some kind of power over me. After drying my face, I changed into my pajamas and lay down on my bed, pulling a pillow against my chest.

The stifling air suffocated me, so I flipped the ceiling fan on, changing it to a higher speed than normal. The cooler air began to circulate, and I took deep, steady breaths.

Lying still, I tried not to think about the man downstairs and the hypnotic pull he seemed to have on me. But it wasn't his touch, or the feel of his mouth on mine, that sent shivers down my spine. No... it was the knowledge that if he hadn't asked me if I was staying... I wouldn't have been able to stop. I'd probably still be down there right now.

That scared me more than anything I'd ever faced in my life.

CHAPTER FIVE

I woke to find the sun streaming into my room. Stretching, I yawned, watching the ceiling fan for a few moments to get my bearings. My thoughts turned to Creed. For a quick moment, I wondered if he was still here, but then I shook my head. Of course he was. Where would he go?

Still, it was enough to get me out of bed and into the shower. Dressed and ready for the day, I hurried down the stairs, glancing toward the couch. Not finding him there, my gaze moved to the kitchen, and I found him sitting at the table, eating a bowl of cereal. He'd changed into the scrub bottoms and t-shirt, probably last night sometime after I left.

Seeing him sent relief coursing through me, shocking me with its intensity. Wanting someone this much had never happened to me before. I was in so much trouble.

"You okay?" Creed asked.

"Oh... yeah. Actually, I feel a lot better. It's amazing what a little rest can do." I stepped into the kitchen and pulled open the refrigerator. "I was going to cook some eggs for breakfast. Do you want some?"

"Sure... I wouldn't pass that up. So you slept well?"

Was that a trick question? "Like a baby." I smiled, hoping to sound chipper like I hadn't been awake and tossing and turning half the night.

"Oh yeah? Me too... especially if you mean waking up at all hours of the night."

I chuckled and took out the frying pan, butter, and eggs. "Want some toast with that?"

"Yes, please."

Before cooking the eggs, I cut up the melon and set the freshly cut pieces on the table. We both tried it out, and Creed declared it the best melon he'd ever had. I got the eggs and hash browns cooked and then took the finished plates over to the table. After grabbing a couple of forks, we both began to eat.

"I'm looking forward to that drive today," Creed said, between bites. "Where did you say it was?"

"It's a slot canyon about fifteen miles from town. That's where I was right before we... uh... bumped into each other. I almost died up there."

His eyes widened. "What happened?"

I told him about the flash flood. "I had no idea it was coming. The slot canyon is called 'Devil's Gulch,' and at the top is a waterfall named 'Angel Falls.' It's a great hike, but it can be deadly if you're caught in a sudden cloudburst. In fact... we ought to check the weather today before we head up there. Just in case."

"Sounds like a good idea." Finished with his food, he scooted back from the table. "While you check on that, I'm going to get ready."

He headed into the bathroom while I cleared the dishes, stacking them into the dishwasher. I checked the weather on my phone, happy to see there were no storms expected. Before I could slip it into my pocket, it began to ring. The caller ID said it was Seth, so I quickly answered. "Hello?"

"Hey Ella. You okay over there?"

"Yeah sure. Why?"

"I heard about Wyatt. Some folks are saying you saved his life. It's kind of a big deal."

"I'm glad I got to him when I did. He was in bad shape, but it sounded like he was doing better last night. Have you heard more about his condition?"

"Not this morning. But, like they say, no news is good news." He chuckled. "The reason I'm calling is about your... uh... guest. I found something that I thought you should know."

The back of my neck prickled. "Okay, what is it?"

"What did you say this fella's name was?"

"Creed... Aiden Creed."

"Oh... then maybe it's not a big deal."

Creed came out of the bathroom and hobbled over to his duffel bag for some clothes. He barely glanced my way, but he must have heard me say his name. Wanting some privacy, I opened the back door and stepped onto the patio. "What do you mean?"

"Well the car is registered to a woman. Uh... let me see. Yeah... it's registered to Avery Creed. But if she has the same last name, it must be his wife."

My heart hitched, and the world tilted. His wife? What? "Oh..."

"Yeah... so... at least we know the car's not stolen. I was worried about that, since he's a stranger and it seemed suspicious, but that explains it." At my silence, he continued. "You okay? He hasn't made the moves on you, has he?"

"What? No... no... not at all."

"Okay... good. You can tell him I got the parts this morning, so I'll start working on it this afternoon. It will still take me a few more days though."

I swallowed. "Okay, I'll let him know. Thanks."

"Sure. See ya."

Shock rippled over me. I disconnected the call and slipped the phone into my pocket, my breath shallow and my lips pinched. He was married? How could he be married? He'd kissed me and... we'd almost made love... and... he was married?

Did that mean everything else about him was a lie? What about the money? Had he lied about that too? What if he'd stolen it? What if he was a criminal... or worse, a killer? What did I really know about him anyway? I knew he played poker... but that could be a lie, too. What about his job? He'd never really told me anything about it. Only that he'd worked as an extra on movie sets, but how reliable was that?

I didn't know a thing about his background. All he'd said was that he'd grown up in L.A., but nothing about his family... and most assuredly nothing about a wife. It hit me that I hardly knew anything about him. My stomach twisted, and I had to swallow several times to keep my breakfast down.

The door opened behind me. "Ella? Are you okay?"

I stiffened. "Uh... yeah. I just need a minute."

"What is it?"

"Just give me a minute. Okay?" That sounded frantic, even to me, but at least it worked, and I heard the door shut. I glanced over my shoulder just to make sure, knowing I had to figure out what to do before facing him.

Should I confront him? Should I call the police? If I did, I'd have to make sure I called when he wasn't able to hear me. If he was on the run, he might do something stupid, and I didn't want to get hurt.

I closed my eyes. What was I thinking? Did I really believe he'd hurt me? That was ridiculous. Maybe he was everything he'd said, only he'd just left out the part about being married. That wasn't quite so bad, although, in light of last night, he was a horrible person for leading me on. But, other than that, at least it meant he wasn't a criminal... or a killer.

There was nothing for it. I'd have to confront him. But maybe it was better to wait until we were in the Jeep. That way, I could take him straight to the police or leave him on the side of the road. That appealed to me, especially since he'd been lying.

My mind made up, I took a deep breath and raised my chin. I could do this. He may be a scumbag, but I'd met scumbags before, and not one of them had gotten the best of me. Still, a tiny part of my heart was breaking, and an even smaller part was crying out that I'd gotten it all wrong. That was the part I wanted to believe the most... but could I risk it?

I stepped into the house, finding Creed sitting at the kitchen table. I tried to put a pleasant expression on my face, but I should have known it wouldn't work. Creed took one look at me and his eyes grew wary. His brows drew together, and he took a sharp breath. "What's wrong?"

Dammit. "It's nothing for you to worry about... I just heard something about a friend in New York." I was a terrible liar... and I knew Creed didn't believe me the moment the words came out.

"No you didn't. I heard you tell the caller my name. So who was it?"

I swallowed. "Oh... yeah..." Damn... I forgot about that part. "Fine. It was Seth from the car shop. He... he told me your car is registered to your wife... Avery."

Creed's brows rose with shock. "What? My wife? I don't have a wife. You think..." He huffed out a breath and shook his head. "I can't believe you'd think I'm married... after last night... I would never..." He shook his head and scrubbed his face with his hands.

"You're not married?"

"No."

"But you were?"

His left brow rose. "What if I was?"

Guilt washed over me, and I huffed out a breath. "I don't know. What was I supposed to think? I don't know anything about you... only that you're a card shark, with a ton of money in your duffel bag, and you're an actor. Maybe that's the problem. You haven't told me much of anything.

"For all I know, you could be a criminal running from the law, or even a serial killer." He opened his mouth to speak, but I raised my hands. "I know it's my fault you have a broken leg and you're stuck here. But I need to know what's going on with you. If you're not willing to tell me that, then you'll have to leave."

He held my gaze and the fight went out of him. He glanced around the room before focusing on me. "You're right. I've been here too long." He bowed his head and closed his eyes. "This has been nice. But it's time for me to move on. I'll call a friend. He can get here sometime tonight."

Shock washed over me. That was his answer? He took his phone from his pocket and put the call through. I wanted to object, but the words got stuck in my throat. Was he really going to leave without an explanation?

"Danny, it's Creed."

I stood close enough to him that I could hear Danny. "Hey man, where've you been? It's like you disappeared."

"Yeah... I needed a change of scenery. Sorry I didn't tell you."

"It's okay. Stuff happens. So, are you back?"

Creed shook his head. "No. Uh... remember that time I helped you out and you said you owed me?"

"Yeah... sure. What do you need?"

"I've been in an accident. It's nothing big, but I have a broken leg and I can't drive. Can you help me out?"

"Uh... sure. What do you want me to do?"

"I need a lift. I'm about five hours away in a little town called—"

He glanced my way, so I whispered, "Sandy Creek."

"Sandy Creek. It's just north of the state border."

I couldn't believe he was really doing this, and I stepped away, frustrated that he was leaving. But what could I do? I had every right to give him an ultimatum. Why couldn't he just talk to me?

"Yeah... that's it. Do you mind coming? Yeah? That's great. I really appreciate this. How soon do you think you can you get here?"

Creed listened for another minute. "Sure. I get that. Just don't tell anyone... promise me. No one can know where I am... okay... good. I'm staying at the medical clinic. It's on the main road... you can't miss it. Yeah... send me a text when you get here." Creed thanked him and ended the call.

With his head bowed and his shoulders slouched, defeat hung over him. He finally glanced my way. "He should be here around midnight tonight. Then I'll be out of your hair."

"Creed, I—"

"No... it's best that I leave. You've done a lot for me, and I appreciate it. Maybe if we'd met under different circumstances..." He left the sentence unfinished and struggled to his feet. Moving to the couch, he sat down and reached for his discarded shorts. "I'm changing my clothes over here... you might want to go back outside."

Anger burned in my chest that he was acting like this. I'd thought we were friends, but I guess I'd hurt his feelings, and now he didn't want anything to do with me. But I didn't think my request was so bad. What was wrong with telling me about his situation, unless he was hiding something? Still, I wanted to make some sort of a peace offering.

"Look… we can still go on that drive. I'll pack us some snacks and water. It will be good to get out."

He glanced my way, considering it, and shrugged. "I guess."

Ten minutes later, we headed out. On the drive to the slot canyon, I slowed to show him where his car had been that day. It reminded him that it was still getting fixed, and he'd have to leave it behind. "I'll leave enough money to pay for it. Could you keep the car for me until I can come back?"

Something inside my chest unfurled. With the car here, he'd have to come back for it, so he wouldn't be totally out of my life. "Of course."

"Thanks."

"Here's the turn-off. It's going to be a little bumpy. Let me know if it's too much."

He nodded, and I turned onto the dirt road. We made it to the fork in the road that led down into the ravine, and I eased the Jeep into the dry creek bed.

"Wow. Seeing it now, it's hard to believe there was any water coming down here. But you should have seen it. It was rushing down so hard and fast that I could hear boulders in the water, crashing downstream."

I took it slow, needing to go around several large rocks that weren't there before. In the winding creek bed, the Jeep only spun out a few times before we made it to the top. Here, the terrain was wide enough to turn the Jeep around, but I had to work at it. Finally pointing downhill, I turned off the engine and pulled on the emergency brake.

"We made it. You want to get out?"

"Yeah."

I took the crutches from the back and handed them to Creed. Several large boulders sat off to the side of the trail, and we made our way over to them. The ground was uneven, and I worried that Creed wouldn't be able to navigate through the rough terrain on his crutches, so I stayed close to his side, ready to lend a hand.

Reaching one of the boulders, he sat down in the shade. From here, we could enjoy the view, looking up and down the canyon. It was another beautiful, sunny day, with the blue sky above and the red rocks and sand at our feet. It surprised me to find green vegetation at the edge of the dry bed. Somehow, it had survived the torrential flood.

I set my small backpack on the ground and reached inside for a couple of water bottles and the trail mix I'd brought. Creed took a long drink and leaned back against the boulder, his gaze taking in the beauty surrounding us.

"Thanks for bringing me here." His light tone held reconciliation, freeing the burden over my heart.

"It's great, isn't it?"

"Yeah."

After sitting in silence for several minutes, I decided to tell him the real reason I was here. Maybe if I opened up, he'd do the same. Even if he didn't, it felt right to tell him the truth. "I told you that I was a trauma nurse in New York City, but you don't know that I got demoted. They sent me here for breaking the rules."

"So it wasn't a transfer?"

"Nope."

"What did you do?"

"I let a man die." Actually saying those words out loud made it sound a lot worse than I felt it was.

At Creed's raised brows, I continued, telling him the story of a drug dealer with ties to the mob who'd killed three women. "One of them didn't die at the scene, so I was caring for her in the hospital. When the killer realized she could identify him, he snuck into her room and finished the job. She had a guard and everything, but he got in anyway, and it happened while she was in my care."

I shook my head and sighed. "So when they brought the same guy into the emergency room a few days later, with three bullet holes in him, I refused to help save his life. He died on the operating table."

Creed's brows dipped together. "What makes you think he wouldn't have died anyway? I mean... sure you have a gift, but it sounds like he was in bad shape."

"Yeah... I know what it sounds like, but... trust me... I could have helped him survive. It's just that he was a killer, and he didn't deserve to live, not when he'd killed so many people."

Creed let the silence hang over us, and then he glanced at me. "Well. I guess I see your point, but maybe that's not your decision to make."

My breath caught. For some strange reason, I thought he'd be on my side. It took me a minute to gather my thoughts and respond without anger or resentment. "Maybe... but it was a hard call, and I'm not sure I'd change anything if I had to do it over."

I glanced up at the sky, noting the clouds as they floated by. "Maybe I deserve to be stuck here after all."

"Hey... I don't think this is too bad." He motioned to our beautiful surroundings. "I think if I could stay here for a while, I'd jump at the chance."

"Now I feel even worse. Thanks a lot." I bumped his shoulder with mine. He smiled, but the hint of sadness in his eyes caught at my heart. "So what's going on? Maybe I can still help you."

He huffed out a breath and shook his head. "No... you don't want to help me... I'm in too much trouble, and I'm definitely not good enough."

He didn't say, *for you*, but I heard it just the same. The bitterness in his tone cut me to the quick, and I sat there with my mouth hanging open. "That's not true. I know you're a good person. You can tell me. I want to know."

He glanced up at the sky, then closed his eyes and let out a sigh. "Fine. First of all, Avery..." He paused to swallow before continuing, "...is my younger sister. She got into some trouble, and I was trying to help her. But she was hurt in an accident before I had the chance. I let her down."

"What happened?"

"She went to Vegas with some friends. While she was there, she bumped into an old friend of mine, Dom Orlandi. He grew up with us in L.A., but moved to Las Vegas with his mom during our senior year of high school.

"We lost touch, but when Avery bumped into him, he offered her a job at one of the hotel bars waiting tables. I guess you could say they were into each other. My mom called to tell me that Avery had decided she wasn't going back to college, and that she planned to stay in Vegas with Dom."

He shook his head. "I knew I had to try and talk some sense into her. She'd taken her time in school, but she'd finally made it to her last semester, so it was a big red flag for me. I wasn't sure what Dom had gotten into since we knew each other, but I knew he wasn't the kind of guy I wanted my sister involved with, and I wouldn't put it past him to be involved in something bad. After the movie shoot I was working on got cancelled, I headed down there.

"Avery was caught up in Dom's world, and she didn't want to leave. I tried to convince her to go back to school, and she said she would, but she just wanted some time off. After a couple of days, I decided to stick around, so I could see what was going on.

"I renewed my friendship with Dom and found out more about him, including who he worked for. His boss, Sonny Dixon, owned the hotel and casino where Avery worked. But that wasn't all, he owned lots of other real estate, and he was a big deal. The more I found out about him, the more I realized he had all kinds of shady dealings going on.

"By then, Sonny had taken notice of Avery, and I knew that if she stuck around, she could end up as collateral damage. So I kept an eye on her for about a week by spending a lot of time playing poker at Sonny's casino. I even developed quite a reputation."

"How could you afford to do that?" I asked.

"Most of the time, I won." At my confused glance, he shrugged. "You learn a lot as a kid on your own, with an aspiring actor for a mother and no father around. I learned to handle myself, and I had a kid sister who I practically raised. Still, I couldn't wait to leave home. Then my mom..."

He shook his head. "She pulled some strings and got me onto a couple of movie sets. It wasn't something I'd ever wanted, but, since I didn't really know what I wanted, it was easy to get caught up in that world. That's how I got started in the business."

I nodded, knowing that, with his good looks and overall sex appeal, he wouldn't have any trouble getting hired.

"It's not like a steady job, but I've done well enough... and Avery..." He sighed. "She hasn't had the breaks like me... but she wanted to get into the business, pretty bad."

He bowed his head. "But being the big, protective brother that I am, I refused to help her. I told her to go to school and make something of herself. I think she hated me for that."

I shrugged. "Yeah... but you were looking out for her. Deep down, she probably knew that."

"Maybe, but even though she'd started college, she had a hard time sticking with it. I think she always wanted a more exciting lifestyle, and now... she'll never get that."

"Why? What happened?"

"One night in the casino, she stopped to talk to me. For the first time there was real fear in her eyes. She told me she'd overheard something she shouldn't have, and she wanted to go home. I told her we could leave right then, but she insisted on waiting a couple of days until Sonny and Dom left for a trip to San Diego.

"The night she spoke to me, a police detective stopped me on my way back to the cheap motel where I was staying. He'd been keeping an eye on Sonny, and he wanted to know if Avery had information about a murder Sonny was suspected of committing a few days earlier.

"I figured that was why she'd been spooked. I told him I was taking her back home and to leave her alone. The next day, she was hit by a car."

He clenched his jaw and took a deep breath to calm down. "She nearly died, but they managed to keep her alive on life support. I was able to move her back to L.A. to a care center, where my mom can watch over her, but it hasn't been easy. She's made a few improvements, but she's in bad shape, and she'll need lots of help. She also didn't have any health insurance, so I've been strapped for cash."

"The money... is that for your sister?" At his nod, I continued. "So... it's not all from winning at poker?" My stomach sank. Had he stolen it after all?

He shook his head. "Not all of it. But it's not what you think."

"Okay... then tell me."

"After getting Avery home, I went back to Las Vegas. I wanted to know if Sonny was responsible for what happened to Avery, and if he was, then I wanted that bastard to pay for what he did. Her accident was a hit and run, and they never found the driver, but I'm sure that Sonny was behind it."

"What about Dom? Was he involved, too?"

Creed let out a breath. "Yes, I'm sure of it, but I think he blamed me for the whole thing. He said it was my fault Avery wanted to leave in the first place."

"But she heard something she shouldn't have, right?"

"She never told Dom about that, and, for whatever reason, Dom doesn't think Sonny had anything to do with her accident. He's probably just lying to himself."

My brows rose. "But you're convinced Sonny did it?"

"Yeah. I talked to the detective again. He seemed to believe it was Sonny, too. But there was no proof."

"Okay. So what happened?"

"Sonny never knew that I was Avery's brother and, by then, Dom wasn't about to tell him. It would mean Dom had held out on Sonny, and he wanted to stay on his good side. So I took a job working at the casino. And when I wasn't working, I was playing poker. That caught Sonny's attention, and he asked if I wanted to work for him."

I nodded, realizing that Creed was serious about making Sonny pay. "I'll bet Dom didn't like that much."

He snorted. "That's true. Dom told me to watch myself, but he said he'd stay out of my way unless I rocked the boat. He wasn't real high on Sonny's food chain, but he's made a lot of progress since then. Anyway... Sonny seemed to like me, and, with Dom vouching for me, he asked me if I'd do a job for him. I told him I would, as long as the pay was good."

Dread ran down my spine. "What was it? Did he want you to kill someone?"

Creed nodded. "Yeah. Sonny gave me a gun and told me to meet this guy in a remote area on the west edge of town. I was supposed to exchange a bag of cash for drugs. Only... once I had the drugs, I was supposed to kill the guy and bury him out there. Then bring the drugs and the cash back to Sonny."

"Did you agree?"

He huffed out a breath. "Of course. At that point I didn't have a choice, but I didn't trust Sonny. I'd noticed him talking about me with his men a few times, but he never said anything to my face. Now I wonder if he found out I was Avery's brother after all." He shook his head. "Or maybe Dom told him."

"So what did you do?"

"I checked out the meeting place. It was a landfill on a dirt road on the west side of town. I figured it was probably a set-up, so I decided to take my chances and run. An hour before the exchange, they gave me the bag of money and told me they'd be watching, so I'd better not screw up.

"That made running a bit of a problem. I didn't want to meet up with the drug dealer, and I certainly didn't want to kill him, but, if they were watching, I had to find a way around it. That's when I decided to take Avery's car instead of mine.

"I'd left it in a parking garage after her accident, just in case I needed to make a quick getaway. So, on the way to the meeting, I pulled into the garage and made the switch. Back on the road, I made sure no one was following me and decided to head to Denver instead of L.A.

"My plans were working fine until the car quit. Then you hit me." He ran a hand through his hair. "I figured this was a good place to lay low for a while, but I've been here long enough. My leg's feeling better, and I don't want to put you in danger."

"Do you think they'll come after you?"

He shrugged. "I don't know, but I need the money to help my sister. I'd planned to send it to my mom, but I never got the chance, and breaking my leg has just made it worse."

He turned my way and reached out to touch my hair. "Then there's you. I didn't expect to find you in the middle of all this."

He pulled back and shook his head. "You're the other reason I need to leave. I haven't wanted to admit it, but I've enjoyed the last few days here with you. I've tried to forget about everything else, since there wasn't much I could do about it, but when you asked me about Avery, it all came crashing back."

I nodded, frustrated that he hadn't shared any of this with me before. "You don't have to go yet... you could call your friend back and tell him you've changed your mind."

"No. It's better if I leave now." He sighed before meeting my gaze. "If I don't go now, it will just be harder to leave later."

Warmth filled my chest. He did care. I hadn't imagined it after all. And now he was leaving? A sudden need to convince him to stay another day or two washed over me. If I just had a little more time with him, it wouldn't hurt so much to see him go.

"I get that, but you really could use a couple more days for your leg to heal. No one's going to find you here." I spread my arms wide. "I mean... look around. You're in the middle of nowhere."

His eyes widened before his lips tilted into a sexy grin that sent palpitations through my heart. "Hmmm... you're not going to make this easy are you?"

"Nope."

He groaned and shook his head, so I pushed my case. "Besides, there might be a better way out of this mess. What about working with the police? You could call that detective you spoke to and tell him what happened. You could give him the scoop about Sonny's business dealings."

"But you're forgetting about the money. I stole it, and I need it for Avery." Sighing, Creed glanced around at our beautiful surroundings. The cry of a hawk sounded overhead, breaking through the silence. "It's so peaceful here. It's like a different world, away from everything."

I took in the red rock formations, framed against the vast expanse of blue sky. "Yeah... it's pretty amazing here."

"There's something I'd like to do."

"What's that?"

His eyes darkened with desire. "Kiss you... right here... in this beautiful place. Then I'll have this moment to remember, and leaving won't be so hard."

Just knowing he had to leave sent all my reservations out the window. I slid off the boulder, turning to face him where he sat, and threaded my fingers through his hair, treasuring its soft, silky texture. His strong arms circled my waist, and he tugged me close. His lips found mine, claiming me with urgency, and I responded in kind, holding nothing back. The kiss deepened, and I couldn't seem to get enough of him.

As I plastered myself against him, Creed slid off the boulder, shifting all of his weight to his good leg. Kissing him with abandon, I threw my arms around his neck, accidentally knocking him off-balance. He began to tip to his injured side, and I realized what I'd done. Not wanting him to step on his broken leg, I desperately pulled him against me, but he was too heavy, and we both went down.

Creed took the brunt of the fall, and I landed on top of him. He let out a groan, and his face contorted with pain. I tried to roll off him, but jabbed in him the stomach instead. He doubled over and let out another groan.

"Oops... sorry." I slipped off him and knelt by his side. "Where does it hurt? Is it your leg?"

"No," he ground out. "My back—"

He held his shoulder, and I realized that he'd landed on a few large rocks. I helped him maneuver off the rocks to a sandier spot, and then raised his shirt so I could take a look.

A red scrape and bruise were starting to form just below his shoulder blade.

"Uh... it's not bleeding, so that's good." His shoulders started to shake, and panic tightened my throat. This must be worse than I thought. Had he broken his shoulder blade?

A strangled sound escaped him and I realized he was laughing. I sat back on my heels with my mouth open. "What's so funny?"

He shook his head. "I can't believe it... of all the stupid things..." He chuckled some more, then flinched with pain. "I think another rock caught me on my lower back... and maybe my butt, too." He glanced at me and narrowed his eyes. "Man... kissing you is painful."

"Hey... it wasn't my fault..." He snickered, but didn't say anything, so I continued. "What about your leg? Did you put any weight on it?"

He cursed under his breath. "I don't know... maybe."

"Does it hurt?"

"Not really," he hedged. "Okay... maybe a little, but not as bad as my back."

"I'd better get you home so I can look you over."

He grinned up at me, raising his brow. "I like the sound of that."

I shook my head, grateful he was joking instead of screaming in pain. I found his crutches and helped him up. Getting to his feet took longer than it should have, so I knew he was hurting more than he let on, and worry tightened my stomach.

On the drive down the creek bed, I kept an eye on Creed, noting his clenched teeth and white knuckles. By the time we got to the dirt road, his face had turned white with pain. We came to a stop before turning onto the main road, and I handed Creed some water. Pulling onto smooth road helped, and he didn't cringe quite so much on the rest of the drive.

I got him inside the house, and he headed straight to the couch. After lying down, he closed his eyes and finally relaxed. I gave him some ibuprofen and let him rest. After waiting a good twenty minutes, I sat on the couch beside him. "Feel any better?"

"Yeah, I think so."

"Good. I need to check you out." At his knowing glance, I rolled my eyes. "Let me take a look at your back."

"Okay." He sat up, and I helped him pull the t-shirt over his head, cringing to find his shoulder swollen and black and blue. "Ouch. That looks like it hurts." He grunted, and I traced my fingers down his back, finding that whole side of him had bruises that continued below the waist of his pants.

"I'm going to get the salve so I can rub it over your skin. The gel mostly helps me concentrate my healing touch, but it might feel good on your skin too."

He nodded. "If it will help me feel better... you can do whatever you want to me."

I ignored his suggestive tone. "I want to take the brace off and look at your leg too. Hopefully, you didn't cause more damage."

He moaned, and I left to get more gel from the supply closet. Unlocking the door to the clinic, I stepped to the closet and flipped on the light. Opening the cabinet, I grabbed a full tube, along with some gauze and moist wipes. As I came out of the supply room, a flash of light reflected off a passing car, hitting me in the face. Glancing out the window, I watched a car drive slowly past the clinic.

It kept going, so I turned to leave, only to catch a glimpse of the car turning around and heading back. This time it stopped in front of the clinic. Was it someone who needed help? I waited for a moment, but no one opened the car door.

As I stepped to the window, the car pulled away from the curb. This time it continued down the street, and I lost sight of it. Had the person finally noticed the closed sign? I checked to make sure the clinic door was locked and hurried back into the apartment.

Creed was lying down on his back with his arm over his eyes. With his eyes covered, I could look at his chest all I wanted, but, as I approached, he began to sit up. "No... stay like that for now. I'll look at your leg first."

Grateful he was wearing shorts, I quickly took off the brace and felt along the shin bone. There was no swelling, and I couldn't feel the dip from the break like I could yesterday. In fact, it surprised me that it felt so smooth, almost like it was completely healed. Had I done that? Normally, I could speed things along with my touch, but this was different.

Of course, most of the time, I only helped my patients once. After they left the hospital, or wherever I'd treated them, nature had to run its course. With Creed, I'd used my touch a couple of times, and, with each use, he'd healed more. Maybe that's why he hadn't hurt his leg earlier. Was it possible to completely heal someone? I had no idea, but it wouldn't hurt to try.

I squeezed some gel onto Creed's leg and massaged his muscles, concentrating on pulling a small amount of heat from my chest and pushing it into my fingers. I settled my hands over the break and pushed the warmth into his leg to soak into his bone.

This time, I felt a difference in the bone. Yesterday, I'd concentrated on knitting the bone together, but today it felt different. I sensed that it needed strengthening, so I imagined fortifying the bone around the break. It might leave a little bump, but it would be strong enough to hold it tightly together until it completely healed.

I focused on the break until I was satisfied that the reinforcements would hold, surprised to find that about ten minutes had passed. The exertion left me panting, and I pulled my hands away to catch my breath. After my breathing returned to normal, I touched the break and felt a bump of bone. Had it worked? Did that mean he could walk on it?

Not wanting to tell Creed until I knew for sure, I put the brace back on and tightened it up. "How does it feel now?"

"To be honest... it got really hot. In fact... it was painful. Now it's just warm."

"Hmmm... that's interesting." Not wanting to dwell on that new development, I continued. "Okay... now I need to check your back. Can you turn over onto your stomach?"

At his nod, I helped him move the pillows so he could lie flat on his stomach. Squirting salve on my hands, I rubbed them together until they were nice and warm. Laying my hands on his back, I massaged the salve into his skin, trying not to push too hard.

The energy at my disposal wasn't as plentiful this time, but I did the best I could and filtered it into his back and down his side. I had to pull his pants down in the back a little to reach the bruise forming on his butt, but he didn't seem to mind.

Naturally, I didn't mind either, and couldn't help admiring his backside, even with the purple bruises. I pushed the last of my heat deep into the swollen tissue. This time, I knew I'd drained all my energy, because I got a little light-headed. I quickly sat down on the floor and put my head between my legs.

"Ella? Are you okay?"

"Yeah... I'm fine. I just got a little dizzy. Must have been all that sun." Soon, the spots in my vision cleared, and the ringing in my ears eased. Feeling better, I glanced his way. "Did the salve help?"

"Yeah... I think so."

"Good." Needing a diversion, I stood up. "I'm hungry. You want something to eat?"

"Sure."

"Okay... you just lie there and rest while I fix it." I rose to my feet, grateful I could stand, even though my legs were a little unsteady. In the kitchen, I opted for something easy and pulled out a loaf of bread, along with the peanut butter and jelly.

To my surprise, Creed came over to help, taking out a couple of plates and setting them beside me. I told him where to find the potato chips, and we soon had everything on the kitchen table. I knew I was famished, but Creed ate like he was starving too.

Catching me staring, he shrugged. "I'm hungry."

"Yeah... I can tell."

We finished eating at about the same time, and a sudden longing pierced my heart. I didn't want him to leave... and it didn't have anything to do with the fact that he was sitting at my kitchen table without a shirt on.

"Uh... it's not too late to call your friend. Just tell him you figured something else out and he's off the hook."

Creed didn't object, so I continued. "Besides, you need to wait for your car to get fixed."

He pursed his lips. "I don't know. I'd like to stay... but I can't help worrying that Sonny might be looking for me."

"They don't even know which way you went. How can they find you?" A chill ran down my spine. "Wait... what about your friend? That guy you called. Is he involved with Sonny? Would he give you up?"

"Danny? No. He doesn't have anything to do with them."

"Are you sure?"

"Yes. He'd never give me up. He owes me too much."

I nodded. "Okay... that's good. So, where will you go?"

Creed shook his head. "Probably back to L.A. After I use the money to pay for Avery's care, I'll figure out what to do next."

I shrugged. "I still think you could stay here a couple more days. At least until your car is done." I held his gaze, willing him to accept my offer.

He let out a short breath. "You're sure making this hard, you know that?" I nodded, and he shook his head. "Okay... you win. Let me call Danny and see how close he is."

A thrill of elation warmed my heart. A few more days with him would keep me warm for a long time. After that, he could go, and I'd be ready.

He pulled out his phone and made the call. "Hey Danny, I don't know how close you are, but... What? Oh... how did you manage that?" He listened for a minute before responding. "So you rented a car?"

Creed met my gaze and let out a sigh. "Yeah... sure. I just need to pack up my stuff, and I'll be ready... yeah... okay, see you soon."

My heart sank. He was leaving after all.

Creed put his phone away and shook his head. "He had a buddy who was flying his small airplane to St. George, so he hitched a ride with him. He'll be here in about ten or fifteen minutes."

"Wow. That's impressive. Is he rich or something?"

Creed shrugged. "Yeah... you might say that. He's one of those guys who knows a lot of rich people."

I nodded, but dread tightened my chest. "Are you sure you can trust him?"

"Danny? Of course. He's harmless." Creed's brow furrowed, but he shook it off and glanced around the room. "I'd better get my stuff together."

He grabbed his crutches and stepped into the bathroom for his toiletries. I couldn't seem to move, but I finally managed to step to the bathroom door. "Do you need a zip-lock bag for all that?"

"Sure."

Back in the kitchen, I grabbed one and took it back, holding it open while he dropped everything inside. Finished, I zipped it up and carried it over to the couch. Creed gathered his clothes, slipping his shirt back on while I unplugged his phone charger and set it on the coffee table next to the salve.

He glanced my way. "Uh... I'll leave some money so you can pay for my car."

"Oh... yeah... right."

He reached into the duffel bag and took out a roll of bills. "This should more than cover it." He handed it over and I nodded, disappointment clawing into my stomach.

"I just realized something," he said. "I don't have your number. Can you give it to me?"

"Sure." He pulled his phone from his pocket, and I recited my number to him. "Send me a text so I'll have yours too."

A few seconds later, my phone chirped. I reached for it, but Creed stopped me. "Don't read it until after I've left."

My brows rose. "Why? Is it mushy?"

He chuckled. "You wish."

A loud knock sounded from the clinic door, and my heart raced. "That was fast."

"Yeah. I guess it's time to go." His eyes held regret, and he bent down to kiss me. I met his lips and wrapped my arms around his neck, kissing him hard, so he wouldn't forget me. Another knock on the door broke us apart. Creed swallowed and bent down to pick up his bag.

"Here. Let me carry that."

"Can I keep the crutches?"

"Yes. You should use them for the next week or two, just to be on the safe side. Hopefully you'll be okay to walk with the brace by then."

At his nod, I picked up his duffel bag and led the way through the connecting door and into the clinic. I unlocked the outer door and pulled it open to find a middle-aged man wearing a Hawaiian shirt and shorts. He smiled and offered his hand. "Hey... I'm Danny."

"Hi."

After shaking my hand, his gaze shifted to Creed, then back to me. He looked me over appreciatively and turned to Creed with raised brows. "Uh... dude... you sure you want to leave?"

Creed huffed out a breath. "Yeah."

Danny nodded, rocking on his heels, like he couldn't hold still. "Okay. Let's get going then." He glanced down the street, then at his car, before turning back to me. Noticing the bag, he reached for it. "I can take that."

For some reason, I didn't want to let it go. He grabbed the straps and tugged it out of my hand, sending me a confused stare. "I'll put this in the trunk."

As he hurried to the car, the back of my neck prickled. That was the same car I'd seen earlier. That meant he hadn't just arrived, he'd been here for a while. Creed started down the steps toward the car, and I grabbed his arm. "I don't think you should go."

Standing at the bottom of the stairs, he glanced my way. "Why?"

"I saw him drive by almost an hour ago, so he's been here longer than he let on."

Danny closed the trunk and stepped toward us. "You coming?"

"Give me a minute." Creed called over his shoulder. "What do you mean he was here?"

I told him about the car stopping in front of the clinic before it drove away in a hurry. "It's the same car. And look at him... he's nervous about something. He keeps looking up and down the street like he's afraid someone is after him."

"I'll talk to him. I'm sure there's a simple explanation."

"Does he know what happened to you?"

Creed shook his head. "No. No one knows about that but you. Look... I've got to go. It'll be fine. I'll call you." He studied my face, his eyes full of regret, before he hobbled toward the car. Danny took his crutches and put them in the back seat, while Creed settled into the passenger seat. It took all my willpower not to run after him.

As he slipped on his seatbelt, he glanced my way, sending me a smile and a quick wave. I raised my hand, and the car took off, racing down the road faster than I liked. A few heartbeats later, it was already out of sight.

Just like that, he was gone.

CHAPTER SIX

I let out a sigh and turned back to the clinic. Emptiness threatened to overwhelm me, shocking me with intensity. How had I become so attached to Creed in such a short time? Locking the clinic door, I stepped inside the apartment, feeling the loneliness settle around me like a heavy weight.

I glanced around the room, looking for signs that he'd been there. I took in the pillows that were piled up on one end of the couch where he'd slept. Two dishes still sat on the table from lunch, and his cell phone charger sat next to the tube of gel on the coffee table. Oops. Guess he'd missed packing that.

I sat on the couch where he'd slept and pulled the light blanket he'd used to my nose, catching his scent. I held it close and laid my head on his pillow. The rest of the day stretched out in front of me like an empty road, solemn and lonely. Besides the laundry, I had nothing to do.

At least I could give John a call and tell him about my burgeoning powers. I reached for my phone and noticed the notification on my message app. It was the text from Creed. With my pulse quickening, I opened the message.

Ella... thanks for the last couple of days. I will treasure them always. PS... I'll be back.

A smile creased my lips. On impulse, I began to type a response. *For me, or the car?* Shaking my head, I deleted that and began again. *And you think I'll still be here?* I let out a breath and deleted that one too. Finally I typed, *Good*, and pushed send.

I waited for a response from him before calling John, but the minutes passed, and disappointment washed over me. He was probably busy talking to Danny and didn't have time to respond. My finger hovered over the camera app. I finally gave in and opened it up.

There it was. The photo I'd snapped of Creed just this morning up Devil's Gulch. He sat on the boulder and looked up at the sky. The next photo was a close-up of his face. I'd caught him before he'd noticed what I was doing. He seemed deep in thought and a little worried.

In the next and final photo of him, he was smiling and carefree. His handsome face filled me with longing, and I shook my head to clear it away. He'd be back. Until then, I might as well clean the house and do my laundry.

With my clothes in the dryer and my kitchen clean, I glanced around the empty apartment. Without Creed here, the space closed in around me, and I could hardly believe how much I missed him. I checked my phone again, but he still hadn't responded to my text, and disappointment washed over me.

Sitting down on the couch, I gathered the blanket he'd used to my chest. It still smelled of him, and I held it close, inhaling his scent, grateful no one could see me. How pathetic was that?

Luckily, my phone began to ring, and hope sprang in my heart. Hoping it was Creed, it surprised me to see the number coming from the Richmond Hospital. "Hello?"

"I need to speak with Ella?"

"That's me."

"This is Jamie Chappell from the Richmond Hospital. There's been a car accident involving your husband, Aiden Creed? He's asking for you."

My husband? And he'd been in an accident? My heart lurched. "Is he okay?"

"He got banged up a bit, but he'll be fine. He wanted us to see if you could come."

"Of course. I'll leave right now, but it'll be about an hour before I can get there."

"That's fine. I'll let him know."

"Thanks."

The drive to the hospital took forever. Even though I made it in a record fifty minutes, the time seemed to drag on and on. I understood why Creed had told them I was his wife, because they wouldn't have called me otherwise. Still, it was a shock to hear it from the nurse.

Now I'd have to play along, but that didn't bother me too much. In fact, if I were honest, I kind of liked it, which was definitely not a good sign. I mean... I'd only just barely met the guy, and now I could hardly wait to see him again? Not good at all.

I pulled into the parking lot and rushed into the emergency room. After explaining who I was, a nurse took me to a curtained-off section in the corner of the room.

She pulled the curtain away, and I found Creed lying there with a bandage on his forehead. He glanced up at me, and his face filled with relief. "You made it."

"Aiden." I rushed to his side, only half acting the part of a distraught wife. "Are you all right? What happened? I've been so worried." I grabbed his hand and held it tightly.

"I'm okay… Danny lost control of the car. We went off the road and ended up in a ditch."

His pupils were dilated, making his blue eyes seem darker than normal. I turned to the nurse. "It looks like he's got a concussion."

She nodded. "That, and some broken ribs, along with a few cuts and abrasions. I guess his broken leg is from earlier. He was lucky. The doctor wants to keep him overnight for observation, but if he's doing well enough, he can go home with you in the morning."

"Okay, good. Thanks."

"I'll let the doctor know you're here." She left, pulling the curtain closed behind her.

I examined Creed with a critical eye. Besides having dilated pupils, his color was much paler than I liked. "What really happened? Where's Danny."

He shook his head, but stopped, grimacing with pain. "Damn fool. Danny's dead." He hesitated before speaking again. "He set me up. He was looking for me this whole time, and I led him right to your door."

"What do you mean—he set you up? Did Sonny send him?"

"Not exactly. I guess Sonny was more upset with me than I thought. He let everyone know I was on his hit-list. Before he died, Danny told me that Sonny offered the money I took to whoever brings me in."

"That's not good."

"Yeah. I don't know how much time I've got before someone else shows up, but I need to get out of here." Creed tried to sit up, but he cringed with pain and fell back against the pillow.

"You're in no condition to leave."

He let out an exhausted breath. "Can you help me? Even if it's just a little? Then maybe we can go."

"I'll do what I can, but I doubt it will be enough to leave today. At the very least, I think you'll probably need to stay the night."

"Okay... just do what you can." He opened his eyes. "Thanks for coming. Sorry about the wife part... but it was the only way I could get them to call you."

"I know. It's fine. I'm glad you called, but you're going to owe me after this... a lot."

Creed's brows rose, then he sent me a small smile. "Okay... you can keep the chocolates."

I let out a huff. "Ha. You'll owe me more than that."

"All right." His gaze caught mine, and his lips lifted in a half-smile. "You can have whatever you want."

I smiled in triumph. "Good. You have a deal. Where does it hurt the most?"

"My head. It's pounding so hard I can't think."

"Okay. I'll start there." I glanced at the curtain to make sure it was closed before I began. Perching on the edge of the bed, I placed my hands on both sides of his head, then closed my eyes and concentrated on pulling the energy from deep inside me and funneling it into my hands.

Gently tracing my fingers over his forehead, I channeled my healing powers into his head. A sense of wrongness led me to the frontal cortex of his brain, and I focused there, sending a pulse of healing power.

I focused it there a little longer, hoping to alleviate some of the swelling that made his head hurt, but I couldn't sustain it for long. I'd already helped Creed once today, and I just didn't have a lot left to give. I pulled my hands away, breathing heavily and blinking to clear my spotty vision.

Unable to stay upright, I rested my head against Creed's shoulder, careful not to jostle him or bump his broken ribs. His hand came to rest on my back, rubbing it with comforting motions. After catching my breath, I sat back up.

"How's the head now? Any better?"

"Yeah... it still hurts, but it's bearable."

I closed my eyes. "Good. I'd do more, but I'm a little tired right now."

"That's okay. You helped me a lot."

The curtain opened behind me, and I straightened.

"Uh... Hello. I'm Doctor Fischer."

I stood to greet him, and he offered his hand. "Hi, nice to meet you. Thanks for taking care of Aiden."

"Of course." The doctor glanced at Creed. "How are you feeling?" He stepped to Creed's side and examined his eyes, flashing a pen light across his pupils. "How's the headache?"

Creed glanced my way. "Not too bad... I mean... it doesn't hurt as much as it did."

"That's good news." The doctor flashed the pen light in his eyes again and nodded. "You've still got a bit of a concussion, but I don't think it's as bad as we first thought." He moved the gown away from Creed's chest to examine his broken ribs. After poking around, he took Creed's chart and wrote some remarks.

"With your concussion and the extent of your broken bones, I'd like to keep you overnight. I know that's not something most people want to hear, but I think it's best for now. I'll have them get a room ready for you. Do you have any questions for me?"

"What are you giving him for the pain?" I asked. The doctor explained the medications and dosage amounts to me and left.

I sat down on the chair beside the bed and took Creed's hand. "You just can't catch a break, can you? Or maybe I should say you're catching too many breaks."

"Yeah... my lucky day. I just wish it didn't hurt so much to breathe." He huffed out a breath, but I could tell it hurt. I wished I could do more to help him, but I was just too drained right now. Maybe, in an hour or two, I could try again.

A few minutes later, the nurse came in to take him to a room. Grabbing his things, I followed behind, not surprised that his duffel bag was among them. After he got settled into his room, and everyone had left, I sat in the chair beside him. "So how did the car end up in a ditch?"

Creed sighed. "When we got to the highway, Danny spilled his guts. I could tell he felt guilty, and he kept saying it wasn't personal, but the money was too good to pass up. He thought I was an idiot to take off with it. Apparently, Sonny's reach goes a lot further than I thought."

He shook his head. "So Sonny's telling everyone I'm a double-crosser, and he wants me alive to make me pay. I waited until I got the whole story out of Danny before I punched him and grabbed the wheel. It didn't go so well after that.

"We crashed, and it knocked me out cold. I didn't come to until they put me on a gurney and hauled me away in the ambulance. After they were done with all the tests and x-rays, I found out that Danny didn't make it. That's when I asked them to call you."

I nodded, wanting to tell him, in the worst way, that I was right about not trusting Danny, but I kept my mouth shut. "Do you think anyone else knows where you are?"

His lips thinned. "I don't know. But I can't chance it. I need to disappear. Do you think your friend at the repair shop has a car I could buy off him?"

"Yeah... he might. But you're in no condition to drive anywhere. Why don't you rest for now? We'll figure this out in the morning, and I'll stay the night with you. Okay?"

Closing his eyes, he nodded. "I think those pain pills are kicking in."

"Good... go ahead and sleep. I might grab something to eat, but I'll be back when you wake up." I watched him, until I knew he was asleep, and then made my way to the cafeteria for some food.

After paying for a croissant sandwich and a bottle of water, I sat down at a small table in the corner. The sandwich tasted so good that it disappeared quickly. Just as I finished the last bite, a woman sat down beside me.

"Ella? Hi, it's Heather. Wyatt's mom? I didn't expect to see you here."

"Oh, hi. Yeah... I'm here because a friend of mine was in a car accident... but he's going to be fine." Before she could ask me about that, I continued, "How's Wyatt doing?"

She shook her head, and her eyes widened. "He's doing really well. In fact, you'd hardly know he had a fractured skull. His recovery has been... well... miraculous."

"That's good news. He was hurt pretty bad, so I'm glad to hear it."

She chewed on her bottom lip. "Would you mind stopping by his room to see him? I think he'd really like to thank you for what you did yesterday."

"Oh... sure. Why not? I'd like that."

The tension left her shoulders, and she smiled. We spoke about the weather and other things until entering Wyatt's room. I followed her inside and found the handsome young man pushing buttons on the TV remote. Gone was the ashen pallor from yesterday, and his eyes held lucid intelligence.

"Look who I found!" Heather said, ushering me to his bedside. "This is Ella. She's the one who helped you yesterday, before the medics came."

His sharp gaze landed on me, and his eyes widened. "It's you. You're the lady in the light." He glanced between me and his mom. "I mean... uh... this sounds crazy, but I remember you. You brought me back."

My breath caught. Is that what he thought? "I don't know about that, but I'm glad I was there. You were hurt pretty bad."

"No... you did. I wasn't just hurt. I'm pretty sure I was dying. Then there was this bright light. It was so warm and comforting... and I saw you pouring the light into me. It saved me." Without thought, I reached for his hand and squeezed. A little awestruck, he squeezed back, not at all embarrassed by our linked hands. "Thank you."

A smile broke out over my face, and joy filled my heart. "I'm glad I was able to help, but... could you do me a favor?" At his nod, I continued. "Let's keep this between you and me, okay?" I looked up at his mom to include her. They both nodded, and I let go of his hand. "I wish I could explain what happened, but I can't. I think that's something you'll have to figure out on your own, but get better, okay?"

At his solemn nod, we said our goodbyes, and I hurried out the door, unsure of anything. How could he remember me? He'd been on death's door, and his eyes were shut the whole time. I swallowed, knowing that something drastic had changed, and I had no idea what it meant.

I'd never had the ability to save anyone like that before, even though I'd tried. I needed to talk to John. Did he know more than he'd told me? If so, why would he keep me in the dark? A shiver ran down my spine. Deep down, I knew I'd just passed a milestone, and this was more significant than I wanted to admit.

Deciding the call couldn't wait, I took the elevator to the ground floor and hurried outside, needing some privacy. I found a small garden area, with a walkway, among several memorial benches. Floodlights shone on a water feature, surrounded by plants and trees, making it a calm spot for people who needed some peace.

At the moment, I was alone, and I quickly put the call through. John picked up right away, surprising me. "Ella. What a pleasant surprise. How are you doing?"

"Uh... I'm okay. No, actually, I'm not. Something's happened, and I don't know what to do."

"What is it?"

I hesitated before blurting it out. "I think I saved someone from death." After letting that sink in, I explained what had happened. "I just left his hospital room. He's doing great, but he recognized me. How is that possible? He never opened his eyes. That's why I called. I need to know what's going on. Did you know I could do this?"

There was a long moment of silence before John answered. "Ella, listen closely. You need to come back home. To New York. Leave first thing in the morning. Don't help anyone else with your gift... anyone. Understood?"

"Why?"

"I can't explain it over the phone. You just have to trust me. Okay?"

"But, what about the clinic?"

"Don't worry about that. I'll take care of it. Just lock everything up and get on the road."

"Uh... that might be a problem." I explained how I'd hit Creed with my car and broken his leg. "He's been staying with me at the clinic, and I've been helping him. Anyway... the point is, his leg's not broken anymore because I healed it... as in... completely healed it. I didn't just speed up the process like I have in the past. I totally healed it."

"Does he know you healed it?"

"Not exactly. He knows it feels better, but I didn't want to tell him it wasn't broken anymore."

John huffed out a breath. "How did you explain it to him?"

"I just told him I have healing hands... same as I've always explained my gift. He just doesn't know I healed him completely."

"Well... I guess that's good. So... what's the problem? Just send him on his way and come home."

I swallowed. "Uh, I can't do that. He was in an accident a few hours ago." I told him about Creed's car accident, leaving out the part where his friend was taking him against his will to see the guy he was running from. He'd be upset if he knew that part, and I just didn't want to deal with it right now.

"Wait," John said, stopping me. "You went to the hospital and healed him again?"

"No... I was too worn out, but... I did help him with his concussion." At John's indrawn breath, I continued. "Don't worry, I didn't heal him, but I was planning on helping him again when I'm stronger, so we can leave."

John didn't say anything for so long, I thought we'd been disconnected. "We?" he asked. "But I don't understand. What's going on? You're saying that he stayed with you for a few days... then left... and now you're at the hospital with him. It sounds like you've left something out."

That was not what I'd expected him to say. "Uh... not really. I mean... he needed my help, so I've been helping him. That's all. I mean... I'm the one who ran him over with my car, so I've felt responsible for him."

"And that's all it is?"

"Of course." That came out a little too loudly, and, with John's silence, I knew I hadn't fooled him for a minute. "Okay... maybe I have feelings for him. I don't know... I just know I can't leave him here like this."

John sighed. "Yeah... okay. Just don't let him know the full extent of what you can do, and come back here as soon as you can. There are some things I need to explain, but it can't be over the phone. When you get back to the clinic tomorrow, call me. Then we can make plans to get you home."

"Okay."

"And Ella... it's important... don't tell anyone what you can do... not even this man you're helping. And, for heaven's sake, stop healing him, especially if he can heal on his own."

"Uh... sure, I get it. I'll talk to you tomorrow." We disconnected, leaving me more confused than ever. What did John need to tell me? He seemed more worried about who would find out than how my gift had changed. Did he know this would happen?

Helping Creed wasn't just an option; it was something I was going to do, no matter what John said. I didn't have a choice. He couldn't go anywhere in his condition and, if I had to head back to New York, where did that leave him? I wouldn't have to heal him completely... just enough so he would be okay without me.

It was full dark when I headed back inside. When I opened Creed's door, his closed eyes cracked open, and I hurried to his side.

"You're back." His breathing seemed labored, and worry puckered my brow.

"How are you feeling?"

"Not so good. It hurts to breathe. I must have moved the wrong way or something."

Worried, I pushed his hospital gown out of the way and gently moved my fingers over his broken ribs. Feeling along the broken bones, I found one that seemed more serious than the others. He winced at my touch, and his breaths came rapid and shallow.

"I think one of your broken ribs may have punctured your lung."

I knew John wouldn't want me to help Creed, but calling for a doctor when I could do something felt wrong. Still, it wouldn't hurt to ask Creed what he wanted. "Do you want me to call for help? Or do you want me to try and fix it with my touch first?"

"You... first."

I nodded, grateful I'd eaten something to replenish my strength. I placed my fingers over the bone and closed my eyes. Finding the heat deep inside me, I focused it from my fingers and into Creed's ribs and lung.

I felt the wrongness right away, especially where the bone had punctured his lung, and it surprised me that his lung hadn't completely collapsed. Concentrating all my energy into his side, I felt the broken rib knit back into position.

With the bone no longer pressing into his lung, I quickly patched up the torn lung tissue and sent a wave of healing power into the whole area. It took several long minutes for the bones to come together. Before everything was completely healed, I let go of the energy and pulled away, gasping for breath.

Opening my eyes, I found Creed staring at me. Sudden dizziness overcame over me, and I quickly fell into my chair. Leaning forward, I rested my head between my legs, hoping I wouldn't topple over. As the ringing in my ears cleared, I heard Creed's voice.

"Ella? Ella? Are you okay?"

"Yeah... I'm good. Almost. Just give me a minute."

My vision cleared, and I slowly sat up. His worried gaze rested on my face, and I managed a weak smile. "That was... uh... intense. Did it work? You feeling better, or should I get the doctor?"

"No... I don't need the doctor."

I let out a breath, and my shoulders dropped. Glancing around, I found my half empty bottle of water, and drank it down, instantly feeling better. Looking his way, I tried to smile. "You need some water, too?"

"Sure. But I can reach it." He managed to pull the wheeled side-table closer to him and took the plastic water bottle in his hand for a drink. After a long pull, he set it back down. "My mind's a little blown right now. What you did..." He shook his head. "I feel so much better."

"Good." I stepped to his side and examined his ribs. "Your injury's not completely healed, which is a good thing, since the doctor might think he's going nuts." I sent him a weak smile, but he just looked back at me like I was crazy... or weird... or just plain scary. "Don't look at me like that."

His eyes widened, and he shook his head. "Sorry. I'm just a little freaked out."

"Yeah... me too." My head felt too heavy to hold up, and I could hardly keep my eyes open.

"Come here." Creed moved over and guided me onto his bed. I wasn't about to resist, and I soon lay on my side next to him, with his arm wrapped around me.

"This feels so good." With my head resting on his shoulder, I felt his fingers move my hair away from my face. As he kissed the top of my head, I relaxed and let sleep overtake me.

The sound of a door opening brought me awake. I turned my head to see the nurse checking Creed's IV and making a note of his vital signs. She caught me staring and smiled. Embarrassed, I began to rise from my place.

"You're fine," she whispered. "I'm leaving."

The door clicked shut, and she was gone. Creed's face had turned slightly away from me, but his deep, even breathing told me he was sound asleep. I carefully sat up and pulled away from him, sliding my feet onto the floor.

He stirred, but didn't wake, and I sat on the chair. The clock read six in the morning, and I decided it was a good time to visit the restroom and grab something to eat.

I came back forty-five minutes later, and found Creed wide awake. He smiled to see me and held up his hand. "See that? They took out the IV. The nurse was a little surprised at how well I was doing, so it wasn't hard to get her to take it out."

"I'll bet." I nodded and sat beside him. "How are you feeling?"

"Ready to go. The nurse said the doctor would be in at seven, so I'm hoping he'll release me."

Before I could respond, the door opened, and a woman brought in a tray of food. She placed it on his stand and wheeled it closer to him. As she left, Creed pulled it over and inspected the scrambled eggs, toast, and fruit. "I'm starving." He dug in, then seemed to remember his manners. "Do you want some?"

"No. I got something at the cafeteria."

He finished up, and we waited for the doctor. "I'm anxious to get out of here," Creed admitted. "I feel almost as good as new. Even my broken leg isn't bothering me." His questioning gaze caught mine. "You did more than help me feel better, didn't you?"

I shrugged, not wanting to give a straight answer. "I think so, but you can't tell anyone, okay?"

"Who am I going to tell? Besides, how would I explain it?" He raised his brow, daring me to answer him, and I pursed my lips. "Yeah... exactly."

The doctor came in with Creed's chart, looking it over. "I just need to do a quick exam, and then you guys can get out of here." He pulled out a pen light and flicked it into Creed's eyes. As he checked Creed's broken ribs, I held my breath. His skin was still bruised, so that shouldn't alarm him, and

Creed even winced when the doctor brushed his fingers over them.

"They'll be sore for a while, so no heavy lifting or any kind of strenuous exercise for the next couple of weeks." He noticed the brace on Creed's leg. "How are you getting along with that?"

"Doing pretty well. I've got some crutches somewhere. Oh yeah... there they are." He pointed to the crutches resting against the wall.

The doctor had some last-minute instructions, and then he told Creed he could go ahead and get dressed. "The nurse will be here shortly to check you out."

He left, and Creed didn't waste any time getting out of bed. I handed him the crutches, and he raised a brow. "Do I still need those?"

"Yes."

With a shake of his head, he tucked them under his arms and stepped into the bathroom. A few minutes later, he came out, ready to get dressed. He moved cautiously, tugging a t-shirt over his head. I helped him pull the shirt down, hoping he wouldn't notice too soon that his ribs were completely healed. I even helped him with his shoes, to keep him from bending over.

The nurse came inside, pushing a wheelchair. Creed grumbled about using it, but, after a stern look from me, he knew it was better not to argue with either one of us. In the parking lot, the nurse helped him into the Jeep, and he thanked her. I slid his duffel bag into the back, along with his crutches, and got behind the wheel.

As I started the Jeep, Creed slipped on his seat belt and shook his head. "My ribs don't feel broken anymore. Not even a little. Do you want to tell me what's going on?"

Dang... I hadn't fooled him. "I'm not sure I can."

"What does that mean?"

"It means that I don't know. I've never completely healed an injury like that before. I think it all changed when I helped Wyatt. It triggered something more inside me... more than I ever had before."

I shook my head. "I called John—my Father. He wants me to come back to New York and said he'd explain everything. So... I guess, as soon as you're on your way, I'm leaving."

His brows rose, and he took a breath. "Oh. So... he knows what's going on with you?"

I huffed. "I don't think he has a clue, but he knows more than I do, so that's where I need to start." Silence stretched between us. It was on the tip of my tongue to ask Creed if he wanted to come with me. But I didn't think he'd agree, and I didn't want to sound pathetic.

He finally spoke. "I guess I need a car. Did you say Seth had a car I could buy from him?"

"He might. I know he planned to work on your car yesterday. He might be done soon, and I can wait to leave for another day or two if you want."

He shook his head. "I don't know. It might be best for me to take off today, before anyone else shows up, you know?"

"Yeah. Sure. Uh..." I took a breath for courage and continued. "You could come with me, if you want." Crap, why did I have to ask him? If he didn't want to, the time we had left together would be so uncomfortable. I should have kept my mouth shut.

His head whipped my way, and he studied me for a minute. Did that mean he was thinking about it? Encouraged, I continued. "We could deposit the money and transfer it to your mom so she'd have it, and you'd be away from Sonny and his people." I shrugged. "You have to agree that New York is a long way from here, and you can stay until you figure out what to do next."

His lips twisted into a small smile. "Well... I guess it's an idea. You do still owe me."

I rolled my eyes. "Whatever."

Although he hadn't given me an affirmative answer, it was close enough, and the tension left. We spent the rest of the drive talking about New York City. Creed had never been there before, and he wanted to know what it was like.

Before I knew it, we were back in Sandy Creek. I pulled into the driveway and parked in the garage. Creed slid out and walked cautiously to the back of the Jeep.

"What are you doing?" I jumped out and met him there. "You're supposed to use the crutches."

He shook his head. "My leg doesn't hurt. It's as good as new. I know you healed it yesterday and didn't tell me." I didn't answer, and his lips twisted. "Why? Why didn't you tell me?"

"I... uh... I wasn't sure if I wanted you to know." At his raised brow, I continued. "This is all new for me, and I don't even understand it myself. How was I supposed to explain it to you?"

The fight went out of him, and he nodded. "Yeah... I get that, but... this is a big deal." He grabbed his duffel bag, and we headed inside. After setting the bag down beside the couch, he found his missing phone charger and plugged it in. "Do you mind if I take a shower?"

"No... go ahead."

"I guess I don't need help this time, unless... " He raised his brows.

I shook my head. "No. I'm not helping."

He frowned. "That's too bad."

I rolled my eyes and headed into the kitchen, grabbing the leftover melon pieces out of the fridge to eat. After he shut the bathroom door, I called John, who picked up right away. "Hi John. I'm back home. I want to drive home from here. It might take a while, but I'd like the extra time to think. Does that work?"

"Yeah sure. And, once you get here, I'll share everything I know. Okay?"

I let out a breath. "Sure. I think I'll stay here tonight and get an early start in the morning."

"Okay. That's a good idea. What happened to your friend? Is he still in the hospital?"

Dang. I was hoping to keep Creed's involvement to myself. "Uh... no. He's here with me."

"Ella... what did you do?"

"What? He needed help, and I couldn't just leave him there."

He let out another exasperated breath. "Yes you could. He's not your responsibility."

"But he is. It was my fault he was hurt in the first place. I couldn't just leave him, especially not with the situation he's in."

"What situation?"

Oh crap, I'd done it now. "Well... uh... you remember that I told you he was in an accident?"

"Yes."

"Well... there was more to it." I took a breath for courage and blustered on. "He's running from some bad guys who want him dead. That's how he got in the car accident. He was trying to get away."

"Are you kidding me? What kind of bad people?" I didn't answer right away, and I could just imagine him flinging his arms up in the air. "I can't believe it. You've always hated people like him. That's why you're there in the first place, because you wouldn't help a criminal. And now you're telling me you're involved with someone like that. What are you thinking?"

"He's not a criminal." I knew it sounded lame, but it was true, and I had to defend him.

John let out a huff. "Dammit Ella." He paused before continuing. "You're just asking for trouble. What are you going to do? You can't leave if he's recuperating at the clinic." I didn't answer right away, and it gave him the time to put things together. "Wait a minute... did you heal him?" My silence was his answer. "Ella."

"What? I couldn't leave him defenseless, especially with these bad guys after him."

"What if you're wrong? What if he's one of the bad guys?"

"I told you, he's not. I'm not that gullible. Give me some credit here."

"I'm not saying that, but I just know how easy it is to make a mistake when your heart is involved."

I gasped. Was he right? Was I being stupid because of my feelings for Creed?

"Fine," John said, bringing me back to the conversation. "What's done is done. If he's well enough to leave, then send him on his way, and you can come home."

I froze, knowing I needed to tell John that Creed might be coming with me. Or maybe I should just keep that part to myself? John was having a hard enough time already. Plus, what could he say if I just showed up with Creed? Not much, right?

The shower turned off, and I knew Creed would be out soon. "Okay. I'll let you know when I'm on my way." I disconnected and put my phone away.

Creed opened the door, looking more energized and fresh than I'd ever seen him. With a towel wrapped around his waist, even the fading bruises on his chest weren't enough to keep me from staring. I was so screwed.

He started toward me, and I backed up until I knocked into the counter. "What are you doing?"

"Angel, when you look at me like that, what do you expect?" He stood close enough that I could smell his clean scent, and my legs got a little rubbery.

His lips turned into a knowing smile, and I flattened my hands against his chest and pushed. "Ugh... you're terrible. Go get dressed."

He chuckled and turned to go. An urge to tease him came over me, and I reached for the towel wrapped around him. It easily came off, and I held it in my hands, my chest catching with shock. What was I doing? Creed froze. Glancing at me over his shoulder, he began to turn around.

My eyes widened. I threw the towel at him and ran up the stairs to my room, slamming the door behind me. With my chest heaving, I shook my head, surprised at what I'd done. What the hell was wrong with me?

I didn't do stuff like that... ever. Sure, I'd had my share of flirting and kissing, but I'd always put my gift ahead of any physical desires I'd had. Of course, being raised by a bunch of priests didn't help. They were always sacrificing for their beliefs.

Is that what I'd done as well? Creed had awakened a new side of me, but there was more between us, right? Or was it all just a physical attraction? I'd decided long ago that I wouldn't enter a physical relationship without commitment. It wasn't worth the heartache.

I'd learned a lot from spending time at the women's shelter. Many of the women came with broken bones, split lips, and fractured jaws. I'd helped with the physical pain, but the emotional pain was beyond my touch.

I had to keep telling them that it wasn't their fault. A few believed me, but some of those poor women went right back to their abusers with some confused idea of love, only to end up back at the shelter if they were lucky, or dead if they weren't.

So what was I doing? A handsome actor like Creed was the epitome of a one-night-stand, and I couldn't ever forget it.

Locking my door, I stripped out of my clothes and took a quick shower. Feeling more in control, I got dressed and pulled my luggage from the closet. Laying the bags out, I began to pack. It didn't take long to fill them up, and I was ready to go. I opened the door, pulling the bags behind me.

Creed sat at the table, finishing off the melon. "I saved you some."

Why did just looking at him fill me with longing? I left my bags and hurried to the table before he ate it all. "Thanks. I want to take the apples too." As I chewed on the melon, Creed studied me, and my brows dipped. "What?"

"I want to come with you."

Those simple words took my breath away, and I choked. Coughing, I swallowed a few times before running to the sink for a glass of water. After a couple of big gulps, I could finally breathe again.

"You okay?" he asked, a small smile on his lips.

"Yeah. I'm fine."

"Good. I've been working out a route." He bent over his phone, and I hurried to his side to take a look at the map. "We're right here... and if we take—"

The back door crashed open, startling us both. Creed jumped up and froze. A tall, lean man with black hair and a wicked gleam in his dark eyes pointed a gun at Creed's chest.

"Hello Creed. You look surprised to see me."

CHAPTER SEVEN

C reed pushed me behind him. "Dom. What are you doing here?"

Dom chuckled. "I'm sure you can figure it out. Sonny wants his money back."

Creed swallowed. "What if I don't have it?"

"Hmm… why don't I believe you?" He pulled the trigger, and a bullet ripped into the wall behind us, right above Creed's head.

We both ducked, and Creed raised his hands. "Shit… Hey man. Cool it. All right? I'll give you the money. Just put the gun away."

Dom narrowed his gaze. "What happened to Danny? He was supposed to bring you to me."

"He's dead."

"You killed him?"

Creed huffed out a breath. "No. We were in a car accident."

Dom's brows rose. "What?" He studied Creed, looking for injuries. "You look too good for that lie. So what really happened?"

"It's true. Danny said he would help me, but, after I got in the car, he said he was taking me back to Vegas. I tried to take control of the car, and we ended up in a ditch. He died."

Dom shook his head. "That's too bad. He was a reliable source of information." His eyes narrowed. "I can't believe you took off with the money. I told Sonny we could trust you, and now it looks bad for me."

"Well, excuse me, but I'm not a killer. Did you really think I'd go through with killing someone?"

Dom paused, then shook his head. "I guess not. But I never thought you'd run off with the money. That was bad form, and Sonny will never forgive you for that."

"So? Are you supposed to kill me now?"

"No. But you could hardly blame me if I wanted to. I vouched for you, so now I have to do whatever Sonny wants, or it's my head on the line. That's how this works. I thought you knew that."

"Oh, I know all about it. You're the one with your head in the sand. Did you think to have this little talk with Avery? Did it ever cross your mind that she might still be okay if you'd mentioned that your allegiance was to Sonny and not her? It might have given her a fighting chance."

"You don't know what you're talking about. She wanted to be with me. It was her choice. You're the one who ruined everything. You shouldn't have come."

Creed opened his mouth, but Dom raised the gun. "Maybe I'll just kill you now and get it over with."

Dom's eyes burned with anger, and I didn't think he was bluffing. "Stop it. That's not necessary. You can take the money. It's right there in his duffel bag."

Dom turned his gaze to me and relaxed his stance. "And who the hell are you?"

"I don't want any trouble. Just... take the money and go."

Dom's dark eyes glittered with interest. "Why are you so eager to help him?" The derision in his tone surprised me. "He's not the good guy you may think he is."

Creed's mouth drew into a thin line, and he sent a glare Dom's way. "Leave Ella out of this. You can have the money, and I'll even come with you, but she's off limits."

Dom glanced between us. His brow furrowed like he was trying to figure something out. "Maybe Ella should come along."

"No. That's out of the question."

At Creed's quick denial, Dom's brows rose. He focused on Creed's protective attitude, easily picking up that there was something more going on. "As much as I hate to admit it, Sonny needs you alive. Maybe if Ella comes, you'll be more cooperative."

Creed shook his head. "I'll cooperate. You don't need her for that. Just leave her out of this."

"Can't you just take the money and go?" I asked.

Dom turned to me. "No. Afraid not. Besides wanting his money back, Sonny's running a high-stakes poker tournament, and Creed was supposed to play for him. That's the only reason he's not dead right now." He glared at Creed. "I guess you forgot about that."

Shaking his head, Dom continued. "I think you might be more inclined to win if Ella's there to motivate you. Unless, of course, I've got this all wrong, and you don't care what happens to her. Just give me the word, and she's not a problem."

He raised his gun in my direction, and I gasped.

"Stop it." Creed lifted his hands in surrender. "I'll do whatever you want. Just don't hurt her." He waited until Dom lowered the gun before he glanced my way. "I'm sorry Ella. I never meant to involve you in this."

"I know. It's okay."

Dom chuffed out a breath, then smiled and shook his head, like the joke was on me. "I don't know how this clown convinced you that he was trustworthy." He glanced at Creed. "What did you do? Tell her some sob story?"

Creed grimaced, catching my gaze. "Don't believe anything he says."

Dom chuckled. "Hey. You're lucky I caught up with you before the tournament. If you'd missed it, Sonny would have spread the word to have you killed, no matter how far you tried to run."

Creed shook his head. "Maybe. So where's your back-up, or are you here alone?"

"Grant's outside in the car, so it won't help you to try anything." Dom took out his phone and called the man. "I've got him. And he has a friend who's coming along for the ride, so come to the house. Pull into the driveway and come all the way to the back."

Slipping his phone into his pocket, he glanced behind me, noticing my packed bags. "Were you planning to run off with this loser?" Sneering at Creed, he continued. "Wow, you're a better actor than I thought, unless she's not as smart as she looks."

"Knock it off," Creed growled. Dom smiled, happy to get under Creed's skin.

The sound of a car pulling into the driveway sent my heart racing. Was this really happening? I couldn't see a way out of it that didn't involve one of us getting shot.

A few seconds later, a man entered through the door, sending Dom a nod. He stood at about five ten, had short, brown hair, and stood straight and tall, like he was ex-military. "Need some help?"

"Yeah. Get that duffel bag, and put it in the back." Dom glanced my way. "I guess you can bring your luggage since it's all ready to go, but only if you hurry."

Shaking my head, I slung my purse over my shoulder and grabbed both my bags. Dom stood beside the back door, ushering Creed out behind Grant. As I passed the kitchen counter, I grabbed the bag of apples and stuffed them in my purse.

Dom raised a brow, but he didn't stop me. At the back door, I took the house key off the ring. As Dom pulled the door shut behind him, I locked it up, wishing it would have been locked before Dom showed up. It might have slowed him down.

Not sure what to do with it, I placed the key under the planter on the deck. Dom raised his brow, and I shrugged. With a shake of his head, he followed me to the black Escalade sitting in the driveway.

Creed waited at the car. He reached down to help lift my big suitcase into the back, his eyes full of regret. My small case followed, and he turned to follow me to the back door of the car.

Dom waited, holding out his hand. "Before we go, I'm going to need your phone." With a sigh of despair, I handed it over. "Yours too," he said to Creed. Dom pocketed them and motioned me into the front passenger seat.

I wanted to object, but his sharp gaze held enough menace that I sucked it up and kept my mouth shut. Creed got in the middle seat, and Dom joined him there. A minute later, Grant pulled onto the road, heading south toward the highway.

I turned in my seat, glancing at Dom. "So... what's the plan here? Are we driving all night?"

"Yes," he answered. "But it won't take all night. We should get to the hotel around three in the morning."

That didn't sound too bad, although it wasn't anywhere near New York, where I needed to go. Dom seemed a little unhinged, but at least he hadn't killed Creed flat out like he'd wanted. Still, I wouldn't put it past him to try it another time.

Now we were heading back to an angry boss. Good thing Sonny still needed Creed, but after the poker tournament, what would happen? Maybe, if Creed won, it would appease Sonny enough to let us live, but what if it wasn't enough?

With so much to worry about, it surprised me that I dozed off. I woke to find the dazzling lights of a city alive with people. I thought New York was amazing, but it was nothing compared to the flashing lights and crowded streets of the Las Vegas Strip.

Passing several famous hotels and casinos, Grant finally pulled into the circular drive of the renowned Mojavi Desert Hotel and Casino. Three tall towers comprised the hotel, and I had to crane my neck to see all the way to the top.

Dom and Creed got out, so I followed their lead, stepping to the back of the SUV to get my things. I was definitely underdressed in my shorts and tee, but since it was three in the morning, and still hot out, it didn't matter too much.

Dom took both my bags, leaving me empty-handed—kind of like he was holding them hostage. Creed held onto his duffel bag, and it surprised me that he still had possession of all the money inside, but I didn't think that would last.

As we stepped inside the swanky hotel, my stomach clenched with nerves. Dom steered us into a hallway behind the registration desk and into a large office. A heavy-set man stood to greet us, and Dom nodded. "Is Sonny awake?"

"No, but he told me where to put these guys. I'll take you on up." He stared at Creed and gave me a quick once-over before heading back into the hallway. We followed him to the elevators. Inside, he touched a keycard over a reader and pushed the button for the penthouse suite.

Wow, did we rate or what? Of course, that meant there was probably only one way in or out, and we were basically prisoners without a keycard of our own. Still, a penthouse suite wasn't too bad for a prison.

We rode in silence, and I managed to catch Creed's attention. He sent me a half-hearted smile, but I couldn't miss the worry tightening his eyes. The doors slid open, revealing an amazing suite of rooms with plush carpet, deep couches, and a breathtaking view. The main room spanned the whole floor, and the far wall had floor-to-ceiling windows overlooking the Strip.

In the short entryway, a half bathroom opened on one side, and, on the other, a doorway led into a kitchen and bar nook. Further into the room, a set of dark, leather couches surrounded a large-screen TV on one wall, and a dining set, with a hanging crystal chandelier in the ceiling above, sat near the windows along the other.

"Don't get too comfortable," the night manager said, casting a sneer at me and Creed before handing Dom a second keycard and leaving the suite.

Dom sighed, glancing my way before he spoke to Creed. "He's right. You're only here because you can't leave without this." He held up the card before sliding it into his pocket. He motioned to the duffel bag containing the money. "I'll take the money now."

Reluctantly, Creed opened his bag and began to pull out the rolls of money. Dom grabbed the nearest garbage can and filled it up, counting it as he went.

"There's a roll missing." Dom glared at Creed and my heart lurched.

"Oh... that's right. I've got it." I grabbed my purse, pulling out a few things before finding it, and handed it over. "Here you go."

Dom grabbed it, unhappy that I'd kept it from him. He dropped it in the bin with the rest and picked it up. "I'm sure Sonny will want to see you first thing in the morning." He sent another glare my way before stepping onto the elevator.

The doors slid shut, locking us in, and Creed turned to me, his eyes full of regret. "I'm sorry I dragged you into this." He ran his fingers through his hair and shook his head. "I had no idea... I really thought I could trust Danny. I never should have called him." He took my hands in his. "I wish Dom wouldn't have made you come. He didn't need to. I would have played in the tournament anyway."

"Yeah... but it seems like he's holding a grudge against you."

Creed huffed out a breath. "Yeah... you're right about that. I didn't realize he blamed me for what happened to Avery. That's just insane."

"Some people are blind when it comes to accepting blame for anything they might be responsible for. Nobody likes to look bad."

"That's Dom in a nutshell. I wish it was different." He dropped my hands and stepped toward the couch. "I wish I could go back and change it all... but now I have to worry that you might die because of me. Staying with you so long was a mistake. I should have left earlier."

"Maybe so, but... it doesn't matter now. Besides, things can still work out. They can't just kill anyone who gets in their way, right?"

He shook his head. "You don't know these guys. And, to be honest, I'm not much better. If there's a chance to get you out of here, I'm taking it. Understand? I got you into this, and I'll get you out."

"Sure... but this isn't all your fault." I stepped toward him. "Don't forget that I'm the one who hit you with my car and broke your leg. You couldn't drive after that, so you couldn't leave. We're in this together, so let's see if we can figure it out together. Okay?"

His shoulders slumped, but he bridged the distance between us and pulled me against him. "I'm sorry." He held me tightly, like he didn't want to let go, but, after a few moments, he stepped away. "We have to do what they say, but I think, if I can win the poker tournament, I'll have some bargaining power. I'll use it to get them to let you go. I promise."

"But what about you? I'm not sure I can just... leave you here."

He shook his head. "I don't know. I'll see what I can do, but you have to promise me you'll leave if you get the chance. Maybe once you're gone, and I don't have to worry about you, I can get away. But I can't do that if they're using you against me. Understand?"

"Sure. I get it."

"Good." He took my hands in his. "I need to close my eyes for a bit. After a couple hours of sleep, I might be able to come up with a better plan."

I could see the fatigue in Creed's eyes and realized he hadn't gotten much rest. Even though I'd healed him, he'd still been through a lot. I glanced toward a set of doors that opened into a large bedroom. "It looks like there's only one bedroom."

"You take it. I'll sleep on the couch. I'm used to it." He smiled at my raised brows and reached for my luggage.

I followed him into the spacious bedroom, admiring the king-sized bed and drawer set, with a desk and chair off to one side, and the wall with floor-to-ceiling windows overlooking the Strip.

I continued into the beautifully tiled bathroom, finding a double-sink and Jacuzzi bathtub. A door on the other side opened into another bathroom, only this one had a fancy tiled shower with all kinds of strategically placed shower heads. Hmm... I couldn't complain about that.

Creed moved to the closet and grabbed an extra pillow, along with a blanket, and stood in the doorway, where he paused to tell me goodnight. "Get some rest."

He took them straight to the couch and began to undress. As much as I wanted to stand there and watch, I managed to shut the door. Suddenly exhausted, I slipped off my shoes and clothes and rummaged through my luggage for my pajamas. After slipping them on, I lay down on the bed, but sleep eluded me.

Sonny had gone to great lengths to get Creed and his money back. If he was anything like the mob-bosses in New York, Creed didn't stand much of a chance. That meant I didn't either. How were we going to get out of this?

Dom had made it sound like Creed hadn't been exactly honest with me, but that was just to get under his skin, right? But now, I had to wonder if Creed had lied to me about the money, or worse, his sister. He wouldn't do that... at least I didn't think so. But Dom had planted a seed of doubt, and it was rearing its ugly head, not helped by the fact that Creed was an actor.

But I was a better judge of character than that. I couldn't believe Creed would lie about everything. I knew he wanted to protect me. That much was clear. He also felt bad about involving me in this mess. He'd even agreed to go to New York with me. Why would he do that, if he didn't care? Was there another reason? I couldn't think of anything at the moment, but I couldn't rule it out.

Now I was in this mess with him, and I wasn't sure he had enough clout to save me. But if he did, I needed to be honest about my choices. What if I had to leave him behind to die? Could I do that? What choice would I have?

It was hard to believe that, just a few days ago, John had told me that I was in that tiny town for a reason, and, if I just held on long enough, I'd figure out what it was. Now look at me, a hostage in a penthouse suite in Las Vegas. How could this be part of a grand plan?

It made no sense at all, especially after the big change I'd been through. Knowing I could actually heal people changed everything, and John had even wanted me to come home. Now I wasn't sure that would ever happen.

The timing sucked.

I heaved a sigh and closed my eyes. Giving in to despair was not the answer. I had to believe that I could get out of this. There had to be a way... I just needed to figure it out.

I fell into a fitful sleep, waking to the early morning light coming through my window. I padded to the view, looking out over the city with its flashing lights that never turned off. What was I doing here? I needed to get back home to New York and the answers John had promised me.

Too bad I couldn't call him. Frustration boiled over, so I decided to take a shower to cool off. The pounding water helped revive me, and I took my time, enjoying the multiple shower heads. Finished, I dried off, and spent extra time on my hair and makeup.

Not sure what to wear, I decided my jeans were okay, as long as I wore a nice top. At least I'd already packed my things before Dom showed up, so I had plenty to choose from. I settled on a v-neck white t-shirt with a golden print design that wouldn't seem too out of place in a casino.

Ready, I opened the door, finding Creed stirring on the couch. Opening the door woke him, and he glanced in my direction, then swung his legs to the floor and rubbed his face.

"Do you think we can get room service?" I asked. "I'm starving."

He chuckled. "I doubt it." He stood and stretched, totally forgetting that he only wore his boxers. While I admired the view, he hitched the blanket around his waist and turned, a sheepish smile on his face. "Uh... do you mind if I take a shower?"

"No... go ahead."

He carried his duffel bag into the bedroom and closed the door. While waiting, I stepped into the small kitchenette and found a bottle of water and turned on the coffee machine. As I glanced over the other amenities, the room phone began to ring, and I rushed to pick it up. "Hello?"

"Hello Ma'am. I'm just calling to let you know your breakfast is on the way. We'll leave it just inside the door."

"Oh... great. Thanks."

A minute later, the elevator door chimed, and a man wheeled in a cart. Seeing me, he smiled. "Enjoy your breakfast." I thanked him, and he promptly left.

Heavenly smells came from that cart, and I eagerly wheeled it over to the table. I made quick work of setting out the plates and utensils. Next, I set the covered serving plates on the table, along with the butter, jam, and syrup. Peeking under the lids, I found bacon, hash browns, scrambled eggs, pancakes, and a plate of fruit containing fresh pineapple, kiwi, grapes and melon.

What a spread. My stomach growled, and I picked up a piece of bacon, but decided to wait for Creed before eating anything else. My wait wasn't long. Creed came out dressed in jeans and a blue, long-sleeved dress shirt.

I stared at his movie-star good looks, unable to take my gaze away for a full twenty seconds. Creed smiled, and I pulled myself together. Was I a total idiot? I didn't want to be just another woman to him, but I was sure acting like a fool. "Uh... breakfast came."

He nodded and strode straight to the table. After sitting down, we began to fill up our plates. We ate in silence, each of us lost in our thoughts. Finished, we piled the dishes back on the cart and I wheeled it over to the elevator doors, leaving it against the wall.

"What's going to happen now?" I asked.

"I guess we wait."

I nodded and stepped toward the windows, looking out across the city. Creed joined me, and we stood in silence. I glanced his way. "Did you think any more about a plan?"

He shook his head. "Nothing came to me. I'll just have to make sure I win the tournament. I think it's the only way to stay alive right now. But I was thinking that if you have a chance to get away, you should take it. Go straight to the police. I'm sure they'd help you. Or at least give you a phone to call your father. Would he be able to come?"

That didn't sound like a man trying to pull one over on me. "Yes, I'm sure he would."

"Okay. Then try and get away, however you can."

I searched his gaze, but the doubt still lingered. "Creed... I have to know. That story about your sister... and the money... you didn't make that up, did you?"

Creed inhaled sharply. "Of course not."

"I'm sorry I had to ask, but Dom made it sound like—I don't know—you'd say anything, and I just needed to make sure."

Creed blew out a breath and closed his eyes. He was silent for a moment before glancing my way. "I get that, but it's all true. Everything I told you is true. I thought I could handle these guys, but I got in way over my head. Now... here we are... and I'm so sorry. I'll do whatever it takes to make sure that you don't suffer because of it. That's a promise. Do you believe me?"

Sincerity shone in his eyes, too real to be faked, and I nodded. Before I could speak, the elevator doors swooshed open. Instead of the staff coming in to take our breakfast dishes, Dom and Grant entered the room, and my heart skipped a beat.

"Sonny's ready to see you," Dom said, directing his gaze at Creed.

Creed straightened his shoulders and stepped toward them. Not quite so eager to leave, I followed behind. At the elevator, Dom stopped me. "Not you."

I opened my mouth to protest, but pressed my lips together and watched them step into the elevator with Creed between them. After the doors closed, I stood in the silence, not knowing what to do.

Letting out a breath, I began to pace across the room. After several long minutes, I remembered the phone on the desk and jerked to a stop. It wouldn't hurt to see if I could use it. I picked it up, but there was no dial tone. Checking the directory beside it, I pushed zero for service.

"Good morning. How may I help you?"

"Uh... hi. I need to make a phone call. Can I get an outside line?"

"One moment, please."

My heart soared, and I listened for the dial tone. The voice came back on. "I'm sorry, but that's not available right now. Is there anything else I could help you with?"

"Uh... yeah." The breakfast cart caught my eye. "I'm done with breakfast. Can you send someone up for the cart?"

"Of course. Someone will be there shortly."

"Thank you."

The line went dead, and I hurried over to the cart, wondering if I could find something to use as a weapon. Unfortunately, there were no knives included, not that I could actually stab someone, but they wouldn't know that.

I rushed into the kitchen nook, looking for something else I could use.

Nothing looked remotely heavy enough, so, instead, I grabbed a bottle of wine from the collection of bottles on the back shelf. If I could hit him hard enough with the bottle, I could get the key card and get out of there. Carrying the bottle, I grabbed the cart and pushed it back to the table.

Just as I got it into position, the elevator door opened. Holding the bottle out of sight, I straightened and glanced up with a smile. Instead of a staff member, Dom stepped out. I froze. "What are you doing here?"

As the doors closed behind him, he stopped to study me. "Why do you look so guilty?"

My mind went blank. Before I could think of something to say, he continued. "Planning to hit me over the head? Is that a bottle in your hand?"

Knowing he'd caught me, I set the bottle on the table and frowned. "Why are you here?"

"It's your turn. Sonny wants to meet you." My mouth dropped open, and he continued. "Come on, let's go."

I crossed the room to his side and entered the elevator. I stepped to the back, as far from Dom as I could get, and we rode in silence to the main floor. The elevator doors opened, and Dom tightly grasped my elbow, leading me down the hallway and past the registration desk. Instead of stopping at the manager's office, we continued to the door at the end of the hall.

After a quick knock, he opened the door and pulled me inside. This opulent office held twice the space of the manager's office. A conference table sat at one end, surrounded by comfortable leather chairs. The other end held a large, dark-wood desk in front of an ornate bookcase.

Side tables with lamps sat in the corners, while a large double door opened onto a courtyard, with access to the pool and greenery. Filmy curtains covered the glass doors and side windows for privacy.

Creed sat in front of the desk, dabbing at a trickle of blood, running from his mouth, with a tissue. Grant stood beside Creed, and an older man sat perched on the desk in front of him. As we entered, the older man glanced up with interest and stood. "This must be Ella. Please, come in and sit down."

Sonny moved to take his chair behind the desk, while Dom led me to the chair beside Creed. As I sat down, Dom stood behind my chair, hemming me in. I swallowed, feeling like a cornered rabbit in a den of wolves.

"Creed and I have come to an agreement, and it involves you." Sonny began. "He's insisting that we let you go after the tournament, provided he wins." Sonny smiled. "He seems to think you're his good luck charm... although he hasn't seemed to be lucky lately."

The sight of his smirk sent anger deep into my stomach. I hated bullies, and he was the worst.

"I just wanted you to know about our agreement, in case you're inclined to take off. As long as you stick around, nothing happens to Creed. But if you should manage to slip away, you will have just signed his death warrant. Am I clear?"

"Yes... of course." I glanced at Creed, but he wouldn't look at me. Catching Sonny's gaze, I asked, "After you let me go, what happens to Creed?"

Sonny's brows rose. "I'm sure we can work something out... as long as he has learned his lesson."

Creed met Sonny's gaze. "Like I said, I thought you wanted me dead."

My neck prickled. What did he mean by that?

Sonny shook his head. "I admire loyalty in my people. I would have given you the benefit of the doubt if you'd just come back to explain. Now I'm not sure I can trust you at all. Consider it your good fortune that Ella's here to keep you in line, as long as you remember that she won't live long if you don't come through."

Sonny glanced at his watch. "The tournament starts in an hour. You'd better get cleaned up. I've registered you to play, but you'll need to sign in, so don't be late."

Sonny stood, signaling that the meeting was over. I got to my feet and followed Grant and Creed to the door, with Dom following behind me. Soon, they ushered us back into our room. Before leaving, Dom said, "I'll be back to get you."

Creed headed into the main bathroom and splashed cold water on his face, wiping the blood from his lip and chin. I followed behind. "Why did you tell Sonny that you thought he wanted you dead?"

Creed held the cold washcloth to his mouth. "I couldn't tell him that I just ran off with the money. That would be a death sentence for sure, so I told him I thought it was a set-up, and that the drug dealer was supposed to kill me."

"Did he believe that?"

"Probably not. But Sonny glanced at Dom after I said it, like he wouldn't put it past him to do something like that."

I shook my head. "I guess anything's possible. Do you believe they'll let me go if you win?"

"I don't know. But it worries me. I may be a good poker player, but I don't always win. Unless they have something in mind to give me an advantage, I could lose just as easily."

"So you knew about the tournament?"

"Yeah, but I'm not the only player on Sonny's list." He shrugged. "I have to admit that leaving Sonny in the lurch appealed to me. I just never thought he'd find me so easily." He pulled the washcloth from his face, and it came away bloody.

"Here... let me stop the bleeding."

His gaze jerked to mine. "Oh... right. That would be nice."

"Let's sit on the bed." He followed me into the bedroom and sat down, tilting his face so I could get a better look. I leaned over him and placed my fingers over his swollen lips, getting lost for a moment in how soft they felt. Closing my eyes, I pulled warmth from deep inside me and sent it pulsing through my fingers into his broken skin.

The heat flared before subsiding, and I pulled my fingers away to find the gash on his lip gone. The bruise forming along his jaw had faded as well. "There." I swallowed, still surprised that I could heal him so completely. "How does that feel?"

Creed shook his head. "Amazing." He rubbed his tongue over his lip. "It's gone... like it never happened."

"Yeah... kind of crazy, huh? It still surprises me." Unable to stop, I brushed my thumb over his lip. With his face so close to mine, it seemed only natural to close the distance and seal his lips with a kiss. My fingers slid from his jaw and into his hair. His hands found my waist, and he pulled me between his legs, deepening the kiss.

Creed fell back on the bed, pulling me down on top of him. Our bodies close, he rolled me onto my back and ran kisses down my neck. Taking my mouth with his, he held me tightly against him.

"You're so beautiful," he breathed. "So perfect." He pulled away, his breathing ragged. "I want you, but I don't deserve you." He cupped my cheek and gently kissed my lips, one last time. Slipping off the bed, he stood, reaching for my hand to help me up.

Standing close, he whispered, "Maybe, when this is over, I'll have time to earn your trust. Will you give me a chance to do that?"

The uncertainty in his eyes caught at my heart. "Yes."

"Good." He kissed me once more before stepping away. "I need to change. Did you bring anything to wear? Like... maybe a dress or something nice?"

"Oh... sure. Let me look."

He nodded before stepping to the closet, where he'd hung a sport coat and a couple of shirts. He unbuttoned his blue shirt and shrugged it off, giving me a great view of his bare chest. Looking at the shirt collar, he shook his head. "I got blood on my shirt, so I'm going to let it soak for a minute."

"Sure." I couldn't take my eyes off him. After he disappeared, I swallowed and picked up my luggage. I placed it on the bed and opened it up. It took me a few seconds to process why I was looking through my clothes. Right... a dress. Now that I could think again, panic set in. I had two dresses to my name, and I couldn't remember packing either one of them.

Creed came back in, and my gaze wandered over his bare chest while he picked out something to wear. He chose a white shirt and slid it over his arms. Now that he was covered, I could concentrate on my task. I rummaged through my bag and hoped my dress was in there. Feeling the stretchy material, I let out a breath and pulled the dress free.

The black dress wasn't anything special, but it would do in a pinch. The stretchy material clung to my curves, and the gathered ruching along the right side seam draped the material across my waist with a slimming accent. The round neckline didn't show any cleavage, but the back dipped enough to seem more daring than it was, and the three-quarter length sleeves made it appropriate for any setting.

I took it into the bathroom to change, hoping my sling-back sandals and some jewelry would dress it up. After slipping it on, I touched up my lipstick and found some silver, dangly earrings in my makeup bag. I took another minute to scrunch my shoulder-length waves a little tighter and sprayed it with a touch of hair spray.

With one last look in the mirror, I pulled the door open and stepped into the bedroom. Creed wore a blue sport coat over his white shirt, and was slipping on his shoes. His gaze landed on me and he froze. "Whoa. Maybe you should stay here. I don't want all the men hitting on you." I frowned, and he continued. "Seriously, it would be too distracting."

I smiled, pleased that he liked what he saw. "Uh... I don't agree with you, but I can stay here if you think it will help."

He shook his head and stood. "No... I want you with me. Sonny was right that I told him you were my good luck charm. He has no idea how true that is. Just having you there will help me... I'm sure of it."

I thought he was grasping at straws, but I wasn't about to disagree. "I sure hope so."

The elevator door swished open. Through the bedroom doorway, we caught sight of Dom and Grant entering the room. Creed sighed. "Guess it's time to pay the piper."

"You can do this." I gave Creed a quick hug, knowing he needed to believe in himself and his skills.

He held me tight before stepping back. With a grave nod, he stepped through the bedroom door, taking my hand and pulling me with him.

CHAPTER EIGHT

D om noticed our tightly clasped hands, and his face tightened. His gaze roamed over me with a critical eye before settling on Creed. His brows dipped together, and he frowned. "What happened to the cut on your lip? I thought Sonny hit you pretty hard, but it looks like nothing happened."

"He put some ice on it," I said. "And the cut is on the inside of his mouth, so it doesn't show."

Dom turned to me, his icy stare sending shivers down my spine. With a haughty nod, he motioned us toward the elevator, waiting to follow us inside.

In the cramped space, Creed squeezed my hand, holding it tightly, all the way down to the main floor, and bolstering my courage. We stepped out into the crowded lobby, and Dom led the way to a large room, just for playing poker.

I counted twelve oblong poker tables, each fitted with golden felt and sitting below spotlight lampshades, which emitted low levels of filtered light. Each table was surrounded by ten deep, velvet-backed chairs, with the dealer's chair in the middle to round out the seating arrangement.

Spectator seating was sparse around the outer edges of the room, but the chairs were plush and comfortable-looking.

Dom directed Creed to the guest services desk to check in, and I trailed along behind. At the desk, Creed found his name and signed the paper. They gave him his assignment at table number twelve. As he stepped away, he took my hand again, offering me comfort.

Most of the players were already seated at their tables, but Creed put it off until the last minute. The final call came for the players to take their seats, and Creed turned to me. "A kiss for luck?"

I smiled and nodded. He leaned in for a tender kiss before heading to his table. As Creed took his seat, Sonny began to speak into a microphone at the front of the room. "Welcome to the first winner-take-all Mojavi Casino Poker Tournament, with the largest jackpot on record of ten million dollars.

"You should have all registered and received your table assignments. Please note that all regular Texas Hold'em poker tournament rules will apply. There will be short breaks between rounds as needed. Anyone who doesn't play by our previously agreed set of rules will be escorted from the room without compensation. That includes cheating of any kind. For that purpose, monitors will be watching throughout the tournament.

"After the first round, the winners of each table will have a dinner break of forty-five minutes. You will then be assigned to one of two tables for the second round. The two winners from the second round will then face off for the chance to win the ten-million-dollar jackpot."

Sonny paused, looking over the room. "Are you ready?" Several people clapped, and a few whistled, bringing a big smile to Sonny's face. "Dealers, take your places." The dealers filed to their respective tables, each wearing white shirts, black pants, and golden vests.

"Monitors come forward." Six people, wearing the same clothing as the dealers, took their designated positions throughout the room.

With a satisfied smile, Sonny gave the final command. "Let the games begin."

A chill ran down my back. This game didn't have any gladiators fighting to the death, but the stakes were just as high. How many other professional poker players had been hired to play in this tournament? Were any of them under the threat of death like Creed? I couldn't rule it out, but I sure hoped it wasn't the case.

The low murmur of hushed talking filled the room, but it wasn't loud enough to distract the players. The dealers all opened a fresh deck of cards and began to shuffle them with expert fingers. All the players had an equal amount of chips arranged in front of them, so they began on a level playing field.

At a couple of tables, a few players introduced themselves to their fellow challengers, and I hoped most of them were there to have a good time, since only one of them would win. Others, including Creed, merely nodded at their competitors and waited for the cards to be dealt.

I took a deep breath and let it out, still shocked at the ten-million-dollar jackpot. Did people really play for that much money? It boggled my mind. Dom stood beside me, and I glanced up at him. "This is going to take a while, isn't it?"

"It sure is. Want to sit down?"

"Yes."

He ushered me to a spot closer to Creed's table. As we sat, I noticed most of the guests wore casual clothes, although I was sure they easily cost more than my entire wardrobe.

My stretchy black dress was nice, but quickly put to shame by the designer jeans and fancy shoes surrounding me, especially if all the diamond jewelry was added to the mix. I didn't belong here, and this madness sent my stress levels through the roof.

"How long does a tournament like this usually last?" I asked.

Dom's brows rose. "Don't you like all the excitement?"

"No."

That brought a chuckle out of him. "It's going to take a while. In fact, it probably won't end until early tomorrow morning." He pointed out the large, flat-screen TV at the end of the room, telling me that all the statistics would be posted there, just like at a sporting event.

"So they're going to keep playing all night?"

"Of course."

"Wow. I know Sonny already explained it, but how does it work exactly?"

Dom explained that once a player lost their chips, they were eliminated. With ten players per table, that could take a while, but it would happen because the blind bets would incrementally increase. The winner would then move to the second round of six players at two tables. The final winners from those tables would have a showdown against each other, leaving only one winner for the jackpot.

"Everyone will come back for the winning round. It will be the most exciting match of the night."

"Yeah... I'll bet. Hey... I know Creed's good, but do you really think he has a chance? I mean... isn't poker mostly a game of luck?"

"It's not just luck. There's a lot of skill involved as well. But I think he has an excellent chance to win."

The way he said it made the back of my neck tingle. "How can you be so sure?"

He smiled down at me. "Let's just say he's in a good spot."

My brows rose. "Oh... so he's been strategically placed?" At Dom's quick nod, I continued, "Because Sonny is running the show?"

"You might say that."

I couldn't hold back the smirk on my lips. "Isn't that... cheating?"

Dom's brows drew together. "Not at all, and you need to watch your mouth if you want to stay here. Understand?"

His threat didn't frighten me like he wanted. It just made me mad. "Sure."

"It still doesn't mean Creed will win." Dom shrugged with feigned indifference. "He's good. One of the best I've ever seen, but that doesn't mean the cards will fall in his favor. Still, if he plays smart, he can pull it off."

"Right." I tried not to sound too sarcastic, but I didn't like the odds. "So what does Sonny need all of that money for, anyway? He's probably rolling in the dough. Why do this?"

Dom frowned. "It's a matter of pride. He invited several of his 'friends' to compete in the tournament, and they were more than willing to put in their share for the jackpot. Now it's a matter of who can win it all, and take home the prize."

"You mean—the bragging rights?"

"Sure. But the ten million jackpot doesn't hurt either."

I shook my head. "Rich people and their money. Why don't they just help the poor or something more meaningful? Games like this are kind of disturbing."

Dom studied me like he was seeing me for the first time. I didn't like his scrutiny, so I asked him a question about the blinds and the little white chip that sat in front of one of the players. Soon, we got interested in the game, and Dom was more than willing to answer any of my whispered questions.

Along with the basics that Creed had taught me, it was enough to grasp what was going on, but I didn't have the slightest idea of what constituted a good betting hand. Skill might be involved, but it was still a game of chance. Bluffing played a major role, but playing for such high stakes on a bluff seemed a little crazy.

Now that the games were underway, I glanced at the other players in the room. Most had their backs to me, so I couldn't see their faces. A lot of them dressed more casually than Creed, without a sport coat or jacket, although a few had taken them off to drape across the backs of their chairs.

There also didn't seem to be a lot of women players. In fact, I only spotted two because of their hair. One near the front had long, blond hair, and another, closer to the back, had a dark, chin-length bob. There might have been a few more with short hair, but it was hard to tell from where I sat.

Creed was surrounded by men, ranging in age from early twenties to late sixties. Several of them began playing with their chips, actually shuffling them together with their fingertips. Those guys had to be the pros who did this sort of thing for a living. I could never imagine a life like that, but they must be used to the pressure.

Creed didn't play with his chips. In fact, he didn't seem concerned about anything. He looked more laid back than I thought possible, considering the stakes. His impassive expression didn't give away a thing, but I was sure he'd been studying the other players and learning their 'tells.'

The first hour, Creed lost as many games as he won, keeping his chips holding steady. A younger player's stack had dwindled, and his upper lip was coated with perspiration. I didn't think he could gain back what he'd lost, and I was sure he didn't think so either.

Going *all in* on the next round sealed the deal. He was one card short of a flush and lost it all. With a heavy sigh, he shoved his chair back and strode from the room, clearly angry and upset. The room went still to watch the first player leave. Then everyone went back to business as usual.

Dom occasionally left my side, but he always came back to check on me. An hour and a half had passed, and I was tired of sitting. Eight of the ten players remained at Creed's table, so it was far from over. As Dom approached, I stood. "Mind if I stretch my legs and maybe go outside for some fresh air?"

Dom's lips twisted. "Sure. Come with me."

I followed him into the lobby, but, instead of going out the entrance, he took me down another hall that opened into the courtyard and swimming pool area I'd seen from Sonny's office. Outside, the heat hit me pretty hard, and I knew this wasn't where I wanted to be.

"Wow... it's too hot out here. Maybe it would be better to head to my room for a few minutes... you know... kick off my shoes and visit the bathroom? If you give me a key, I promise I'll come right back. I just need a break."

Dom's brows rose. "Give you a key? Are you serious? That's not going to happen, but I'll take you up for a few minutes."

I sighed before nodding, and followed him back into the hotel. A few minutes later, we entered the penthouse suite, and I went straight to the bathroom. It was the only place I'd have any privacy, and I just needed to be alone. I kicked off my sandals and wet down a washcloth with cold water. I held it to my forehead for a few seconds, then touched up my makeup.

After rummaging through my luggage, I made a quick decision to change into more comfortable clothes. I could wear the dress for dinner if I needed to, but, as a spectator, my jeans and shirt were fine, as long as I kept the jewelry on. I slipped my purse over my shoulder and hoped Dom wouldn't notice. If I got a chance to run, I'd need my credit cards and driver's license.

I came out of the room to find Dom talking on his phone. Seeing me, his brows drew together. He finished his call and shook his head. "Why'd you change?"

"Have you ever tried wearing high heels and walking in them for hours?"

"No."

"Well... they hurt my feet, and I wanted to be more comfortable." At Dom's scowl, I continued. "You said this would take all night."

"Fine. But you'll have to change back to the dress for dinner and the last match. Sonny expects it."

"Sure. If Creed makes it to the last match, I'll be happy to."

"You'd better hope he does, or you're both dead."

Part of me wanted to throw something at Dom. "How can you work for such a rich bully?"

Dom let out a sigh and sat down on the couch, in no hurry to leave. "You're a doctor, right?"

I sat on the edge of the couch across from him. "No. I'm a nurse... well, an RN... a registered nurse. But nursing is what I do. I used to work as a trauma nurse in New York City."

"New York? What brought you out here, especially to that little dinky town in the middle of nowhere?"

I let out a breath. "It's a long story."

"We've got time."

"Let's just say I made a mistake, and I'm taking a break."

He frowned. "So what happened? You get hooked on prescription drugs?"

I sucked in a breath. "What? No. I'd never do that."

He smirked. "Well... you can't blame me for thinking that was the case. It happens to a lot of doctors. So, what did you do?"

"I don't think that's any of your business."

"Probably not, but I'd like to figure you out." He studied me for a minute, and I squirmed under his gaze. "In fact...

if I were to guess, I'd say you don't think you did anything wrong."

How did he know that? I slumped lower in my seat. "Maybe not at first, but now... I can see their point... even though I'd probably do the same thing again."

His brow lifted. "So... where were you headed when we showed up? Back to New York?"

"Uh... maybe."

"And Creed was going with you?" Seeing the answer in my face, he shook his head. "He's better than I thought... convincing you to take a chance on him like that? I mean... you don't seem like an easy person to con, so how did he do it? I guess he's good-looking and all that, but I'd wager he's hardly your type. You seem too good for someone like him."

"What do you mean, 'like him'? At least he's nothing like you."

"Maybe not," he agreed. "But at least you know what you're getting with me. Creed? Well, you don't know the half of it."

I shook my head. "I'm confused. Why do you even care?"

His brows rose, like I'd hit a sore spot, and he frowned. "I don't."

"Is it because of what happened to Avery?"

Dom sucked in a breath, and his face turned stormy. "I don't know what Creed told you, but he's the one to blame for what happened to her. The accident was bad enough, but he just couldn't leave well enough alone."

Unease prickled my neck. "What are you talking about?"

Dom's eyes narrowed. "You don't know? What did he tell you anyway?"

"He said she was involved in a hit-and-run and suffered some life-threatening injuries. I don't know the extent of it, but I think he said she was on life-support for a while. It sounded like she was doing well enough that he moved her back to L.A. where she'd get better care."

Dom sighed heavily. "Her injuries were life-threatening. The only thing keeping her alive was the life-support, but that's because she suffered serious brain damage. I told Creed to take her off the machines, but he wouldn't do it. I knew she wouldn't want to live like that, you know?"

Standing, Dom shoved a hand through his hair, more disconcerted than I'd ever seen him. "Creed moved her to a facility in L.A. that would keep the machines going. After she'd been there a week, I think his mom finally talked him into pulling the plug.

"Miraculously, she kept breathing on her own. I guess he took that as a sign that she might get better, but I don't know how. From her initial diagnosis, she hardly had any brain function left."

He caught my gaze. "What do you think? Can someone recover enough to have any kind of a normal life after an accident like that?"

I glanced away. "It's highly improbable."

He nodded. "That's what I thought. She'd be better off dead, but try telling Creed that."

"I understand what you mean, but Creed's in a tough spot. I think he feels responsible for her."

Dom stood, shaking his head. "Then he should let her go. Death has to be better than the life she has now."

"Maybe it seems that way to you, but if there's any hope of saving her, I'm sure it's hard to let go. Maybe she's made some progress that you don't know about. Do you know anything about her current condition?"

"No, but it doesn't seem possible that it would change enough. You just said so yourself." He stepped toward the elevator, done with our conversation. "We should get back."

I followed behind him, knowing it probably wasn't a good idea to upset the guy who might end up killing me. But I couldn't figure him out. Was he a killer or just full of hot air? He obviously cared about Avery. We stepped into the elevator, and I met Dom's gaze. "Would you really kill me?"

He blinked. "What kind of a stupid question is that? Of course I would."

"And you wouldn't even feel bad about it?"

He huffed out a breath. "No. Because then I wouldn't have to listen to your stupid questions."

I folded my arms and stepped back to lean against the back of the elevator. As we got closer to the main floor, I figured this might be my only chance to make a run for it. Once the doors opened, I could shove past Dom and take off out the front door. I wasn't sure how far I'd get, but, in the crowds of people, it might work.

What about Creed? Playing in the tournament, he was safe enough for now. If I could get away, I might be able to get some help and come back at the end of the tournament and rescue him. If I told the police what was going on, they might help me.

The doors slid open and I straightened, ready to run. Only Dom didn't step out. He turned to face me, slapping the penthouse suite button with his palm.

The doors slid shut, and my heart raced. "What are you doing? We need to get back to the tournament."

Dom shook his head. "No... I'm afraid not. I've been too lax with you. All this time I thought you cared about Creed, but I guess I was wrong."

"Of course I care about him. What are you talking about?"

"You were going to run. Don't try to deny it. You changed your clothes, and you've got your purse."

I opened my mouth to deny it, but the glint in his eyes stopped me. We rode in silence until the elevator doors opened. He gestured for me to head into the room. I didn't move, worried that once I was in there, I'd never come back out.

Dom reached for my arm to drag me in, but I jerked out of his grasp. "I'll change back into the dress, and leave my purse here. I'll do whatever you want. Just don't leave me here. I need to know what's going on. Creed needs me. I'm... I'm his lucky charm. He said so himself."

Dom shook his head. "It's too late for that. Are you coming out, or do I have to drag you out like a spoiled brat?" At my widened eyes he stepped right up into my space, and I backed into the corner. His steely gaze bore down on me, and I knew I only had seconds before he followed through on his threat.

"Okay, I'll go." Resigned, I stepped around him and stalked into the room. "I'll change back into the dress. Just... don't leave me here. All right?" I turned around to plead my case, but the doors slid shut on his satisfied smirk.

"Dammit." Now what was I supposed to do? I hurried back into the bedroom and threw my purse into my luggage. It had given me away, and I never should have chanced taking it. Now I was stuck here with no way to know if Creed was winning or losing.

Not knowing if or when someone would come to get me, I quickly changed back into my black dress, hoping Creed would insist that I return. I paced the room for nearly an hour before finally giving up and turning on the television.

I changed the channel nearly as often as I got up and paced the room, but nothing happened. Still, I hoped that, once it got close to the dinner hour, someone would come for me.

Hours later, I knew dinner had come and gone. I grabbed an apple from my purse and ate it, watching another hour go by. As the sun began to set, I pulled a chair over to the windows and sat down. Dusk turned the sky gray, and I watched the lights below begin to sparkle in the twilight. The Strip lit up after that, and I began counting all the red cars, then switched to counting the white cars.

Bored of that, I let out a breath, feeling a weight of despair settle in my stomach. I knew this was a form of punishment, but it seemed like they had forgotten about me. Didn't Creed want to know where I was? Shouldn't he insist they come and get me?

What if he'd lost? Was that why they'd left me here? Were they trying to figure out how to kill us and make it look like an accident?

I didn't know how long I sat in the dark before I heard the welcome sound of the elevator doors swooshing open.

"Ella?"

"Creed." I jumped up from my chair, racing across the room to him. "Are you okay? They wouldn't let me come down." I touched his face, and he leaned down to pull me against him, kissing me with passion. I pulled away to come up for air. "What happened? Are you still in?"

"He won the first round."

Surprised, I jerked back to find Dom standing beside the elevator doors. He flicked on the lights and stepped toward us. "I see you changed."

I glanced down at my dress. "I told you I would."

"Get your shoes. You're coming with us."

Relief spilled from me. "Okay."

"I need to change my shirt," Creed said, following me into the bedroom. He shut the door behind us and locked it, leaving Dom on the other side. "What happened? Why did they leave you up here?"

"Dom brought me up because I wanted to change into something more comfortable. After I changed, I grabbed my purse and... I had this crazy idea that maybe I could run when we reached the lobby and get some help. Before I could even try it, Dom figured it out and brought me up here and left me."

Creed nodded, but his lips thinned, and I knew I'd disappointed him. "I wasn't going to leave you... I would have come back... with help."

"I know." He shook his head. "It's fine, Ella. Even if you didn't come back, I would have understood."

I dropped my gaze. "I just made it worse. I've been going crazy up here, wondering what was going on."

He pulled me against him. "Just stay by me from now on, okay?"

"Yes, of course."

"Good."

Creed quickly rid himself of his jacket and shirt. He pulled out a deep maroon shirt and began to button it up. "This last round shouldn't take as long because they're raising the blinds. But it's still nerve-wracking. At least I'm not playing against the blond."

"Who?"

He tucked his shirt into his jeans and explained. "At dinner, some of the others were talking about her. Apparently she won pretty quickly at her table, and rumor has it that she has a reputation for never losing. Dom told me something weird about her, and I don't know if I believe it, but he said she has... premonitions, or something crazy like that."

"What do you mean?"

"He said it's like she has some kind of psychic power that helps her know if she'll win the round." He sighed. "I know it sounds stupid, but that's how he explained it. If it's true, and we both make it to the final round, I'll need all the luck you can send me."

Creed stepped to the bathroom. "I'll be right back."

My mind flew back to my last few days in New York. I'd met someone who worked with the police and seemed to know more than a normal person could. Didn't she say she had premonitions? But it couldn't be the same person. What were the odds that our paths would cross again? Not likely, that's for sure. Still, I couldn't wait to see for myself. Shaking my head, I slipped on my shoes.

Creed came back out and took my hand. "I told Sonny I wouldn't play without you beside me. That's why Dom brought me up here. But... there's another reason I needed to see you."

"What's that?"

He let out a breath, and I could see the fatigue in his eyes. "I have a splitting headache. I'm sure it's from the pressure of the tournament. I was hoping you could help me with that."

"Of course. Sit down on the bed." As he sat, I placed my hands on either side of his head. Closing my eyes, I sent a pulse of healing energy into him, feeling my way to the pain. His sigh of relief let me know it had worked, and I pulled my hands away. "Better?"

"Yes... so much better. Thank you. I might have a chance now." He took my hand. "Ready?"

"Yes."

Creed pulled the door open, and we headed out. Dom scowled before stepping to the elevator, unhappy Creed had locked him out. Inside, we stood apart from Dom, still holding hands.

I glanced up at Creed. "So you've already had dinner?"

"Yes. But I'm sure Dom can get you something."

Knowing Dom would hate that, I shook my head. "Oh... that's okay... I'm not that hungry."

"I'm sure he wouldn't mind." This time Creed's tone had an edge to it.

I peeked up at Dom. "Uh... maybe a roll or something would be good?"

With twisted lips, Dom tilted his head. "I'll see what I can do."

I barely refrained from rolling my eyes at his blatant lie. The doors opened, and Dom followed us out. Grant had been waiting, and joined us, not letting us out of his sight until we had entered the poker room. Stepping inside, surprise washed over me to find the room totally different.

Most of the tables had been moved out, leaving only two set up in the middle with rows of seats on either side of the tables. A few players had taken their seats, but not all, and I scanned the room for a woman with blond hair.

Near the back, I found her, and my breath caught. It was Shelby, the woman I'd met in New York. She'd been working with the police, and she'd helped capture the killer... the person I'd let die, and the reason I was here.

Beside her stood the tall, dark, and dangerously handsome man she'd brought to the hospital, but I couldn't remember his name. Without thinking, I stepped toward her.

She glanced up and spotted me, and her eyes widened. "Ella?"

We both rushed toward each other, meeting in the middle of the room. "Shelby. It is you. I wasn't sure."

"Oh my gosh! What are you doing here?"

"I'm with someone..." I glanced at Creed, who stood behind me, rooted to the spot.

She followed my gaze and looked him over, nodding appreciatively. "You're with him?"

"Uh... yeah, Creed. He's playing in the tournament."

"I know..." Shelby glanced from Creed to Dom, then back to me. "Is he playing for Sonny?"

"Yes... he is. I guess you're playing too? How did you get into this?"

"Uh... I came with my Uncle Joey... uh Joe Manetto. He's an associate of Sonny's and bought into the game." Her brows drew together, and she lowered her voice. "Are you in trouble? I mean... that guy standing by your friend looks kind of nasty... if you know what I mean. And Sonny is probably worse."

Before I could answer, Sonny spoke into the microphone. "Players, take your places. It's time for round two to begin. If you're not seated within the next two minutes, you will forfeit your spot." He was looking straight at Shelby and me.

"I'd better go. Let's talk after this round, okay?"

"Sure." As she hurried away, I noticed tall, dark, and handsome standing nearby. He'd stood apart from us, allowing us some privacy, but now he joined me. "You're that nurse from New York." At my nod, he continued. "I'm Ramos. I brought Hawk in to see you?"

"Yes, of course, I remember you. Uh... nice to see you again. Well... it looks like I'd better go." Ramos made me more nervous than anyone I'd ever met. He had dangerous vibes shooting off him in spades, and I didn't like it one bit. Something in my primal brain told me to stay far away from him, and I intended to do that.

Creed waited near the poker table, so I hurried to his side. "How do you know them?" he asked.

"I met them at the hospital in New York."

"Oh... were they part of your... uh... problem?"

"Yeah... kind of, but not in a bad way. Shelby—"

"Players, take your seats or you will forfeit your spot." Sonny's loud voice startled me, and I jumped.

"Good luck, Creed. You can do this."

"Thanks." He squeezed my hands and gave me a quick kiss before taking his seat. I glanced around, realizing that a lot of people had noticed our kiss. I tried to keep my expression calm, even though my heart raced and my palms began to sweat.

Dom took my wrist and pulled me to a chair on the front row, beside him. His face held an ugly scowl, and his body practically vibrated with anger. "What the hell?" He hissed. "You know them?"

His grip tightened on my wrist, and pain caught my breath. "You're hurting me." His grip relaxed, and I tried to pull my hand away, but he held on tight, waiting for my answer. "Yes... I know them... but just in passing. Let me go."

Exhaling, he dropped his hold, and it took several minutes before he'd calmed enough to speak. "Let's take a walk." He reached down to grab my wrist again, but I tightly folded my arms before he could.

"No. I'm staying right here. And, for your information, I met them over two months ago in New York at the hospital where I used to work. That's all. Now leave me alone."

His jaw jutted out, and I figured he wanted to beat the crap out of me. I squirmed in my seat, shifting as far away from him as I could, and hoped he'd cool off before he got the chance.

I glanced Creed's way. He sat to the dealer's right, and his worried gaze caught mine. He'd witnessed my exchange with Dom, and his jaw tensed. With his eyes narrowed, he looked ready to leave the game and punch Dom in the face. As much as I wanted him to do that, I pushed down my fear and sent him a nod, pouring all the determination into my expression that I could.

His face cleared and he nodded back. Grateful he understood my message, I smiled. He winked in response, clearing away my worry and settling something inside of me. Whatever happened, I wasn't alone, and neither was he. Somehow, we'd figure this out.

CHAPTER NINE

D om's phone chirped with a text. After reading it, he slipped from his chair and paced to the service desk where Sonny stood. They spoke in whispers, but darted glances my way, and I knew Dom was relaying the information I'd given him about Shelby.

Sonny's face tightened, and I followed his gaze to the man sitting beside Ramos. He had to be Shelby's Uncle Joey. He was a distinguished-looking gentleman, with a head of thick, white, wavy hair. His dark eyebrows and strong jaw gave him a commanding air.

Ramos bent to whisper to him, and Manetto glanced in my direction, catching me staring. I returned my gaze to Sonny and watched his scowl deepen. Manetto followed my gaze, glancing over his shoulder to see Sonny glowering at me.

From all the whispering and staring going on between them, it was easy to see that they weren't on the best of terms, and I'd just stepped in it by speaking with Shelby and Ramos. Now what?

A few seconds later, Ramos left his seat. I watched him with growing alarm as he came toward me and sat down in Dom's vacant chair. I glanced Dom's way and found his face tightening with anger. In a way, it satisfied me that Ramos had gotten under his skin. But, on the other hand, it probably just made things worse.

Ramos didn't speak to me, and I noticed him watching Creed with interest, almost like he was studying his playing style. I didn't like that at all, since it meant he could tell Shelby what he'd observed, giving her an advantage that Creed wouldn't have.

Of course, since they were playing at different tables, it didn't matter unless both of them won. But what if they did? I leaned closer to Ramos and spoke in a low tone. "I think you've upset Dom. That's his chair. Maybe you'd better leave."

Ramos's lips tightened, but he didn't look my way as he spoke. His voice was so low, I almost didn't hear him. "Are you in trouble?"

I waited until Dom wasn't watching us before I answered. "Maybe."

Ramos's head dipped just a fraction. Then he began to speak to the man on the other side of him, like that was the reason he'd sat in the chair. Not a fan of Dom's dirty looks, I glanced toward the back, where a long table offered tidbits like crackers and cheese, along with several flutes of champagne and bottled water.

Creed's current poker round ended, so I slipped away and headed to the food table. I filled a small plate with several crackers, topped with cheese and olives. I quickly ate the crackers, grabbed a bottle of water, and headed back to my seat, just in time for the dealer to play the flop of the next game.

Thankfully, Ramos chose that moment to return to his seat, and it wasn't long before Dom came back to sit by me. He didn't say a word, but his imposing presence set my nerves on edge. I concentrated on the poker match, to offset my worries, and sent all the good vibes to Creed that I could.

In the next round of betting, one of the players risked everything and went *all in*. Three of the other players had folded, which left Creed and another man to call, raise or fold. The other guy called, and Creed took his time. After glancing at his cards, Creed doubled the bet.

The guy who'd called tried not to react, but he rubbed his nose, and I figured that was a tell, although I didn't know if that meant he was bluffing, or if he had a good hand. After several tense moments, he threw in a bunch of chips to call, nearly depleting his stash.

Did this mean Creed might lose? I held my breath as the dealer turned the river card. It was a lousy four, and my heart sank. I hoped Creed hadn't been betting on that card. In fact, the dealer's hand showed a seven, a jack, two fours, and a ten. That gave him two fours, but it was hardly a winning pair.

The players revealed their cards. With the fours, the guy who'd gone all in had two pair, aces high. The other one who'd called Creed's bet had two pair, kings high. Could Creed beat that? Creed turned his cards over to reveal two fours. Then it hit me that he had the winning hand, with four of a kind. Hot damn!

My breath whooshed out. Creed had done it. That was intense, and relief washed over me. The player who'd gone *all in* was now out of the game, leaving five to continue. Would Creed's luck hold? The next few rounds weren't as exciting, but Creed's stack continued to grow, and I began to relax.

During this time, I kept an eye on Shelby's table. Her stack of chips was pretty big too, and it looked like she had a good chance of making it to the final round. I watched her, hoping to see how she played so I could give Creed a tip or two. During the three rounds I observed, I noticed that when she didn't fold, she usually won the hand.

It also didn't look like she ever bluffed. Why was that? Was it because of her premonitions? I wasn't sure how that could work with poker. Wasn't a premonition like a vision or a feeling of something about to happen? How could that help her win at poker? There must be something to it though, because she kept taking the pot with relative ease.

I focused back on Creed's table, and my stomach tightened to see him lose the next two rounds. Tendrils of worry ran down my spine and stayed there until he came back to win the next game, taking a bigger pot than the previous games.

I realized that was due to the blinds going up, which also kept the game from slowing down. After the next game, another player ran out of chips, leaving four to fight it out. Creed continued to do well, and, to my relief, another player dropped out, leaving him with the biggest stack of chips and three others to play against. My heart soared. He might just pull this off.

At Shelby's table, it had come down to two players, and she had the bigger stack against a man with sweat rolling down his face. As the dealer turned the river in the game, Shelby threw down her cards, face-up.

All the spectators sighed at once, and the dealer pronounced her the winner, loudly proclaiming that she was now qualified to play in the final tournament.

The man playing against her sputtered and stood, throwing down his cards and swearing loudly. His face turned red, and he pointed a finger at Shelby. "You're cheating." He glanced at the dealer. "She should be disqualified. She's been cheating this whole time."

Ramos stepped to the man's side, his face a mask of granite, and his tone a quiet snarl. "You need to stop. Right now. Before you regret it."

The man jerked back and dropped his hands to his sides, but he didn't back down. He pointed at the monitor. "You." His upper lip rose in a sneer. "You need to check the cards. And I insist you do a sweep under the table for anything hidden there, like a mirror or extra cards."

I hadn't noticed the monitor before now, but he'd been watching the whole time, and he stepped to the man's side. "I've seen no evidence of any cheating going on by the lady or anyone else."

"That doesn't mean anything. I insist you check the cards. Check the cards, damn you!"

Dom stepped toward the man, holding his hands out in a placating gesture. "Sir. May I remind you that you agreed to the terms of play long before the games began? Let me be clear. If you won't abide by them, you will lose any chance of ever playing in a poker tournament in this casino again. Do I make myself clear?"

At that, the man clamped his lips together, barely holding in another outburst. Dom called a security guard to escort the man out of the room, and he left with a red face and an angry stomp.

As he neared the exit, I glanced Shelby's way, finding her massaging her temples with her fingers, like she had a headache. Ramos knelt beside her and spoke. Standing, he motioned to the monitor. After a brief conversation, Ramos helped Shelby up, and they left the room.

If she had a headache, they'd probably arranged for her to take a break. Since Creed's table still had four players to sort through, there was time for her to rest. I knew I could help her with my gift, but not under these circumstances. Besides, under Dom's watchful eye, I'd never get the chance anyway.

About ten minutes later, Ramos returned and sat down by Shelby's uncle. It was easy to see that Manetto was Sonny's biggest competitor. It might be nice if I could talk to Shelby and find out what was going on. Maybe she was here under duress too? I shook my head... that didn't seem likely, but I'd still like to know.

Since Ramos had asked me if I was in trouble, he must have noticed the bad vibes between me and Dom. Did that mean he'd be willing to help me? With Ramos and Shelby on my side, Creed and I might have a chance to survive this mess... unless Manetto wouldn't let them help. But if he and Sonny were enemies, it could happen.

It probably all came down to who won the ten-million-dollar jackpot. So... maybe it wouldn't be so bad if Creed lost?

I turned my focus back to Creed's table, watching with interest as his game progressed. One more player left, leaving three altogether. Luckily, Creed still had more chips than the others, so that was good, but it went back and forth a few times, leaving me a little worried.

Finally, another player lost. Now it was between Creed and the last man at the table. Without a name, I'd been thinking of him as "Shaggy Hair." The guy was heavy set, and looked like he was made out of stone. His hair was the only incongruent thing about him, but it tended to hang over his eyes, and I figured that was the point.

Without seeing his brows twitch, or much of an expression in his eyes, he was hard to read. I checked the stats and found out his name was Harry. I tried not to snicker, but, with the hair in his eyes, it certainly fit.

The tension in the room rose, and anxiety filled my stomach. Could Creed pull it off? Harry won the first two games, making a sizeable dent in Creed's pile of chips. As my stomach began to churn, the tide turned in the next game, giving Creed the lead.

After the flop, the betting took a turn. Harry toyed with his chips and stared at Creed. His lips twitched a couple of times, and he went all in. My breath caught. Creed hadn't taken his eyes off Harry, and I knew he'd seen the twitch. Did that mean Harry was bluffing?

Creed waited for nearly a minute, keeping his focus on Harry. Without taking his gaze away, he pushed all of his chips into the pot. This was it... the moment of truth. The dealer played the river, throwing out a ten, adding to the ace, nine, four and eight.

Pursing his lips, Harry flipped over his cards, revealing an ace and a king, giving him a pair of aces. My heart raced. Had Creed just lost? Creed turned his cards over, showing a jack and a queen. My breath caught. Was that a straight? Had he just won? I jumped from my chair with a whoop. Hot damn! He'd won! The ten gave him a straight.

After the dealer proclaimed him the winner, Creed pushed away from the table, offering his hand to Harry, who shook it once with a curt nod. Creed came straight to my side and pulled me into his arms. "Did you see that?"

"Yes. I can hardly believe it."

As Sonny announced the final match between Creed and Shelby, Creed pulled away, shaking hands with some of the other players who congratulated him.

"We'll take a twenty minute break," Sonny continued. "And the final round will begin at midnight."

People streamed out of the room, and Sonny stepped to Creed's side, clasping his shoulder. "Well played. That was a nail-biter, but you pulled it off." He shook his head. "I don't know how you did it, but it worked. Go take a break. This last match will be the hardest of all, and I want you ready."

After a curt nod to Sonny, we followed Dom to the elevator and straight to the penthouse floor.

"I need coffee," Creed said, before heading into the bathroom. I got the pot going, and Creed returned, grabbing a mug.

I quickly stepped into the bedroom, before Dom could stop me, and changed my heels for ballet flats. After visiting the bathroom and freshening up, I sat beside Creed and Dom at the table. They both glanced my way, and I knew they'd been talking about me.

"So, what do you know about Shelby?" Creed asked. "Anything that will help me beat her?"

I let out a breath and shook my head. "She's got something going for her. I guess she calls it premonitions, but that seems like such a careless explanation for what she does. It's like she has a sixth sense about things. At least, that's how she explained it to me when we met at the hospital."

I shrugged. "I don't know any more than that. But I think if you try to keep your mind clear, that should help."

"What do you mean?"

"I don't know... she's really good at reading people... so try to keep your emotions quiet. Maybe she's like a clairvoyant and can pick up feelings? That might explain some of it."

"Okay... I'm not sure what that means, but I'll do my best."

"You need to win," Dom said. "You might say Sonny and Manetto have some history between them, and it's not good. There's a lot at stake for Sonny, and it would go a long way for you if you won. In fact, I think it would just about guarantee that you and Ella could leave with your lives. Since you're his last player left, it's up to you."

"Last player?" I asked. "You mean he had others besides Creed playing in the tournament?"

"Of course. None of them were as good, but he had to hedge his bets." He turned to Creed. "And if you're thinking of throwing the game to spite Sonny, just remember that Ella's continued good health is at stake."

"I'm aware." With a flat stare at Dom, Creed finished up his coffee. Glancing between them, I knew that the friendship they'd once shared had turned them into bitter enemies. Creed set down his mug and stood, taking my hand. With a twist of his lips, Dom strode to the elevator and pulled out his key card.

Creed tensed, dropping my hand and ready to make a move. I grabbed his arm, knowing that a fight with Dom was the last thing we needed. Even if Creed got the key card from him, there was no way we could leave the hotel without being spotted.

Creed let out a breath and took my hand. Dom stepped inside the elevator, missing the whole thing. We followed him inside and rode to the main floor in silence. The doors slid open, and we followed Dom out, with Grant falling into step behind us.

I angled my head toward Creed and whispered. "Just do your best, and we'll figure this out."

He closed his eyes and nodded. We entered the poker room with ten minutes to spare. Once again, the room had changed, with one poker table in the middle of the hall and chairs spread out on either side of the table. The room was crowded with people, all of them interested to see which of the two finalists would win the jackpot.

In addition to the setup, a video camera was positioned above the table, transmitting the game to the big screen on the wall so everyone could see the action.

The back table had even more refreshments on it, including a shrimp bowl, cheese, and caviar. There were also mini cakes and cookies in parchment cups, as well as fruit tarts with whipped cream. It all looked amazing, but, with my nervous stomach, I couldn't imagine eating any of it.

The crowd parted slightly as Shelby and Ramos entered the room. She looked refreshed, and she'd changed into a different dress. It was a striking, royal blue color and fit her well, showing off her slight form and drawing everyone's attention.

"Shelby!"

Shelby turned to gape at the man who'd called her name, and I recognized him as the guy who'd accused her of cheating. How did he get back in here? His big smile held remorse and a touch of shame.

"My dear lady," he began. "I'm so sorry for my terrible behavior. I made a complete ass of myself. It was totally uncalled for, and I apologize. Will you please forgive me?"

Shelby didn't return his smile. In fact, her brows drew together, and she took a couple of steps back. The man's expression changed into an angry sneer, and he lunged at her. She easily pivoted out of his way, and someone yelled that he had a knife.

Ramos jumped into the fray, putting himself between Shelby and her attacker. The man jabbed at Ramos, who blocked the assault. In a flash of movement, Ramos grabbed the man's wrist and pivoted inside his reach so the blade pointed outward.

With a sharp twist to the man's wrist, the knife fell to the floor. Keeping a strong hold on his wrist, Ramos maneuvered the man down onto the floor, face first. With his knee on the guy's back, Ramos twisted the man's arm behind him. The attacker screamed out in pain, but Ramos didn't let up until a security guard slapped handcuffs on his wrists.

With the drama over, the guards escorted the wobbling man out of the room. Shelby stood beside Ramos, her face full of worry. Taking a better look, I realized blood seeped from Ramos's arm. I started toward them, but Dom pulled me back.

"Where do you think you're going?"

I shook his hand off my arm. "He's injured. I'm a nurse. I can help."

"No. The staff here at the hotel will help."

I ignored Dom and stepped away. He reached for me again, but this time, Creed pushed his arm down. "Let her go."

"Ella," Shelby called. She beckoned to me, and I hurried over.

Blood dripped from the knife wound on Ramos's forearm, and Shelby's face had gone completely white. I wasn't sure who to help first. "Shelby, sit down before you faint."

Her uncle stood nearby, and I summoned him to Shelby's side. "Make her sit down with her head between her legs. I'll take care of Ramos."

I turned my attention back to Ramos, and he raised a brow, surprised that I'd taken charge so quickly. I pursed my lips and called a staff member over. "I need a towel or a cloth napkin." She pulled a cloth from her waist and handed it over. "Is there a first-aid kit around here somewhere?" I slapped the cloth over Ramos's dripping arm and pulled it tight to stop the bleeding.

"Yeah. There's a first aid kit in the supply closet," she said. "I'll get it."

"Okay. We'll head to the women's restroom. Bring it to me there."

She nodded, and Ramos followed me to the restroom in the lobby, just outside the poker room. "Hang on, and let me make sure it's empty."

Inside, a woman dried her hands with a towel. I checked the stalls and found them empty. She left, and I motioned Ramos inside, pulling him to the sink. I took off the cloth and held his arm under the running water. He winced, but didn't make a sound.

"It looks like you might need some stitches. Do you want to go to the hospital?"

"No. Just bandage it up so I can get back to the tournament."

"Okay." I pulled some paper towels from the dispenser and blotted the cut to see it better. The wound was deep and nearly three inches long. The server came inside with the first aid kit. "Thank you. Will you stand outside and keep the ladies away until we're done?" She agreed and left.

"Hold your arm over the sink while I get the things I need." Unzipping the kit, I found everything I needed except a needle and thread to sew him up. "I'm going to spread on some antibiotic gel before I apply the bandage."

He nodded, and I got to work. Drawing on my healing powers, I gently rubbed a dab of gel over the deep cut, sending heat into the wound. Finished, I pinched the skin back together, holding it tightly, and applied a little more gel, continuing to use my gift.

Concentrating, I traced my forefinger along the cut, pushing healing light into the wound. The bleeding stopped, and the skin held together like I'd glued it shut. I tried not to gape, but I'd never done that before. Afraid that Ramos could see what I'd done, I quickly placed another piece of gauze over the wound.

"Can you hold that while I get the tape?"

"Sure." He placed his hand over the bandage, holding his arm closer to his chest.

I ripped the plastic packaging off the tape and caught Ramos peeking under the gauze pad. "Don't do that. It needs to stay air tight to keep it from getting infected."

His eyes narrowed and his brow lifted. "It actually looks pretty good, almost like you glued it together. That must be some kind of miracle gel you've got there."

Flustered, I jerked my gaze away from his and found the edge of the tape, deciding to ignore his comment. "This is that stretchy tape. It sticks to itself, so it won't pull your arm hair out."

I carefully wrapped the tape over the gauze and around his muscled forearm. Finished, I cut the tape with the small pair of scissors in the kit and smoothed it out. "There. That should take care of it for now."

Ramos tugged the sleeve of his black dress shirt down over the bandage, only leaving the cuff rolled up. "Guess I won't need any stitches after all."

Was he testing me? "Uh... I think you're right... it wasn't as bad as I thought. Leave the bandage on until you need to shower. Then you can take a look at it and decide if it needs more attention. I put a lot of antibiotic gel on it, so it shouldn't get infected."

I busily put the first aid kit back together so I wouldn't have to look at him. He just stood there studying me like I was crazy, and I finally glanced up. "Okay... we can go now."

As I moved past him, he reached out to stop me. "Ella... wait." He dropped his hand from my arm. "Thanks. It doesn't even hurt. Shelby told me you had a nice touch. Now I know what she meant."

"Uh... good. I'm glad I could help."

"So tell me what's going on. Maybe I can help you."

I shook my head. "I don't think so. Creed's playing for Sonny, and if he doesn't win, Sonny's not going to be too happy with us."

"Has he threatened you?" I nodded. Ramos's lips thinned. "I figured as much."

I opened my mouth to explain, but the door flew open, and Dom stepped inside. "Are you done in here?"

I jumped a little and clutched the first aid kit to my chest. "Yes. I just finished up. Has the game started?"

"No. We're waiting for the two of you. It seems that Shelby and Creed won't play until both of you are out there."

"Oh... then I guess we'd better get going." I skirted past Dom and out the door. Ramos managed to follow behind me, leaving Dom in our wake. Had Ramos done that on purpose to protect me? My heart softened toward the handsome devil. Yes, he was totally dangerous, but I'd take him over Dom any day.

As we stepped inside the tournament room, Shelby hurried toward us. "How is he?"

"Good. It wasn't as bad as it looked."

"Thank you Ella," she said. "I'm so glad you were here."

"Yeah... me too. That guy who attacked you was so scary. But... you saw right through him and got out of the way. I would have been taken totally by surprise, especially with his apology. I never thought he'd try to hurt you."

"I know... it was definitely a surprise. Listen..." She stepped close to whisper. "Whatever the outcome, I'm here to help you."

Her blue eyes held earnest sincerity, and hope rose in my chest. "Thank you."

She nodded and quickly strode away. "Hold your horses. I'm coming."

I glanced up to find Sonny with his mouth open and his hands on his hips, like he was ready to call the game. He shook his head and announced the final round, declaring the game underway.

Creed had already taken his seat, but he caught my gaze. I nodded, sending him an encouraging smile, and hurried toward the chairs. There were a couple of empty seats on the front row, and I took one of them, with Dom following behind me to sit in the other.

I glanced at Creed, sorry I hadn't been able to tell him that Shelby and Ramos were on our side. But maybe it didn't matter. He still needed to play to win, but at least I wasn't quite as worried that we'd both die if he didn't.

The first couple of rounds were nothing to get excited about. It was like both Shelby and Creed were getting a feel for the other's style of play. The next game wasn't much different, with Shelby folding after the flop. It surprised me that she folded so quickly, almost like she knew she couldn't win.

The next two games, she played more aggressively, not just calling Creed's bet, but raising him. It became apparent that, when she raised the bet, he needed to fold, because she always had the winning hand.

I could see how someone would think she was cheating. It was like she knew what Creed's cards were. But that didn't make sense, even for someone with premonitions. Her stack of chips grew, and Dom began to fidget in his chair.

After the current game ended, Dom left, heading Sonny's way. They spoke for a few moments, and Sonny nodded his head, agreeing with whatever Dom had suggested. Sonny beckoned a game monitor to his side and, a few minutes later, he called for a ten minute break in the play, surprising everyone in the room.

The game monitor stepped to the poker table and asked Creed and Shelby to stand. She began to inspect the table, looking on the floor beneath it and on the underside where someone could tape a card or two. Declaring it clean, she announced that they could resume their play.

While Creed and Shelby took their seats, I glanced at Ramos and Manetto. I expected to find them angry and offended, but they hardly seemed bothered, almost like they'd expected it. Maybe they did. If Shelby played poker using her premonitions, it probably happened a lot, and she was one hell of a poker player.

Her stack grew, and Creed began to sweat. He couldn't seem to catch a break. The next game looked close, with both of them betting and raising all the way to the river. So far, the dealer's cards consisted of a ten, seven, queen, and four. It didn't look like much to me, and I couldn't understand why they were betting so high.

The dealer turned the card, showing a jack, and Creed let out a breath. He turned over his cards, showing a pair of jacks.

Shelby shook her head, clearly surprised. Her cards showed a queen and a ten, giving her two pair. The jack was the only card that would have given Creed the win, and he got it. As the dealer moved the chips his way, he actually smiled. Now he had the advantage.

It didn't last long. Shelby won the next three games, chipping away at Creed's lead. It didn't look like she was taking any chances, and the round moved quickly in her favor. It frustrated me, because every time Creed bet higher, like he had a good hand, she folded before we even got to see his cards.

With Shelby's pile of overflowing chips, it came down to the final game. I didn't see how Creed could win, unless he went all in and beat her. On the river, he did just that. I hoped that Shelby would fold, to give him a chance to get back into the game, but she called instead. Creed turned over his cards, revealing two pair, kings over tens. Shelby beat him with a straight, and the tournament was over.

Creed didn't seem surprised, and he congratulated her with a sincere smile while they shook hands. As she stood, the spectators applauded. Sonny was frozen in place, his face a mask of disappointment. As several people in the crowd congratulated Shelby, Sonny finally stepped to the podium.

One of the staff members brought out a beautiful crystal trophy, featuring three stacks of crystal poker chips in differing colors. The crystal chips balanced on each other with their edges touching like they were falling from the sky.

It was beautiful, which surprised me since this was a poker trophy.

"The winner of this year's Mojavi Casino Poker Tournament goes to Shelby Nichols." Sonny motioned to Shelby, and she joined him at the podium. He handed her the trophy, and they posed for a couple of pictures.

Another staff member brought out a big, cardboard money order prop, with "ten-million-dollars" written on it. It bore Shelby's name, and Sonny presented it to her. As they stood together, a photographer had them pose and took several photographs.

I had no idea the tournament was such a big marketing tool for the casino, but it probably brought in a lot of people eager to watch someone win that much money. Of course, only the high-rollers could afford to play, or pay someone to play for them, since the buy-in had to be at least fifty grand. But that was just a guess. I honestly had no idea.

Sonny showed no outward anger that he'd lost, but he didn't seem too happy either. With the ceremony over, he encouraged people to stay and enjoy the night in the casino. Finished, he whispered something to Shelby before Manetto and Ramos joined them. While Manetto and Sonny spoke together, someone took my arm in a firm grip.

"Time to go," Dom said, pulling me away.

I glanced over my shoulder to look for Creed, but I'd lost track of him in the crowd. "Wait. Where's Creed?"

"Sonny needs to talk to him."

I planted my feet and struggled against his grip. "But—"

"He'll join us in the penthouse suite, as long as you come willingly."

His threat sent a shiver down my spine, and I quit fighting against his hold. As we neared the exit, I couldn't find Shelby or Ramos in the crowd. How were they going to help me now?

We entered an elevator filled with several people. With all the stops, it took longer than usual to reach the top floor, and the mounting tension filled me with dread. The doors opened into the suite, and I stepped inside, with Dom following closely behind.

"Get your things. You're leaving tonight."

"Where?"

"We don't need you anymore, so we're taking you back to your place."

That sounded like a lie to me, but what did I know? "What about Creed?"

He shrugged. "That depends on Sonny, but I wouldn't get my hopes up if I were you."

"You and I both know that Creed couldn't have won that game. I don't know how she does it, but Shelby's unbeatable."

"Yeah, I got that. But it doesn't matter anymore. Now get your stuff."

I hurried into the bedroom and changed into my tee and jeans, stuffing the rest of my things into my bags. Would Dom really take me home? Or was this just an easy way to get rid of me? Finding Creed's duffel bag, I decided to pack his stuff too, just in case I could convince them to let him leave with me.

I also wanted to see if he had a weapon tucked away in his bag. Even a pocketknife would be better than nothing. Voices sounded from the other room, and relief coursed through me. Was Creed here? I pulled the door open a crack to find him arguing with Dom.

"... she doesn't know anything. I never told her any of it, so she's not a problem you have to take care of. Just let her go."

"But Sonny was pretty adamant—"

"Yeah, but that was before he knew she had ties to Manetto. Don't you think they'd get involved if anything happened to her? Sonny doesn't need that right now."

Dom glanced past Creed and noticed me listening at the door. Creed turned, stiffening to see me. He turned back to Dom. "So we have a deal?"

"I'll see what I can do. Get packed. I'll be back."

Creed didn't move until the elevator doors closed. He slumped with relief and turned my way. His gaze met mine, and he pursed his lips, coming toward me with troubled eyes. "I think I bought you some time. I just hope it's enough to get you out of this."

I stepped back to pull the door open, and he came into the bedroom. Seeing his bag on the bed, he continued to pack up his things.

"What were you talking to Dom about?"

He hesitated slightly, then continued packing. "Dom was worried that you'd go to the police, so I tried to convince him that you didn't know anything about Sonny's organization... which you don't. I told him I'd stay, and Sonny could do whatever he wanted with me, as long as he let you go."

Creed dropped his shirt into the duffel bag and caught my gaze. "There's more I didn't tell you, and it's about the tournament. It's the other reason I took off. Sonny's whole reason for the tournament was to scam Manetto. He's Shelby's uncle, the older guy with the white hair." At my nod, he continued, "I was supposed to win, no matter what it took to do it."

"You mean... like cheat?"

"Yes. But from what I knew about Manetto and his organization, I stood a better chance of living if I took off. Manetto has a reputation, and I thought Sonny was crazy to try and scam him. But when Dom caught up to me, I didn't have a choice."

I nodded, and he continued. "It's worse. You know that guy with the knife? He's one of Sonny's men. He was supposed to hurt Shelby."

"What?"

"Yeah. I think Sonny was desperate enough to put him up to it. In the rules Sonny created, it states that if anyone is unable to play due to being late, or sick, or injured, they forfeit their spot in the tournament.

"That knife play was a last resort. I think they may have tried some other things, but I don't know for sure." He glanced at his feet.

"I know Sonny gave me every advantage he could to help me beat her, but it wasn't enough. I got the impression that Shelby had some idea that Sonny was coercing me to play. You know?"

"Yeah… you're right. Shelby and her bodyguard, Ramos, both asked me if I was in trouble."

Creed sucked in a breath. "What did you say?"

"I told them I was, and she said she'd help me… us."

His eyes widened with surprise, and he sat down on the bed. "I wonder how she planned to do that?"

"Who knows?" I shrugged, sitting beside him. "It's probably too late for that now. So what happens next?"

"I don't know. I think Dom would have a hard time killing you. I'm not sure he'd go through with it, so he might try to talk Sonny into letting you go."

My brows rose. "I'm not so sure, but I did get him to talk about Avery. I think he cared for her, so he's not totally heartless."

"What did he say?"

"That he thought you were wrong, and he didn't have much hope that Avery would recover. He thinks you're just prolonging the inevitable and you should have pulled the plug on her life support." Creed winced, and I continued. "You made it sound like she could get better, while Dom thinks she'll never recover. He said she has significant brain damage."

Creed's brows rose. Then he nodded. "Good. I wasn't sure we'd fooled him."

"What?"

He met my gaze. "Look... I'm not supposed to tell you this." He glanced toward the elevator door and lowered his voice even more. "She's not out of the woods, but she's talking and making progress. We're hoping she'll recover enough to testify against Sonny. The detective working on the case thought it was best to keep Dom in the dark so they wouldn't try anything."

My brows creased. "So why did you come back here? And what about the money you stole?"

He huffed out a breath. "I still needed that money to help Avery. The extent of her injuries is pretty bad, and her life from here on out is not going to be easy. She might never walk again. Besides that, I needed to know if Sonny was still planning to kill her. The money was just... I don't know... an opportunity to get back at him. I figured, once he was arrested, no one would care where that money went."

He shook his head. "I don't know when... or if... that's ever going to happen, so it was a stupid thing to do." He met my gaze. "Just promise me you won't tell them about Avery... okay?"

"Of course not."

He shoved a hand through his hair and stood, pacing the room. "Listen... if I don't make it out of this... would you maybe... go see her?"

My eyes widened. "Don't say that."

He stepped toward me, taking my hands in his. "Once they let you go, it would make it easier for me to stay if I knew you would... just... see if you can help her. I don't expect you to heal her... but... I just thought it wouldn't hurt to ask..."

"Creed... of course, I'll see her, but I can't guarantee anything. I can't promise that I can help her, or even do anything to make her life better. I just don't know. I'm sorry."

"No... don't be. It's a lot to ask. And whether you see her or not, it doesn't matter so much, as long as you can get away. If I have to stay, that's fine. I've made my bed and all that... but you... you're special... I mean... you're amazing.

"What you can do is... nothing short of miraculous. You need to get away from all this so you can help people. I think that, if I were the cause of your death, I'm pretty sure I'd go straight to hell, and I mean that in a very literal way. So I have to protect you... I have to get you out of here, no matter what it takes."

"Don't talk like that. Maybe Sonny will let both of us leave. Besides, I still want you to come to New York with me."

"You do?" A surprised smile played on his lips. "I'd like that." Our gazes met, and he pulled me up. "Can you forgive me for dragging you into all this?"

I nodded. "Yes. I mean... I'm the one who ran you over, right? Maybe we were supposed to meet." His brows rose, then he smiled, and something inside me melted a little.

"I don't believe in fate, but I'm glad we met." He pulled me into his arms, holding me like I was fragile and precious. His lips found mine, and his kiss held tenderness, along with a touch of sweet regret.

The elevator doors opened, and we pulled apart. I studied Creed's handsome face, wanting to memorize everything about him, and hoping that this wasn't our last moment together. His eyes full of remorse, Creed pulled away and stepped into the other room to face Dom.

My heart heavy, I followed behind him.

Dom stood inside the room. From his grim expression, it didn't look like either one of us would make it out alive.

CHAPTER TEN

"We're leaving," Dom said.

"Both of us?" Creed asked.

At Dom's nod, Creed caught my hand, and my heart raced. Did this mean we were both going to live, or both going to die?

Dom's lips thinned. "Yes. Both of you. Get your bags and bring them, we won't be coming back here. I'll explain everything on the way."

Did that mean there was hope? Rushing back into the bedroom, I threw my purse over my shoulder and grabbed my luggage. I rolled it out ahead of Creed, and Dom opened the elevator doors. After we stepped inside, Dom pushed the button for the parking garage.

"I don't know why, but Manetto made a deal for you. Sonny accepted, so I'm taking you to make the exchange."

That was unexpected, but I wasn't about to complain. The doors opened, and we followed Dom to the black Escalade. After throwing our bags in the back, we got in the back seat.

Dom drove out of the garage and onto the Strip, heading north.

"Where is the exchange happening?" Creed asked.

"At a restaurant. Manetto insisted on a neutral spot. It's not far."

"Do you know anything about the deal?" I asked.

Dom let out a breath. "I don't. We'll find out when we get there. Since Manetto doesn't trust Sonny, he's insisting that you be there before he makes good on the deal."

I thought that was smart of him. The fact that he was willing to make a trade for us kind of surprised me. Shelby must have more influence on him than I thought, which was good for her if he was a mob-boss type. In fact... maybe he was a mob boss.

If that was the case, her whole involvement made a lot more sense. If he was her uncle, she probably helped him out a lot. But, hadn't she been helping the police in New York? So how did that work? If she helped both the police and a mob boss, I couldn't imagine how she did it. I'd only met Creed a few days ago and, from what I'd seen of this side of life, I wasn't sure I'd want to deal with it on a daily basis like she did.

Maybe her premonitions helped, but what a crazy life. Still, I had to admit that, even with everything going on, I knew she was a good person. Unlike most people I'd met lately. Of course, who was I to judge?

A niggling voice in the back of my mind reminded me that I'd done my fair share of bad things by letting the killer in New York die. And getting sent to the middle of nowhere to think about it had thrown me into a whole new world.

Now look at me, sitting in this car on the way to a meeting between two mob bosses who were making a deal about whether I lived or died. Yeah, this was a little nuts, and not at all how I expected things to go when I got sent away.

I glanced at Creed, noting the perfect symmetry of his handsome face. He felt my stare and met my gaze. With a reassuring nod, he picked up my hand and squeezed it. My heart lurched a little just from being so close to him.

Where did these feelings come from? Was it because I was so physically attracted to him? Or was there more to it? Did he feel the same way about me? Or was he just sorry he got me into this mess? Now he wanted me to help his sister. But what if I couldn't? Would that be the end of it?

I probably shouldn't even plan on him coming to New York with me. Whatever happened with his sister, he'd most likely want to stay with her.

Thoughts of heading to New York without him sent a pang through my heart. I couldn't imagine taking the journey without him. But... had he agreed because he was motivated by something else? He'd said he wanted to earn my trust, but was that because he wanted me to heal his sister?

Dom pulled the car into a restaurant parking lot, and nervous tension filled my stomach. He pulled all the way around to the back of the building. At two in the morning, there were still plenty of cars, although this area wasn't anywhere near the Strip and all the crowds.

We followed Dom to the entrance and passed through the main dining area into a private room in the back. Sonny and Grant sat on one side of the table, with Shelby, Ramos, and Manetto on the other.

Sonny stared daggers at me, probably because my friendship with Shelby was the cause of his surrender to Manetto. Shelby sent me a smile, looking relieved that I was there in one piece. What had Sonny planned to do anyway?

"There," Sonny said. "You can see they are unharmed, and they will be free to go once we are done here." He looked at Dom. "Did you bring their luggage?"

"Yes sir."

"Good." He turned to Manetto. "Are you satisfied? You will agree to our deal?"

Manetto took his time answering. He whispered something to Shelby, and she nodded. Turning back to Sonny, he gave his answer. "On one condition."

"What's that?"

"It seems that you took Ella from her home. I believe it's only fair that she has the ability to return, so she'll need one of your cars."

Sonny's nostrils flared before he sent Manetto a curt nod. "That can be arranged."

"Good. Then we're done here."

My curiosity grew. Manetto didn't seem the type to give Sonny back the ten-million-dollar jackpot, so what was the deal he and Sonny had made? Shelby could tell me, and I hoped I'd get the chance to ask her.

Now that it was over, Sonny and Grant stood to leave. On the way out, Sonny pulled Dom aside and whispered something to him. Dom nodded and watched them leave.

Manetto stood, planting his stern gaze on me, and I knew he'd done me a favor I'd probably never be able to repay. "Uh... thanks Mr. Manetto. I don't know what you just did, but I'm in your debt."

His face lit up with a smile. "You're welcome. Glad to help a friend of Shelby's."

His gaze landed on Creed, and the smile evaporated. "You're lucky you're with her, or you'd probably be dead."

Creed's brows rose at his bluntness. Before he could respond, Manetto continued. "But you're a hell of a poker player, even if you tried to cheat." At my gasp, he gave Shelby a nod. "Shelby seems to think you're worth saving, so I'll leave it at that."

Creed swallowed. "Thanks... uh... both of you."

Manetto held out a business card to Creed. "Here's my card. I'd like to keep in touch."

"Of course." Creed took the card, Manetto's meaning clear. He was now beholden to another mob boss, and I couldn't help shaking my head. When did it ever stop?

Shelby came around the table to my side, sending me a reassuring smile. Filled with gratitude, I gave her a quick hug. "Thanks for helping us out. I hope it didn't cost your uncle too much."

Shelby laughed. "No... Uncle Joey's still pulling the strings. Don't worry about him." Her admiration for Manetto was easy to pick up. Ramos joined us, sending me a quick nod.

"How's the arm?" I asked.

"Good. It doesn't even hurt anymore. Should I take off the bandage so you can take a look at it?"

"Uh... no, no, you don't need to do that. I mean... leaving the bandage on as long as possible really helps with the healing process, and it keeps all the bad bacteria out, so you should leave it for now. Maybe even until tomorrow. Okay?"

His brow rose in a challenge. Shelby smacked his arm. "Stop baiting her. I told you she has healing hands. I'm sure it's doing a lot better than if someone else had treated it."

"You've got that right." He said it sarcastically, like it was an understatement. Then his gaze focused behind me, and I turned to find Creed and Dom speaking in hushed tones.

"I wonder what they're saying."

Shelby cocked her head. "Probably something about letting you take the Escalade? Oh... and Creed wants to get your phones back."

How did she know that? "Huh... and you got that from your premonitions?"

Her eyes widened, but she quickly recovered. "Yeah... mostly."

I let it go. "Well... it would be nice to get my phone back. They took it last night, and John's probably frantic."

"Who's John?"

Oops. "Uh... he's my... uh... representative with the hospital board. They want me back in New York." At her raised brows, I continued. "They sent me away after that guy died. You remember him, right?"

She nodded. "Yeah... Tony Bilotti. I remember how upset you were."

"Right... anyway, it's a long story, but now they want me to come back. Creed had planned to go with me."

Ramos narrowed his eyes. "You sure you can you trust him?"

I swallowed. When he put it that way, it sounded like a stupid idea. Creed hadn't been totally honest with me, so why should I trust him now?

"I think you can," Shelby said to me. "At least he cares deeply about you... uh... seems to care, I mean."

My eyes widened, and my doubts cleared. "You think so? I wouldn't mind having some company, you know?"

"Sure. I totally get that." She glanced at Manetto and nodded. "Sorry, but we need to go now. Let's keep in touch." She pulled a card from her purse and handed it to me. "That's my number. Call me after you get to New York. Okay?"

"Yeah. I will. And... I don't know how to thank you—but if there's ever anything you need, please let me know."

"You bet... just be sure to call me so I'll have your number."

"I will." As they headed toward the exit, I joined Creed and Dom. "What's the plan?"

Dom frowned. "It looks like Sonny's letting you take the Escalade. You just need to drop me off at the hotel, and you're free to go."

"Really?" I glanced between them, and Creed nodded. A sudden lightness filled my chest. "Okay. Let's go." We followed Dom back to the car. He took the driver's seat, saying he'd drive us back.

I smiled at Creed, unable to hide my relief. I wanted to discuss our plans, but not with Dom listening. Nearly to the hotel, Dom's phone rang. He quickly answered.

"Yeah... I'm on my way... but... yes... I understand." Dom listened for several seconds before heaving a big sigh. "... okay... sure... no... no I can do it... Yes... I'll take care of it."

Disconnecting, he glanced over his shoulder at us. "Sonny wants you to take a different car, so I'm supposed to take you to his place."

Next to me, Creed stiffened. "His house?"

"Yeah. His garage is full of cars. I guess he's got a Subaru he wants you to take." Dom shrugged. "I think he likes his Escalade too much to give one away, but don't worry, the Subaru will work just fine. He takes good care of his cars, so it'll get you back to your place without a problem."

"We can keep it?" I asked.

"I guess so. At least, that was the deal."

Creed caught my gaze, his lips lifting in a smile. "We could take it to New York. It might be better than the Jeep, right?"

My worries eased, and I let out a breath. "Yeah. Probably a lot smoother ride."

Dom drove into a residential neighborhood lined with palm trees and streetlamps. Turning down a quiet lane, he pulled in front of a gated driveway. After he entered a code, the gates swung open, and he continued toward the large mansion sitting majestically at the top of a small hill.

The circular drive swung past the mansion to a six-car garage. Dom pulled in front of the garage doors and hit the opener attached to the sun visor. As the garage door opened, he turned off the Escalade.

"I want my phone back," I said. "You know where it is?"

"Oh... right." He opened the glove box, rummaging through it, and pulled out both of our phones. "Here."

I checked my phone for messages, but, after so long, it was dead. Shaking my head, I slipped it into my purse and followed Dom and Creed into the garage. The Subaru sat at the end of the line of cars, looking nothing like the high-end cars around it.

Dom turned to us. "Why don't you get your luggage, and I'll find the keys. They're supposed to be here somewhere."

With enthusiasm, we grabbed our stuff and took it into the garage to the Subaru. By then, Dom had found the keys, and he unlocked the back, helping Creed stack our luggage inside. As he shut the hatchback, I could hardly believe we'd done it. We'd actually made it out alive.

We moved to the front of the car, and Dom handed Creed the keys. Dom took a step back toward the Escalade and hesitated. With a shake of his head, he pulled a gun from under his jacket.

"Sorry guys. But Sonny changed his mind."

Creed and I both stepped back, bumping into the car. "What are you doing?" Creed said. "You can't kill us. What about the deal with Manetto?"

Dom shook his head. "I guess Sonny thinks your death is worth it. You took off with the money, Creed. For no good reason. Then you lost the tournament. Sonny doesn't like losing, especially to Manetto. Then to have Manetto threaten him unless he let you go... it was the last straw. He couldn't take it."

"Wait." Creed raised his hands. "You don't have to go through with this. Just let us go, and you'll never see us again."

"Sorry, but I can't. You know how this goes. If I don't do what Sonny says, he'll kill me. You were my responsibility, and you got away, so now I have to make it right. I don't want to die. Don't you see? I have no choice."

As he raised his gun, Creed raised his hands in a pleading gesture. "No... wait. Just think this through. At least... don't kill Ella. If you have to kill me, do it, but let Ella go. She hasn't done anything to Sonny.

"You can convince him that my death is enough, I'm sure of it. And letting Ella go will keep Manetto from coming after him. You can make him see that, right? He's smart enough to figure that out, and he'll thank you for doing it that way."

Dom hesitated. "You make a good point, but what's to stop her from going straight to the police?"

"You should be more worried about what Manetto will do to you. You kill her, and he'll come after you. Your life will be over. He's not someone you want to mess with. You've heard what he's like."

"Maybe... but Sonny's not much better." Dom raised the gun.

Panicked, I held my hands out. "Stop! Dom... no. You can't kill him."

He shook his head, glancing my way before focusing on Creed. "Look Ella... I'll let you live, but that's as much as I can do. One of you has to die for Sonny to be satisfied, so it's got to be Creed."

"No. Please. Please Dom... don't do it. Let us go... just tell Sonny you killed us, he doesn't need to know."

Dom clenched his jaw, clearly upset. "He'll know. He always does." Dom's eyes turned flat, and I knew he wouldn't listen to me. Creed was going to die.

"It's okay, Ella," Creed said, turning his head to look at me. "I don't mind, as long as you live." He glanced back at Dom. "Promise me that she'll get out of this alive." Dom didn't answer, so Creed raised his voice. "Promise me!"

Dom's lips thinned with disgust. "Damn you to hell. Now she'll love you forever." He raised the gun and fired.

In the split second before Dom pulled the trigger, I jumped in front of Creed. A strong force ripped into my chest, throwing me back into Creed's arms. Intense pain took my breath away, and my legs buckled beneath me.

"Ella! No!"

As I slid to the ground, Creed yelled my name, but I could barely hear him over the sharp pain that consumed me. I took a shallow breath, but it hurt so much that tears sprang from my eyes.

"Breathe Ella, breathe." Creed's eyes glistened. "Don't die on me. You can't die."

Dom knelt at my side, his face white, and his dark eyes haunted. "Why? Why did you do that?" He pulled my shirt away, revealing the bloody wound above my left breast. "Shit." Still holding the gun, he raised it to shoot Creed.

"No," I wheezed.

Dom met my gaze, giving Creed enough time to knock the gun away. Stepping over me, Creed swung his fist, hitting Dom in the jaw. Filled with raw anger, Creed pounded Dom with his fists, hitting him again and again. Under the barrage, Dom sank to his knees. With one vicious kick to his head, Dom went down.

Panting, Creed rushed back to my side. "Ella. Hang on. I'll take you to the hospital. Just stay with me."

Creed bent down and slipped an arm under my neck. I focused on his grief-stricken face and managed to lift my hand to his cheek. Taking a shallow breath, I spoke. "I don't think I'm going to make it."

"Yes you will. You have to."

I closed my eyes, struggling to speak. "It's okay. I'm not afraid." My vision swam with dark spots, and my ears pounded with the beating of my heart, getting slower and slower. Someone spoke, and I could just make out Creed's voice.

"Please don't die, Ella. Hang on... Ella!" His breath caught, and he made a choking noise.

I tried to keep my eyes open but, even so, darkness filled my vision. Through a small pinprick of light, I felt Creed kneeling over me and heard his pleading voice. "God... please... don't let her die. She needs to live, God. Please. I know you need her. Let her live."

Creed's voice sounded ragged and broken. At that moment, I wanted to live more than anything. Not for me, but for Creed. I fought against the darkness, struggling to pull in one last breath, but my strength gave out, and the darkness closed over me.

All at once, the horrible pain left my chest. As I surrendered to death, a flash of peace washed over me. Somehow, it felt familiar, like it had happened to me before. It seemed ages and ages ago. The thought faded, and light enveloped me, filling me with incredible warmth.

The warmth expanded, starting in my chest and rolling through my body on a wave, extending all the way from my head to the tips of my toes. Time stopped, and I reveled in this peaceful existence, letting the wave of heat overtake me.

I couldn't say how long the moment lasted, but all at once my lungs expanded, and I sucked in a deep breath of sweet air. Awareness flickered into my mind, and I felt the cold, concrete floor under my body. Creed held me tight against his chest, but the sound of my indrawn breath caused him to pull back.

"Ella?"

It took everything in me to take another breath. Then my heart began to pound, quickly at first, until it settled into a slow, regular beat. I managed to open my eyes. Creed's tormented gaze widened with astonishment. He froze for a second before jerking into action.

With shaking hands, he pulled off his shirt and held it to my still-bleeding wound. Surprising me with his strength, he picked me up and carried me to the passenger side of the car. Bracing me against the car, he managed to open the door and set me on the seat inside, lowering it back as far as it would go.

Creed hurried around to the driver's side and started the car. He pulled out, racing down the driveway, only to stop at the gate. Even though the gate opened automatically, it opened so slowly that Creed cursed under his breath. Once we were clear, he stepped on the gas and pulled out onto the street.

"I'm taking you to the hospital. Just hang on, okay?"

I nodded, unable to speak.

The neighborhood streets were dark and quiet at this time of night. I closed my eyes, concentrating on my breathing and a new chill that seemed to penetrate deep into my bones. In a desperate move to push away the cold, I searched for the energy of healing power deep inside of me.

Finding nothing, panic began to set in. I looked deeper, concentrating with my remaining energy to find it. Was it gone? Not willing to accept that, I explored in more depth, finally coming to rest on a few tangled threads of light. There, amid the threads, a small seed of power rested.

Filled with determination, I cradled that seed, covering it with all the warmth I could muster. In the cold, it threatened to slip my boundaries, but I held it tight, sealing it in so it could survive.

"Ella? We're here. You still with me? Hang on."

Creed's words sent warmth into my heart. Other voices joined his, and I felt several experienced hands move me from the car onto a gurney. I managed to open my eyes to see their faces, with Creed at my side. Passing through the emergency doors, I closed my eyes against the bright lights.

We didn't slow, and I heard someone speak. "Sir... you need to wait out here." The noises and sounds of the emergency room penetrated my awareness. A needle was inserted for an IV, and a blood pressure cuff was strapped around my arm.

I knew everything they were doing, but in my impaired state, I couldn't respond. Instead, I returned my attention back to that tiny seed of light. An oxygen mask covered my nose and mouth, and I breathed in the pure air, funneling the energy deep into the seed.

To my relief, it began to grow, expanding until it pushed away the cold. With a deep sense of well-being, my awareness expanded. The beeps of the machines turned into a regular rhythm, and those working on me paused.

"Holy mother of God... Look. The bullet's right there. Hand me those forceps. Quick."

The clang of a bullet hitting a pan rang through the room, along with an audible exhale from nearly everyone there. "Okay. Let's patch up the wound."

"Wait... is she even asleep?"

I heard all of this, but I couldn't open my eyes to save my life. I wanted to tell them to forget about putting me out, since I was out of the woods, but someone must have realized I was still semi-conscious. The next thing I knew, darkness engulfed me.

"Ella?" I opened my eyes to find a nurse looking down at me. "There you are. How are you feeling? Any pain?"

I took a deep breath, only feeling a twinge from my chest. I tried to speak, but only managed a croak. Clearing my throat, I tried again. "Not too bad."

"Any dizziness? Nausea?"

"No."

"Good. Would you like some water?"

"Yes."

"Let's raise the bed up first." She pushed the button on the side of the bed, raising me so I was in a sitting position. She handed me a cup of water with a straw, and I quickly drank it down.

"Thank you. How long have I been out?"

"Oh... about forty-five minutes. Your husband has been asking about you. Shall I send him in?"

Oh... she meant Creed, and my eyes filled with moisture. "Yes, please." She patted my arm and left. I took in the room and realized I was still in the ER. My chest was covered with a big bandage, and I remembered that they had pulled the bullet out before everything went dark.

Wanting to take a peek at the wound, I pulled the tape away and found a small line of skin glued together and resting under a clear piece of special adhesive tape. My head fell back, and I let out a breath, relieved that my skin hadn't magically closed up.

Having the bullet practically pop out of the wound was bad enough, but the skin coming together would have caused them all to panic.

The curtain parted, and Creed came inside. He wore a blue, scrub top someone had given him, and his worried eyes filled with relief to see me.

"Creed." I opened my arms, and he rushed into them. He held me for a long time, careful not to squeeze me too hard. Feeling him so close brought tears to my eyes, and I swallowed several times to hold them back.

He pulled away, his own eyes filled with moisture. "How are you feeling?"

"Better." I patted the side of the bed, and he perched beside me.

"I thought I'd lost you." He blinked a few times and swallowed. "I thought you died back there. Was I wrong?"

"Uh... No... I think maybe I did... but... that was..." I swallowed, unable to continue. I closed my eyes, overcome by everything that had happened, and Creed wrapped me in his arms again. After a few deep breaths, he pulled away.

"I'm so sorry this happened."

I shook my head. "It wasn't your fault." He glanced away, and I knew he didn't believe me. "Creed. Look at me." He pursed his lips and met my gaze. "I'm okay now. We got away, and we're both okay. Let's concentrate on that."

He nodded. "I had to tell them that you got shot as we were leaving the restaurant. I said some guys tried to jump us in the parking lot, and I brought you straight here."

"Okay."

He licked his lips and glanced at the bandage on my chest. "Does it hurt?"

"No. I was afraid it was all healed up, but they glued the skin together and it's under some special tape. I wonder what the doctor thought of all this."

"I spoke with him. He was... a little spooked... I think. He said the bullet must have passed through something before it hit you, because it didn't go in very far."

"Did he say anything about when I can leave?"

"Yeah. They just wanted to make sure you were recovered from the anesthesia, and then they'll release you."

The tension drained away, and I nodded. "That's good news. Did you—"

The curtain moved aside, and the doctor came in. He wore blue scrubs and carried a clipboard. Smiling, he introduced himself. "How are you feeling? Still groggy?"

"Uh... not really. I'm tired, but I hardly have any pain."

"Good. You were lucky. We think the bullet must have passed through something before it hit you, because it barely penetrated your skin. I still can't get over it. At first we thought you were dying, and then..." He shrugged, unable to explain it. "Do you remember anything?"

"No... not really. I think I must have passed out. Maybe it was the shock?"

He nodded. "That's probably what happened. I'm just glad it wasn't as serious as it seemed."

"Yeah. Me too."

"Okay. Let's get you checked out." He explained how to take care of my wound, telling me that I'd need to leave the clear tape on and not let it get wet. "Also, no driving, or making any big decisions for at least twenty-four hours."

"Got it." I thanked him again, and he told me the nurse would be back to take out my IV and finish checking me out.

It took another hour before the nurse checked us out. In the meantime, a police detective took Creed's statement, since I didn't remember anything, and told us he'd be in touch.

By then, a bone-weary exhaustion had crept over me, and I was fighting to keep my eyes open. Since they'd cut away my bloody shirt, they gave me a scrub top to wear home. The nurse pushed me out in a wheelchair, and it was a relief to finally get out of there.

Creed helped me into the car, and I leaned my head back against the cushion, totally drained. Even though I'd mostly healed, I'd expended a lot of energy, and I could hardly wait to lie down and close my eyes.

Creed got in the car and glanced my way. "I'll find us a motel to crash in."

I nodded and he started the car, driving away from the hospital and back onto the southern end of the Strip. Before long, Creed pulled into a motel that didn't look too bad, and hurried inside to register. Finished, he drove the car around to the back of the building and came to my door to help me inside.

I liked leaning against him, and, even more, I liked that he was taking such good care of me. After unlocking the motel door, he directed me to the bed. I wanted to crash, but he wouldn't let me lie down until my shoes were off and the bed was turned down.

As I crawled beneath the sheets, I let go of my worries and welcomed the darkness of sleep.

CHAPTER ELEVEN

S unshine hit me in the face, and I rubbed my eyes. Pulling them open, I glanced around the room, taking in the cheap prints of the Las Vegas Strip hanging on the walls. Something warm pressed against my back, and I turned my head to find Creed sleeping beside me.

I still wore the scrub top the hospital had given me, so I pulled it away to look at my wound. The skin looked pink and new, so I tugged the tape off and rubbed my finger over my skin. It was smooth and even, with only a hint of a scar.

I may have used my own power there at the end, but I knew something else entirely had brought me back to life. What was it? Why had I survived? And what did it mean?

All kinds of possibilities flowed through my mind, but how could any of them be real? I wasn't an alien or a supernatural being. I was just a normal human being with a different kind of gift. Besides, I'd heard of a few others who had a healing touch as well, so that part wasn't totally unusual.

Of course, something had changed in the last few days. I hadn't just helped Wyatt or Creed, I'd actually healed them. But I knew I hadn't pushed the bullet out of my heart. Was it the light that had filled me? Where had it come from? The process had still worn me out, but it wasn't the same as when I healed others. So what was going on?

Creed stirred beside me, and I turned to snuggle against him, my head resting on his chest. He pulled me close, his cheek resting on the top of my head. "How are you doing?" His scratchy voice rumbled in his chest, tickling my cheek.

"I'm okay… amazingly okay."

He drew a deep breath. "During the night, I kept re-living what happened. Just thinking about the moment you got shot still makes me sick to my stomach. When you stepped in front of me…" He swallowed. "I think my heart stopped. Why did you do it?"

I thought it over and realized I'd acted instinctually. "I… I guess because I didn't want you to die."

He sighed, rubbing his hand across my back. "Did you have any idea what would happen to you?"

"No. Not a clue."

His throat moved, like he had a hard time swallowing. "But I'm not worth it."

Appalled, I rose onto my elbow to gaze down at his handsome face. "Of course you are."

"No." He shook his head. "I keep seeing it in my mind. The moment you took that bullet for me… it hurt my heart. Seeing you get shot like that. It was… horrible… the worst thing I could ever imagine. You died." He held my gaze, his clear blue eyes searching mine. "You quit breathing, and your heart stopped. I'm sure of it."

Nodding, I sank back down beside him. "I know."

Now he rose up to his elbow to look down at me. "And now… look at you." Noticing my missing tape, he pushed away the material to inspect my wound. "It's healed." He heaved out a breath. "Did you heal yourself? Is that how you survived?"

As crazy as it seemed, I couldn't take credit for something I didn't do. "No. It was something else, a power beyond my own. I felt my heart slow, and then it stopped. The pain left, and it felt... peaceful... like I was somewhere else. Then a flash of bright light surrounded me. It filled me from my head to my toes.

"That's when I started breathing again. But it wasn't over. The pain came back, so I concentrated on my healing energy." I shook my head. "I couldn't find it at first, and it scared me. I was so cold, but I latched onto the warmth inside of me, and it began to spread."

I sighed. "When I got into the emergency room, the doctors checked my wound and saw the bullet just inside my skin and pulled it out. They seemed shocked. I was still conscious, so they gave me something to knock me out."

"So... where did this power come from? Was it God?"

"I don't know... " Something about the light seemed familiar, but I couldn't place it. Until I knew more, how could I explain it to Creed?

But why would God bring me back? It made no sense. People didn't come back from the dead like that, at least not unless they were blessed by a priest or something. That's what I'd been taught all my life, so why had it happened to me? "Maybe John will know."

Creed nodded. "Well, whatever the reason, I'm so grateful it happened." His eyes held tenderness and yearning. Leaning close, he captured my lips with a gentle kiss, melting my heart. A second later, he pulled away, his brows drawn together in concern. "Am I allowed to kiss you?"

My eyes widened. "What do you mean?"

"Well... I don't know. You're not like anyone I've ever known... and you came back from the dead. Does that mean you're like... an angel or something?"

My brows rose. "No... of course not." I shook my head, but the worry in his gaze demanded a better answer. "To be honest, I don't know what it means. We can only hope that John has the answers."

"What if he doesn't?"

I shrugged. "Then we'll just have to trust that the answers will come. I mean... there has to be a reason, right?"

"I don't know. That's your thing isn't it?"

"Don't you think things happen for a reason?"

He opened his mouth and shut it, thinking it through. "I'm not sure. I mean... I'd like to think that we're all part of something bigger, but then stuff happens... like Avery. Was she supposed to get hit by a car and nearly die? Is someone you love supposed to get cancer and die? That just doesn't sit well with me."

"Yeah. I know what you mean. But isn't that just part of life? I guess it's—" Creed's phone began to ring, and my stomach tightened with worry.

"I'd better get that." He scrambled off the bed and picked up his phone from the small table in the corner where he'd left it to charge. He glanced my way before answering, his expression wary.

"Dom. What do you want?" Creed pursed his lips and shook his head. "Why? So you can feel better about shooting her?" After another long pause, he spoke again. "Look... I'm done talking to you. I don't care what Sonny does. Tell him we're both dead if you want, just... don't call me again."

Creed ended the call and glanced my way. "Dom wanted to know if you pulled through." He came back to the bed and sat down. "I didn't tell him one way or the other, but I probably shouldn't have answered the phone in the first place."

"Do you think he's still planning to kill you?"

He scrubbed his face with his hands. "I don't know, but I'm pretty sure he's running scared. Sonny wanted me dead. Since that didn't happen, I can't imagine Dom will go back to tell Sonny he messed up. He might try to bargain with Sonny from a distance, but he'd be better off disappearing for a while."

"I guess that goes for us too."

"Yeah, but there might be a problem with the Subaru. If Dom actually tells Sonny I'm still alive, I wouldn't put it past Sonny to tell the police it was stolen."

My breath caught. "Dang. That doesn't give us many options. Do you think we could make it back to my place before that happens and switch with the Jeep?"

He considered it. "I don't know. If Dom thought we'd do that, he could be waiting there to finish the job. The only option I can think of is to steal a different car."

I shook my head. "But that's no different than driving the Subaru." I slowly sat up, grateful my head didn't spin.

Standing, it surprised me that I felt as good as I did. In fact, I felt better than ever. What did that mean? "Let's get cleaned up and go. Once we're on the road, I'll give Shelby a call and tell her what happened. I think her uncle can make sure Sonny behaves."

"That's a great idea." Creed closed the distance between us. "Just to be clear, we're headed to New York, right?"

"Yes." Uncertain what he meant, I looked up at him. "Unless you don't want to go with me."

"Of course I do." He paused, his mouth opening and closing like he wanted to say something.

"What?"

He took a deep breath. "I just had this thought that maybe we could visit my sister first. L.A.'s not that far from here, but... it's in the wrong direction, so I understand if you don't want to go."

"Creed I... I don't know what's going on with me. I need to figure this out, and John's the only way." I caught the disappointment he tried to hide, and remorse flooded over me.

He glanced out the window and nodded. "Yeah... you're right. I shouldn't have brought it up, especially after last night."

I sighed. "I need to shower. Let me think about it."

"Sure. Your bags are over there by the door. Which one do you want?"

"I just need the smaller one."

He picked it up and set it on the bed. After grabbing my toiletries, I found some clean clothes and headed into the bathroom. Shutting the door, I leaned against it and let out a big sigh. Was it wrong of me to want to head home? I wasn't sure I could help Avery, but that shouldn't stop me from trying.

I turned on the shower, to warm up the water, and took off my clothes. Catching sight of my reflection, I stopped to stare. My face seemed paler than normal, but it was the tint of purple in my blue eyes that shocked me. Normally, it was hardly noticeable, but now it stood out. What did that mean?

Shaking my head, I stepped into the shower, letting the hot water wash away the tension. I needed answers, and heading to L.A. wouldn't get me any closer to them. Still, it would give me the chance to see Avery and find out if I had any healing powers left.

After that, I could take a plane to New York. I'd probably get there faster that way than driving across the country, and I wouldn't disappoint Creed. Would he still want to come with me? Maybe not. As much as that saddened me, I had to remember that it was probably for the best. This was my problem, not his. He'd just have to promise me to keep it a secret, but I had no doubt that he would.

I finished up and quickly toweled dry. After getting dressed, I combed through my hair and took my stuff back into the room. "It's all yours."

Creed was watching the news on TV, but, with my appearance, he jumped up and hurried into the bathroom with his clean clothes. I sat at the desk with the mirror above it and applied some face cream and a touch of makeup, then scrunched my wet hair before putting all my things back in my bag.

Before long, Creed came out of the bathroom, his hair still wet and carrying the leg brace. He wore a pair of jeans but no shirt, and my heart raced at the sight of him.

"I probably don't need this anymore, do I?"

"No." I shook my head, a little distracted by his bare chest.

"Good." He pulled a t-shirt out of his duffel bag and slipped it over his head. Shoving the brace inside, he zipped the bag shut and glanced my way. I'd been standing there like a statue, and his lips twisted into a knowing smile. "You ready to go?"

My face turned red. "Uh... yeah. I just need to put these things away." I stuffed my dirty clothes into my bag, along with my toiletries, and zipped it up. I found my purse and slipped it over my head.

"Don't forget your phone. I charged it up for you." He pointed toward the small table in the corner.

"Oh... thanks." I grabbed the phone and charger, taking a second to look at my messages and finding several missed calls and texts from John. "I need to call John. He's probably worried about me."

"Sure. You can call him while we drive."

Creed stepped toward the door, but I caught his arm. "Wait." He turned toward me, his eyes wary. "I was thinking that we could see Avery first, since we're this close."

"Really?"

"Yeah. Then um... I could take a plane to New York. It would probably get me there faster anyway, right?"

"Uh... yeah." His face clouded. "So, you don't want me to come with you?"

"I don't know. What if I can't help her? Would that change your mind?"

Creed dropped his duffel bag and faced me. "Of course not. I want to be with you."

Relieved, I nodded. "You're sure?"

His lips tilted up and he shrugged. "Yes. Besides, I want to see this through. I want to know what's going on. Maybe not as much as you do, but I bet I'm pretty darn close."

I twisted my lips. "So that's the only reason?" He opened his mouth to speak, but I cut him off. "Be careful what you say to me."

He shut his mouth and narrowed his eyes. "I don't think you're ready for the truth."

"And what truth is that?"

He shrugged. "Just... that I'm madly in love with you." He held his breath, waiting for my response. That alone gave me pause, knowing that this was more serious than the teasing remark he'd made it out to be.

"Hmm... maybe there's hope for you after all. But only time will tell."

He huffed out a breath and picked up his duffel bag. "And here I am, laying my heart at your feet, and that's the best you can do? Pathetic." He pulled both my bags out the door, and I followed behind, my heart thumping in my chest. His feigned outrage gave me more hope than I dared to admit. I swallowed and tried to calm down, but his off-hand remark shook me. Did he mean it?

As we loaded the car, I calmed down enough to think again. A little voice in the back of my mind yelled at me to tell him I loved him back, but the practical side said there was plenty of time to figure this out, and I needed to be patient. That side won out, and I concentrated on what I needed to do next.

Creed drove around to the motel office and stepped inside to check out. While he was gone, I pulled out my phone and put my call through to John. He picked up right away.

"Ella... why haven't you called me? I've been so worried. Are you okay?"

"Yes, I'm fine. Something came up and I couldn't use my phone." I sighed, not sure what to tell him. "Listen, I'm headed to L.A. with Creed. His sister is... uh... she was in an accident, and I told him I'd see if there was anything I could do for her."

He sputtered a reply. "But—"

"I know you don't approve, but I need to do this. As soon as I'm done, I'll catch a flight to New York. Something else has happened... and I'm hoping you'll know what's going on. There's so much I need to tell you."

A long sigh escaped him. "Okay... that sounds ominous. Can you give me a hint?"

I couldn't get the words out. It all seemed too strange. "I... I'll tell you when I get there."

"All right. Is Creed still coming with you?"

"I think so."

He hesitated. "So tell me... is he involved in all of this... whatever it is you can't tell me?"

"Yes." I glanced up to find Creed coming out of the office. "Look, I've got to go, but I'll let you know when my flight will arrive. And... Father... say an extra prayer for me."

"Gabriella... are you sure you're okay?"

"Yes... I'm good... it's just... I'm a little scared."

"About Creed?"

"No, no... it's this other thing."

"All right. I'll light a candle, too."

"Thanks. I'll call you soon." I disconnected, sorry I couldn't tell him more.

Creed got in, and we pulled out of the parking lot. He took the road out of town that headed toward L.A. My stomach chose that moment to growl, reminding me that I hadn't eaten for a long time.

Hearing it, Creed smiled. "Guess we'd better get some breakfast."

"Sounds good to me."

We pulled into a road-side diner and spent a short half hour ordering and eating our food. Surprising me, Creed pulled out some cash and left it on the table. "Where did that come from?"

He quirked a brow. "You didn't think I'd give it all to Dom, did you?"

I chuckled and shook my head. "Where did you hide it?"

"My duffel bag has a few special compartments inside. I always make sure they're full of the green stuff."

I should have known, but it still surprised me.

We got back in the car and headed out. I'd never been this far west before, but the land was pretty dry, and there wasn't much to see. "How long of a drive is it?"

"It's about four hours from here, so not too bad. Of course, it will probably take another forty-five minutes after that to get to Avery's care center."

I checked my phone for the time. "Then we should get there around three?"

"Yeah. I thought we could spend the night at my place. Then catch a flight to New York tomorrow. How does that sound?"

"That sounds really good." Should I tell him I loved him now? "I'm glad you're coming."

He grinned. "Yeah, me too." He reached over and took my hand, giving it a tight squeeze. "Did you call John?"

"Yeah. He was worried, but I told him we'd be flying out tomorrow."

"How'd he take it?"

I shrugged. "Good, I guess. I didn't tell him much, only that we'd talk when we got there."

"But what about me?"

"Well... he wasn't too happy about that, but he knows you're involved in all of this, so he'll get over it." Wanting to change the subject, I continued. "I guess I'd better give Shelby a call. We don't want Sonny to try anything before we get there."

I found Shelby's card and put the call through. She picked up right away. "Hi Shelby, this is Ella."

"Ella. How are you?" She greeted me enthusiastically, telling me that she was back home, and asked how I was doing.

"That's why I'm calling." I explained that Dom had tried to kill Creed, leaving out the part where he shot me instead, and told her Creed had wrestled the gun away and knocked him out.

"We left him there, and now we're on our way to L.A. Since Dom didn't do what Sonny wanted, we were worried that Sonny might try again. Maybe I'm just being paranoid, but I thought if your uncle knew what had happened, he might talk to Sonny and straighten him out."

"Holy hell. Sonny is a stupid idiot. Uncle Joey's not going to be happy to hear that. You did the right thing to call me. I'll let Uncle Joey know. I'm sure he'll want to have a word with Sonny."

"Thanks so much."

"Of course. I'll call him right now. Let me know if Sonny tries anything. If he knows what's good for him, he won't. I'll be in touch." We said our goodbyes and disconnected.

I glanced at Creed. "I think that should do the trick."

"We're lucky that you know her. Tell me how you met again?"

"Sure." I spent the next hour telling him all about my involvement with her murder case and the detective with whom she'd worked. After that, we spoke about my work at the hospital and all the training I'd gone through.

Next, I asked Creed about his career and the movies he'd been in, which were a lot more than he'd let on. The time flew by. Before I knew it, we had entered the outskirts of the city. Creed's phone rang, and his brows drew together. "Hey Mom, what's up?"

He listened for a few seconds before shaking his head. "You're not making any sense. Hang on a minute." He expertly changed lanes and pulled off the nearest exit, taking a right and following the road to a parking lot.

After stopping the car, he spoke into the phone. "Okay. What's going on... uh-huh... yeah... wait, is she okay?" He heaved out a sigh and closed his eyes. "Sure. Look... I'm not far. I can be there in about half an hour... yes, really. Don't panic. Is the doctor there? Yeah? Then I want to talk to him. Yeah, half an hour. Okay, bye."

He set down the phone and shook his head. "That was my mom. She said Avery's had some sort of episode or something... I couldn't understand what she was talking about, so I don't know what she meant."

"That's not good."

"Yeah... she told me I needed to drop everything and come to the center. It was almost like she thought Avery was in real trouble." He ran his hand through his hair. "I think it surprised her that I was so close. It's a good thing we are, because, if it's serious, maybe you can help her."

"Sure. I'd like to try."

"Thanks, Ella." Worry tightened his brow. Entering traffic, he managed to turn around and get back on the freeway. We drove in silence the rest of the way, Creed's shoulders tense and his jaw set. I reached over and squeezed his arm. "She'll be okay."

The tension left his shoulders, and he relaxed a bit. "Thank you."

We pulled into the parking lot of a one-story building with "Franklin Memorial Care Center" emblazoned above the entrance. It was just after four in the afternoon, and we both hurried inside.

Creed took my hand, holding it tightly. He told the lady at the desk who he was, and she buzzed the door open to the rooms. We followed a long hallway to the end and turned left. Avery's room was the last one at the end of the hall.

I braced myself, not sure what we would find. Creed hesitated at the door, doing the same. After a glance my way, he dropped my hand and opened the door, stepping inside. I hesitated in the open doorway, wanting to give Creed a moment to greet his mother and sister without intruding.

His sister lay in the bed, which had been raised to a sitting position. She caught sight of Creed, and her mouth worked, but no sound came out. A stunning older woman, with porcelain features framed by long, dark hair, sat in the chair beside her. She looked up, but, instead of joy, her face tightened with fear.

Creed stepped closer, but stopped at the end of the bed, his gaze caught by someone who stood just out of my sight.

"Creed. I didn't expect you to get here so fast."

Dread ran down my spine, and my heart raced. It was Dom.

"What are you doing here?" Creed positioned himself between Dom and his family.

"Relax. I'm just paying a friendly visit to your sister. Your mom was kind enough to let me in." With his back to me, he stepped into my view and gestured toward Avery. "She's doing so much better than you told me. I wish I would have known. I would have come to visit her sooner."

Dom had no idea I stood behind him. I considered rushing inside and whacking him over the head, but I didn't have anything to hit him with.

Creed held his ground. "What do you want? Did Sonny send you to finish the job?"

"I think he'll be glad to know Avery is doing so well, unless you'd like to come with me for a little chat? I'm sure I can be persuaded to forget I know she's awake and talking."

"Dom... leave... Creed... alone." Avery's breathy voice caught everyone's attention. "I...I promise... not to testify... but you... you can't... hurt him."

"Baby... I'm afraid you don't understand. It's me or him. I can leave you out of it, and you can testify against Sonny all you want, but, for now, I don't have a choice."

He turned to Creed. "You've already lost Ella. Don't do the same with Avery."

I'd heard enough. "Lost who?" I strode inside, tired of Dom's threats.

Dom's eyes bulged, and he gasped. Stepping back, he sputtered. "What the hell? How are you still alive?" His gaze focused on my chest, looking for a bandage or something to indicate I'd been shot.

"Things have changed, Dom." I put all the force into my voice that I could. "I think you need to call Sonny before you do anything you might regret."

"Why... what's going on?"

I shook my head. "Forgetting my connections already?"

His face paled. "Manetto?"

"That's right. He knows what you did. How long do you think you've got before he sends someone after you? I think he'll go for Sonny first, so that gives you a little time."

Desperate, Dom quit the act and stepped my way, his eyes dark and angry. "It's not my fault you stepped in front of Creed. I was going to let you go." He looked down at my chest again, shaking his head. "Look... I'll leave. Just tell Manetto I'm not a problem anymore, and you'll never see me again."

"Why should I do that?"

Faster than I could imagine, he grabbed me around the neck in a choke hold and pulled me against his chest. He pressed his forearm painfully into my neck, making it difficult to breathe. In his other hand, he held his gun pointed toward Creed.

"Maybe I can't hurt you, but I can hurt Creed and his family. Now take out your phone and make the call."

I choked and gasped, struggling against his hold. "You're... cho... choking... me."

Dom relaxed his hold, and I caught my breath. Keeping one hand on his arm, I felt for my purse with the other, rummaging inside for my phone. Before I could find it, I realized I could feel Dom's pulse and energy through my touch on his bare skin.

Could I stop him with my touch? I'd never considered using my power this way, but what choice did I have? Concentrating on his energy, I found the spark of light coursing through his body. Without thought for the consequences, I tugged at the light.

Normally, I pushed light into someone who needed my healing energy. This time, I began to pull it out, slowly at first, then with a yank. Dom's hold on me loosened, and the gun fell out of his hand.

As Creed kicked the gun away, Dom collapsed to the ground, his face mottled red and his mouth open and gasping. He clutched his throat as he struggled to breathe, and his eyes bulged with fear and horror.

Shocked at what I'd done, I knelt beside him. Touching his face, I sent a pulse of light back into him. He gasped in a breath and turned onto his side, heaving in deep gulps of air and coughing loudly.

"Ella? What happened?"

Creed stood beside me, but I couldn't spare him a glance. Part of me was appalled, but another part of me had relished it. "Uh... I don't know... he just collapsed." I reached for Dom, but he backed away.

"Don't touch me." His clipped words held fear and shock. Recovered enough to stand, he lurched to his feet and backed away, his arm outstretched to fend me off. Reaching the door, he grabbed the handle and pulled it open. Still facing me, he backed out into the hallway.

Creed glanced my way, confusion in his eyes, then he rushed to the door and out into the hall. I couldn't seem to move, still shocked at what had happened. Creed came back a few seconds later, shaking his head. "He's gone. I got to the hallway in time to see the main doors shut behind him."

I swallowed. "Uh... that was..." I shrugged, not quite sure what to say. I met Creed's searching gaze and shook my head. "I'm not sure what happened."

Creed pulled me into his arms. "I can't believe he tried to kill you again."

His touch brought me back and I sagged against him. As I held him tight, tears gathered in my eyes, and I fought to push them away. What had I done? Had I almost killed someone? No... I'm a healer. I don't hurt people. I would never do that.

"It's okay, Ella." Creed soothed, misunderstanding my tears. "He's gone. He can't hurt you again. I'll make sure of it."

Nodding against his chest, I took a deep breath and pulled myself together. I didn't kill anyone. In fact, Dom was a dirt bag. He got what he deserved. That little scare might do him some good. I pulled away. "I don't think he'll be back."

Creed nodded and turned toward his mother and Avery, his arm tightening around me. "Well... now that he's gone, let me introduce you all. Mom, Avery, this is Ella... Ella St. John. We sort of... ran into each other a few days ago, and I convinced her to come home with me. She's in the medical field, and I was hoping she might have some ideas that will help Avery."

Creed's mother stood and offered her hand. "I'm Lauren." She glanced between us, taking in Creed's possessive stance and how closely we stood together. Focused on Creed, she narrowed her eyes. "Are you sure that's the only reason she's here?" He opened his mouth, but nothing came out. Her lips twisted, looking so much like Creed that I nearly gasped. "That's what I thought."

Turning to me, she continued. "My dear, thanks for coming... I'm not sure what you can do for Avery, but I appreciate anything you have to offer."

She glanced at Creed, her face filling with regret. "Aiden... I'm sorry I let Dom in, but I didn't know... he said you'd told him he could visit her, so I thought it was all right. I should have known..."

"Mom... it's okay." Creed stepped to his mother's side and pulled her into a hug. "I'm sorry I've been gone so long. I shouldn't have gone back to Vegas. You were right."

She shook her head. "You're here now. That's all that matters."

I glanced Avery's way, finding her eyes bright with tears. I stepped to the side of her bed and took her hand. "It's nice to meet you Avery. Creed's told me a lot about you."

"I...hope...it's...not...all bad."

My brows rose. "Not all of it." I smiled, and she tried to smile back, but it took more effort than it should, and only part of her mouth moved.

Creed stepped to the other side of the bed and kissed her cheek. "Hey sis."

"S'nice to... see... you."

Creed swallowed and tried to talk, but could only manage to nod. Wanting to help him out, I glanced around the room and noticed both a wheelchair and a walker. "Have you used the walker much?"

"Not...yet. But I'm...trying."

"That's good." I glanced at Lauren. "Is she doing physical therapy every day?"

"Yes. They want her to get as much mobility back as she can. But she gets tired really fast."

Creed ran his fingers through his hair, and I caught the pain in his eyes to see Avery like this. He glanced my way, and his pain turned to hope. I took a deep breath, overwhelmed by his expectations. Her injuries were extensive, and they had happened a few months ago. I wasn't sure I could help her.

"Mom, let's give Ella a moment alone with Avery." Creed urged Lauren out the door. "I could use some coffee."

"Oh... all right." She sent me a wary gaze before smiling at Avery. "We'll be back."

After the door closed, Avery spoke. "This... is hard... on... the... them."

I nodded. "Yes. I'm sure it is. Do you mind if I examine you?"

"No. Go... a... head."

I began with her legs, testing her reflexes and muscle-strength. I didn't need to do this, but it was necessary if I didn't want her to know when I used my gift. It encouraged me that she could talk at all. It meant there was a greater chance that she could heal and regain control of her motor-skills. Still... it was a long road to recovery, and it might never be complete.

Finishing that part of my exam, I moved to her shoulders and neck. I hadn't used any of my energy to this point, knowing the damage was mostly to her head. As I massaged her muscles between her head and shoulders, I called the light from inside me and pushed it into my fingers.

At first, nothing happened, but I persisted, moving my hands to the sides of her head. I immediately felt the damage inside and directed a pulse of power into the area. I met resistance, almost like a barrier that deflected my energy. It was most likely scar tissue, and I wasn't sure I could get through.

Not wanting to push too hard, I eased the power into a small trickle, navigating through the tissue until I found a spot thin enough to penetrate. Keeping full control of my power, I sent it in small waves through the barrier and into the damaged area.

I kept the flow going as long as I could, feeling the minutes slip by. Soon, the strain became too much, and my strength flagged. A part of me realized that, if I kept this up, I would drain my power to the point of no return. Pulling back, I left my hands on her head, probing with my gift to see if anything had changed.

The damaged part of her brain began to pulse here and there, in little bursts of activity, almost like tiny lightning strikes. It wasn't healed, but it was beginning to come back. How much... I couldn't say. Only time would tell.

I pulled my hands away and quickly sat in the cushioned armchair Lauren had vacated. My ears buzzed, and I had to put my head between my legs. After a few minutes, I sat up and looked at Avery. Her lips were parted, and she blinked several times.

Turning her head my way, her brows drew together. "I feel strange... like I've been asleep for a long time and I just woke up."

My breath caught. She hadn't slurred her words. Swallowing, I nodded. "That happens sometimes after a... treatment. You might feel more energetic for a bit, but you need to take it slow and give your body time to adjust."

"Okay." She moved her head back and forth, then raised her hand to scratch her chin and gasped. "Did you see that? I touched my face." Tears gathered in her eyes, and her gaze caught mine. "And I'm talking. I'm actually talking. What did you do?"

Smiling, I patted her hand. "Can I ask a favor?"

"Anything."

"Don't tell your doctors about my visit, okay? Let's just keep this between the two of us."

She took a deep breath. "But... how is this possible?"

"I believe it's a God-given gift."

"Does Creed know that you can do this?"

I smiled. "Yes... so... this needs to stay between the three of us. You mustn't tell anyone else, not even your mom. Can you do that for me?"

"Of course."

"And... whatever you do, take it slow... your body needs time to relearn everything."

She swallowed, her tears flowing freely now. "I will. Thank you. I don't know what you did, but... thank you."

"I just helped you out a bit. The rest is up to you." I pulled a tissue from the box beside her and patted the wetness from her cheeks. "There. You should get some sleep. That's the best way to let your brain heal."

She nodded, and her eyes fluttered closed. Relaxing, she fell into a restful sleep.

Exhausted, I wanted to sleep as well. That had taken a lot out of me... just like all the other times. What did that mean? Would I wither up and die after using my energy this way? Was it taking years off my own life?

I watched her for a long moment, grateful I could help, but staggered by the implications. At least helping her had balanced out the moment I'd hurt Dom. What I'd done to him still shocked me, and I could hardly believe my power could harm someone. Unease crept through my stomach, but I pushed it away, too tired to think about what it meant.

Totally drained, I let out a breath and closed my eyes. Pulling my feet onto the cushion, I laid my head on top of the armrest and gave in to sleep.

CHAPTER TWELVE

"Ella?"

A touch on my shoulder woke me. I sat up, blinking the sleep out of my eyes. "You're back."

Creed knelt beside me, concern on his face. He glanced at the bed, then back at me. "Hey. Avery's sound asleep. Is she okay?"

"Yeah." I looked behind him. "Where's your mom?"

"She was worn out, so I convinced her to go home." He took in Avery's sleeping form. "Did it work? Were you able to help her?"

"Yes. I think she can recover now, but it's going to take some time."

"Really? You think she'll get better?"

"I think so."

His eyes lit up, and he pulled me right out of the chair and into his arms. "Ella... I don't know how to thank you." He crushed me against him until I could hardly breathe.

"Squishing... you're squishing me."

"Oh... sorry." He relaxed his hold and lowered me back to my feet. "I'm just..." He swallowed, overcome. "Can I wake her up?"

I understood his eagerness to see the change with his own eyes, and I hoped he wouldn't be disappointed. Had I done enough? I wouldn't know until she woke up. "Yeah, sure."

Not hesitating, Creed nudged her shoulder. "Avery." Her eyes fluttered open. "How are you doing?"

She took in a deep breath and blinked, her eyes widening. "I feel like I've just woken up from a dark fog." She moved her arms, lifting her hands to her face. "Look at that. I can move my arms." Her face held wonder. "I need to see if my legs work."

Creed caught my gaze, his eyes wide and his mouth open. "Is that okay?"

"Her muscles are weak, but sure."

Grinning, Avery grabbed Creed's arm as an anchor and slowly pulled her legs to the edge of the bed. Not satisfied to stop there, she grabbed both his arms and stood. Her legs trembled with the effort, but her smile grew, and tears filled her eyes.

Stepping away from the bed, Creed held her tightly so she wouldn't fall. With his help, she walked to the closet before her strength gave way. Creed tried to pick her up, but she wouldn't hear of it. "No. Just give me a minute to catch my breath."

He waited patiently until she was ready, then he helped her walk back to the bed. She sat down on the edge and breathed heavily before struggling to get her legs back up on the bed. Creed tried to help her, but she stopped him. "No. I want to do it."

She worked hard to lift her legs, and managed to raise them off the floor, but the effort cost her. Creed helped her at the last minute, and she gratefully flopped back onto the pillow.

She grinned at Creed, and tears streamed down her face. "Man... I am so out of shape."

He nodded, unable to contain his own tears at her progress. She glanced my way. "I feel better than I have in a long time. If I were in shape, I think I could walk right out of here."

Just hearing how easily she spoke sent relief over me. "I have no doubt that you will, but please take your time. Your doctors and nurses will be shocked if you progress too quickly." I shook my head. "They'll be shocked anyway."

She nodded. "They'll think it's a miracle."

"I think it is." Creed caught my gaze. "Ella's like... an angel."

"No I'm not." They both looked at me like I was some kind of heavenly being, and I didn't like it. "It's not like that at all. I've been given a gift. I don't understand it, but I'm not anything like an angel." If they knew what I'd done to Dom, they'd believe me. But I couldn't talk about that right now.

Avery closed her eyes. "That wore me out. I think I need to close my eyes for a bit."

"Sure." Creed stepped beside her and pulled the blanket under her chin. "Get some rest. I'll come back and visit you tomorrow."

"I'd like that." She smiled up at him before glancing my way. "Ella." She swallowed. "Thank you." She held her hand out to me.

I stepped beside her, grasping her hand. She opened her mouth to say more, but I interrupted. "Get some sleep, and don't forget to take it easy, okay?"

"I won't tell anyone, I promise."

"Good." I stepped toward the door, watching Creed kiss her on the forehead. He joined me and we left the room, heading down the hall to the nurses' station. Creed stopped to tell them we were leaving, and we continued down the hallway.

At the double doors, we stepped outside, and Creed took my hand. As we walked toward the car, his concerned gaze met mine. "Are you okay? Your hand is freezing."

"Helping her took a lot out of me, especially after yesterday. But I'll be fine in a bit. I might need something to eat, though. And after that, I could use some good, uninterrupted sleep."

"I think I can help with that." Creed pulled me under his arm, and we walked side-by-side into the balmy evening air.

It was more humid here than in Sandy Creek, and I enjoyed the salt-scented breeze. "Are we close to the ocean?"

"Yes. You want to see it?"

"Sure do."

He smiled. "There's a nice little restaurant near the beach. I'll take you there. Maybe we can eat outside on the deck."

"That sounds heavenly."

Creed drove through the busy streets, glancing my way every once in a while like he was checking up on me. He didn't speak, so I closed my eyes, resting my head against the seat. A few minutes later, I felt the car slow, and I opened my eyes to see the ocean in the distance.

That woke me up, and I straightened to get a better view. Creed pulled the car off the road and into a parking lot beside a shabby restaurant. The wooden structure had been painted white, and the paint was weathered and worn.

He parked in a spot overlooking a small cliff above the ocean and got out. As I stepped onto the gravel, an ocean breeze wafted over my face, filling my senses with that salty ocean smell. I inhaled deeply, and the fog lifted from my brain. Turning my head, I smiled at Creed. "This is just what I needed."

"Good." He slipped his arm around me, and we strode into the restaurant together. The inside had a rustic feel, but was a lot nicer than I'd expected, with white tablecloths on the tables and large windows overlooking the bay.

We approached the front desk, and the hostess's eyes widened. "Creed! It's been ages. I heard you took a job in Vegas. Are you back now?"

"Oh... hey... yeah, for a few days at least."

Drinking in the sight of him, she bobbed her head. Her gaze turned to me, and her enthusiasm waned, but she glanced back at him and smiled. "Glad to hear it. I'll find you a table."

"We'd like to eat outside on the deck. Do you have a table there?"

She hesitated, but quickly recovered. "Of course. Follow me." She grabbed a couple of menus and took off. Creed dropped his arm from around my waist, and I followed her through the tables to a patio door.

A couple of steps took us out onto a large wooden deck, surrounded by a weathered, wooden fence. A canopy of brightly colored patio umbrellas kept the sun off the tables, and we followed her to an empty table beside the fence. The view was spectacular, with the patio on the edge of the short drop-off, giving us an unfettered view of the ocean.

Sitting down, I glanced at Creed. "Wow. This is amazing."

He smiled back, barely acknowledging the hostess's comments to enjoy our meal. "I thought you might like it."

"You must come here often."

His head tipped. "Uh... yeah. This is a favorite spot of some of my colleagues after a long day of working on the set."

"I can see why."

A waitress came over and filled our glasses with ice water. After telling us the specials, she left, and I drank most of my water before picking up the menu. "So, what's good here?"

Creed made a couple of suggestions, and I settled on the shrimp scampi. After we placed our orders, I sat back in my chair, letting the breeze blow away my fears. "I wasn't sure I could help Avery." I shook my head. "She had some serious brain damage."

"But... she'll get better, right?"

"Yes... with time, which is a good way to have it happen, since I wouldn't want anyone to know that I'd had a hand in it. I'd rather the doctors thought it was an act of God."

"Yeah." He looked toward the ocean before resting his gaze on me. "Maybe it was."

I nodded. "I'm beginning to think so, but why me? If I were an angel, it might make sense, but I'm far from that."

Creed took my hand and smiled, making my chest flutter, and I knew I couldn't tell him the rest of the story. What would he think of my touch if he knew I could hurt him just as easily as I'd healed him? Worse, Creed's eyes held a new reverence in them I hadn't seen before, and I wasn't sure I liked it.

Squeezing his hand, I smiled. "You know what I want?" At his raised brows, I continued. "I want to watch every single movie you've ever been in. I want to see what you look like on the big screen."

Sitting back in his chair, he chuckled. "Sure... but it's nothing compared to the real deal."

I nodded and smiled. "I'm sure you're right, but I want to see if you were telling me the truth."

"About what?"

"That you can't act."

He snickered and shook his head. "Uh... yeah... that's what I'm afraid of."

I smiled, happy that he wasn't looking at me so strangely. I wasn't anything special, not by a long shot. Our food came, distracting me from my worries, and we spent the rest of the meal talking about his acting jobs.

"What was the very first show you were in?"

As he regaled me with his experiences, my strength began to return, and I enjoyed this respite from bad guys, poker, and injured people. He told me several great stories, and we stayed longer than was necessary, both of us enjoying this beautiful spot and our time together.

The sun began to set, and Creed took me down a boarded walkway to the sandy beach. I stepped out of my sandals to feel the warm sand beneath my feet. It wasn't the same as my desert sand, but it still nourished something deep inside of me.

We walked along the edge of the waves, holding hands and watching the sun set. As the last of the sun's rays sank behind the horizon, we stopped. Creed stood behind me and wrapped his arms around my waist. I leaned back against him, letting the peace of the moment wash over me.

As the light disappeared, Creed turned to face me. Cupping my cheek with his warm palm, he bent down and kissed me. This kiss seemed different from the last one we'd shared. I still felt the passion, but it held a touch of awe in it as well, almost like he was afraid to overstep his bounds.

Creed pulled away and took my hand, stepping back the way we'd come. Neither of us spoke, enjoying the breeze and the sound of the ocean waves. Full dark had settled around us, and we carefully stepped back up the trail to the car. Creed opened the door for me, and I sat down, leaning my head against the back rest with a sigh.

Creed picked up on my weariness. "I know you're tired, but, lucky for you, my place isn't too far from here."

He was right. Five minutes later, we pulled down the driveway of a small bungalow, following it around to the back. He parked the car off to the side of a two-car garage with a staircase leading to an apartment above it.

Creed gestured to the apartment. "I live up there. It's small, but it works. My friend owns the property, and he rents it to me for a good price."

"Nice." A place so close to the beach couldn't be cheap, and I realized he had to be doing a lot better financially than he let on. Creed jumped out and began to unload our luggage, taking his duffel bag, along with my larger bag. I grabbed my small bag and followed him up the long staircase to the second floor.

After he unlocked the door, he flipped on the recessed lighting and hurried inside. I followed, surprised by the artful décor. It was a little stuffy, and Creed quickly opened a couple of windows. A kitchenette, with tall, white cabinets and dark granite countertops, sat along the nearest wall, with a laundry room on the other side of the entrance. A small bathroom, with a shower stall, backed the laundry room.

A black leather loveseat sat in front of a large, flat screen TV. A wall separated the space between the TV and the kitchenette. On the other side of the room, a closet and drawer combo separated the entertainment area from a queen-sized bed with a lamp on an end table.

Painted in gray, with white trim, the whole apartment reminded me of a set-up I'd seen at a furniture store for small spaces. Wherever it came from, it worked great. The vaulted ceiling even held skylights that would let in plenty of light during the day. "Wow. This is a nice set-up for such a small space."

"Yeah... I like it." Creed set his duffel bag next to the couch, along with my large luggage bag. "It's been a while since I was here last, so it might be a little dusty."

"I don't mind, but I think I might change into something a little more comfortable."

"Sure. Go for it."

I took my bag into the bedroom area, grateful the closet shielded me from view, and quickly shrugged off my shirt and shorts. I found my large nightshirt, and pulled on some boxer shorts to go with it, grateful to leave my shoes beside the bed.

Stepping back to the living area, I found Creed puttering around in the kitchen. He opened his refrigerator before checking his cupboards. Glancing my way, he frowned. "I'm sorry I don't have anything to offer you to drink. I must have finished the last of it off before I left. I could run to the store."

"That's okay. I'm fine." I rounded the furniture and sat down on the couch, finding a stash of DVDs. Most of them were alphabetized, and there weren't many that I recognized. After looking through them, I didn't think I'd seen them before, but I hadn't watched many movies lately, so maybe that was why. "Are you in all of these?"

Creed brought a couple of glasses of ice water to set on the coffee table, and knelt by my side. "Yeah... most of them." He shuffled through several movies until he came to the one he wanted. "I think this is the best one to start out with. At least you should get a kick out of it. It's called "Hell Spawn." Have you seen it?"

My brows rose. "Uh... nope."

He frowned. "Really? Well, you've been missing out."

"Right." I smiled. "Okay... let's go for it."

Creed grinned like he was pulling something over on me, and I hoped he wasn't in some awful love scene. I would absolutely hate that. As the movie began, he sat beside me and slipped his arm around my shoulders. Unable to resist, I snuggled against him, enjoying his fresh, clean scent. Feeling relaxed, I focused on the movie.

The opening scene began in a church, showing the back of a priest, kneeling in front of an altar, with his dark head bowed in prayer.

A loud, rattling bang echoed through the chamber, causing me to jerk in surprise. It did the same to the priest. He flinched before he stood straight and tall. As he turned to face the doors, I got my first look at his handsome face and gasped. "Oh my gosh! That's you."

On the screen, Creed's face held worry, then his countenance changed to fierce determination. The pounding increased, and he took a deep breath, like he knew the doors wouldn't hold for long. Reaching to his side, he pulled a sword from under his priestly robes. As he withdrew it from the scabbard, the sound of steel rang through the chamber.

The pounding stopped, and Creed stepped toward the church doors. He took up his position in front of the double doors and shifted into a fighter's stance. Barely audible, he began to chant words in Latin. I couldn't make them out, but the cadence sounded familiar.

The pounding started up again, and Creed's chanting grew louder to match it. All at once, the doors flew open. Several dark-clothed men, with unnaturally glowing, red eyes, rushed inside, carrying swords of their own. Creed began to move with athletic grace, bringing his sword down and around, cutting through those who attacked him.

He held them off for several long minutes, killing several, but there were too many, and they soon had him surrounded.

He fought with all his might, but it wasn't enough, and the attacks broke through his defenses. He grunted with each wound he took and struggled to stay on his feet. In the end, it was no use, and his sword clattered to the ground.

The battle suddenly stopped, and the attackers parted for their master. A tall man-like creature with horns and fiery red eyes stepped inside the church. He stood in front of Creed, and his rasping voice echoed through the chamber.

"You have vexed me long enough, priest. Now it's time to die."

The creature raised his sword of red-hot steel and plunged it into Creed's chest. Creed's body arched, and he cried out in pain before falling to the ground. As the light left his eyes, he muttered three words. "Si dis placet!"

The scene went dark, ending with the sound of demonic laughter.

I pulled away from Creed and turned to face him. "You were amazing, but I hated it. I don't like watching you die."

He pushed the pause button and grinned. "I did pretty good, huh?"

"Yes. Did you have to learn all those moves with the sword? You looked great killing all those demons."

"Thanks." He smiled. "Yeah, I've done a lot of training with martial arts. I spent most of my free time in the dojo growing up, so that's how I got the part in that movie. In fact... it's why I'm in a lot of the movies I've been in."

"That's cool. You looked pretty awesome in that priest's robes too, and I was impressed with all that Latin you were speaking."

"Yeah? Do you know what I said at the end?"

"Of course."

His brows drew together. "You know Latin?"

I huffed. "Uh... yes..." I pointed at my chest. "Raised by a priest."

"Oh... right."

He pursed his lips, and I narrowed my gaze. "Don't you know what you said?"

He scratched his chin. "Of course."

I knew he was totally bluffing, and now I also knew his tell for the next time we played poker. "Okay... good. I don't think a real priest would say that... but whatever." I was messing with him, but he deserved it if he hadn't bothered to find out.

He shook his head. "Okay... so maybe I forgot. There was all that Latin before the attack as well. I had no clue about that either. Why? What does it mean?"

I wanted to think of something good, but it took me too long, so I just went with the truth. "The Latin you used at the beginning came from the mass. Those few words you said at the end mean, God save us."

"Wait a minute. That makes total sense."

I grinned. "I know. Gotcha."

"You little devil." He pounced on me and began to tickle my ribs. I laughed and shrieked, squirming to get away. I lurched to my feet, but he grabbed me around the waist and pulled me back down, pinning me with his body. His lips found mine, and we kissed between heaving breaths.

Creed pulled away, his eyes full of desire. He nuzzled my neck, trailing kisses down past my collar bone toward my chest. His lips found the smooth skin where the bullet had hit me. He froze and pulled away, studying the pink color and the smooth texture. Sitting up slightly, he touched the new skin with his fingers.

"Does it hurt?"

"It's a little tender."

His gaze met mine. "It scares me to think that you should be dead... you would be dead... if not for some... miracle... or divine intervention. Are you sure you don't know why it happened?"

I nodded. "Yes, I'm sure. John knows something... at least that's what it sounded like, so I have to get home."

"We'd better book you on the first flight out tomorrow."

My breath caught, and I sat up, dislodging him. "Book me... what about you? I thought you wanted to come."

Creed let out a breath and sat still beside me, his eyes full of doubt. "I do, but... I don't want to be in the way. Don't get me wrong, I'm happy to come, and I will, if that's what you want. But this is beyond me. It's between you and your father... and... I guess... God."

He shrugged. "I'm nothing special, and I don't want to be the reason you don't get the answers you're looking for."

"What do you mean? You think you're not worthy or something?"

He huffed out a breath. "I know I'm not." His gaze caught mine. "I've done some things I'm not proud of, and I think if we had met any other way, you wouldn't have wanted to help me. I mean... I'm sure you would have helped me, but then you would have gone on with your life, and I'd just be a side-note in your memory."

I shook my head, suddenly exhausted. "But Creed... it didn't happen that way. We're here now... together. We've been through a lot. I don't even care if you believe in God, and I understand if you're not comfortable coming with me. But don't throw away what we have because you're afraid."

He stiffened. "I'm not afraid of what we have. I'm afraid of what you are."

Shock rippled over me. I had no idea he felt that way, and I winced inside.

He ran his fingers through his hair. "You died and came back to life. I guess I'm having a hard time dealing with that. I mean, I'm glad you did, but you did it for me. What if you weren't supposed to?"

My mouth dropped open, and I struggled for the right words. "I guess that's a good question, but I think you're wrong. I think we were supposed to meet. I don't understand the rest of it. I'm not even sure John will know what's going on. But... this is my path, and I have to see it through, and I'm going to do whatever it takes to get to the bottom of it."

Creed rubbed my arms. "I didn't mean it like that... I'm glad we met, whether we were supposed to or not. This part of the journey is about you, and I don't know how helpful I'd be." He shrugged. "Maybe it's because this whole mess is my fault, and I'm not sure how happy John will be to see me. That probably makes me a coward, but you're practically an angel."

"Creed... I'm not an angel. And I get it. It's just... I'm worried about what will happen after I leave. Will you forget all about me?"

His brows dipped and he shook his head. "How can you say that? Of course not. If you don't come back, you'd better believe I'll track you down. You're not getting away from me that easily."

"Oh yeah?"

"Yeah. Besides, you're the only one who will watch my movies with me."

I grinned. "You have a point."

"Damn straight. Speaking of which... you want to finish the show we started?"

"Uh... only if you come back from the dead."

He met my gaze, and we both laughed. "That's kind of ironic. Usually something like that only happens in movies... until you."

"I know. Pretty crazy, huh?"

"Yeah. Well—I guess that means we can continue the show then."

"Are you serious? You come back to life?"

He chuckled. "Yeah... but I return as a spirit to warn the main character."

I relaxed. "Oh... got it. Then I'd rather see a different movie... preferably one where you don't die."

His lips twisted. "Well... to be honest, I'm mostly in action shows, and I think I die in them all. It's about the only thing I'm really good at."

He was completely serious, so I hid my smile and nodded. "Well... you did a good job in the first one, so that makes sense. I still want to see you in another movie."

"There is one where I'm alive a little longer, but I'm not sure you'll want to see it."

"Why not?"

"There might be a woman and lots of kissing involved. But if you're okay with that—"

"No." I shook my head and held up my hands. "That's okay. Let's go for an action flick."

Grinning, he picked another movie and slipped it into the DVD player. We settled back to watch. After the title came on, I perked up.

"Hey. I've seen this one. I liked it."

"Yeah? I'm one of the guys in the biker gang that comes to kill the main character. Remember the fight at the bar? That's my scene. I get killed there, but I get to ride in on a motorcycle. That was a lot of fun."

"Cool." We started the movie and settled in on the couch. Soon, I was snuggled against Creed's side and enjoying the little tidbits he had to offer about the action behind the scenes. To me, that was almost more enjoyable than the movie.

When his scene came, I didn't recognize him at first. They made him up to look quite rough around the edges, but his muscled physique and toned abs certainly fit the bill. I could see where he might even move into a bigger role at some point. He certainly had the looks and the body. But I hoped it never happened.

Creed died again, but he was on the screen a lot longer this time. After that, the show wasn't as interesting to me. Toward the end of the movie, my eyes got heavy, and I couldn't keep them open. I drowsed a bit, until Creed pushed me into a sitting position, and I blinked my eyes open. "Is it over?"

"Yeah. Let's get you to bed."

With his strong arm around my waist, I let him lead me to his bed. I slid under the covers and closed my eyes. A few minutes later, Creed lay down beside me, his chest against my back. Sighing deeply, I fell into a contented sleep.

The sound of a door opening woke me, and I opened my eyes. Creed came inside with a couple of grocery bags. He set them on the counter and began to put the contents away. I stretched and stood, feeling almost back to normal. After coming back to life, and healing someone, I'd count that as a win. Maybe that meant using my healing powers wouldn't shorten my life.

"Hey there," I said. "Looks like you went to the store."

"Yeah. I thought I'd make us some breakfast."

"Sounds good." I grabbed some clothes and underwear and hurried into the bathroom for a quick shower. Fifteen minutes later, I exited the bathroom and found breakfast waiting for me on the kitchen island. Creed was already eating, so I hurried to sit down beside him.

"This looks amazing."

He grinned. "Thanks. I found a flight to New York this afternoon. Do you want to book it?"

"Yes. Let me get my phone." I brought it up on my app and entered all the pertinent information. Next, I called John to tell him when to expect me.

"So your friend isn't coming?" he asked.

"No. It's just me."

"Okay… I guess that makes things easier. Call me when your plane lands."

"I will. See you tonight."

Disconnecting, I smiled at Creed, trying to sound positive to hide my disappointment that he wouldn't be coming with me. "Okay. I'm all set. I need to be to the airport around one. Can you take me?"

He waved his fork. "Of course."

He finished up and glanced my way. "My agent called. I've got some offers for work coming up, so I told him I was available."

His declaration surprised me. "Oh… that's great."

He nodded. "Yeah. I guess it's back to real life now."

Real life? What did that mean? Life without me? "You know… I don't know what's going to happen, but… I'm sure there's plenty of work in the hospitals around here."

He let out a breath and turned to face me. "I like the sound of that."

Before I could respond, his phone rang. He glanced at the caller ID, and his brow creased. "It's Avery's care center." Pushing the button, he answered. "Hello? … Who? No … I don't want him to see her. He has? No. Let me talk to him."

Alarm washed over me. I met Creed's gaze before he spoke. "Dom… what are you doing there? No… Avery's… You've what?" He let out a breath. "Yes… I know…. good… but stay away from her. I mean it. It's over." Creed looked at me. "Yes… she's here… Dom…" His mouth twisted while he listened. "Good… I'm glad you know that… here she is."

He handed me the phone, and I took a breath before answering. "Yes?"

"Ella. I had to know, so I came back. It's true."

My heart skipped a beat. "What's true?"

"I know what you can do. You should be dead, and I've seen Avery. She's… better… not all the way… but the change is remarkable. They're saying she might even make a full recovery. I never would have believed it, if I hadn't seen her yesterday. It's because of you, isn't it? You did something."

I didn't answer, so he continued. "You did something to me too... but it wasn't as nice." I gasped, but kept my mouth shut. "I know you don't want to talk about it, especially not with me. I probably deserved it. Hell... I've been an ass. But, for what it's worth, thank you for helping Avery.

"There's one thing I need to tell you. Tell Creed that Sonny called me off. Manetto got to him, like you said he would. I'm going back to Sonny... but tell Creed that Avery's secret is safe with me. I won't tell Sonny about her... in fact... if Sonny gets any ideas that she's able to testify, I'll do what I can to stop him, and I'll let Creed know. That's a promise. Will you tell him?"

"Sure... but why don't you tell him yourself?"

"You and I both know that he won't listen to me."

I sighed. "That's true. Okay. I'll tell him."

"You're... a fascinating woman. I hope we can meet again sometime, as long as you don't try to touch me. Goodbye Ella." The line went dead, and I handed the phone back to Creed.

"What did he want?"

"A lot... but first... he knows... he knows that I helped Avery." It didn't scare me too much, since he also knew that I could kill him with a touch.

"Did he threaten you?"

I shook my head. "No... he thanked me for helping her... but... there's more." I explained what Dom had said about Sonny and keeping Avery's secret. "Can we trust him?"

Creed stood. "I don't know, but I need to see Avery. I need to make sure she's all right." He checked his watch. "There's just enough time to run over there before I have to take you to the airport."

I nodded. "Okay. I'll get my bags packed, and we can go." I spent the next few minutes getting my things together. Since I'd hardly used anything, it was easy to pack up. I took a few extra minutes in the bathroom to fix my hair and makeup before brushing my teeth. Finished, I packed up my toiletries and was ready to go.

As Creed pulled my luggage down the stairs, I glanced back at the apartment one last time before closing the door. Would I ever come back here? I sure hoped so, but a lot of it would depend on what John had to tell me.

We didn't speak much on the way to the center, both of us worried about Dom and his interference. After parking, I scanned the area for any sign of Dom, or a big, black Escalade. Creed had the same idea, and, after a moment of checking, he motioned toward the doors. "Guess we might as well go in."

Inside, we went through the process of signing in before heading through the double doors to the patients' rooms. Creed knocked lightly at Avery's door before opening it and stepping inside. She wasn't there, and his face tightened.

Hurrying back out, we found one of the nurses in the hall. "Do you know where my sister is? Avery?"

The man nodded, his eyes widening. "You mean the miracle girl? Yeah." He shook his head. "She's in the therapy room. I'll take you."

"Why did you call her that?" I asked.

"Because her condition changed overnight. She woke up this morning a different person." He motioned toward the therapy room. "See for yourself. She couldn't even walk more than a few steps yesterday. Now look at her."

We stepped inside the room and found Avery walking slowly between two wooden railings. She wore white sweat pants and a sweatshirt that swallowed her tiny figure. Using the rails for balance, her steps were sure and true, with only a small hesitation as she moved, like her muscles were weak more than impaired.

The therapist helping her exclaimed that her progress was amazing. "You keep this up and you'll be out of here in a week."

Avery grinned, her face lighting up. She turned around to walk back and caught sight of us. "Creed! Look at me. I'm walking."

Creed swallowed and strode to her side, his chest heaving and his eyes wet. He couldn't speak, so I stepped beside him and took his hand, smiling at Avery. "You're doing great."

She nodded. "Yeah... even better than last night. I can't walk on my own yet, but I'll get there."

The therapist shook his head. "I've never seen anything like it. She's doing so much better. It's like her brain just started firing on all cylinders... you know? It's a freakin' miracle."

"That's amazing." Creed glanced my way. "Whatever happened, I'm certainly grateful."

Avery came to the end of the rails and stopped, her chest heaving from the effort. "I think I'm done for now."

The therapist quickly brought the wheelchair over for her, and helped her sit down. "Yeah. You don't want to overdo it. But I think we should work on some other strengthening exercises a little later. Sound good?"

"Yes. I'd like that. Shall we say around one this afternoon?"

He chuckled. "Sure. I'll come get you."

"Great." She turned to Creed. "Want to wheel me back?"

He nodded and began to push her out of the room. She weakly waved to several people on the way back to her room, and all of them had huge smiles and wide eyes, each marveling at the change in her. I held her door open, and Creed pushed her inside.

"You need help getting in bed?" he asked.

She shook her head. "I've had enough of lying in bed. I think I'll stay right here."

He grinned before turning serious. "I got a phone call from Dom, so I wanted to check on you. Was he here?"

"Yeah." Her excitement dimmed. "He asked to see me, and I wanted to hear what he had to say. I probably shouldn't have let him in, but... I thought he cared about me once."

"What did he say?" Creed asked.

She shook her head. "At first he seemed shocked, then he asked about you, Ella. I don't know what he knows, but he asked me if you did something. I told him I didn't know what he was talking about, but I'm not sure he believed me."

She sighed. "I thought maybe he wanted to apologize for what happened to me, but all he could talk about was you. I told him thanks for stopping by, but he could leave, and I never wanted to see him again."

Creed stiffened. "Did he try to hurt you?"

"No." Avery straightened and caught Creed's gaze. "You don't think I'm in trouble do you? Is Sonny coming after me now?"

"I don't think so. Dom told Ella that he wouldn't tell Sonny about you, but I think I'll give the detective a call and see how the case is going. I'm also going to tell the front desk not to let anyone else in to see you who's not on the list. I'll be right back."

Creed left the room, taking his phone out of his pocket.

As the door closed, Avery glanced my way. "Did Dom really say that?"

"Yes. I think he's had a change of heart. If Sonny has any ideas about you, I think Dom will let us know. You should be safe. The best thing you can do is get better."

She nodded. "I'm planning on it. You've given me hope, Ella. I don't understand what you did, but I'll never be able to thank you enough."

I shook my head. "I appreciate that, but just think about it as a gift... just for you... and let's leave it at that."

She took a deep breath, overwhelmed with emotion. "If you say so."

"I do. Just get better."

"I will." We sat in silence for a minute, then her gaze caught mine, and her head tilted with curiosity. "I haven't seen much of Creed for a long time, and I have no idea what he's been up to. Want to fill me in?"

"Uh... I think he should tell you about that."

Her brows drew together. "Okay... is it because it's about me?" I nodded, and her lips flattened. "I see. I guess he probably did something stupid, then." I nodded again, and she rolled her eyes. "Well... at least tell me how you met."

I smiled. "Yes... that I can do." I told her that I hit him with my car in a rainstorm, and she could hardly believe the coincidence. "At least it just broke his leg."

Before I could continue, Creed came back inside.

"Is everything okay?" Avery asked.

"Yes, for now." His brow furrowed, but he sent her a smile. "They have a solid case against Sonny, and it looks like everything's moving in the right direction. They still need your testimony, but the detective said they have an inside source who will keep them informed if anything comes up, so he's on top of it. I don't think we need to worry about your safety."

"That's good news," Avery said.

"Yes... it is." Creed nodded. "And with the extra security here, I'm sure you'll be fine." He glanced at the clock. "I'm sorry Avery, but we've got to go. Ella's catching a flight to New York, and I need to take her to the airport."

"New York?"

"Yeah," I said. "That's where I'm from."

"Oh. Uh... okay. Will you come back?"

"I hope so." With her hopeful gaze pinned on me, how could I let her down? No matter what happened, I'd come back, if only to see her walk on her own.

Creed bent down to kiss Avery on her forehead. "I'll stop by on my way back."

"Okay. I'm sorry you have to leave so soon, Ella. Try and come back, okay?"

"I will." I sent her a smile and followed Creed into the hall. His arm came around my waist, and I snuggled against him, wondering how long it would be before I could do this again. I reluctantly let him go and climbed into the car.

We hardly spoke as he drove me to the airport. When we reached the drop-off point, he pulled my luggage out of the trunk, while I stood on the curb. Setting it beside me, he pulled me into his arms for a tight hug, and I tried to memorize how he felt against me.

Stepping back, he cupped my face with his hands and his lips found mine. I kissed him with all the pent-up worry and longing I had. After another quick hug, he pulled away.

I wanted to promise him that I'd be back, but I also wanted him to promise me that he'd come find me if I didn't. I swallowed. "Goodbye Creed." I turned to walk away.

"Ella..." He grabbed my arm. "This is only for now... right?"

"Yeah, sure."

"No... I mean it."

"You do?"

"Yes. I love you."

My brows rose. "Really?" At his solemn nod, I swallowed. "I love you back." I dropped my bags and threw my arms around his neck. After another bone-crushing hug and a quick kiss, I grabbed my bags and hurried into the airport.

CHAPTER THIRTEEN

The long flight became even longer with the change in the time zone. After adding three hours, it put me in New York just after ten p.m. I put a call through to John that I'd arrived, and he insisted I take a taxi into town. I'd planned on using the subway, but I decided not to argue, grateful I wouldn't have to wander around, dragging my luggage.

During the hour-long drive into the city, I rolled down my window and inhaled all the familiar smells and humid air that was New York. Even this late at night, the streets were ablaze with lights, sounds, and crowds of people. It didn't soothe me like I'd expected.

Did I actually miss the peace and quiet of Sandy Creek? Maybe I just needed a couple of days here to get back into the swing of things. Of course, how long was I going to stay? Nothing was certain, and I hated not knowing what to expect. Would John even want me to stay? What about my job? Would management insist on sending me somewhere else?

The taxi pulled up in front of the apartment building, and I spotted John waiting on the steps. I got out, and John pulled me into a hug. "Gabriella! It's so good to see you. I've been so worried."

"It's good to see you too."

John helped me retrieve my bags, paid the cab driver, and hurried back to my side. He grabbed the large bag and looked me over. "Well... you don't look any worse for wear. After your call the other day, I wasn't sure what to expect."

"I know. It's been crazy, but I'm fine. I just... there's a lot I need to tell you."

"I'll bet. Come on. Your apartment is rented out, but one of my neighbors is gone for a few days and said you were welcome to stay there. I hope, by the time she gets back, we'll be able to find you more permanent lodgings."

I didn't want to set John straight, so I just nodded instead. I'd grown up with John in this apartment building, so it was as close to home as I'd get. Several years ago, John had downsized to a one-bedroom apartment, so I couldn't stay with him anymore. Even though he was my 'real' father, we had to keep up appearances.

He led the way up the stairs to the third floor, hauling my big bag, while I took the smaller one. I'd forgotten how musty the building smelled, and I didn't remember the stairs being so worn or the walls so drab. Everything had a worn-out feel to it. When had that happened? He unlocked the apartment just two doors down from his, and I followed him inside.

I glanced around, noting that the décor was on the feminine side, with a few frilly doilies and ruffles on the couch. The elusive citrusy smell of air freshener gave the room a pleasant feel, and it relieved me to have a homey place to stay. A small kitchen stood on one side of the apartment, with the living area on the other. The bedroom, bathroom, and washroom spanned the area along the back.

"I set out some clean sheets on the bed. Since I didn't know if you'd be hungry, I got a sandwich from Leni's for you. It's in the fridge, along with a quart of milk. I left some cereal for you on the counter. We'll figure out the rest tomorrow."

"That's great. Thanks so much."

"Of course." We carted my luggage into the bedroom, and John stepped back into the main room. It was almost midnight, and, from John's tired eyes, I figured talking could wait.

"Shall we talk tomorrow?" I asked.

Relief flowed from him. "If you don't mind. Now that I know you're okay, it can wait, but that doesn't mean you're off the hook. I want to hear everything. Got that?"

"Sure."

He ducked his head. "I know you have a lot of questions for me as well, so I'll answer them all, nothing held back, I promise."

"Thanks. What time works?"

"I have a meeting in the morning. Why don't you come by around one in the afternoon? Come to my office and we'll talk. I'll explain everything then." At my nod, he handed me the keys to the apartment. "Goodnight munchkin."

That brought a smile to my lips. "Goodnight... Dad."

I was supposed to call him Father, so using Dad flustered him. But tonight, I caught a hint of sadness before he rolled his eyes like he always did. What was that about?

After shutting the door, I automatically locked the deadbolt and turned the lock on the doorknob. I ate a couple of bites of the sandwich, but I didn't have much of an appetite, so I put it away, deciding to get ready for bed. After changing the sheets, I plugged my phone into the charger and called Creed.

His warm voice soothed my worries, and it was nice to hear him talk about Avery and the progress she was making. "I wish you could have seen my mom's face when she stopped by this afternoon. She... she burst into tears. Between her and Avery, it was a sob fest."

"I can imagine. I'll bet you shed a tear or two as well."

"Me? Hell no. I don't cry." He paused. "Mom asked if it was anything you'd done, and I told her it wasn't. I'm not sure she believed me, but I know she won't say anything."

"That's good."

"So, did you and John talk?"

"No." I sighed. "It was too late when I got here, so we're talking tomorrow afternoon."

"You have to wait that long?"

"Yeah. He has a meeting in the morning, but I'm meeting him at the church around one. But... that's one my time which is three hours ahead of you."

"Oh," he said. "That's right. What church is it, anyway? I don't think you ever told me."

"It's called The Cathedral Church of St. John the Divine in Manhattan."

"Oh... okay. Uh... that sounds like a big deal."

I chuckled. "It is. You ought to look it up."

"So is that where you grew up?"

"Basically... yes. There's even a school on the property that I attended, along with several other buildings. It became a designated landmark just a few years ago, and the cathedral is amazing."

"Oh. You're making me wish I would have come with you." He sighed. "Even Avery chewed me out. She called me an idiot. Me—her awesome, big brother."

"Hmm... I think I like her more and more."

He groaned, sending shivers up my spine and making me wish he was here. "Well... since it's so late there, I'll let you go, but call me tomorrow. I need to know what John says, okay?

Or better yet, just come back here and tell me in person. I miss you already."

"I miss you too." I worried that John would insist on secrecy, but I wouldn't let that stop me from telling Creed. Still, it would have been easier if he was here. "Good night, Creed."

"Goodnight... Angel."

I smiled and disconnected. After placing my phone on top of the nightstand, I turned out the light and settled under the covers. In this strange bed, sleep eluded me. I worried that John wouldn't have any answers. Then I worried that John's answers might mean my life would change, and I could never go back to Creed.

Of course, that was nothing compared to the knowledge that I could kill someone with my power. How could I ever tell him about that? Of course, I'd never start killing people, but what would he think about me then?

Between that, and my imagination running away with me, it took a long time before I could drift into sleep.

I slept until ten, and it felt wonderful. Of course, back in Sandy Creek, it was only eight, and in L.A. it was seven, so ten wasn't really sleeping in. I took my time eating the rest of my sandwich, perusing a few newspapers on the table.

Before I knew it, an hour had passed, so I hopped into the shower and got ready for the day. I dressed in warmer clothes since I wasn't in the desert anymore. I topped my jeans with a white lace camisole, tucking it in and wearing a tan belt. I added a navy blue duster sweater over it, which dressed it up a bit, and seemed the perfect choice for my meeting with John.

Glancing in the mirror, I saw that my eyes seemed more purple than normal, but maybe it was just a trick of the light. With time to spare, I spent longer than usual on my hair and makeup. With dark eyeliner and mascara, my eyes seemed to pop, and I liked the effect.

In a break from my normal lip gloss, I added a touch of red to my lips. Pleased with the results, I practiced a sultry smile and wished Creed was here to see me. Just thinking about him sent a thrill through my chest. What was that saying? Absence makes the heart grow fonder? I shook my head. I'd just been with him yesterday. It hadn't been that long.

With time to spare, I decided to visit the cathedral for some peace. Slinging my tiny hip purse over my shoulder, I strolled across the block, amazed at how noisy the city was with honking cars, sirens in the distance, and a never-ending crowd of people. It had never seemed so crowded when I lived here, but now it nearly overwhelmed me.

I stepped inside the cathedral, and the noise drifted away. Glancing up at the towering ceiling, I released my breath. Turning back toward the Great West Doors, I tilted my head up to take in the Great Rose Window that never failed to inspire me with its stained-glass beauty.

Reverence filled my soul in this sacred place of worship, and the cares of the world drifted away. I passed through the nave, marveling to know it was the longest in the United States. At the moment, it held a couple of amazing sculptures of two phoenix birds hanging in perpetual flight above my head. Their shimmering colors of purple, blue, red, and gold, with their long tail feathers floating out behind them, brought a smile of awe to my lips.

From there, I entered the great choir and organ section and continued toward the high altar. Here, the references to St. John the Divine were infused into the building with his symbol of the seven stars and seven candles. They were also echoed in the seven lamps above the high altar.

I stood there taking it all in for a few moments, and then bowed my head in meditation. I'd never questioned my trust in a supreme being. For me, I found comfort in my belief, and it never occurred to me to question my simple faith. I prayed for answers and hoped they would come sooner, rather than later.

Soon, the time came to leave, and I headed back to the front entrance. Leaving the cathedral behind, I descended the outside stairs, and my attention was drawn to a man climbing the steps to the great doors. Something about him set my nerves on edge. He seemed agitated and was muttering to himself, but I couldn't hear his words.

Despite the warmth of the day, he wore a heavy grey coat and a cap, with one hand held under the coat against his side. I cast my gaze at the wide steps surrounding the cathedral entrance, noting the many people who sat in the sun, reading, or eating a late lunch.

More people filled the sidewalks, hurrying as they always did to their destinations. As I watched, I caught sight of a familiar face coming toward the cathedral, and my heart raced. Creed? Was that him? What was he doing here?

He looked up at the cathedral and caught sight of me on the steps. His face broke into a huge grin, and I waved. I took a step in his direction, and a loud crack sounded from somewhere behind me, causing my heart to jump. I ducked, hearing two more rapid cracks.

I knew that sound and clutched my chest in response, almost feeling the burn of a bullet enter my skin. I swallowed, knowing I hadn't been shot, but terror nearly overwhelmed me. Several people began to scream, and the crowd burst into panic, running for cover.

I scrambled down the steps toward the side of the building, out of harm's way. Reaching relative safety, I glanced toward the street, my stomach clenching with dread. Where was Creed? I caught sight of a familiar figure taking cover behind the traffic light pole in front of the cathedral.

It was hardly wide enough to protect him, and he ducked down from a standing position as more shots rang out. His head swiveled in my direction, and relief washed over me. So far, he was unscathed, but he was in a precarious position.

I sent him another wave, hoping he understood that I was okay, and he nodded. Above me, the agitated man I'd seen stood in front of the great doors, waving a gun. He pounded on the doors, yelling incoherent words. In a fit of rage, he turned back toward the street and fired two more shots.

A woman fell in front of the steps, not far from me, clutching her leg and letting out a scream. Her body grew still, and I didn't know if she was dead or if she was trying to keep from getting shot again. The shooter began yelling "kill me" over and over.

The woman on the stairs moved, clutching her leg, and pulling herself toward me. Afraid that the gunman would shoot her again, I ducked to the ground as low as I could and crawled toward her. She caught my gaze, and her eyes widened. She mouthed the words, "help me." I sent her a nod and glanced up at the shooter, hoping for a chance to help her while he wasn't looking.

A couple of police officers approached, keeping low and taking cover in front of some garbage bins. They yelled at Creed to stay put and concentrated on the gunman, shouting at him to drop his weapon.

Two more gunshots sounded. I flinched and lowered my head. The yelling continued, and I glanced up to find the woman closer to me, and reaching out a hand. Blood seeped from her thigh, and I knew she didn't have a lot of time before she bled out.

I glanced at Creed, then back at the woman. I pulled my legs under me to lunge for her, hoping to pull her to safety before the gunman took another shot. As I lunged for her, I heard a shout from Creed. He stepped away from the safety of the pole and yelled at the shooter, providing me with the diversion I needed to help the woman.

With my heart in my throat, I sprinted to the woman and grabbed her arm, surprised to find a police officer right beside me to help take her weight. A single shot rang out, and I fought to keep my focus on helping the woman instead of glancing Creed's way.

What was he thinking? I prayed that he hadn't been shot, not having time to check before five more shots rang out, but these sounded different and came from the police officers. As we pulled the woman to safety, the officer met my gaze. "Can you help her?"

"Yes. I'm a trauma nurse."

He glanced toward the cathedral doors. "I think the police got the shooter."

"Is anyone else hurt?"

"I don't think so."

Relieved, I pushed up my sleeves and found the wound on the woman's thigh. As I applied pressure to stop the bleeding, I closed my eyes and drew on my healing energy, pushing it into the woman's leg. I instinctively knew that the bullet had gone straight through her leg, but it had also nicked her femoral artery.

With blood pouring from the wound, I directed my energy into that spot and patched the blood vessel, sealing it back to normal. The wound still gapped open, but at least the bleeding had slowed, and I knew she would survive.

"What can I do?" the officer asked.

"The bullet missed her femoral artery, so she'll be okay, but we need to bind the wound."

Before he could get help, another officer joined us with a first aid kit. I told him what I needed, and he handed me the supplies. I used sterile wipes on the wound, and soon had it covered and wrapped with gauze. Once the wound was secure, and the bleeding under control, I used the wipes on my hands to get as much of the blood off me as I could.

I felt a familiar presence behind me and turned to find Creed. Not hesitating, I fell into his arms. "Are you okay?"

He held me close. "Yes. I'm fine."

"That was a big chance you took. You scared me to death."

"So did you."

I nodded, knowing he spoke the truth, and pulled away to look into his beautiful, blue eyes. "What are you doing here?"

His lips twisted into a wry smile. "I wanted to surprise you."

I huffed out a breath. "Well... you certainly did that."

The paramedics joined us, and I told them about the woman's injury and what I'd done. They quickly took over the woman's care. As we stepped out of the way, the officer who'd been helping me came to my side. "I saw what the two of you did. That took balls."

He glanced at Creed. "I thought you had a death wish until I realized your girl here was trying to pull the woman to safety, and you were providing a diversion. That was pretty gutsy."

"I'm glad it all worked out," Creed said, slipping his arm around my waist and helping me with my sudden case of the jitters. At least I wasn't light-headed from using my healing energy on the woman.

Another set of paramedics carried a gurney to the top of the steps where the gunman lay. Did I need to go up there and help him too? I sure didn't want to. "Is he still alive?"

"Yes... he is for the moment," the policeman answered.

I pursed my lips. "Should I see if I can help?"

The cop glanced my way and shook his head. "No. He took a bullet to the head... maybe two. He's not long for this world, and it's not something you'd want you to see."

I glanced Creed's way, unsure of what to do. I didn't want to get in trouble again for not helping a killer, but maybe this was one of those times I could stay out of it.

Creed caught my gaze. "I think he's right."

Relieved, I sent him a grateful nod.

"You both put your lives on the line to help that woman." The police officer said. "It's not something I expected."

"We're just glad it worked out okay," Creed said. "If that's all, I think my... girl needs to find a place to sit down."

Hmm... what was Creed about to call me? He'd called me his wife so many times lately, I'd almost expected it. His stance shifted to shield me, and his possessive grip around my waist tightened. His attentive concern helped push away the blood and horror of the shooting, and my shoulders relaxed.

The officer nodded and hurried away to do some crowd control. Creed held me close, still shielding me from view, and I leaned against his side, careful not to get my bloody hands on his clothes.

"Where can I take you?" he asked.

"I was just about to meet up with John. That's where I was headed when all this happened. It's that way." I motioned him onto the path around the cathedral to the back property. Several people from that direction began to stream toward the commotion, and I found John in the group coming toward us.

He caught sight of me, and his shoulders sagged with relief. "Ella? I heard all the sirens. Are you okay?"

"Yes." He glanced at Creed and frowned, so I rushed to explain. "Father... this is Aiden Creed. He decided to come after all." I shook my head. "But his timing was lousy. He almost got killed by that shooter."

John's mouth dropped open. "What happened?"

As I explained the incident, John led us back to his office. I finished up in time to take a seat in my favorite chair in front of the window. Creed sat down in the chair beside mine, dropping his familiar duffel bag on the floor. I reached up to tuck my hair behind my ear and realized I still had blood on my hands.

"Uh... can you excuse me a minute. I need to wash my hands."

"Of course," John said.

I sent Creed an apologetic smile. "I'll be right back."

He didn't look too happy that I was leaving him alone with my father, but he nodded just the same. After a thorough washing, I felt much better and hurried back to the office. John had taken my chair, and the sight of the two of them talking to each other reminded me of all the times I'd been in the hot seat.

John spoke to Creed with a stern voice, but Creed seemed to take it in stride. Seeing me, John ended his words in mid-sentence, and I sent him a withering glare. "You guys talking about me?"

"I'm just making sure Creed knows where I stand as your father. I don't want him to get any ideas."

I glanced at Creed, fully expecting him to roll his eyes or something. Instead, his lips twisted into a wry smile. What was that about? "I want him to stay and hear what you have to tell me. He knows everything anyway."

John huffed out a breath. "Yes, I gathered that." He glanced at Creed. "But what is said in this room stays in this room. Got that?"

"Yes sir... uh Father."

John's brows drew together. "Are you a religious man?" Creed shrugged, opening his mouth to speak, but John cut him off. "The truth."

"No sir... uh Father. I'm not."

"Then you might have a hard time with what I'm about to tell you."

"I respectfully disagree." Creed glanced my way, and his eyes softened. "Nothing you say will surprise me... even if you say she's an angel. I'm already half-convinced of that."

John's brows rose, and a hint of a smile touched his lips. Then he frowned, motioning for me to take his chair. I sat, grateful that confrontation was over, and happy to rest after the shooting on the steps.

"You look a little shell-shocked," John said. "There's water in the staff room. I'll get us some."

"Thanks."

John left, and I relaxed into my chair, gazing out at the pleasant view of the gardens. "This was my favorite place to sit when I came to visit John. We had a lot of intense conversations in here."

"It's nice." Creed glanced around the office. "If a bit intimidating."

I smiled, noting the walls filled with books, some of which were probably older than both of us. The dark wood paneling lent the room an air of antiquity, which was both comforting and intimidating. "I guess that's the whole point, right?"

"Yeah." Creed nodded, his eyes softening with understanding.

John returned with bottles of water for all of us. We thanked him, and I drank down nearly half the bottle before coming up for air. John waited patiently, taking his seat behind his large desk and sitting forward with his fingers clasped together in front of him.

"I am glad that you're both all right," he began. "I can't believe what just happened. I guess it's shaken me up a bit, too."

I studied John, noticing that his naturally blond hair had more gray at his temples than I remembered. His face bore deeper creases as well, but his eyes held the determination of someone with enough faith to face anything.

"Well... let's get on with it." He leaned forward, capturing my gaze. "Why don't you start by telling me what's been going on. Start with meeting Creed, since that seems to be when everything changed."

John was one of those few people who listened with all his heart, and I knew he would only interrupt me when he wanted to understand something in more depth. Telling him everything didn't worry me so much as finding out what it all meant, and why it was happening now.

True to form, John drank it all in, his face only losing color when I told him about getting shot and my brush with death. He took a breath to speak, but I told him there was more, continuing the story and even confessing how I'd pulled the energy from Dom.

Creed hadn't known about that, and his mouth dropped open. As understanding dawned, he nodded, realizing the truth behind it.

"I put it back, but not before he fell to the ground and struggled for breath." I swallowed and shook my head. "It came so naturally to me that it's kind of scary. I mean... it was the only way to stop him, but I've always used my gift to heal, and then... I did that."

I caught John's gaze. It was now or never, so I might as well confess. "You sent me away because I wouldn't help a known killer. What are you going to do with me now that I have the power to kill so easily... with just a touch of my finger?"

John sat back in his chair, his brows drawn together and his face pale. "This is troubling, and I don't have the answers, but I think it's time you learned about your background. I think it will help shed some light on all that's happened." He let out a breath. "But the knowledge will come with a price."

My eyes widened, and he hurried to explain. "Not as much for you... but for me. I haven't been totally honest with you. I hope you will forgive me, but circumstances have changed, and it's time you knew the truth."

My heart began to race, and I knew, instinctively, that what he had to tell me would change my life. I only hoped it was in a good way.

"Gabriella, the circumstance of your birth is not what you thought. I'm your father in every way that counts, but one. You were brought to me by a special messenger from the diocese of the church. He was very specific that I raise you as my daughter, and he made sure everyone knew that this was sanctioned by those in authority.

"The truth is... I don't know the conditions of your birth. The messenger who brought you placed you in my care. He had a birth certificate listing your name and the name of your mother, but the name listed as your father is not mine, even though I said it was. I'm sorry, but I'm not your biological father."

Shock pounded into my head, and I got a little dizzy. "Then who is?"

He shook his head. "I don't know. That's where things get muddled."

How could this be real? How could John not be my father? I'd never considered him as anything other than my dad. I mean... we even looked alike. Why had he been given the responsibility to raise me? And why lie about it?

"I don't get it. Why all the secrecy?"

"That my dear... I don't know. But there's something else I need to tell you." He licked his lips and took a deep breath. "When you were about five years old, you... took a fall." He glanced down at his desk and rubbed a hand over his face.

"It was bad... and it was my fault. Back then, my office was on the third floor. You were playing there, and something caught your interest outside the window. I don't know how it happened, but you ran to the window for a better look. As you leaned against the glass, it popped open, and you tumbled out."

He closed his eyes, clearly reliving that horrible moment. "I ran down to the courtyard and found you lying in a puddle of blood. It came from the back of your head. I checked your pulse, but there wasn't one, and you weren't breathing."

He swallowed, and tears came to his eyes. "It was my fault, and I cried out in anguish, praying to God to save you. That's when he came... the same messenger who'd left you with me. He placed his hands on your head and spoke in a language I didn't know. As soon as he finished, you began to breathe again.

"You opened your eyes and looked up at him, raising your little hand to touch his face. He kissed your hand, and you smiled. He helped you to your feet, and you hugged him so tightly that it brought tears to his eyes. After he kissed your forehead, you turned to me, asking me if you could play outside for a little while. It was like nothing had happened.

"I could barely nod, and I watched as you skipped along the walkway. At a loss for words, I glanced at the messenger who stood beside me. He nodded at me, without judgement for my mistake, holding only compassion in his gaze. I was about to thank him, but you called to me, telling me to come and look at something... a bug... I think.

"When I turned back, he was gone. Through the years, I've watched for him. I thought I may have seen him out of the corner of my eye a few times, but he was never truly there. Still, I always hoped he was watching over you."

I shook my head, hardly daring to believe it was true. If I'd come back from the dead as a child, maybe that's why it had seemed familiar after I got shot. That feeling was something unearthly, and having it happen again must have rekindled the memory.

"Maybe that's why you came back this time as well," John said. "Maybe he was there, and he brought you back."

"No. He wasn't there. I would have remembered." I glanced at Creed. "You didn't see anyone like that did you?"

"No."

John nodded and glanced out the window, his hands clasped together. "Not long after that incident, your gift manifested. You were so young, but it seemed like second nature to you. The first time it happened, you had found a butterfly with a broken wing. You touched it with your finger, and the wing became whole again."

He smiled. "I can't tell you how many bugs you fixed. You tried it on a few dead bugs, but it didn't work, much to my relief.

"Everyone in the diocese knew about your gift, and that's why we pushed you to study medicine. You took to it like a fish to water and made us all proud. I think that's why... when you refused to help that man... it was suggested that you needed a change.

"None of us wanted you to take what you could do for granted, or worse, make you too proud for your own good. We all believe that your healing power is a gift from God."

I nodded, understanding for the first time exactly what he meant. "Do you know who the messenger was?" John didn't answer, so I continued. "Do you think he could be my father?"

John shook his head. "He seemed like a regular person, but he has to be much more than that."

"Like what? An angel?"

"I don't know."

We sat in silence, each of us lost in our thoughts. Besides learning that John wasn't my father, what did it all mean? Why did I defy death, not once, but now twice? What was the purpose of my gift? Even more important, what was I supposed to do now? Work at a hospital like I'd been doing?

"Why me?"

John shook his head. "I don't have the answers to that. I suppose that's something you'll have to figure out for yourself."

"But how will I know what those answers are? Are you telling me everything? Is there more to this that you're not saying?"

"I'm sorry Ella." He spread his hands in a placating gesture. "I don't have the answers. I would tell you if I did."

I frowned, not content to let it go. I needed to know why I was still alive and what was expected of me. I didn't want to figure it out on my own. I wanted someone to tell me what was expected, because I didn't want to mess up.

On the other hand, would I be happy with that? Happy to let someone else run my life? I was stubborn enough that I didn't want to be tied down to a life I didn't choose. So what was it going to be?

"You've given me a lot to think about," I told John. "But there aren't a lot of answers to go with it."

"You're right. I'm sorry I can't give you a clear path to follow, but I think it must be your choice."

I shook my head. "I'm not sure I want to make that decision. What if I get it wrong, or what if I don't like it?"

He shrugged. "It wouldn't be the first time. I mean... you're not perfect, and it's easy enough to make a mistake. But I have confidence that you can learn from your mistakes." He caught my frown and smiled. "Sorry, but I'm just trying to keep you humble."

"Thanks." I glanced Creed's way and narrowed my eyes, daring him to say something, but he seemed lost in his thoughts. My heart sank. Was this a deal-breaker for him? Not that we'd made any commitments, but he'd come all the way to New York for me. Would he regret it and change his mind?

The room suddenly felt too small, and I stood, needing some fresh air. "I need to take a walk. Clear my head. You know?"

"Yes. Of course."

Creed stood as well, taking my hand and offering me a small smile. "I'll come with you."

He was so earnest that my heart soared. Maybe this hadn't scared him off after all. I nodded and glanced back at Father John. "We'll be back in a few minutes."

"Sure. Just don't go too far. There are still some things I'd like to discuss."

"Okay." There was more? I wasn't sure how much more of this I could take. I was already drowning in self-doubt and overwhelmed by the whole thing.

We left the building and strolled through the grounds. Creed held my hand, but didn't speak, allowing me the time I needed to come to grips with everything I'd just heard. We circled the grounds twice before I even noticed where we walked. Passing an enclosed garden, I stopped, remembering all the times I'd played there as a child.

A short gate opened into the walled-off space, and I eagerly entered this sanctuary of green plants, trees, and herbs. Forgetting my worries, I stepped along the stone path, touching the plants and smelling the familiar scents of lavender, basil, and mint.

Turning to Creed, I smiled. "I forgot all about this garden. Isn't it lovely?"

He nodded, but his eyes rested only on me. "Yes. Lovely."

I knew he meant me, and my face flushed. "So, what do you think?"

"It's a lot to take in."

"I know. I wish I had more answers."

"Your father... uh... John... explained a lot. You're... special. Maybe that's why I keep following you around."

I smiled, and my heart picked up speed. "So... this isn't scaring you off?"

His brow puckered. "No. But I do wonder if you'd be better off without me. Most of the trouble you've gone through lately is because of me. I don't know if I'm good for you."

I took his hand and pulled him toward the stone benches in the corner under the birch tree. "I'm glad you came, but it's still hard to believe you're standing here with me. When did you decide to come, anyway?"

"After I spoke to you on the phone last night, I booked the first plane out I could get. I thought it would be a nice surprise."

"It certainly was, but seeing you so close to that gunman scared me to death."

He nodded his head. "Yeah. That was nuts. Luckily, the shooter wasn't aiming at me. Everyone scattered, and I took cover behind the pole. It seemed like a good idea at the time, but I should have kept running."

"Yeah... that was too close."

"I kept thinking that, if I happened to get shot, you'd save me. That gave me the courage to draw his fire and give you a chance to help that woman."

"Yeah... it worked out, but if you'd been shot..." I shook my head. "I would have helped you first... and I'm not sure I could have saved the woman, too. It was a big risk."

"Yeah... but he never would have hit me. I ducked back long before he fired the gun. Besides, it also gave the police the opportunity to shoot him."

"That's true, and there wasn't a moment to spare. The woman was bleeding out, so it was perfect timing."

He smiled. "Well, then I guess we make a pretty good team."

His infectious smile tugged at my heart, and I grinned back. "I can't argue with that."

The gate opened, and I glanced up, expecting to see John. Instead, a tall man, dressed in jeans and a dark blazer over a white, button-down shirt, stepped inside. Something about him caught my breath. He seemed to glow with strength beyond this normal existence.

His dark eyes and hair, along with his dark olive skin tones, marked him as someone with a middle-eastern heritage. But his eyes set him apart. They blazed with light, and I knew immediately who he was.

CHAPTER FOURTEEN

"**G**abriella."

He smiled, and my heart nearly burst. "It's you."

I stood, unable to stop my forward motion into his arms. Hugging him was like hugging light itself. I stepped back, surprised that I had tears in my eyes. He looked exactly the same as my five-year-old self remembered him.

"It is good to see you." His pleasant voice held a trace of an accent, and he glanced at Creed, who stood with confusion.

"It's him..." I told Creed. "...the messenger."

He sent Creed a nod of acknowledgment before motioning to the bench. "I am here to answer your questions and give you some guidance. Please sit down, and I will explain everything."

We sat on the benches, with the messenger facing us, and he smiled again. "First of all, let me introduce myself." He waited a heartbeat before continuing. "My name is John." His smile widened at my raised brows. "But you would know me best as St. John the Divine."

My mouth dropped open. What? Had I heard him right? St. John the Divine was an apostle of Jesus who had lived nearly two thousand years ago. This man couldn't be him. Was he nuts?

The earnest expression on his face, along with that special light in his eyes, forced me to hold my tongue. In fact, the longer I sat beside him, the more I realized how different he seemed. So much light filled him that he fairly glowed with it.

"But... you're not even dressed like a Saint."

His face broke into smile, and he chuckled. "No. I am not. Can you imagine how much attention that would bring to me?" He shook his head. "Let me explain, and then you will understand why I must keep my identity a secret.

"You have probably heard the story that I was the only apostle who was not a martyr for the cause. That part is right. At the end of Christ's ministry, he asked all of his disciples what they wished for. I was the last, and I must admit that I was ashamed that my wish was so different from the others.

"You see... they all wished to give their lives for his gospel. To show that they were willing to give everything they had for him and his kingdom."

He shook his head. "He came to me, and I could not speak, but he knew the wish of my heart anyway. He blessed me and granted my wish: that I would tarry on the earth, and minister to the people, until he came again.

"My body was changed to a different state so I would not taste of death. I am not a resurrected being, but I am not entirely mortal either, thus my ability to remain alive these many years. As you can imagine, I have seen many things since that day, and I have done my best to fulfil my calling. That is why I have revealed myself to you, Gabriella. You have been given a special gift."

My mouth went dry, and I had a hard time swallowing, but I managed to whisper. "I don't understand."

He leaned forward, his arms resting on his thighs and his hands clasped together. His eyes held such earnestness that there was no room for doubt, even though my mind screamed that this couldn't be real.

"Among other things, I minister to those in need of special blessings—the downtrodden and the less fortunate. On the day of your birth, I found your mother, not two blocks from here. She was young, and had run away from an abusive situation.

"In that dirty alley, she lay on the cold cement in the final stages of labor, too weak to call for help. I managed to get her to the hospital, where I sat beside her and comforted her while you were born.

"It was a beautiful moment to see you come into the world, and, just as abruptly, to watch her leave. I wanted to heal her, but I was forbidden by the spirit to do so. The attending doctors and nurses assumed that I was your father, and I did nothing to correct them.

"They checked you over and kept you for a few hours, asking me to fill out the forms for your birth certificate. Your mother had told me her name was Gabrielle, but that was all I knew. So I named you Gabriella after her and used my name as your last. Gabriella St. John.

"I have to admit, I found it hard to let you go." He shook his head. "I kept you for two weeks. But I knew I could not complete my ministry and raise a child, so I brought you here. Because this church is named after me, I have a special influence with those in charge.

"Father John was a young priest at the time. I knew his heart, and I knew he would make a good father for you. Even so, it was hard to say goodbye, but I knew you would have a chance for a wonderful life here."

My brows dipped together. "So Father John knows who you are?"

"No. Even the bishop does not know my identity, but after revealing a portion of my power to him, he gladly followed my guidance." He waited for me to nod before he continued.

"Five years later, I received an impression that you needed me. As I came onto the grounds, I heard John's cry and rushed toward him. You were lying broken and lifeless on the ground, and he was sobbing. I reached down to bless you, and an unexpected power poured from my soul, healing you completely and bringing you back to life.

"I knew then that you were one of the chosen."

He stopped speaking, and my mind reeled with shock and surprise. I felt the blood drain from my head, and, if not for Creed's arm around me, I may have slid to the ground in a puddle of shock.

The apostle's eyes twinkled with apology. "How are you doing? Shall I continue?"

I swallowed and managed to sit up straight. "Uh... yeah. Just give me a moment." He nodded, and I caught my breath, unsure I'd heard him right. Had he said I was one of the chosen? What did that mean? Chosen for what? Needing to know what came next, I gave him a nod. "Okay... I'm ready. Please go on."

He studied me for a moment before nodding. "I need to add that I am not the only one who was given this gift to tarry on the earth. There are others from different walks of life that remain also, but altogether, we are only a small handful, and, in this big world, it is not enough.

"Through my sojourn, I have been granted helpers, those with special gifts of healing. The last person with this calling died over a hundred years ago, at the end of a long life. I was not sure I would be given another until you came along.

After your fall and healing, I have observed you from afar, waiting for the right time to introduce myself.

"When you refused to help that man a few months ago, I knew that a change was in order. You needed a place for quiet introspection, away from the noise and the fast pace you had grown used to. So you were sent to that beautiful desert land, full of sand and shadows.

"I think the slower pace helped you contemplate your purpose and appreciate the gift you were given. It was not meant as a punishment, but rather, a time for growth. Am I right?"

I nodded. "Yes... it helped me see what was important to me, and how much I wanted to use my gift to help others... and of course... I wondered what it all meant."

He straightened, nodding his approval. "During that time, I began to receive visions of you. It is through them that I know of your recent journey, and that you crossed paths with this man." He nodded at Creed.

"He also brought you many unexpected opportunities for growth, along with their many consequences. I believe that is what allowed your gift to grow and develop. Your hardships caused you to blossom. The deciding factor in determining your destiny happened when you took the bullet meant for him."

He gestured at Creed, his assessing gaze studying him before returning to mine. "That act sealed your chosen status and is the reason that you were brought you back to life."

At my widened eyes, he nodded with solemnity. "Gabriella, I need you to realize that you have a greater gift than many others who were called before you. That means it comes with a greater responsibility for the welfare of those you serve."

His words struck fear into my heart. I glanced away, unsure of how to tell him about the dark side of my gift. What would he think of me then? Would I still be chosen? Or would the gift be taken away. "But... there's something... you... you don't know... about me."

I swallowed and couldn't seem to meet his gaze. He placed his finger under my chin, compelling me to raise my eyes until they were level with his. "What is it, child?"

The compassion I found there gave me the courage to tell him my dark secret. "There was a man who threatened me and Creed's family. He began to choke me while he pointed a gun at Creed and his sister. I... I used my gift to... pull the light out of him; just the opposite of how I heal people. He couldn't breathe, and he fell to the ground choking. He dropped the gun, and released me."

I held St. John's gaze, pleading with my own. "I didn't know I could hurt him like that. As soon as he fell, I pushed the energy back into him so he could breathe again. There was no lasting harm... but I'm sure it's not the way God intended me to use this gift. If that changes things—"

I dropped my gaze again, knowing I wasn't worthy. How could a chosen healer also use this gift to hurt someone? It was only right that I lose the gift, even though the idea tore me apart inside.

"My child." I raised my gaze to his, hardly daring to hear his verdict. "This is troubling, but... it is not a reason to forfeit your gift. I believe God needs you, and wants your life to be preserved."

He glanced between me and Creed. "But I worry that if you use your gift too many times in that way, it could darken your soul. If the worst were to happen, and you took a life in defense of your own, there would be allowances, but I do not know how it would affect your calling. As a healer, it would be best if you never reached the point where you had to kill someone."

He shook his head, clearly troubled. He took a deep breath and grew still, his eyes closed in prayer. I hardly dared move and added my own faith to his, asking God for direction.

Several tense moments later, his eyes flew open, and his face cleared. Glancing between me and Creed, he turned the full force of his attention to Creed. "It is you. Now I understand your involvement." He glanced between us, and his lips rose in a gentle smile. "What brought you here, Aiden Creed?"

Creed didn't hesitate. "Ella." He took a quick breath. "I mean... that sounds simple, but it's not." He caught my gaze and shook his head, as if it didn't make sense. "I feel... drawn to her. When I'm with her, I feel like my life has a purpose. It's almost like fate... but I don't believe in fate. Maybe it's just that I want to be with her, more than I want to be anywhere else."

St. John smiled. "Some people might call that love."

Creed's face reddened a bit, then he shrugged. "I suppose that's true." He met St. John's gaze. "So what are you trying to say?"

St. John smiled again. "I am saying that you and Ella are meant to continue this journey together. Ella is the chosen healer for this time, and you are her chosen protector. It means that your role will be to keep her safe from harm.

"The days ahead are perilous. And Ella's path will not be easy, as you have seen. Today's event in front of the cathedral was just one example of when she needed you. It may not seem like much, but it is part of a pattern for your future. Are you willing to help her, protect her, and sustain her in the ways she will need in the coming days?"

Creed took a deep breath, and his brows dipped together. Then he turned to study me, and his expression cleared. I braced for his denial, but he surprised me and took my hands in his. "I don't know exactly why, but this feels right.

In all my life, I've never felt so certain of anything. So... yes. As long as there is breath in my body, I will be there for you."

I blinked, and sudden tears filled my eyes. My heart began to race like I'd just run a marathon.

St. John caught my gaze. "Gabriella, will you do the same for this man who has given you his heart?"

My breath whooshed out, and my heart filled with so much love I could hardly contain it. "Yes. Always."

He nodded. "Then I have done what I came for. Your calling as the chosen healer, and his as your protector, will set you on your path. Where that takes you is up to you."

I shook my head. "Wait. What does that mean? Where do we go from here?"

He ducked his head, hiding a smile. "That is always the question that I cannot answer. I can only set you on the path. Free will, with all its consequences, is of utmost importance. Until the end of this dispensation, certain knowledge is hidden for that reason. But I can tell you this much..."

He took my hand, holding it in both of his. "You are needed now. Your healing powers will change the course of the world, but it will happen slowly. One person at a time. You may not understand why or how. But your belief and prayers will see you through."

That sounded overwhelming and not specific at all. "But how will I know who to help? I can't possibly help everyone."

He nodded his agreement. "That is true. Not everyone can, or should be helped. Like your mother. I wanted to save her, but I was not allowed. You will know the feeling when it happens to you."

He squeezed my hands and his eyes filled with tenderness. "This may be hard for you to hear, but you were sent away because the man you refused to help could have stopped an evil person if he had lived. His death nearly cost the life of another with a special gift. Do you understand?"

"Oh. I didn't know."

"But you do now." He waited for my nod. "Do not be troubled. All is well."

His compassion and forgiveness sent the guilt of my mistake out of my heart, leaving me free from the burden of this knowledge. "Thank you."

He nodded and smiled, pleased that I understood. "Now, I must go. There is much to be done, but, because of you, my burden is lighter."

"Wait... I don't know if I'm ready. What if I have questions? Can we talk again?"

He smiled indulgently and stood. "I am sure we will cross paths again. We are connected, you and I, but for now, your path is your own. Rely on your faith, and you will find your way. And you are not alone. You have Aiden Creed, and you can always talk to Father John. Tell him what I told you."

"Can I tell him who you are?"

St. John hesitated before nodding. "Yes. He has been faithful in his stewardship. He deserves to know, but it must go no further."

At my nod, he placed his hand on Creed's shoulder, and they locked gazes. Understanding passed between them, and they clasped hands, giving each other a quick hug and pat on the back.

St. John turned to me, and I rushed into his arms. Our short embrace ended too quickly, but I felt his love and trust in me and let him go.

"God go with you." With a quick nod and a smile, he turned on his heel and passed through the gate.

Creed stepped beside me. We exchanged glances, both of us overwhelmed by what we'd learned. Suddenly, I wanted to see St. John one more time. I hurried out of the garden to look down the path, but he was gone. Creed joined me, taking my hand.

"I feel a little ... lost. He left so quickly and, now that he's gone, it's like there's an empty spot in my heart." I stepped into Creed's open arms. His warmth soothed me, relieving the emptiness of St. John's leaving.

I glanced up at him. "I'm so glad I have you." I studied his handsome face, looking for any sign of regret. "It's a lot to take in, right?"

"Yeah." He bent his head lower and kissed me, his lips warm against mine. The kiss stirred my heart with love and warmth.

"What do we do now?" I asked.

He swallowed. "That's a good question." He pulled me back into the garden, and we sat down on the bench. Studying me, he took my hands. "I guess you're pretty close to being an angel after all. And it looks like I'm stuck with you."

My lips twisted. "Yeah... but I think it's more that I'm stuck with you, so I guess we'll just have to make the best of it."

He nodded. "True... I think I got the better deal."

I smiled. "Well... I won't argue with you about that."

He sighed. "Angel... I can't imagine the rest of my life without you." I opened my mouth, but he spoke over my protest. "I know it won't be easy... but life never is... whatever we face, as long as we're together, I'll count myself a lucky man."

"I love you, too." I raised my lips to his and pressed my body tightly against him. To know that he was mine sent my reservations out the window. All my doubts vanished, and my heart soared with hope. I wasn't alone, and neither was he. We had each other—and a lifetime to figure out where to go from here.

"Gabriella!"

I jerked my head back, finding Father John not two steps away. When had he come in? Twisting my lips, I disentangled myself from Creed's lap and straightened on the bench. "Hello Father."

"What's going on here?"

"Well... he started kissing me and—"

"That's not what I meant." He shoved his hand through his hair and I cringed.

"Uh..." I glanced at Creed, at a loss to know where to start.

Creed's lips twisted into a sardonic smile and he stood, pulling me up to stand beside him. "Ella and I are together now."

John's brows rose. "Is that so?" He caught my gaze, and alarm skittered through my chest. I sent him a firm nod, and he continued. "Hmm... very well. When shall I plan the wedding?"

Creed swore under his breath, and I couldn't hold back my astonishment. John pushed his advantage. "Your vows? Unless you're not serious?"

"Father, this is too—"

"What? It looked to me like you were ready to make a commitment."

My breath caught with indignation. "You're being kind of pushy, aren't you?"

His shoulders sagged, and he took a step back. "Yes. I suppose I am. I'm sorry. But there's a reason. You're my daughter, and I'm a priest. Besides that, you two have been gone a long time, and I was worried. When I found you in here, kissing like that, I over-reacted. Can you blame me?"

"No. Of course not."

"Okay." John glanced between us. "What's going on with you two? What's happened?"

"Let's sit down," I said, beckoning him to the bench. "We have some things we need to share. First of all, the messenger who healed me all those years ago... came right through that gate to talk to us not more than twenty minutes ago."

John inhaled sharply. "He came back and now he's gone again?" At my nod, John's brows drew together. "I'm sorry I missed him. What did he tell you?"

"He explained that I've been chosen to help him, and the purpose of my healing gift is to help others. He wasn't real specific about who I was to help, only saying that I would be an influence for good in the world."

John nodded, but his lips turned down. "This isn't anything new. I've told you that many times."

"Yes... of course. But... it explains why I have this gift in the first place. The messenger healed me as a child, like you said, and it changed everything."

John's shoulders dropped. "And he spoke to you... and Creed? He explained everything?" His lips twisted and he shook his head. "Forgive me... I'm just disappointed that he didn't talk to me too." He caught my gaze. "Is he... an angel?"

"No. He's not an angel... but he's pretty close. He's St. John the Divine."

John's eyes widened, and his brows rose in shock. Before he could question me, I told him everything, including St. John's admonition to keep his identity a secret. I explained the many things St. John had said about his mission, his connection to me, and those like me who'd come before.

"Hmm... I suppose it all makes sense now," John said, rubbing his chin. "But I never... St. John the Divine... I'm still in shock that he's... walking the earth... among us."

I nodded. "I know... it certainly wasn't anything I ever expected."

We sat in silence for several moments, each of us mulling it over. Suddenly John's head jerked up, and his brows drew together. "Did you tell him everything? How you hurt that man... did you tell him about that?"

"Yes Father... it was hard... but he understood. He didn't like it much, but that's where Creed comes in. He asked Creed to be my protector."

"Your protector?"

"Yes... to help me to avoid those situations in the first place, and to watch my back."

John caught Creed's gaze, his eyes narrowing. "Oh? And you agreed?"

"Yes sir... uh Father."

John's brows drew together, his gaze thoughtful. "Well... I guess that answers a lot of our questions. It also helps me understand a few other things..."

At my widened eyes, his lips turned up. "But we'll go over them another time. This is a lot to think about, and you need to decide where you go from here. Do you have any ideas?"

I caught Creed's gaze. "Yes... I do." I glanced between them. "I think we need to go back to L.A. for now, and... there's something else. I don't know what it is exactly, but... I think I need to return to Sandy Creek." That surprised John, and Creed's brows rose as well. "But we can figure it out after we get back to L.A."

Creed nodded. "That works for me."

"If that's what your heart is telling you, I think you should listen," John added. "And while you're at it, think about my suggestion. I know it's too soon right now, but I believe exchanging vows would strengthen your bond. You might need it in the days ahead."

I glanced at Creed before meeting John's gaze. "It's interesting that you say that, because a part of me feels like we've already exchanged vows, with St. John the Divine as our priest."

John's eyes widened. "What did he say?"

"He asked us if we would love, honor, and support each other. We both agreed."

John rubbed his chin. "Hmm... I don't think it gets more sanctioned than that. I mean... he's a Saint, so you're probably right."

I smiled at Creed, reaching out to take his hand. His lips twisted, and I wanted nothing more than to kiss that crooked grin off his face.

Watching us, John jumped to his feet. "I know what to do... follow me." He left the garden, his stride filled with purpose. Confused, we followed him to his office where he stopped to grab Creed's duffel bag. Handing it to him he glanced my way. "You have your ID?"

"Yes." I'd slung my small purse over my shoulder before I left, and it was still there. "Why?"

John ignored me and moved to his filing cabinet. Pulling out a folder, he glanced inside before nodding. "Okay, let's go." He was out the door and striding all the way to the street where he raised a hand to call a taxi.

"What are you doing?"

Almost like magic, a taxi pulled up, and he opened the door. "Get in." Before I could protest, he jumped into the front seat, surprising the driver. As John spoke softly to the driver, I slid into the back seat, and Creed followed me in, carrying his duffel bag.

As soon as the door shut, the driver drove away. He glanced over his shoulder at us, and a big grin broke out on his face.

Unease washed over me, and my brows dipped together. "Where are we going?"

Father John turned to look back at us, a satisfied smile on his face. "To the justice of the peace. You already feel married, so I want to do this right." He sat back in his seat. "And there's no better time than the present."

I gasped. He was serious. Creed blinked a few times, completely caught off guard. He turned to me and shook his head, then a slow smile spread over his lips and he began to chuckle. "I guess we're doing this."

"Yeah... I guess so."

The taxi pulled to the curb in front of the courthouse. John marched up the steps into the building, expecting us to follow. Creed took my hand, and we followed more slowly behind him. After getting directions, we soon stood in front of a clerk for a marriage license.

John produced my birth certificate from the folder and asked for my driver's license. He turned to Creed and held out a hand. "We need two forms of ID."

"I have my driver's license and my passport." Luckily, his passport was in his duffel bag, and they accepted it as his second form of ID.

After filling out the information, we turned in the form. The clerk smiled at us. "You came in at the perfect time. Normally, it takes a few days, but I can get that ready for you in just a few minutes. Take a seat, and I'll call you when it's done."

"Uh... thanks." I smiled at her and sat between John and Creed in a waiting area. John's face practically glowed with pleasure, and I couldn't help smiling. "You're pretty pleased with yourself."

He sat forward, casting his smile at both of us. "I had no doubt it would all work out."

Creed snorted. "I guess you don't mess around, do you? I never thought I'd get married, but this takes the cake. It's like you're holding my feet to the fire."

John's face held no regret. "It's better not to anger the man upstairs."

Creed shook his head, glancing my way with remorse. "I didn't even get to ask you to marry me."

John didn't miss a beat. "You can take care of that right now... on your knee."

I let out an exasperated sigh, completely embarrassed. Before I could object, Creed surprised me and took a knee, right there in the waiting room. Taking my hand, he spoke. "Gabriella St. John, I love you with all my heart. Will you marry me?"

Everyone in the room gawked at us, including the clerk who came to the window with our marriage license. "Yes. I will."

Creed stood, pulling me to my feet, and planted a big kiss on my lips. The room exploded with spontaneous cheers and lots of clapping. The clerk called Creed's name, and we broke apart.

As we stepped to the window, the clerk's face held wistful longing. She drank in the sight of Creed's dark good looks and sighed. "When are you getting married?"

Before I could answer, John stepped beside us. "I know this is unusual. But is there a justice of the peace available now?"

I thought he was pushing his luck, but the clerk's eyes widened, and she fairly squealed with excitement. "You know what? I think so. Let me check."

I looked at Father John with my mouth open. He just shrugged. "God's errand."

Before long we were in the next room waiting for a judge. A woman entered, still throwing the judges robes around her shoulders. She smiled at us, her eyes widening slightly to see John in his priest robes. She glanced around for another person and pursed her lips. "You need another witness."

"Let me get the clerk," John said, stepping out of the room. A few seconds later, he came back in with the young clerk, her cheeks flushed pink with excitement.

The judge soon began with each of us repeating our vows, and ended with those famous words about kissing. Creed kissed me before she'd even finished speaking, and the clerk nearly fainted.

We all signed the document, and it was over. After thanking everyone, we stepped out of the building and onto the busy New York street, totally and completely married.

John hailed a taxi, and we made it back to the church barely an hour and a half after we'd left. Before heading back to his office, John hugged me tightly. "I'm grateful to have a daughter. Not many priests can say that."

He shook Creed's hand. "I'm grateful for a son-in-law too. Take care of Ella."

"I will."

John nodded and smiled. "I think my neighbor will be gone for two more nights, so make the most of it. Oh... and come see me before you leave. I have some things I need to tell you both."

Before I could ask him what he was talking about, he turned on his heel and strode away. Glancing at Creed, I shook my head. "Could this day get any more complicated?"

"I don't know how." He chuckled and took my hand. "Is there a nice, romantic place I can take you for dinner?"

My eyes lit up. "Yes."

"Good. I need to ditch my duffel bag."

"The apartment's not far, we can stash it there."

We took the stairs to the third floor, and I hardly noticed the shabbiness of the walls, or anything else for that matter. The only thing that seemed to register in my mind was that we were married. It had all happened so fast that it didn't even seem real. But at least now when Creed called me his wife, or I called him my husband, it would be the truth.

"I hope you're okay that I kept my name," I said, over my shoulder.

"I'm glad you did. It wouldn't seem right otherwise. Hey... maybe we can have a proper celebration in L.A. with my mom and Avery."

"I'd like that."

I fumbled with the lock, and Creed put his hand over mine to steady it. His warm touch sent my pulse racing. As soon as the door shut behind us, Creed dropped his duffel bag and pinned me against the door, capturing my lips with his.

"I've wanted this for so long," he said, trailing kisses across my face and down my neck. His lips captured mine again, and there was nothing tentative about it. This kiss was like fire, burning me with heat and passion.

I responded in kind, holding nothing back, weaving my arms around his neck and feeling the heat of his touch burn through me like a wildfire. His hands slid under the back of my camisole, the heat branding my bare skin, and I groaned against his mouth.

He pulled away, his gaze scorching mine with desire. Still breathless, he scooped me up into his arms and stepped toward the bedroom. Surprised, I let out a yelp, and couldn't resist a chance to tease him. "Wait... the couch is back there."

He jerked to a stop, and his expression turned dark. "What?"

Trying to look innocent, I raised my brows. "I just wanted to point out that you never have to sleep on the couch again."

He practically growled. "You're going to pay for that." Stepping into the bedroom, he dropped me onto the bed and began to tickle me. I tried not to shriek too loudly and managed to hold him off for about two seconds. I quickly turned the tables by kissing him soundly and pulling off his shirt. After that, I quit thinking all together.

Later, I snuggled against his warm body, at peace and totally content. As I stroked my fingers across his bare, muscled chest, I marveled at how far we'd come. We'd been through so much together, but really our journey was just beginning.

"I'm so glad I ran into you."

His chest rumbled with a low chuckle. "I never thought I'd say it, but so am I."

"There is one thing that's puzzled me."

"What's that?"

"Just... you know that road you were driving on when I hit you? It's one of the least traveled stretches of road in that whole area. It's not even the right way to go from Las Vegas to Denver. Did you get lost or something?"

"That's... " Creed froze before leaning up on his elbow. He looked down at me, his eyes wide. "You won't believe this."

"What?"

He shook his head. "I stopped at a gas station to fill up and went inside for a Coke. A man was mopping the floor in front of the machine, and I had to wait for him to get done. While I waited, he apologized and asked me where I was headed. I told him Denver, and he told me about a shortcut. He said it went through some beautiful country, and not many people took that road."

The hairs on my neck stood on end.

"I never would have gone that way if he hadn't told me." He licked his lips. "I didn't see the resemblance until just now. He looked so ordinary... but it was him. St. John. I'm sure of it."

He lay back down, pulling me close, and we held each other tightly, both of us in a state of wonder and shock. After several minutes had gone by, I twisted my head to look up at him. "What a day this has been. Did you ever expect to be married to me when you left L.A. this morning?"

"Not quite. I had hoped we'd end up in bed together, so at least that part worked out."

I smacked him. "That's not what I meant."

"Oh yeah?" He leaned over me, pinning me down with his body. "I know you wanted me from the beginning. The first time you told me to take my pants off, it was pretty obvious."

I huffed out a protest and began to struggle against him, but he held me down.

"Admit it. You couldn't take your eyes off me."

"You're terrible. That's exactly why I didn't want to get involved with someone like you."

He froze. "Like me?"

"Yes. You're way too handsome for your own good, and I'm not..." I pressed my lips together. "I'm not even in your league."

His eyes softened. "Is that what you think?" Shaking his head, his earnest gaze roamed over my face, catching at my heart.

"Angel... you're the most beautiful woman I've ever known, and believe me, I've met a lot of beautiful women. If anything, I'm the one who doesn't deserve you."

I took a breath to protest, but he held me down. "You mesmerize me with one look. You occupy all my thoughts and dreams. You've taken on my burdens, even when you didn't need to. Since knowing you, I've found a purpose to my life I've never had before."

His lips brushed mine, and he moved to kiss my forehead, my eyes, my chin, and down my throat to the skin of my healed wound. After placing a tender kiss there, he captured my gaze, his eyes dark with emotion. "I love you Gabriella... with all my heart."

My lips found his, and my heart swelled with love for this beautiful man. I didn't know what the future held, but, with him beside me, I knew I could face it.

There was much to ponder about the role I had been given, and St. John's words seemed vague and mysterious... and even a little frightening. There was even more that I could get wrong, and so many mistakes I could make.

But I was stronger with Creed beside me, and that gave me hope for the future, whatever it held.

FROM THE AUTHOR

T hank you for reading **Angel Falls: Sand and Shadows Book 1**. If you enjoyed this book, please consider leaving a review on Amazon. It's a great way to thank an author and keep her writing!

Desert Devil: Sand and Shadows Book 2 is now available on kindle, kindle unlimited, and paperback! Turn the page for a sample!

I am also working on the next Shelby Nichols Adventure. If you are new to the series, please check out **CARROTS: A Shelby Nichols Adventure**, featuring Shelby, Ramos and Uncle Joey. It's the first book in the series, and it's available in paperback, ebook, and audible formats. Also in Kindle Unlimited. Get your copy today!

For news, updates, and discounts, sign up for my newsletter here. By signing up you will receive a FREE ebook, Behind Blue Eyes: A Shelby Nichols Novella. Sign up today!

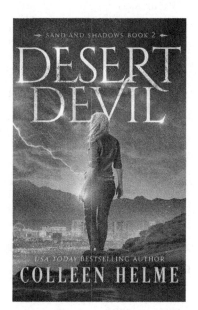

DESERT DEVIL

Sand and Shadows Book 2
NOW AVAILABLE
Read on for a Sample

I stepped down the hallway and paused in front of room two-one-two-seven. At three in the morning, most of the patients were asleep, and it was relatively quiet. Taking a breath, I pushed the door open and stepped inside.

The boy lay quiet and still, hooked up to several machines. The halo around his head held his neck in place and kept him from moving. His curly, blond hair was pushed back from his forehead, and, even with his eyes shut, his dark, long lashes went on for days. For a fifteen-year-old, he looked small and helpless, surrounded by all the machines that monitored his vital signs.

This was the first time I'd been able to visit him, but I'd been drawn to this room since my first shift at the hospital. I'd had to wait until now, when things had settled down, before I could visit him without drawing unwanted attention. I still didn't have a lot of time, so I stepped to his side and took his hand.

To my surprise, his eyes fluttered open and his gaze met mine. I smiled to put him at ease. "Hey Tucker, I'm Ella. I didn't mean to wake you."

"S' okay." He blinked a few times, trying to wake up.

"I just wanted to see how you were doing. Is it okay if I sit with you for a minute?"

"Sure."

"You can go back to sleep if you want."

"It's all I ever do anymore."

I smiled. "That's because sleeping will help you get better."

Tucker's breath hitched and his eyes brightened. "You think I'll get better?" The desperation in his tone sent sorrow into my heart. Through no fault of his own, this poor boy had broken his neck in a freak accident.

The doctors had little hope that he'd ever walk again. Tucker's parents had been devastated, but this young man had put on a brave face, telling everyone he'd be okay and he'd walk out of this hospital and prove them wrong.

Now, alone with me, his eyes filled with tears, and worry tightened his brow. He'd tried to be brave for his parents, but now he couldn't hold the emotion back.

As he blinked his tears away, I tightened my grip on his hand. "I don't see why not. You just have to give it some time, and let your body heal. Can you do that?"

He tried to nod his head, but couldn't with the halo around it, and pursed his lips instead. "I think so."

"Good. Now try not to worry. Close your eyes and go back to sleep. Everything's going to be okay."

His eyes closed and a tear rolled down his cheek. "What does that even mean?"

"It means that it's okay to be scared, but don't lose hope, you're stronger than you think. Now rest and go to sleep." He glanced at me with half-closed eyes. I smiled and sent him a reassuring nod. He let out a breath and his eyes dropped shut. He relaxed and, a few seconds later, his breath came deep and even.

Now that he was asleep, I closed my eyes and concentrated on my connection to him. Still holding his hand, I placed my fingers against his wrist and felt the beat of his heart. Sending my awareness through our connection, I traveled up his arm to his neck and centered on the source of his injury.

There, I felt the swollen tissue, and the herniated disc that had damaged his spinal column. Through surgery, the disc had been successfully treated, but the injury to his spinal cord was irreparable.

Using my gift, I sent my healing power into his neck, starting with the swelling and proceeding to the injured nerves of his spinal column. Stimulating the nerves and bringing them back together was a slow process, but soon, the tissue began to regenerate. I sharpened my focus, pouring all my energy into the tissue, until it had strengthened and fully reconnected.

Several minutes later, I knew the moment the injury had completely healed. The swelling was gone, and the vertebrae reset, allowing his neck and the rest of his body to resume its normal position and functionality. My breath whooshed out of me, and I pulled my focus away.

Opening my eyes, I panted, feeling like I had just run a marathon. Thankfully, Tucker's eyes were still closed. As I studied him, I noticed that his face held a slight flush of healthy color that hadn't been there before. With his spine restored, he'd be able to walk again and live a normal life.

Totally exhausted, the exhilaration of using my gift to help him gave me the strength I needed to get up and walk out of there. With one last glance at his peaceful face, I opened the door and stepped into the hallway.

Holding the outside door handle, I made sure the door closed without the usual loud click. I turned to leave and nearly crashed into a cart being pushed by an orderly.

"Oh! I'm so sorry," the woman said, covering her mouth with her hand. Her long dark hair was pulled back into a low knot at the base of her neck, and her dark eyes flashed with embarrassment. "I didn't see you there."

"It's okay. I was just... I was trying to be quiet."

"Of course." She nodded, glancing at the door. "That's the poor boy with the broken neck. How is he? I feel so badly for him."

She stepped down the hall in the same direction I needed to go, so I moved beside her. Still a little weak, I couldn't quite keep up with her pace. She noticed and slowed her step, sending me a look of concern. Before she could ask if I was okay, I picked up the conversation where she'd left off.

"I know. It's heartbreaking, isn't it? But maybe with some therapy, he'll get some of the use of his arms and hands back at least."

"That would be something. I pray for him every day. Such a tragedy."

"Yeah, for sure." I'd never seen her before, but she acted like she knew me. Maybe she'd been in one of my patient's rooms and I'd missed it. Orderlies like her were nearly invisible in a hospital this size, but I usually wasn't so preoccupied that I couldn't be friendly. "I don't think we've met. I'm Ella St. John."

"Oh... it's nice to meet you. I'm Reyna Torres." Her surprise that I'd introduce myself seemed genuine. "I've only worked the night shift for a few days, but I'm always happy to make new friends, although... I have to say that I've heard of you."

"You have?"

Her eyes widened. "Oh... nothing bad of course. It's all been good. I mean... you're new here so people have talked about you a few times. But in a good way. You're a really good nurse... at least that's what everyone says." Her gaze met mine and she gave me a rueful smile. "So... I'm happy to run into you."

I chuckled. "Yes... well... it's nice to meet you, too, Reyna. I guess I'll see you around."

She nodded and continued down the hall, while I stopped at the bank of elevators. I pushed the button for the main floor and stepped inside, grateful to be alone so I could lean against the side and catch my breath.

END OF SAMPLE

DESERT DEVIL: Sand and Shadows Book 2
is now available from Amazon. I hope you love it!

ABOUT THE AUTHOR

USA TODAY BESTSELLING AUTHOR

Colleen Helme is the author of the bestselling Shelby Nichols Adventure Series, a wildly entertaining and highly humorous series about Shelby Nichols, a woman with the ability to read minds.

She is also the author of the Sand and Shadow Series, a spin-off from the Shelby Nichols Series featuring Ella St. John, a woman with a special 'healing' touch. Between writing about these two friends, Colleen has her hands full, but is enjoying every minute of it, especially when they appear in books together.

When not writing, Colleen spends most of her time thinking about new ways to get her characters in and out of trouble. She loves to connect with readers and admits that fans of her books keep her writing.

Connect with Colleen:

Website | Amazon | Facebook | Bookbub | Twitter | Instagram | Shelby Nichols Consulting | Amazon Series Page

Made in the USA
Las Vegas, NV
26 May 2022

49392876R00194